The Greater Infortune

The Connecting Door

Rayner Heppenstall

VP Festschrift Series:

Volume 1: Christine Brooke-Rose
Volume 2: Gilbert Adair
Volume 3: The Syllabus
Volume 4: Rikki Ducornet
(Edited by G.N. Forester and M.J. Nicholls)

Reprint Titles:

The Languages of Love
The Sycamore Tree
The Dear Deceit
The Middlemen
Go When You See the Green Man Walking
Next
Xorandor/Verbivore
by Christine Brooke-Rose

Three Novels — Rosalyn Drexler
Knut — Tom Mallin
Erowina — Tom Mallin

New fiction:

Mirrors on which dust has fallen — Jeff Bursey

other Verbivoracious titles @

www.verbivoraciouspress.org

The Greater Infortune

/

The Connecting Door

Rayner Heppenstall

Verbivoracious Press

Glentrees, 13 Mt Sinai Lane, Singapore

This edition published in Great Britain & Singapore

by Verbivoracious Press

www.verbivoraciouspress.org

ISBN: 978-981-09-6761-1

Printed and bound in Great Britain & Singapore

The Greater Infortune first published in the UK as *Saturnine* by Secker & Warburg (1943), and revised and published by Peter Owen (1960).
The Connecting Door first published in the UK by Barrie & Rockliff (1962).

Contents

Introduction

JULIET JACQUES

The two novels presented here, *The Greater Infortune* and *The Connecting Door*, were both originally published as halves of a pair, although not with each other. They were both released in the early 1960s, as author Rayner Heppenstall turned fifty, although *The Greater Infortune* was a revision of his *Saturnine*, first issued in 1943. They represent Heppenstall's engagement with two literary genres, one quite archaic and quintessentially British; the other aggressively modern and apparently French.

I write 'apparently' as *The Connecting Door* was Heppenstall's attempt at a British answer to the *nouveau roman* or 'anti-novel', making waves across the Channel. The movement had no manifesto or fundamental principles, instead being an invention of critics who saw similarities in works by Michel Butor, Marguerite Duras, Robert Pinget, Alain Robbe-Grillet, Nathalie Sarraute, and Claude Simon. All opposed to the 'traditional' novel and to social(ist) realism, they eschewed dramatic plots, coherent temporality and deep character psychology, focusing instead on the properties of concrete objects and the mundane, random nature of everyday life.

Heppenstall was frustrated with Britain's post-war literary scene, dominated by the formally reactionary 'Angry Young Men' in drama, 'kitchen sink' novels and the conservative style of Philip Larkin in poetry. In 1961, he published *The Fourfold Tradition*, a critical text that examined differences and drew parallels between 'traditional' and 'experimental' literature in Britain and France. 'In this country,' he wrote, 'there is too little technical enterprise. We have endless conventional novels,' concluding that the *nouveau roman* was far more interesting than anything happening in his native land.

Born in Huddersfield in July 1911, Heppenstall had always felt a great affinity with French culture. He studied English and Modern Languages at the University of Huddersfield, spending a year in Strasbourg, before moving to London in 1934 to further his literary career. After two volumes of poetry, a book on critic John Middleton Murry and *An Apology for Dancing*, he published his first novel, *The Blaze of Noon*, in September 1939. The novel was overshadowed not just by the outbreak of the Second World War, but also by scandal—the *Daily Express* took exception to the overt sexuality of its narrator, blind masseur Louis Dunkel, calling it 'the most explicit British novel since *Lady Chatterley's Lover*'.

Gradually, *The Blaze of Noon* attracted the attention of critics, who understood that besides D. H. Lawrence and Henry Miller, Heppenstall's chief influences were French—modernist authors such as Louis-Ferdinand Céline, Henry de Montherlant and Pierre Drieu la Rochelle, politically inclined towards the right. In May 1967, Hélène Cixous published an article in *Le Monde* on 'le roman éxperimental en Grand Bretagne', stating that the new developments in French literature originated in England, and specifically that 'il *[Heppenstall]* à inauguré le *nouveau roman* dès 1939 avec *The Blaze of Noon*'.

Certainly, *The Blaze of Noon* anticipated the way in which the key *nouveau roman* works took place within their narrator's reflective consciousness, examining the relationship between the internal workings of the psyche and shifting, unreliable versions of 'reality'. It was translated into French as *L'Embrasement di Midi* in 1947 but Heppenstall did not believe that any of the post-war French modernists read it; Jean-Paul Sartre coined the term 'anti-novel' for Sarraute's *Portrait of a Man Unknown* just one year later.

Heppenstall had not intended to write any more novels, but the unexpected success of *The Blaze of Noon* led him to explore the form further. It was "not the work of a literary theorist," he wrote; his guiding principle was that film had assumed the nineteenth-century novel's exteriorised narrative function and that literary prose "would do well to become more lyrical, more inward." His next novel, *Saturnine*, did just that, blurring the boundaries between Alick Frobisher's reality and the excesses of his restless imagination, but for all the modern social science included in the narrative, set in London at the end of the 1930s, he revived the old term 'picaresque' (coined in 1810) to describe it.

'The essence of a picaresque novel is . . . that it is told in the first person by a social parasite, rogue, picaroon or anti-hero and . . . that it has no formal plot but that the episodes simply follow each other serially,' wrote Heppenstall in his memoir, *The Intellectual Part* (1962). Its episodes—drawn largely from his own life—encompassed bankruptcy, homosexual acquaintances, the birth of a daughter and a drunk and disorderly charge, peppered with astrological asides, political reflections and moments that blur the line between reality and fantasy. Written in lyrical prose, its plot explored the effects of modernity on a bourgeois, bohemian man, who felt under the spell of the planet Saturn and his friend Richard St. Hilda, whose interest in scientific empiricism contrasted with his own obsession with 'irrational' beliefs and systems. Its tension, (and considerable humour) sprang from the friction between Frobisher's endless reflection on his own tumultuous psychology and the world around him collapsing into war.

Like its predecessor, *Saturnine* provoked outrage. Drama critic James Agate, a long-standing adversary of Heppenstall's, labelled it "a book more dangerous than bosh," infuriated by a passage reading: 'Everyone stinks of excrement and putrefaction. That goes for you and me, for the Prime Minister and the Hangman, for the Queen of England, the little princesses and the Queen Mother, for all the war-lords of Europe.' But unlike the *Standard*'s journalist, Agate had no media platform, so his indignation about a minor character's untimely iconoclasm roused little public interest.

Saturnine fell beneath the critical radar because of its tiny print run (just 1,650 copies, due both to wartime rationing and concerns about its incendiary content) and Secker & Warburg's failure to publicise it, or deliver a promised reprint. However, Julian Symons stated in one of the few published discussions of Heppenstall's work that "there is nothing else like *Saturnine*'s mixture of philosophical reflection, near-mysticism, triviality and fact in modern literature"—certainly, few novels captured the chaos that enveloped late-Thirties London with such verve.

The text demonstrated a wry awareness of its own fragmented nature, and the difficulty of sewing its strands into any structure, sometimes attacking itself. 'It seems as if I were telling four or five stories at once, but that is how it was. I can imagine this story divided up between four or five different novels.' The protagonist admits that his own narrative is essentially uncontrollable, stating that: 'Any attempt at all-embracing consistency would be dishonest (and I believe that it is always so in life and that all novel-writing is dishonest in its degree.)' In this, Heppenstall anticipated, and most likely influenced B. S. Johnson, who insisted that all 'fiction' should be drawn from a writer's life and that 'Telling stories is telling lies'.

Saturnine was the first of two novels about the war; Heppenstall wrote most of its follow-up, *The Lesser Infortune*, during his service but it was not published until 1953. It seemed more conventional, an apparently autobiographical account of Frobisher's time in the army, during which he had a mental breakdown. While this meant that many strands of *Saturnine*'s narrative were terminated, and Heppenstall was dissatisfied with it, *The Lesser Infortune* was delicately written, with its detached ruminations on army life and subdued political engagement pointing towards the *nouveau roman*, which was just starting to be identified by literary critics.

A revised edition of *Saturnine* was finally issued in 1960, by Peter Owen, as *The Greater Infortune*. This heralded an increased rate of literary productivity, as Heppenstall had become frustrated that his day job, as a producer for BBC Radio's Third Programme, had curbed his output during the preceding decade. Here, Heppenstall distanced himself from his protagonist, changing Frobisher's name to Leckie, primarily as "A number of readers took both *Saturnine* and *The Lesser Infortune* to be more autobiographical than they are and in some cases formed (while one or two critics expressed) conclusions unflattering to myself . . . Myself the most respectable of men, I now think it advisable, if only to make it clear that my central figure is indeed a fictitious personage, to give him a background more distinctly not my own." (He did not help his cause with moments in *The Lesser Infortune* where Frobisher's life is complicated by publishing a novel called *Saturnine,* but his plans to revise that along with its prequel failed as it was technically still in print with Jonathan Cape.)

After publishing just three novels in twenty years, Heppenstall found the inspiration to relaunch his career. 'The *nouveau roman* had given me courage . . . I felt able, without misgiving, to do what I had long wanted to do,' he wrote in *The Intellectual Part,* about *The Connecting Door.* 'To a lapsed poet, it was very attractive, with its tightly formal structure, its spaced repetition of certain themes *[and]* its classical regard for one or other set of unities.' Having foreshadowed the *nouveau roman,* he was now following it: he met Butor, Duras and Sarraute, who praised *The Greater Infortune,* and Robbe-Grillet, who became the chief influence upon his fiction.

The Connecting Door challenged readers to disentangle three simultaneous planes of time, and to work out which characters existed in the present-day reality and which as the central figure's memories, with incongruous and disorienting signifiers throwing the temporal sequence into constant doubt. Its events, inspired by three trips Heppenstall made to Strasbourg in 1931, 1936 and 1948, resisted easy chronology in an experiment with past-tense narration, developed across several aborted novels.

The novel's prose aspired to 'neutrality', but unlike in Robbe-Grillet's *Jealousy,* the narrator *did* act in the story, highlighting the process of writing by meticulously recording details about his surroundings. Harold Atha details his relationships with physical objects but tries to avoid pathetic fallacy, rarely using adjectives and avoiding the reflections on ideas and emotions that typified Heppenstall's narrators. Passages on sites of post-war political meaning describe their features, without stating a position on the atrocities that generated their significance. However, this façade of objectivity disguised a highly subjective novel that, as with his previous works, queried the position of the self in a complex society and the unreliability of memory.

The Connecting Door, like *The Greater Infortune*, was paired with another novel. In *The Fourfold Tradition*, Heppenstall had explored French 'experimental' writing and its conclusion in the *nouveau roman;* looking at British Modernism in the same text, he looked at 'stream of consciousness' and inner monologues in Joyce, Woolf and other English-language authors. *The Woodshed,* also published in 1962, picked up where *The Connecting Door* left off, with Atha returning to Britain in 1948 as his father is dying, and remembering his childhood in Yorkshire.

In many senses, *The Woodshed* was a backward-looking work. It was *The Connecting Door* that made Sixties critics mark Heppenstall out as an 'experimental' novelist and see his earlier novels in the context of the *nouveau roman*. Cixous praised *The Connecting Door*, noting that 'l'auteur abolit la différence entre les temps de réflexion et les âges du sujet avec un sens dramatique de l'humour"[*]; Anthony Burgess also reviewed it favourably. In *The British Novel Since the Thirties,* Randall Stevenson wrote: 'in the manner of Robbe-Grillet, it remains a puzzle, raising and frustrating the possibility of creating a plausible pattern for its events . . . offering only a series of 'connecting doors' into irreconcilable planes of time or reality.'

In *The Intellectual Part,* Heppenstall explained his methods, perhaps offering too many clues into the mysteries of *The Connecting Door*. I will not reproduce that explanation here: instead, I shall leave you, the reader, to explore and enjoy the uncertainties and complexities behind it, and *The Greater Infortune,* and to decide for yourselves how much Heppenstall anticipated the works of Robbe-Grillet and others, and how successful he was in following them.

---

[*]   The author abolishes the difference between the reflexive time and the subject ages with a dramatic sense of humour.

THE GREATER INFORTUNE

To Muriel Spark
A reviver of faint hearts

Saturn is cold, dry and barren; it is the
Greater Infortune; Mars being the Lesser
. . . Mars is hot, dry and barren.

Alan Leo's *Astrological Manuals*, No. IV

ONE

Sam Thorpe died in October, 1938. His death would more properly have befitted some distinguished student of the eighteenth century. As the poet Gray had prophesied of himself, Sam Thorpe died of an apoplexy and was found fallen out of bed, with his head in a chamberpot.

This death terminated my brief career as an enlightened industrialist. Sam Thorpe had taken me into partnership for two reasons. In the first place, he had continued to feel that sense of obligation to my father (I have never discovered its origin) which had long before made him insist on helping to send me to an expensive school. In the second place, I was understood to be artistic, and Sam Thorpe had conceived the idea that money could, in 1937, more easily be made out of taste and discernment than out of plain hardware. Thorpe and Leckie, Ltd., was founded to appeal to that small body of the well-to-do which liked its saucepans streamlined, its trays and small tables made of glass and steel, the profile of its tumblers round at the bottom. In the prospectus which I drew up, we proudly declared that this was the age of industrial design and that we were no mere commercial enterprise but would strive in our own way to create the beautiful.

I had been given pretty much of a free hand, not only with new lines and their advertisement but with the organisation of our London premises. Sam Thorpe, spending most of his time in the Midlands, had nevertheless kept larger financial matters under his own control. When my portly benefactor died, I was forced to declare myself a bankrupt. This was in its way a glamorous condition. Money had always frightened and delighted me. I found it exotic like Arabia. My career as nominal *gérant* of Thorpe and Leckie, Ltd., had been a piece of improbable adventure.

However, the court proceedings were soon over. Sam Thorpe's posthumous creditors took their one and sixpence in the pound. And then I was depressed to find myself once again in that state of chronic penury from which I began to feel I ought never to have emerged.

Such as it is, my sense of humour failed me. Alison, my still quite recent wife, went to an agency and got herself a temporary typing job at two pounds ten a week. She also set about finding a cheaper flat. I did nothing. Or, rather, I went away.

I had arranged, some time before the collapse, to spend a fortnight in Somerset with Tom Johnson, an amiable and surprisingly well-read solicitor. He was a junior partner in the firm which had not quite managed to save Thorpe and Leckie. He drove me down to his farm. For a fortnight, I stood about in wet grass at agricultural sales, drank cider, explored Wookey Hole, poked around Stonehenge and the antiquities of Wells.

It must have been the 27th of November when Tom Johnson drove me back to London. At any rate, it was a Sunday. At three o'clock on the Monday morning, I was awakened by what appeared to be a ball of red-hot metal embedded in my back, a little to the left side and possibly an inch above the waist.

I staggered out of bed, cursing. My reaction to physical pain has always been characterised by impatience, and that night, or rather, that morning I excelled myself. So did the pain, I must admit. It was intense enough to send me downstairs with diarrhoea and then to drag me up to the bathroom again to vomit. It went on for three-quarters of an hour, during which I groaned, raved and kicked the furniture over, doubled myself into a fist and strained at the ceiling, drank China tea and swallowed aspirins. When the temperature of the ball of metal had subsided and it was no more than a sullen, droning weight in my back, I returned to bed with a hot-water bottle.

Alison had wanted to ring up a doctor during the night. At eight o'clock, she was all for getting a doctor on her way to work. I would have none of it, partly because of the expense and partly because of my conviction that a man's diseases were of his own creation and should therefore be of his own curing, a conviction no doubt bound up with the feelings of guilt by which disease is sometimes attended in childhood.

The second attack took place on Saturday of the same week, at seven o'clock in the morning. This time, Alison would not listen to me. I was made to have a doctor. Alison rang up Richard St. Hilda, who lived in one of the Bloomsbury squares, and asked him for the name of his doctor. A few minutes before the doctor arrived, Richard St. Hilda himself came to see me. The doctor, who was a quiet, smiling Jew, prodded my back and abdomen, made me bend, jotted down my medical history, which was negligible, told me to stay in bed for a day or two and said he was not certain whether I had stony kidneys or a form of muscular rheumatism, but would try me with a diet and a bottle of medicine first and, if I liked, send me to hospital for an X-ray later.

Illness was at this point a perfectly satisfactory refuge. I particularly enjoyed denying myself red meat and strong drink. Sweetbreads, whiting and grapefruit purified my consciousness, and I suffered less from anxiety than even before the collapse of Thorpe and Leckie. I had two occupations. First, I played chess both with Richard St. Hilda and with one of two young men who lived in a state of married bliss across the road and the other of whom lent me his spare overcoat when I was allowed out of the house. In the second place, I studied astrology. Indeed, as I see it in retrospect, this was in the most literal sense the purpose of my illness, that it forced upon me a period of rest in which to study astrology. I had dabbled a little during my career as a tycoon, but I was not yet able to delineate and judge a horoscope. Now Richard St. Hilda asked me what books I would like from the London Library, and I had him collect me the available works on astrology, especially those which gave the methods of precise mathematical computation. I memorised symbols and categories by writing them out large with a paintbrush on sheets of paper which Alison then fastened to the wall with drawing pins. I had her go round in her lunch hour to Messrs. L. N. Fowler of Ludgate Circus to buy me Raphael's Ephemeris for this and that particular year. I had her and Richard St. Hilda and one or two others who came to see me write home to know the time and place of their birth. I myself wrote to Aunt Sheena, my only known surviving relation, in Paisley. As it turned out, she was able to tell me my own birth-time within an hour. When I was out of bed, I used a drawing pin and a piece of string to draw enormous circles on the wall to either side of the fireplace, and in these I set out my own horoscope and Alison's with the symbols coloured in crayon to the colour of each planet and each zodiacal sign. According to the textbook rules, my horoscope was a bad one, full of squares and oppositions, that is to say of planets at angles of 90° and 180° to each other in the zodiacal belt. Particularly ominous was a conjunction of the two malefic planets, Mars and Saturn, in the sign Taurus, with Mars in close opposition to Jupiter. According to a small green book, this configuration betokened the native's death through falling masonry. I felt a bit depressed, but luckily I was still at this moment sceptical of the traditional lore and had in any case heard that in the horoscopes of highly developed souls much may be read in a spiritual sense which to a grosser nature would have physical import.

The great frost of 1938 began on December 20th, the date of my first visit to the Middlesex Hospital. It had snowed a little on the previous day, but now the ground was hard and brilliant. More snow was falling. I had not had any third attack, but the doctor thought it would be a good idea if I had an X-ray, and so did I. I went round to Richard St. Hilda's flat in my borrowed overcoat and asked him if he would drive me to the hospital and keep me company while I waited my turn for examination. Richard St. Hilda's flat was luxurious and warm. Two Siamese cats played together on the tasteful carpet. It was Tuesday. I thought it would be interesting for Richard to visit the outpatients' department of a London hospital and there gaze upon the face of the poor.

After I had taken off my shoes and been weighed and had made water into a bottle, I had my interview with the lady almoner. I told her that I was A. W. Leckie, married, of Marginal Road, N.1, and that I was at the moment unemployed (I did not confess what frightful Christian names the 'A.W.' stood for). She thought that I need not pay anything now, but that I would perhaps remember the Middlesex Hospital when I had a job. After that, I was shut in a small room with three dressing gowns, no heating, a large tram-driver and a little man who did not like undressing in front of other people. We shivered together there for half an hour, after which the tram-driver and I were called into a room divided by a curtain on either side of which stood a bed covered by one small red blanket. I lay shivering in one bed, the tram-driver in the other. From the other side of the curtain came a murmur of voices discussing the tram-driver's physique. A hollow, drumming sound was followed by explanation in an authoritative voice that the tram-driver's chest was in a very poor condition.

The authoritative voice said:

'Wait a minute.'

A young doctor with spectacles and a dark moustache stepped through the curtain and tapped my chest. I made a very musical sound. The doctor called his students through the curtain.

'There,' he said, 'that's something quite different.'

One after another, the students tapped my chest and exchanged appreciative glances.

The young doctor passed an asthete's hand down my breastbone.

'Beautiful formation,' he said.

They agreed murmurously.

Everybody trooped back to the other side of the curtain.

Later, students began to come in one at a time and do things to me without anybody watching. Some of them wound about my arm an object like the sleeve of a strait-waistcoat with a clock attached to it. Others pushed sharp instruments into my arm and began to draw out my blood. Eventually, the whole group returned together, and the doctor set everybody pressing his fingers into the soft of my belly and my back to see if they could find a place where it hurt, after which I was told to dress and sent back to the room where I had first had a specimen of my urine taken.

Three hours had passed. I was cold and depressed. A student unfastened my trousers and began to paint certain of my parts with a fluid the colour of tropical sunsets.

I asked:

'What is that for?'

The student said:

'We need a sterile specimen.'

I have never liked having those parts of me roughly handled, even by young women. Perhaps I had what is called a castration complex. There were other symptoms of it. For instance, in the period immediately preceding my renewal of contact with Sam Thorpe, I had worn my hair long. At Ambleside, I had shown religious symptoms for a while and would meditate freely upon the cross and the crown of thorns, the scourging, the speared side and the nail-torn hands and feet. Most ominous of all, I was never able to whistle.

'Excuse me,' I said. 'I'm afraid I'm going to pass out.'

The astral body withdrew itself in anguish, and my physical body fell heavily to the floor, knocking the bottle of sterilised urine out of the student's hand.

I returned to consciousness sitting on the floor with the arms of a particularly attractive nurse about my shoulders.

'Poor fellow,' she said. 'It must have been waiting all that time in the cold.'

Then a beautiful incident took place. This nurse's charming fingers began to button up my trousers. They were very gentle upon my flesh, and her voice was gentle. My trousers were of blue corduroy.

I climbed to my feet and adjusted the clothes about my waist.

The nurse said:

'Don't hurry. Sit here until you feel really well.'

She put a chair under me, and when I was sitting on it with my head pressed down between my knees, she laid her hand on my shoulder and afterwards stroked my hair.

'It's quite late,' she said. 'Your friend left a message to say that he would be at Schmidt's in Charlotte Street.'

I could have stayed all day, but I thought that perhaps this angel among women had other courtesies to perform. I went round to Schmidt's, where Richard St. Hilda was drinking coffee. He had eaten turkey, and I had turkey now at his expense. He said that here they served a coffee which I should be allowed to drink because it was caffeine-free, and after the meal he bought a large tin of it from the emporium next door to the restaurant for me to take home.

Like many other pocketbooks, mine has always been full of privately interesting scraps of paper. If anybody had searched it in those days, he would have found visiting cards which I have sometimes passed as my own, a Communist Party card which had expired six years before, the membership card of an all-in-wrestling club in Kilburn, the timetable for trains between Dukinfield and Manchester, the photograph of a grey seal, a purse calendar published by the British-Israel World Federation, in which is written, 'Let it ever be remembered that this race was "elected" and redeemed for a great and divine purpose, . . . not to be a menace but a blessing to all people, . . . to stand for "justice and judgment," God's instrument in establishing the earth in righteousness,' and (for years, most proudly treasured of all) a yellow paper summoning me to attend a police court in the direction of Islington to answer charges of being guilty whilst drunk of disorderly behaviour. He would also have found this:

THE MIDDLESEX HOSPITAL
PREPARATION FOR
(1) RENAL X-RAY
(2) GALL BLADDER

Take one ounce of Castor Oil or two Vegetable Laxatives on *Tuesday, Dec. 20th*, night.

Take half-ounce of Castor Oil or two Vegetable Laxatives on *Wednesday, Dec. 21st*, night.

On morning of examination, take tea, bread and butter only for breakfast.

Come up for X-ray examination at 10.30 *a.m.* o'clock on *Thursday, Dec. 22nd*.

Name of Patient, A. W. Leckie.

(Show this slip to Porter in Hall on arrival and he will direct you.)

I chose two vegetable laxatives, and on Thursday morning my tripes must have been as pure as those displayed in the windows of a Lancashire fish and chip shop. I remember little of this occasion. I remember sitting in my socks, shoes and a dressing gown reading *Punch* for 1916 and that the jokes were about sailors on leave courting young women with boas around their necks. I remember that sharp instruments were again pushed into my arm and that I was afraid lest the X-ray apparatus to which I was strapped should burn something inside me. I remember that the last photograph was omitted and that I was rushed away to make room for a man with red gashes crisscrossing his back in such a manner as to suggest that he had recently flagellated himself with steel wire or fallen backwards through a shop window. I went to the hospital a third and fourth time. I saw again the nurse who had stroked my hair and buttoned up my trousers. She was friendly and remembered my name, but she was gone before I had myself sufficiently under control to be capable of asking her out for the evening, and on the day of my last visit she was not in attendance at all. I remember the face of the poor. I remember otherwise pretty young women with running eyes. I remember the old regulars who, having once been given a card, had come here ever since on whatever pretext they could invent for a little gossip and a little excitement. I remember a man with a beard and a stiff white collar who made himself a nuisance because he was terrified of being forgotten and of losing his turn in this waiting crowd of more vigorous people. I remember sullen young men in mufflers, whose bitterness had drained the blood from their faces and attacked their vitals. I remember a bedraggled old thing with peroxide hair and a tattered fur coat who truly thought that she ought to be given precedence over these common people and who seized by the arm every nurse who hurried past and demanded in a genteel voice if the doctor had been fully informed of her presence. I remembered the nurses. I loved even those who were plain and had less of themselves to sacrifice.

So far as I remember, nothing that happened during the parties and jollification of that new year has direct bearing on the story. It may be that I had to be confused for a while by this world's apparent friendliness, or it may be that I had to have this happy level from which to descend with more dramatic effect. For it was as if everybody I ever knew had decided in one impulse to come and renew their friendship with me. From Wales, Cornwall and the Ridings of York they came, and each of them brought me at least one new acquaintance, among them a professional photographer who made his living by photographing mortuaries for a refrigeration company and a long-haired, bad-tempered Singhalese with filleted fingers who was starting a highbrow journal in London. On New

Year's Eve I had been given a clean bill of health. I had no stone. It had been no more than a form of muscular rheumatism. My illness was a joke. So was my bankruptcy. A painter from South Wales told me about his aunt who passed stones every month or two and kept them in a tin which she brought out and displayed to visitors. We drank hard, and everybody paid but me. It was fair enough. I had, not long before, been able to give talented people little jobs, drawing advertisements or making up rhymes to go with them. Though for the moment down on my luck, I was a popular man. For ten days, our flat (if our new rooms could be described as a flat) never contained less than a dozen people except at those moments when all of us were together in a near or distant public house or when some of the party had gone home for the night and others were stretched out sleeping in rows upon the bathroom floor.

Marginal Road was old and decrepit, but what we now lived in had been a finely planned, early-Victorian house built without foundations straight on the clay. It was covered with ivy, and from our top-storey window at the back we looked out upon a row of Lombardy poplars, behind which lay the pinnacles of London churches. Along the whole row, these eaves sheltered not sparrows but pigeons, and a beating of wings caused one frequently to look up from a chair and see in the window a Japanese screen full of delicate birds' heads and broad fan tails. The flat below us remained empty the whole time we were there, and the ground floor and basement gave refuge to soft, smiling Indians, a tall Jamaican negro and a number of sinister little men in jerseys who stole my books when I was out and were reputed to be Trotskyites. Alas, this flat did not stand up well to that winter's frost when every pipe was frozen and the local plumber became a millionaire overnight. The wind blew up between the black-stained floorboards, and if I held out my hand I felt it marked across with bars of cold air. It was damp, too. Papers lying about curled into a scroll, and the banister left drops of water upon the hand. Marginal Road was in fact condemned. The leases had expired, and each house was now let in separate flats at a cheap weekly rent. It was intended to pull down the whole long street and rebuild it in imitation Georgian. One or two of the houses were already being demolished. The main length of Marginal Road was saved first by recurring political crises and then until quite recently by the war, during and for ten years after which it remained there, a museum one-third populated, half of its windows broken with a stone by small boys who had left, and again come back to live in London, some of the windows then boarded up.

Despite the state of these houses, despite my horoscope and despite the fact that part of the ceiling had fallen at the fine house Alison and I lived in after we were married, nobody was more surprised than I when the ceiling fell at Marginal Road. It was Sunday morning, the 5th or the 15th of January, 1939. Alison was preparing lunch. I was sitting in an armchair, trying to do a funny drawing which I thought I would send to *Lilliput* or *Passing Show* if it still existed. There was a sound like that of mice in the wainscotting, but rather louder, as if two rutting mice were having a fight. It grew louder still. It was like hail or dry leaves blown against the windowpane. I looked on all sides and at last over my head and was in time to see a crack open in the ceiling. Nobody was there to admire the athletic feat by which I reached the door in time, but it was considerable.

After lunch, Alison swept mouse-black powder off the furniture, and I moved furniture into the bathroom. Perhaps a third of the ceiling had fallen. The plaster was heavy and did not crumble in the fingers. A piece of it had dented the wooden arm of the chair in which I had been sitting. We left the plaster and dust upon the floor and locked that room up.

In the morning, I went round to Richard St. Hilda's. It was still very cold, but the snow had thawed. Richard's Siamese kittens were playing with a toy lamb made of wool, which had been put in a stocking for them on Christmas Eve. Their eyes were running, but they did not seem to mind.

Richard St. Hilda was a large, beautiful man with a round, blossoming face. His dark hair was thin, but waved lightly and was combed back from a forehead of the utmost benignity. A deprecating lift of the eyebrows sometimes creased this forehead, and there were horn-rimmed spectacles over eyes which were blue. A slow, highly fastidious manner occasionally crumbled to reveal a grinning schoolboy. Richard St. Hilda sat in his dressing gown beside the fire.

On the other side of the fire sat another young man, also in his dressing gown. The name of this young man was Derek Sutler. He was dark, slender and exotic-looking in the manner of Serge Lifar. His eyelashes were long, and he was playing with a model aeroplane.

Derek Sutler came from the neighbourhood of Bristol. Having, at the age of fourteen, been seduced in the same week, at Weston-super-Mare, by his favourite uncle and aunt, he had grown up somewhat ambiguously sexed. When Richard St. Hilda discovered him, Derek's hobby had been collecting (perhaps also wearing) ladies' underwear. Three years of Richard's company had in some way settled him, so that he was now proposing to get married and join the Royal Air Force.

It could not have been expected that Richard St. Hilda would exert this beneficent influence, for Richard himself (a product of Charterhouse) was of a homosexual disposition. Having once, at Oxford, essayed the physical practice of sodomy, he had, however, decided that he would never really like it and so looked for gratification in other spheres. He and Derek shared a bedroom, but what went on between them there may be assumed to have been blameless.

I told Richard about the ceiling.

He said:

'You can always come and live here if you think you'd like it.'

Richard St. Hilda's voice was remote, his speech frequently unintelligible. It was as if he found words too coarse to express the subtleties of his intention. In time, one developed a fairly accurate sense of what he was saying, but it was not easy for comparative strangers, and if he asked for six lemons in a shop he was as likely as not to be served with four bananas. After a certain amount of conversation upon general topics, he began to have doubts and said:

'I doubt whether you would like it, you know . . .'

But it was arranged. I did not feel able to set up house again just now. Alison would go to her sister's in Bayswater. I would come here and live in the basement with the grand piano and the handmade gramophone. For purely diplomatic reasons, I also insisted on paying ten shillings a week for my keep, so that I should feel less beholden and might thereby avoid the peril of resentful sensations. In a month or two at most, I knew that I should not have ten shillings, but in the meantime it was an investment.

In Marginal Road, we left several hundredweights of dust and plaster upon the floor. The door of that room was locked. Once or twice before we left I opened the door to display the ruin to a visitor, on one occasion to a schoolmaster I had known some years earlier who also in the meantime had taken up astrology (he attributed the astrological revival to the large number of recent occultations of Uranus). A fortnight or so after Alison and I had left, I walked up Marginal Road and saw that there were again curtains in the top-storey windows. People were living there between the floors that I had blackened and the ceiling that I had whitened and a builder's man lately patched. I fancied these people would not distemper over my horoscope and Alison's, for they were carefully and perhaps even beautifully done. There, I fancy, they stood for many years, on either side of the fireplace, proclaiming to anybody with the knowledge to read them that here lived a tall, mercurial girl and a man three parts fire, four earth and two water, a man without air, an obsessed man.

Two

Among the new acquaintances I had made in the new year were two who had just come to London from Paris. They were Edgar Voysey and Gabriel Fantl. Both were small men turning prematurely bald. Edgar Voysey was American and had private means, blue, solemn eyes, a noble expression on his face and an eloquence which took no account of its audience. Gabriel Fantl had no particular nationality and lived on his wits. His mother was French, his birthplace Vienna and his passport Czech. He had been an officer in the Austrian army during the Great War, had led men both into Russia and into Roumania and had not fired a shot. After the Treaty of Versailles, he had begged for his bread in Berlin and had then moved to Paris where he had spent the last twenty years in the company of Americans. He was frail, garrulous, brown-eyed and reputed to have more women by the month than any known man. He had come to London because he wanted a change and because the English were known to have more money than the French, and the tide of Americans was ebbing from Paris. Edgar Voysey had come to London to attend lectures at the Institute of Mystical Science off Tottenham Court Road and in particular to sit at the feet of a Professor Dr. Unradt whom many considered a greater than Rudolf Steiner.

In January and February, 1939, I spent a good deal of time attending lectures with these two. My other occupations were debating philosophical questions with Richard St. Hilda and dining at the pleasanter London restaurants with him. Richard had read philosophy at Oxford without taking schools. His idol was R. G. Collingwood, whose *Speculum Mentis* showed more signs of wear than any other book on these many shelves. My only philosophical training had been three years' apologetics at Ambleside with the Franciscans, so no doubt I was suitably cast in the part of naïve realist.

Richard St. Hilda's own views were unemphatic like his speech, and this, too, was a sign of fastidiousness. Fantl always remembered him as the man who put *Swan Lake* on the E.M.G. gramophone, flung open the french windows and stood on the balcony inhaling the night air. Richard expected that one day he would find the truth in a book. I did not. I sometimes grew angry with Richard on this score. I became dogmatic. It was, of course, understood that I had superior intuitions. These, together with what Richard described as the taste of reality, I was understood to have acquired as a result of the shifts that members of my southward-trekking family (including, after my father's death, myself) had been put to at various times. These seemed to Richard St. Hilda to lie in the order of iron necessity, an order in which he did not feel at home.

Towards the end of February, Richard took a cottage in Kent for the summer. It was a cottage that I knew. In fact, the owner of the two cottages had been my friend, not his, but Richard had a quite phenomenal capacity for fluttering the hearts of middle-aged ladies and had completely undermined my position. This particular middle-aged lady was the daughter of a High Churchman of the aesthetic period. She had fire-screens, talented children and old-fashioned flowers. Her friends called her Effie. She had been patted on the head by Aubrey Beardsley and might easily have stepped out of a novel by Virginia Woolf. There was a ribbon in her hair and fairies at the bottom of her garden. Most of her money went in the form of allowances to her talented children, and she always let one of her two cottages furnished (furnished in the Edwardian-Bloomsbury taste) for the summer. They were beautiful cottages and had at one time been one house, later divided. In the attic was a great king-post. In the hall was an open fireplace, with a chimney two yards wide.

Richard had taken this cottage for Alison and myself, so he said. Indeed, his first intention had been to give us a cottage to live in indefinitely.

He and Alison drove down to Kent on Saturday, March 10th. I promised to follow on Monday or Tuesday. I had, I said, a man to see tomorrow. Alison and Richard took the Siamese kittens with them in a basket with a wire grill. The names of these kittens were Tit and Nit, Burmese (we understood) for one and two. They were beautiful, but tiresome. The sight and smell of the meat and fish cooked for them, the smells they themselves produced after meals in a peat box in one corner of the drawing room, the fact that in cold weather their eyes secreted a phlegm thicker and brighter in colour than that spat out on the pavements by men going early to work, their frequent vomiting on the carpet, the trouble that had to be taken to enclose them in an airtight box with a dish of steaming Friar's Balsam in order to protect them from influenza, all made me feel rather glad that now they would be in the country where they would perhaps lose themselves or be mistaken for rabbits by a gamekeeper.

But my real reason for not going down to the cottage at the same time as Richard and my wife was that I hoped over the weekend to see a young woman whom I had first met at a party given by Richard the week before. Richard St. Hilda's parties always took a peculiar turn. After a certain amount of gin had been consumed the conversation would become extremely cosmic in a rather sophisticated way. This was very likely Richard's own doing. He thought, I fancy, that the whole truth might after all be found not in a book of philosophical writing but in the ecstatic utterance of a sophisticated person while drunk. On this particular occasion, Richard had paired me off with this young woman, telling us that we were parallel lines which met at infinity. His grounds for this supposition were that she and I were both children of nature, she having been brought up in the slums of some Canadian city. Afterwards, everybody drove off in two cars to the Café Royal. In the back of one car, I am told that I savaged this young woman. I certainly remember looking up from her and observing that the other car was exactly alongside and that the young woman's husband, a dentist, was staring through the window at me with murderous eyes. However, the rest of the evening had passed off without incident, and the following day Richard still thought that we ought to get along and meet at infinity.

I pointed out to him the existence of the young woman's husband, who was a tall, brawny Canadian.

Richard said:

'That'll be all right. He's just a cork who'll float with the tide.'

So I stayed behind, intending to see this young woman when both Richard and my wife were fifty miles away. I did not see her. When I rang up, she had gone away for the week. But at the Institute of Mystical Science, that Monday, there was a farewell meeting for its principal, Dr. Leopold Gloss, who was leaving on a lecture tour in the United States. I decided that I would go to this function instead.

Thus was I prepared to receive my first clear insight into the miraculous operations of fate.

I feel I must add here that the young man in Marginal Road whose overcoat I was now wearing had also been at Richard St. Hilda's party and that he also had directed a fragment of cosmic wisdom at me.

Quite without apparent cause, he had suddenly come up to me and said:

'Leckie, the past is man's worst enemy. I should like to abolish memory, particularly for you.'

The Institute of Mystical Science stood at the top of a very tall building in Phelps Place, which is near Heal's. A lift went up as far as the floor below, and then it was necessary to walk up one flight of steps to a top landing where the visitor was confronted by a bewildering succession of swing doors on violent springs. Between every two swing doors, receiving knocks from both sides as one door or the other opened, stood little pockets of young people talking mainly about places they had recently visited. One or two key personages moved incessantly backwards and forwards.

One of these was the oldest student of the Institute, a young man of thirty-four or so, who greeted any stranger to the place by saying to him:

'*Sie sind Deutsch?*'

If the stranger looked bewildered, shook his head or merely smiled, the oldest student said:

'*Donc, vous êtes français?*'

The stranger was not French.

'*Se habla español?*'

Alas, no.

'*Parla italiano?*'

Oh dear. Oh, dear.

'Ah, then you must be English. So am I.'

The oldest student, still smiling, would take the stranger by the arm and lead him round, introducing him, asking him every now and then what his name was.

For myself, I had already found a way of disinfecting this monster. On entering, I would slap him on the back with so much cordiality, that for the next five minutes or so he was incapable of foreign languages, by which time I had safely entered into conversation with somebody else.

Edgar Voysey and Gabriel Fantl had not yet arrived. I passed through all the swing doors into the main room, where elderly ladies were sitting down on some of the hundred or so plain, wooden chairs. The walls of the room were studded with large, singularly shaped picture frames holding pastels and watercolours which seemed to have been done with a solution of potassium permanganate and from which, upon closer examination, faces stared out with mystically exalted eyes, or formless bodies, wreathed in smoke, stretched out imploring hands. The room also contained a grand piano on which were pieces of woodcarving in the form of ashtrays and flower vases. Against this piano leaned Professor Dr. Unradt, with a piece of paper in his hand.

Professor Dr. Unradt was Aquarian man. Heavily built, his face was yet the height of refinement. His complexion was pale, his nose pinchedly small, his eyebrows starting upward across his temples. The usual subject of his discourses was history and in particular economic history. For him, gold was ruled by the sun and the vagaries of the gold standard a reflection of the sun's path through the parts of Heaven. He lived not in years or centuries, but in aeons, and yet the detailed information with which his mind was crowded would not have disgraced the historian of a single period.

For some reason, I had never found it possible to enter into conversation with Professor Dr. Unradt. I regarded him with admiration and fancied him in private a lovable man, but when on two occasions I had begun to speak to him my tongue had faltered.

Now I contented myself with a half-smile and the respectful, rather hushed greeting:

'Good evening, Professor Dr. Unradt.'

After which, I moved across the room and stared into one of the potash watercolours, portraying the bliss or possibly the sufferings of the dead. These pictures were the work of elderly ladies who would not otherwise have put brush or crayon to paper. I forgave them.

Edgar Voysey and Gabriel Fantl arrived. With them was a tall, blonde girl of the English middle class, blushing and contorting her rosebud mouth as she spoke. Her name was Irene. Edgar Voysey went straight up to Professor Dr. Unradt and engaged him in the discussion of some ticklish point connected with the threefold nature of man or perhaps it was the historical importance of Philippe le Bel. Fantl brought Irene to me.

'Well, how is it, huh? This is Irene,' he said. 'You ought to know her.'

'I'm fine,' said I. 'How do you do?'

'Do you come here quite a lot?' said Irene.

The room began to fill up. Voysey, Fantl, Irene and I sat in a row up against the wall. The room became very full, indeed. People were sitting on the floor. Young women were sitting two on a chair. After a while, the door leading to the fire escape was opened to let in air.

First to speak was Mrs. Verity, the Institute's secretary and, some said, the source of its finances. She lectured on the Akashic records, the angelic hierarchies and the symbolism of Christmas. In collaboration with a young German woman, Fraülein von Stubenau, she also instructed students in the painting of mystical pictures and in a form of dancing. She had rosy cheeks and an effusive friendliness, but it was rumoured that she had been miraculously rejuvenated and that her real age was quite extraordinary.

Dr. Leopold Gloss then made his farewell speech. He was a tiny, frail man who looked scarcely incarnate. The pulse was visible even in his eyelids, and one felt that at any moment those eyelids would flutter and he would be dead. Strangely, as he spoke, he became fully alive. Towards the end of his discourse, his animation faded again. How he would complete a lecture tour in America, I could not imagine.

He was followed by Fraülein von Stubenau, girlishly sincere and in difficulties with the language.

Professor Dr. Unradt came up to the front of the room, and the clearing of throats ceased.

His speech had the tone of a funeral oration. Leopold Gloss, he said, and he, Josef Unradt, had been associated with each other since their days at the University of Vienna. They had worked together in Austria, Germany, Switzerland, Holland and for the last eight years in England.

For most of his auditors tonight, the crucial point of Professor Dr. Unradt's speech was its conclusion.

He spoke of the mission of the English people.

'To which to belong,' he said, 'I have the honour since today.' Everybody cheered. Their own Professor Dr. Unradt was now a fully naturalised Englishman.

But for me the crucial point was this.

Earlier in his discourse, Professor Dr. Unradt had said: 'There are now in this room some that I have known before, although it is not known to them.'

While he was saying it, his eye had rested gravely on me.

Now I must be careful to give this remark and its effect on me neither more nor less than their due weight. First, I must say that at the moment its conscious effect on me was not great. At the same time, it may have stirred my subliminal depths, and I must certainly offer this as a possible explanation of what follows.

Before the assembly broke up for refreshments, a thin, steel-bespectacled person called Siegmund Laufer played the piano. He played Beethoven's *Appassionata* Sonata, very fast, and afterwards the *Scenes of Childhood* by Robert Schumann. During this recital, my eye wandered. It lighted successively on two young women, with either of whom it would have been pleasant to flirt. One of them was a pink little thing full of endearing solemnity, a daddy's girl. The other was a maturer creature, a little out of place here, a brunette of perhaps twenty-eight. I made up my mind that, when the music was over, I would attach myself to this young woman if possible, and if not, to the other. The music finished. Two or three girls and the oldest student of the Institute came round with lemonade, mint tea, little plates of biscuits and a tray on which to put money for these things at the rate of twopence for each item. People got up and moved about. I got up and moved about. Gabriel Fantl was not allowed to get up and move about. Edgar Voysey began talking to him about the threefold nature of man or possibly Philippe le Bel. I went for a breath of air on the roof outside the door leading to the fire escape, and then I came back and began manoeuvring for the chance to approach one or other of my two young women. A young man who had been talking to the more attractive of the two, the maturer woman, turned away. She was free. I seized a spare cup of mint tea from somebody's tray and made across the room to offer it to her. At that moment, I saw 'Thea'. All other young women disappeared from my thoughts, and I spilt at least half of my cup of mint tea upon the floor. I was transfixed. 'Thea' was standing by herself, but I could not for the life of me have approached her.

Instead, I had to go round looking for Irene and stuttering at her:

'I say, there's a girl. Over there. I want to talk to her, and I daren't. Get into conversation with her, please. Then I'll come up, and you can introduce me.'

Irene grinned.

'Please, I said. 'I'll do anything for you. By the time I'm capable again, she'll be talking to somebody else.'

I gibbered.

'Watch me,' said Irene.

She walked across to 'Thea', said that it had been a lovely day, but terribly cold for the time of year, and asked her if she came here quite a lot. I circled round them like a dog circling round someone who had just threatened to kick it, and then I approached. 'Thea' had seemed to chafe a little at Irene's conversation, but she was sympathetic towards me, and I found myself talking to her without difficulty. She was Viennese and had been a dancer, but had given up dancing. She had been in Vienna when the Germans marched in and had in fact left Austria only last June.

'It must have broken your heart,' I said.

'No,' she said. 'There was very little of Austria left, before that.'

Her voice was sensitive, tranquil, heady, her English good. She had studied dancing for a while in London with a great Russian teacher whose name meant something to me. We talked about him.

People were going. The room was less full than it had been five minutes ago. 'Thea' thought she must get her clothes. I waited. When she came in sight again, I asked her to come out and drink coffee somewhere.

'I'm sorry,' she said. 'I'm with somebody else.'

Inwardly, I collapsed.

I waited for Edgar Voysey, Gabriel Fantl and Irene. 'Thea' was standing three yards away from me, also waiting. A young man in a large black hat joined her, and they went out. As she passed me, 'Thea' wished me good night in a friendly, shy voice and I believe (but it was not easy to be certain in the rather poor light between so many swing doors) blushed.

Fantl, Voysey and Irene assembled, and the four of us went out to a small restaurant.

That is the whole incident, recounted as sharply and circumstantially as I can do it.

What I have omitted is not circumstantial but essential. It is this. Just as Professor Dr. Unradt knew that he and I were not strangers, so I knew that 'Thea' and I were not strangers. This knowledge had risen up in me slowly and with perfect certainty as I talked to her. Moreover, I knew in what relation we had previously stood to each other, that she had been in some way subordinate to me and that I had used her cruelly.

Fantl and Voysey were not trivial people. They were characters from a comedy, but they were not trivial. I was not so sure of Irene, so I kept my mouth shut.

Except that I said:

'I must see that girl again. I have to go down to Kent this week. If any of you meet her again, please, please make it plain that I must see her.

It was Fantl who christened her 'Thea'.

Irene was certain that 'Thea' had said she lived in the same house as Siegmund Laufer, the pianist.

Fantl said that she was not his type. She was too ethereal. He said:

'I know the type, huh? It is very common in Vienna.'

We left it at that. Voysey went on talking. He talked about the seven cultural, the seven geological and the seven astronomical epochs. We separated, and I went back to Richard St. Hilda's flat.

I tried hard not to accept my knowledge, for it was already painful to me.

I said:

'There are perfectly reasonable explanations for your feeling. This girl is attractive, extremely attractive. She moves like a dream, and I could myself imagine that the legs and the conical breasts had been turned in a lathe. A thought concerning reincarnation had been inserted into your mind, and you attached to it the next intense feeling which presented itself. This phantasy of having met the beloved in a former life is a common one in cases of romantic love. You were jaded and stale. Since you married, you have experienced no particularly intense feeling with regard to any young woman. Latent intensities gathered to a head tonight because of the unusualness of the occasion and because, as I have already observed, this girl is by the most ordinary standards out of the ordinary.'

I said:

'Even if this wholly rational explanation does not satisfy you, there is still the possibility of true affinities of a more generalised kind. Perhaps this is your "ideal woman". Astrologically, for instance, it may be that your natures are exactly compatible. Did you by chance observe the young man in whose company this girl went away? He was not unlike you.'

I said:

'Her pallor, that alone was sufficient to draw to a focus your images. Professor Dr. Unradt, Dr. Gloss and Professor Laufer all display this same pallor, a spiritual and not a physically sickly complexion. This, combined with the undoubted grace and, if I may say so, the unambiguous maturity of her body, fired your imagination.'

But it was no good. I knew what I knew.

I sat up late and wrote the following at about four o'clock in the morning:

TO PROF. SIEGMUND LAUFER,
c/o THE INSTITUTE OF MYSTICAL SCIENCE,
PHELPS PLACE, W.1.

DEAR PROFESSOR LAUFER,

After your recital last night, I was in conversation with a young woman who, I feel certain, said that she lived in the same house as yourself. I have something I wish to send her, but I omitted to discover her name or (with certainty) her address. She was Austrian and had left Vienna in June of last year. Herself formerly a dancer, she would remember that we talked about the Russian teacher, Legat (what I am anxious to send her are, in fact, some drawings done by Legat during his last illness). She was rather pretty, blonde, of medium height, dressed in a blue, flowered frock, and of a pale complexion.

I enclose a note addressed to this *inconnue.* If someone answering to the description does indeed live in your house, perhaps you would be so kind as to give her this note.

In conclusion, may I give myself the pleasure of thanking you for your playing last night and of saying how much I admired it.

Yours sincerely, A. W. LECKIE.

For two, three and four days I waited for a reply, and then with a leaden heart I packed up a few things and travelled down to Kent. I could do no more. 'Thea' did not attend regularly at the Institute of Mystical Science. If she were there again, Fantl, Voysey or Irene would speak to her for me. I did not think she would be there again. I think I can even say that I knew she would not be there.

Three

Effie's two cottages stood in direct line with the Druids' telepathic way across England. I do not know how this fact had been established. There were Druids' stones quite near, but I do not know what monument in the opposite direction was communicated with. Even if Effie's cottages stood in a geometrically straight line, as the crow flies, between two druidical sites, it is still not established, so far as I know, that telepathic communication takes the same flight as a crow and not, for instance, one of Einstein's bent lines. However, this was the explanation advanced for the presence of so many ghosts in such a small house. They were as it might be frozen here by the power of the Druids' thought.

In our cottage, there were three ghosts. The first was an ordinary poltergeist, which lived on the landing and knocked over lamps, furniture and so forth. The second was De Quincey. It had come to Effie's bedside one night, announced itself by name and implored Effie to stroke its hair. The third was half man, half beast.

When I went down to Kent on March 17th, I was in too apathetic a frame of mind to be even politely interested in Effie's ghosts, and certainly I never asked which ghost belonged to the room in which Alison and I slept.

It was during the first week after I arrived. That is to say, about March 22nd.

I awoke with a feeling of oppressive dread. My eyes knew immediately in which direction to turn. At the foot of my bed were glinting eyes embedded in a round, black object rather larger than a man's head. This may have been the entire creature or only that part of it which was visible above the foot of my bed, I cannot be certain. It was vaguely unclean and, I could imagine, covered with hair like that of a rather threadbare black retriever dog. I was afraid, but not paralysed.

Alison had not awakened. I called to her. Her bed was against the opposite wall, and the reading lamp was on her bedside table. I asked her if she saw anything and then told her to put the light on. Alison saw nothing, and I saw nothing now.

When the light was again turned off, I laid my head on the pillow and prepared to go to sleep immediately. I was still afraid. Mainly, it was the uncleanliness of the creature which affected me, and my fear was the fear that I should have experienced if I had known there was a rat in the room, the fear that it might gnaw my face.

The following day, Richard did in fact advance the theory that the apparition had been that of the King rat which appears only once in a hundred years.

It was, however, in this room that the ghost spoken of as half man, half beast, existed. This, as I say, I did not know at the time. Now I learned too that Effie was not the only one who had seen this particular apparition in this room. The wife of one of her talented children had slept here and had also seen it and had experienced a precisely similar emotion, and this young woman, now living in a house only half a mile away, was a hard-boiled musician whose life consisted for the most part in managing a husband no less full of whimsies than his mother.

Everybody laughed at Effie's ghosts, even those who had seen them. I myself laughed at this one.

Richard St. Hilda murmured something or other to the effect that the Druids must have been telling each other dirty stories.

My secret thought was this:

'There is more evil in me than I knew.'

For a day or two longer, I kept the thought of 'Thea' at bay. I drove around with Richard St. Hilda, drinking, playing darts, making friends with both gentry and folk and listening to their dull, rustic conversations.

Richard and I continued to debate philosophical questions. It frequently seemed as if Richard thought that I knew the truth and would not tell it to him, but his occupation lay in undermining whatever convictions I may have had for the reason that he had none of all. So I began to see.

In the country, Tit and Nit were charming. Awful smells and disgusting articles of food do not matter in the country. Tit and Nit played among the shrubs and the smaller plants, their white and brown bodies in sinuous movement, their cries like the sound of seagulls or distant lambs in this thin air. Logs were kept in a small tub by the fire. Tit, the male,* developed a taste for sitting in this tub. He looked very pretty sitting in it, as if he had been posed for a photograph.

The first flowers appeared, in the garden a pink almond, squills and a yellow doronicum, in the woods a few primroses on very short stems.

Alison was happy. She liked trees, flowers, dumb animals and nature and had always chafed a little at London.

There were beauty spots and places of historical interest. Effie and her daughter-in-law gave a party together. A partition between the two cottages was opened. Effie put her grey hair in ringlets and tied a vermilion ribbon about it. People came from London. Afterwards, everybody went round to the daughter-in-law's house where she and Effie's talented son played piano duets, including some of the latter's own compositions. These two held advanced opinions about music and

---

* The erstwhile male. In February, both cats had been doctored. They went to the vet's on Saturday afternoon, came back on Sunday afternoon with their fur wet and smelling of anaesthetic and in the evening were playing hard again. I must take advantage of this footnote to record, too, that during these weeks in Kent Tit also saw a ghost. He was sleeping in his basket by the fire. Quite suddenly he awoke and turned his eyes to the window. Alison was in bed. Richard and I were up late, talking. Tit paced the room in every direction and growled like a dog, his red-glinting, blue eyes turned the whole time towards the window. This went on for twenty minutes or more. Richard turned the light out. Neither of us saw anything, but Tit went on staring. I stroked him and found that he was in a sweat. It was more frightening than seeing a ghost oneself. Even Effie tried to explain this away. What she called 'a rough man' had returned to the neighbourhood. He was a notable frightener of young girls and had on one occasion sent the tough daughter-in-law screaming back to the house. Effie thought that perhaps this 'rough man' was on the prowl in her garden and that Tit had heard and possibly seen him. Thus do sexual phantasies take precedence over ghostly ones in a fluttering lady's mind.

thought that Beethoven, for instance, was very dull and that Brahms, Wagner and Tschaikowsky were not composers at all. They admired Duke Ellington and the less familiar Viennese waltzes. Mozart they were still just able to listen to. They served a claret cup in breadbins.

At six o'clock in the evening, Alison, Richard and I went round to the other cottage and listened to the news on Effie's wireless. After the six o'clock news, Richard and I walked up the road to the Hoppers' Arms.

The thought of 'Thea' closed in upon me.

I shut out everything else. This image had a finer, more brilliant colour than any that had previously existed in my mind. I have found that erotic images can be of four kinds. First, the despairing images which the adolescent forms of women rather older than himself. These are frankly obscene and tend to degenerate into the grotesque. Second, the first love images. These are intrinsically obscene because they attribute to the beloved object qualities which do not exist. Third, the desire images of the adult. These are without any trace of obscenity because they are strictly purposive. In the imperfect adult, they may degenerate into one of the first two kinds, but in themselves they constitute the normal series of images cast up during a course of action. Fourth, the limit-of-possibility images. There is a biological scale of values, and the adult male is capable of recognising in a particular female his erotic superior. He cannot fail to regard her as desirable, but there is no despairing quality in his image of her, for his character is sufficiently well tuned to permit him at the outset to shut off the flow of emotion towards an impossible object. My image of 'Thea' was none of these four. It was more living, and I do not think there are words for it. The nearest I can approach to describing my emotion in the face of it is to say that it was like aesthetic emotion intensified. It was as if a man should regard a picture, read a poem or contemplate a beautiful action and find in it so much revelation of his own life that he cried aloud. His cry would be composed only in part of pure wonder. The rest would be intolerable anguish because he saw the form of his life exhibited with a definition which he in his actual lifetime would not be able so much as to indicate. Thereafter, he would become a saint or a drunkard or else die quickly.

But this music is pitched higher than I want it to be at the moment. I must continue with the demonstrable facts.

The weather was still cold, and no doubt the cottages were damp. I again caught a chill. This is understatement. I took so much cold on the stomach that I could not use food at all. My bowels turned to water. The muscles of my back began to ache again, and my neck was stiff. Catarrh threatened to choke me. My head, my limbs and my genitals ached.

I said:

'This is the planet Saturn which has me in its grip.'

I said:

'This is the death to which my whole life tended. I must accept the full implications of what I know. Never have I subscribed to any doctrine because it gratified, comforted or exalted me. I must now subscribe to a doctrine which is my death. In this lifetime, I did not reach a sufficient level of development to be vouchsafed complete knowledge of past lives, but 'Thea' was shown to me, and I was permitted to know that it was a wrong done to her which had drifted like sand into the delicate machinery of my fate. I cannot make amends to her directly. That is not permitted. Even to see her a second time is not permitted. Nothing is now permitted except to die in full knowledge and with full consent. Now the planet Saturn will slowly chill me to death.'

The conclusion of this phase was bewildering. Even now I do not know whether I was hallucinated or whether this incident did in fact take place. Certainly, there was a suggestion of uncleanliness to disturb my consciousness. The apparition had been unclean. Tit and Nit had worms. They could be seen dragging themselves across the carpet by the front paws, trying to ease the irritation of their little fundaments. More grotesque and disturbing still, the chief affliction from which Effie suffered, despite her ringlets and ribbons and the Japanese glasses tinkling prettily at her open windows, her old-fashioned flowers and the fairies at the bottom of her garden, was piles. However it may be, I have the distinct visual impression of myself waking in the night with nausea. My throat gaped, and out of my mouth came a large worm and lay wriggling upon the pillow. That such incidents do take place, I know. Later, I examined several books of reference and discovered that among the many species of worm which infest man there is one which lives in his large intestine and does occasionally escape at night through the nose or mouth. It is called the round-worm, and its eggs are swallowed from a bad water supply or with cress grown in foul water. My visual memory further shows me looking distractedly about the room for a piece of paper, terribly anxious to be rid of this creature before Alison awoke. I found a piece of paper from a cigarette packet, inserted it beneath the off-white, ringless worm, opened the window, dropped worm and paper out into the garden and went to the bathroom to gargle and smoke a cigarette. The following day, I left my bed, walked into Tonbridge and bought myself a vermifuge from some chemist's shop. Hallucinatory or real, there was no repetition of the incident. Indeed, I suddenly became well, and resolved that I would have nothing more to do with reincarnation or for that matter with any form of supernatural life, come what might.

Richard St. Hilda took pleasure in the company of sailors. One of his private treasures was a sailor's cap. It lay in a drawer at the flat in Bloomsbury along with photographs of handsome young negroes, and on the wall of the dining room was a line drawing of a French sailor boy with a pouting mouth. Chatham was not very far away from our part of Kent, and while I lay in bed wrestling with the planet Saturn, Richard had been to Chatham twice. There he had located the public houses in which sailors danced, sang and in general lived the romantic, carefree life that we expect of sailors, and in one of these he had made the acquaintance of a young sailor called Bill. After paying for a great many drinks, he had driven Bill out along the landward wall of the docks and drawn the car up against the kerb.

Bill had said, rather bitterly:

'Well, I suppose this is your big moment.'

Richard's way of putting it was:

'Here I thought I had picked up a sailor, and I found myself confronted with a subtle, complex personality.'

Bill had recently married. A girl in Folkestone had got herself in the family way by him, and he had been induced to make an honest woman of her. He did not very much like the sailor's life. He was happier in the dance halls of Folkestone. He was fond of the girl whom he had married and who was now about to make him a father, but he did not like being tied to her, either.

Richard said:

'I shall buy him out of the Navy. Then I will get a small boat, and we shall sail round the Greek islands.'

I saw Bill twice. I also saw his wife. Allison and I drove to Folkestone with Richard, and the five of us went to a dance hall together. There was a sixth person, another sailor with wicked, shifty eyes. Bill's wife was extremely handsome. She had the nobility of countenance and manner that working class beauty may present during the last two years before it is finally conquered by housework, child-bearing, neighbourly quarrels, anxiety and the dreary environment. She was very anxious to please. When I said that she must let me know the time of her child's birth and I would cast its horoscope, her tilted face turned towards the verge of tears. I danced with her, very careful not to jolt her great belly.

Later, Bill and the wicked sailor came to the cottage and were fed on eggs and bacon. In a fortnight, Richard's romantic phantasy was exhausted. He saw no more of Bill and dreamed no more of the Greek islands. Instead, he reverted to a previous intention that, when his lease of Effie's cottage was up, he and I should go to Paris and the South of France for a couple of months.

Day by day, the news on Effie's wireless became more heavy with foreboding. The wicked sailor informed us that two German submarines had appeared in the Medway.

Our closest neighbours were the Abells, who lived in the middle of a small orchard adjoining Effie's garden. This orchard had at one time belonged to Effie, but she had sold it to the Abells (who were her brother, sister-in-law, nephew and niece) at a very low cost, and they had come and built a house in it. Their house was built of rough-hewn timber in the form of a Swiss chalet. Since the orchard was perfectly flat and Swiss chalets are not built on flat ground, the Abells had moved a great deal of earth and had a mound built in the middle of the orchard. The timbers which supported the house in front straddled across the hollow from which the earth for the mound had been taken, and the front windows were therefore on a level with the flat orchard, just as they would have been if the house had been built flat. The house was called Cherry Orchard.

The four Abells, in order of seniority, were called Herbert, Frances, Eric and Caroline. Including Caroline, who was only fifteen, they were all pictorial artists except Eric who, in the first assertion of his male independence, had learnt to play the flute. For a while, Richard St. Hilda had wondered whether to take Eric also to the Greek islands, but Eric had refused before he was asked. He was an agreeable young man and stayed at Cherry Orchard with his parents as little as he could.

Herbert Abell had a stiff, military bearing, an energetic manner and voice and a large, aristocratic nose. At the age of eighteen he had been seduced by an Italian nobleman and taken round the minor courts of Europe as the Italian nobleman's secretary. He was completely dominated by his wife, who called him Harbutt, but retained a certain interest in things of the flesh.

Frances Abell was a pinched little thing as strong as a horse, and behind pince-nez she concealed the eyes of a stoat.

She yearned for popularity, which she felt was her due, and while a man still thought he was safe in the 'Mrs. Abell' stage, she would say to him:

'I'm afraid everybody calls me "Frankie", you know.'

This was untrue. One or two had been trapped into calling her 'Frankie' to her face, but nobody behind her back called her anything but 'Frances Abell', severely in full.

At the age of fifteen, Caroline was physically mature and obstinately shy. This was the fault of her mother who still kept her in very brief, childish frocks, so that she had something of the perverse and rather horrible attraction of the principal boy in a pantomime. She was a large, handsome child, with clustering, fair hair and big, golden legs. She was presumably born under Aries. I found her disturbing and was rather ashamed of the fact. Alison said that I had no need to be, for the girl was obviously of an age to be desired or she wouldn't be that shape.

Frances and Harbutt were great lovers of nature. Harbutt told us how during the first March sunshine he had gone out sketching the woods in the morning and, coming to a hollow full of drifted leaves on which the sun lay, had flung himself down among the leaves and remained extended there until lunchtime. The Abells' first definite attempt on us was when they came round after supper one evening, dressed up in great boots and carrying walking sticks, and said that they were going out to listen to the nightingale and perhaps we might care to come too. I had met them before, both down here and on two occasions at a concert in London, and I exerted myself to prevent them now acquiring Richard.

I said:

'I know that these creatures have souls, just as we have. All the same, one is not the Archangel Michael and ought perhaps to refrain from confronting evil beyond one's powers.'

But it was no good. On Easter Monday, we and the Abells went out picnicking together, and Richard, Alison and I were being made to play drawing games with coloured chalks. Caroline sat beside me, those wonderful legs extended on the grass, scratching designs on the golden bloom thereof with the stalk of a piece of last year's corn-stubble. There was a circus at Tonbridge, and the following day everybody went there. On Wednesday, the Abells gave a party, and we played further drawing games.

For the time being, I had exorcised 'Thea'. But a worse devil came in and took her place. I refer to the money devil, my old familiar, no doubt the noon-day devil of which the Psalmist speaks. Now, it is one of the elementary facts of existence that no man willingly contains a devil. He will try to exteriorise and as it were incarnate it. Thus the German race had tried to incarnate its devil in the Jews. One wondered if it might not succeed in the end. The Jewish race might indeed become devilish, and then it would destroy Germany. In the meantime, the Germans were unable to drive their scapegoat out into the desert in the manner of antiquity. On the contrary, the more they exteriorised their racial devil, the more desperately they seemed to cling to that in which they had tried to incarnate it. As soon as a considerable number of Jews had left the country, they clearly wanted to march into Poland in search of new Jews, choosing Poland because Poland had more Jewish inhabitants than Germany itself. In the same way, I tried to incarnate my devil in Richard St. Hilda.

There were a number of facts to justify the attempt in appearance. For instance, Richard St. Hilda had made several financial promises which he had not kept. I had first met him before the foundation of Thorpe and Leckie, Ltd., and for the scantiest of reasons he had straightaway regarded me as a considerable genius. He already had a painter (one of the two young men in Marginal Road), and felt perhaps that he ought to have a writer, too, though I had published only a handful of rather brittle poems, and was at the moment hawking a short novel called *A Lamentation of Women*. When I married and Sam Thorpe was offering to take me into partnership, Richard had offered me thirty shillings a week so that I could stay out of the business world and 'do my own work.' This was the same amount as he gave his painter, but to date he had managed to enjoy my company free. Some intuition told me that, once Thorpe and Leckie, Ltd., had been rejected, Richard St. Hilda would invoke his overdraft, as he had already several times done when a small sum in ready cash was in question. After the collapse of Thorpe and Leckie, Ltd., the offer of thirty shillings had been renewed. I still attached no importance to it. It was mentioned from time to time and had in fact been supposed to start from the beginning of March, but at the time of this story it was the case that I had on no occasion received so much as a brown penny from Richard St. Hilda. During January and February, it was I who had paid him ten shillings a week. At this moment, both my wife and I were apparently living at his expense, but if one looked at it in another light one observed that, in Alison, he had acquired a first-class cook and housekeeper for the price of her and my keep and that he had contrived this by stating in the first place that he was taking a cottage for her and me and that he would visit us only once in a while at the weekend.

All this I could at a normal moment have forgotten. For a short while, I myself had been in a position to help a few gifted young people to jobs for which they were unfitted, and I liked the sensation of being a patron of the arts at little expense to myself. But this was not a normal moment. Apart from anything else, I had just reached the last three pounds of the money I had saved from Sam Thorpe's wreckage. In another ten days, I should be completely penniless and a prey to anything that Richard St. Hilda or another cared to put across me. Richard chose this moment to confuse me with yet another promise. I had not believed any of his former promises. I did not now believe that I should go to Paris and the South of France at his expense. Nevertheless, I had spent fifteen shillings on having my passport renewed.

The Abells helped, of course. Richard was never at his best in the company of other people. Frances Abell made a fuss of him, and he became quite ridiculous. It was no doubt the case that middle-aged ladies were as necessary to him as he to middle-aged ladies, but the silly, strutting fellow he became irritated me more each day. Irritation would not have mattered, but I was also depressed.

*

Easter Monday was on April 10th. It was on Wednesday of the following week that I cast the Abells' horoscopes and that Richard St. Hilda exhibited his face without spectacles. That was April 19th. On April 18th, 1939, Venus stood in opposition to Neptune, my rising planet. Mercury was stationary and turning on its tracks. The moon came first to the parallel of Saturn and later in the day to the square of Mars, and on the 19th there was first a conjunction with Saturn and, in the early evening, a partial eclipse of the sun followed immediately by the square of Pluto. The following morning, the 20th of April, the sun was in the square of Pluto, and the new moon was moving first towards a conjunction and later towards a parallel with Uranus.

Morning and afternoon of Wednesday, April 19th, were spent in driving Effie round to see the cherry blossom, which was already in its full glory and the plum blossom with it.

Richard St. Hilda brought his Leica with him and wandered off among the trees of one great stretch of orchard, taking photographs. We ate our lunch beside a rather smelly pool in which stood an iron bedstead and where, according to Effie, vipers could be seen swimming at this time of the year.

Away to our left, men were spraying the trees, and a cloud of pea-green or turquoise sulphur stood upon the air with a rainbow across it. Effie talked about a place close at hand called 'the lost field', not because people could never find it but because, however many times it was ploughed, it yielded nothing but a crop of stones. After that, we walked through the woods, and Effie rebuked a woodsman for cutting trees with the sap already in them. Richard insisted on us following a fair-haired young man in a white sweater who turned out, at a closer view, to have the features of a gargoyle. It was a hot day.

Richard, Alison and I walked up to the Hoppers' Arms at half-past five. The Abells were there, looking at the eclipse of the sun through pieces of smoked glass. Richard St. Hilda and I played our usual three games of darts. Richard won. He had beaten me more and more frequently during the last few weeks, and he began to strut.

I said inwardly:

'All right. I'll beat you again when I have money in my pocket.'

The Abells finished with the sun and came inside. They made us play skittles instead of darts. Skittles seemed to me a ridiculous, noisy game, and I had not practised at all. The talented daughter-in-law and her husband came in. They had been gathering cowslips.

After half an hour of skittles, there was conversation. Alison, Harbutt Abell, Caroline and Effie's son formed one group. Frances Abell, the daughter-in-law, Richard St. Hilda and I formed the other. Alison went back to the cottage to prepare supper. Harbutt Abell took Caroline with him and went too. Effie's son went. Richard, the daughter-in-law and Frances Abell talked about their personalities, their psychic experiences, their shyness in company and cognate subjects. Apropos I can't remember what, Richard observed that I knew a little astrology. Frances Abell at once implored me to go round to Cherry Orchard with Richard after supper, and before I knew where I was I had promised that I would if I were paid for the horoscopes.

On the way home, somebody appealed to me for confirmation of an opinion about some aspect of personality.

I said:

'I'm sorry. I have two pounds ten in my pocket. I exist below the level of these discussions.

At supper, Richard thought that I ought to regard Frances Abell as a person.

I said:

'That is not my world.'

Richard wanted to know what was my world.

I said:

'A world of complete lawlessness, a chaos without policemen. Then I should know how to deal with a middle-class imbecile like Frances Abell. I should slit her throat and steal her purse.'

Richard St. Hilda ruffled his hair, and his large, sun-bruised face bore a mixture of frown and boyish grin.

I still bore charitable feelings toward him, for I remember that I said:

'I should steal your purse, too. But I wouldn't slit your throat.'

I decided that I wouldn't go round to Cherry Orchard after all. Richard went by himself. Five minutes later, Frances Abell came through on the telephone and implored me once again to go round. I cursed and went. I arrived at the Swiss chalet with a little pile of ephemerides and astrological reference books under my arm.

Astrology led back to personalities. Richard St. Hilda was asked to take off his spectacles, and Frances Abell said that his eyes were very beautiful. It was at this moment that my devil became fully incarnate in Richard St. Hilda. I had never seen him without his spectacles before, and it was a revelation. This was the glazed, upper-class English eye in perfection, the right eyebrow, finely marked, set in a curve of permanent disdain above the expressionless blue film. This was Richard St. Hilda, at last. And I had taken him for the amiable buffoon he wished to seem.

I thought:

'The face of the poor is well-known. This is the face of the rich, which deserves to be better known.'

The following morning, I stayed in bed longer than usual. When I came down, Richard was sunning himself at the door in nothing but his shoes and a pair of linen trousers. A healthy, bronze sheen had begun to come upon his plump shoulders and little, puffy dugs with their few strands of silky hair. A bit of exercise and hard living, and he would be a magnificent creature, for he was over six feet tall.

I thought:

'The sun does not shine upon the rich and the poor, the just and the unjust, equally. It is because of his money that Richard sits there enjoying the sun, while I overslept with misery. That is why his face is plump, ruddy and without a single line, while mine, at the same age, is deeply scored, set hard and very pale. He shuts me out from the light of the sun.'

After my late breakfast, I set myself down to see a clear picture of my own life and what I could now make of it. The *status quo* was unpleasant, the *status in quem* unimaginable. After so many years of trying to find myself a place of some kind in the world, here I was reduced to the growing boy's condition of helplessness again. Certainly, I must cease to give even a half-credence to Richard St. Hilda's promises. For him, making promises was part of a private game. As to using some technique myself and flattering, cajoling or blackmailing Richard, that I was temperamentally unable to do. My instinct of self-preservation was strong, but not so strong. I must face the problem directly.

Frances Abell rang up to say that she and Harbutt were going to London for the day, and perhaps Caroline might come and have lunch with us.

'Yes, of course,' said I.

I went out into the garden. There were two lawns, separated by flower-beds and a path. On one of the lawns, Richard St. Hilda was now sitting in a deckchair, reading Hegel. I began to pace up and down the other lawn.

So far as I could see, there were no possibilities at all. I should no doubt be allowed to join the Army, if I could bear it. At twenty-six, I was too old for the Navy. The Marines, perhaps. There I should have a red band round my cap and once in a while a sight of the sea. I did not know whether there was an age limit for the Marines, but I fancied not. My colleagues would hate me, but I could perhaps get used to that.

I would bear the Marines in mind. A waiter, no. I should start trouble with the first customer who insulted me. I could not afford a taxi or a set of paintbrushes, and I was untrained for any of the normal proletarian jobs. I could not even have got a job as an underling in the trade in which

I had for a short while been a master. I should need a great deal of practice before I could operate any machine tool whatever.

The harder I thought about it, the more impossible anything became, and I felt that I understood the German cry against encirclement. I developed a phantasy. I thought that henceforward I would go through the world with a rope about my neck like the Burghers of Calais. If anybody were impolite enough to ask me about it, I would explain that I was herein expressing my true condition and that I expected the moment to come soon when that condition finally worsened beyond endurance, upon which I should simply attach the free end of my rope to a tree or something of the kind and jump. I felt that to appear everywhere costumed in a rope would in some way act as a talisman or phylactery, removing me from anxiety and despair because I had so fully expressed and thus come to the end of these things and because the means of a quick deliverance were so tangibly to hand.

I saw that Caroline had arrived. With a great air of consideration for her years, Richard was greeting her upon the other lawn. Shortly afterwards, Richard began moving in and out of the cottage, carrying things out for lunch on the lawn. I felt real hatred for him. I scowled as it were with my whole body, feeling the scowl crease not only my forehead but my bowels and heart.

In the end, Alison came out, too, carrying a tray. She called to me, as she passed, that lunch was ready. I walked across to the other lawn and greeted Caroline, who was dressed in a white, lilac-flowered frock which took away the golden tint and lent a certain pallor to her large, beautiful limbs. To any question, she answered with a shy but definite monosyllable, so there was no conversation.

Richard went in again to fetch a flagon of cider.

As he came back with it, he said in his blithest tones: 'I'm afraid there isn't enough for you, Leckie.'

He filled up Caroline's, his own and Alison's glasses and then handed me the flagon. I put it down on the grass beside me. I was quivering with mad rage.

There were bread, cheese, pickles and a sweet.

The last thing Richard said was:

'Leckie, cut me a piece of bread, will you?'

I was keeping myself under control. I meant to cut this bread. I picked up the breadboard and the knife. The knife slipped out of my fingers. I picked up the knife, and the bread slipped out of my fingers and was rolling about in my lap. I could not hold anything. Richard St. Hilda was grinning at my discomfiture. I must control myself. A sweat came out upon my eyelids. I tried again to make the bread stay on the platter while I took the knife in hand to cut it. I dropped everything between my knees. I picked up the loaf. I did not know what to do with it.

Four

I walked down Charing Cross Road, and in one of the side-streets near Foyle's there was a street entertainer. He was a Scotsman, short, dark and brawny, dressed in dirty grey flannels, dirty white plimsolls and a clean white slip which displayed his weather-browned, tattooed arms and bushy, black chest to the best advantage. His act was unusually simplified. The only apparatus was a long rope, which the little Scot kept tying in a loose knot, to show us how easily it slipped. Then he turned suddenly brisk. He clapped his hands three times, slipped the loosely knotted rope over his head and invited eight strong men to come out of the audience and have a tug o' war, with him in the middle of it. They were allowed and indeed encouraged to pull as hard as they could, the only condition being that they must not jerk on the rope.

The Scotsman's face turned red, purple and finally black, and then he waved a hand limply to tell his impromptu assistants to stop. By the time he had wiped the foam off his mouth and recovered sufficiently to take up his collection, most of the audience had disappeared, including the eight men. He came round among the rest of us, stroking his neck, which was red and scaly like a turkey's, and muttering savagely, in broad, sibilant Clydeside, that if we thought he did this for his own private amusement we were bloody well mistaken.

As a matter of fact, an act as simple and direct as this had got on the halls about three years before. I think it was in Islington I saw it. The man simply came up to the centre of the stage, with a spotlight on him, and announced that he was now going to fall flat on his face, without in any way using his hands to soften the fall. Every light went out except the spot. The side-drums began to rattle. The man stood to attention with his arms stiffly to his sides. He leaned forward a little. The spotlight changed to green. The drums reached a climax. The man fell flat on his face, just as he had promised. Attendants came in and carried him off. Music began. The lights came on. A compère walked on to announce the next act. And that was all.

Perhaps it was the same man, coming steadily down in the world. And perhaps he had once been a great acrobat or juggler until, through drink, drugs, love or the death of a partner, he lost his nerve or damaged one of the fingers of a hand.

To read the newspapers nowadays, you would think that violence in London was new. Islington has never been very quiet. That last summer of peace, I saw a man running out of a side-street there, with his throat slit from ear to ear. The police of those days found their lives made very difficult in Islington. To see trouble coming was sometimes all they could do. A policeman had walked into the Players' Club not long before and advised us to get all the girls away as quickly as possible, for there was a gang of lads outside, all very drunk and getting themselves into the mood for mass rape. I saw one of the girls into a taxi, and she told me next day that the taxi-man had driven her into a mews near where she lived in Kensington and asked her if she were broad-minded.

But this is about the music hall, not yobboes. I want to introduce Flora Massingham. I went to the Calgary with Clifford, and there she was.

Clifford was a faded old thing with false eyelashes. So many years of greasepaint had pickled him. He was such an old whore, so tough at heart and inured to all life's tragedies that nobody else but me dared to be seen around with him. Yet he was full of good humour. He would say he'd been fifteen years in a circus and never lost a spangle. If you drove with him along a bumpy road, he'd say he was used to bobbing up and down.

He'd say:

'I dance on my right leg, I dance on my left leg, and in between the two I earn a living.'

When he was a bit drunk, he'd whoop and cry out: 'Another port, and I'm anybody's!'

That summer, he was going round the halls looking at acts and booking those he liked for a fortnight's season in Monte Carlo, where he and his friend had once run nude shows for the English and American visitors. We arrived at the Calgary at about twenty past nine, and there was Flora Massingham on the stage. She wore a huge turban and a long blue train spangled with stars and signs of the zodiac. At first I could not believe my eyes, but the voice, too, was Flora's, her great, bleating contralto. She was waving a long wand with an enormous crescent moon at the end of it.

I had no sooner taken this in than the music struck up and the curtain was coming down.

I said to Clifford:

'That's Flora Massingham.'

Clifford looked at his programme and said:

'Mme. Zostchenko, dear.'

He added:

'It's not a very good act, is it? I don't think I'm going to book it, dear.'

So many people must have known Flora Massingham in one capacity or another, and it may be that to most of them this theatrical interlude is unknown. They may even be tempted to doubt my assurance that it ever took place. Many will remember her only as the discreet owner of quite a smart bookshop with a political slant, but also with one room upstairs to which recommended customers might be admitted in their search for *curiosa*. That was a late phase. I had known Flora Massingham at a time when kings and royal dukes, great gamblers, great harlots and Labour ministers heard the truth babbled upon her whisky-laden breath.

Whether at heart I believe in numerology, psychometry, traceries in Egyptian sand or palmistry, I should always have found it difficult to say. But I do most certainly believe in the power of a woman like Flora Massingham to wring truth out of the practice of all or any of these arts. I have seen things in a crystal with her. Some years before, I had seen what would happen to me if I did not give up Maimie Joyce.

I left Clifford and went round backstage. I took Flora out to a public house nearby. She was as fat and pink as a pig at Christmas. She had given up whisky and taken to pink gin.

Clifford joined us.

Flora Massingham wanted to know:

'Who's he?'

I said:

'He was fifteen years in a circus and never lost a spangle.'

'I'm an acrobat, dear,' said Clifford. 'I dance on my left leg . . .'

'He's booking acts,' I said.

'I've got an act he can book.'

'Come off the halls,' I said. 'Even Clifford doesn't think you're good.'

'I don't mean me, Leckie. I know an act Clifford'll want to book.'

It was in a little private theatre off Bayswater Road. There were about twenty people there, and most of them seemed to know each other. Flora whispered something to a pious-looking old lady at the door, and they let us in.

I must again strain my reader's credulity. I find it difficult enough to believe myself, when I think of it now.

It was one of those acts in which a conjurer saws a young woman in two. Clifford knew all about that act. So, as it happens, did I. You have two young women in the box, and only one of them is shown outside it.

Clifford yawned.

He said:

'Your friend's crazy, dear.'

The only thing was that this conjurer didn't have two young women. When he'd finished sawing, he showed us the inside of the box, and there was his young woman sawn in two.

Clifford was still yawning. He hadn't noticed.

I said:

'Well, what's the explanation?'

Flora Massingham said:

'There isn't any explanation. He just saws them in two. He has a different young woman every week.'

Somebody screamed and was told to shut up.

Flora Massingham said:

'Come on, we'd better go. You're not supposed to hang about afterwards.'

Oddly, Flora Massingham had never been to see all-in wrestling. I took her to Blackfriars on Saturday evening.

The first fight was a pity-fight between two young lads. One of them had a face like Dick Sheppard or the Duke of Windsor, and he was there to appeal to the maternal instincts of the women in the audience. He seemed to be a complete novice, but of course he was game and put up a good show in the first three rounds. Then his opponent began to pull him through a series of Boston grabs, Indian deathlocks and scissors on the head, until the lad was crying out with pain and banging his hand on the mat, and a tender-hearted section of the audience was on its feet demanding that the fight be stopped. In the end, both his legs were twisted up with his opponent's in a complicated leg-lock which the referee and both seconds tried to disentangle for ten minutes without success. One of the lad's feet was broken, and he had to be carried off. He was sobbing his heart out, but by this time the audience had become properly acclimatised and tired of its own pity and could be trusted to respond in the correct manner to whatever took place in the succeeding fight.

I hardly remember the second fight. It was between the Iron Duke and somebody I hadn't seen before, who wasn't too good. The Duke was a local hero, and I knew his style too well to think of watching him at work upon an inferior opponent. In addition to which, if he will forgive me for saying so, his deeply furrowed brow always seemed to me to be a little out of place in the wrestling ring. I always felt that he was really an intellectual man and that he ought to be occupied with problems of law, religion or statesmanship. I opened my copy of *The Weekly Sporting Review*, turned to the section headed, 'With the Grapplers', and, in the dim light from a great square lamp over the ring, read through all the items of gossip about Bully Pye and 'Villain' Jack Pye, Canadian Earl McCready and Bob ('Legs') Langevin, Tiger Daula and Rajah Ranji from our Indian Empire. There was a photograph of 'Man Mountain' Dean, now doing well in Hollywood, being balanced upon one hand by Joe E. Brown. I was still reading, bemused by the professional, much syncopated, inverted-comma-besprinkled prose of the 'mat-men', when Flora Massingham, beside me, drew in her breath and then puffed out her lips in an explosion of annoyance.

'Oh, just look . . .'

One of the wrestlers for the third fight was already in the ring. He was a popular fighter, and I had better not mention his name because it will seem as if I were holding him up indirectly to opprobrium. His opponent too was just now climbing over the ropes, and it was he whose appearance had caused Flora Massingham to cry out.

She calmed down and said:

'It's Joe Passiful, lad. He oughtn't to be on this job.'

I looked at her and smiled.

'Any more than you ought to be on the music halls.'

'Shut up,' she said.

Joe Passiful was billed in the programme as 'Elbow' Enrico of Italy, and as such I knew him.

'He's never been to Italy in his life . . .'

I could believe that. He was a great, slow, blond creature, rather like the policeman in an American comedy, and his act was pure dirt.

The audience had started booing and hissing him before he got into the ring. He climbed in with a brutal sneer on his face, making the Fascist salute. The crowd howled at him. He made as if to jump down from the ring again and attack the crowd. One or two of the young men stood up and put up their fists and told him to come along, then. He beat his chest, narrowed his eyes, sat down in his corner and emptied his water bottle in one draught.

As the fight went on I could see that Flora Massingham was really suffering, and it was hardly to be wondered at, if 'Elbow' Enrico was indeed Joe Passiful and a friend of hers. No man suffers such pure indignity as the 'dirty' wrestler, who is at one and the same time getting hurt in the ring and insulted by a hooting mob and who knows that wrestling audiences will tire of him far more quickly than they tire of those whose act is 'clean.' I knew that it would be tactless to suggest going out while the fight was on, but that is what I wanted to do. One of the least pleasant features of being a 'dirty' wrestler is that you've got to be really dirty some of the time. And Joe Passiful did everything. He kneed his popular opponent in the groin, gouged his eyes, twisted his ears, threw him by the hair, bit him. On the other hand, when his opponent tortured Joe Passiful, the audience cheered the roof off.

One woman kept screaming out:

'Let him die!'

Everybody else shouted:

'Swing him!'

Or:

'Break it off, and give us a bit!'

Flora Massingham pressed her head down and kept muttering into her vast bosom:

'Oh, the things they've made you do, Joe. The things they've made you do . . .'

His opponent began to get the upper hand, for the 'dirty' wrestler is not allowed to win. He got Joe Passiful in a combined arm-lock and back press and tickled him until he roared, then knuckled him behind the ears, pounded his fat, wobbling paunch, pulled out the hair on his chest. The audience went crazy with joy. There was a fall, and when his opponent got up Joe Passiful lay on his back, gasping.

'Let him die!' screamed the woman somewhere at the rear of the hall.

Flora Massingham said:

'I won't murder that woman. I won't ...'

A moment later, and the fight was over in an uproar. Joe Passiful got up and started appealing to the audience, making the Fascist salute at them as they cat-called and jeered at him. Then he lost his temper, picked up the referee, a small tough man, flung him out into the audience, picked up the sawdust tray from his corner and chased his popular opponent round the ring, banging him over the head with it until he dropped and then bursting into tears, leaping over the ropes and, with a last swipe at the referee who was just climbing back, running off to the dressing rooms amid a demonstration from the crowd that was like the fury of a lynch-mob or a small country that has just declared war.

The lights went up.

Flora Massingham sat beside me looking completely dazed for a moment and then shook her head violently several times and smiled.

She said:

'I think I'll go and have a talk with Joe ...'

The first fight after the interval was a lovely fight between Jim Anderson and I forget whom, but it wasn't Jack Dale. I think the finest wrestling match I ever did see was between Jim Anderson and Jack Dale of Brixton, but tonight the young Scotsman had another opponent. It was a clean, swift fight from beginning to end. There was plenty of forearm hitting, butting and catapulting oneself off the ropes with both feet forward, but for the most part it was pure throwing and holding, with two healthy young bodies giving out all they had at the highest possible speed.

At the beginning of the last fight, Flora Massingham came back, bringing Joe Passiful with her. They both sat beside me for a moment or two, and then in the penumbra somebody noticed that it was 'Elbow' Enrico and started hissing at him and muttering insults. Joe Passiful coughed.

He said:

'I better go. Else the boss'll have at me for sittin' front of the house, and I got to be paid. I got to fight today afternoon, and I want to sleep. I better not wait. This is my lodgings. Mostly I'm in of a morning.'

He gave Flora Massingham a card and pushed his way out. He was panting, hopelessly out of condition even by ordinary non-athletic standards. Flora Massingham clung to his hand for a moment and smiled up at him as if he was Clark Gable and she just Betty Smith of Wimbledon.

But what we talked about after the fight is the important thing. It was a large, bright public house, with a glitter of tinted bottles and silver that made a man feel his drinking was a noble occupation. Flora Massingham's broad face, with its pallor, its occasional rosiness, its uncovered bronze hair and its distinctively nacreous eyes, turned here and there in the light. Her large, blushing arm tilted to the same light a glass of pink gin. The cat of the house came and jumped up on her knee. It was a large, Persian eunuch, with lemon eyes and a luxurious, greenish grey coat. At the first touch of Flora Massingham's fingers it blinked its eyes, and its head fell sleepily down into her lap. It purred and went on purring, its purring interrupted only for a second every now and then, during which it must have fallen briefly asleep with contentment.

I said:

'Cats don't purr except when human beings stroke them, do they?'

'I shouldn't think so.'

'And yet,' I said, 'purring is a very highly specialised development in cats, wouldn't you say?'

'I suppose . . .'

'Then the body of a cat is largely created for the purpose of responding to man's caresses. The cat's association with man was decreed from the beginning.'

Flora Massingham said:

'But is man's lack of independence, the complete interdependence of man and other creatures, new to you?'

And it was at this point that I learned that I was not alone in my recent phantasies of uncleanliness.

Flora Massingham said:

'The earthworm we know is necessary to the soil, its irrigation and fertility. Without it man would starve. But I also remember that when I was a little girl in Cape Town my parents had a book of etiquette and information called *Jack's Reference Book*. In there I discovered that forty-seven species of worms are known to infest man himself. The commonest of these were indeed solely created for man or by man, for they infest only him *and do not reach maturity at all unless man gives them access to his body*. The tapeworm in its immature condition lives in the muscles of the pig and only achieves the condition of maturity when the pig's flesh, in an undercooked state, is consumed by a human being. The tapeworm then develops four suckers in its head, attaches itself by these to the intestinal wall and remains stationary there in the small intestine, a creature of anything from five to twelve feet in length, absorbing into itself the nourishment with which it is bathed by an increasingly hungry *host*. The threadworm reaches man by way of his drinking water or watercress and inhabits his large intestine in great numbers, occasionally escaping singly through the anus at night, a white, capillary creature about half an inch long. The roundworm lives in small numbers in the small intestine. It is like an earthworm in size and shape, but of a dirty white colour and devoid of rings. Like the threadworm it comes from watercress and water. Occasionally it escapes through the mouth or nose, and only when this happens can the animals presence be diagnosed.'

It is sometimes necessary to make stupid remarks in order to keep a conversation moving at the right tempo. I made a remark more appropriate to Richard.

I said:

'Well, when you're dead, I mean, you're all worms.'

Flora Massingham continued:

'I wanted some conception of sin which would embrace the creation by man of this filth in his own body. I even wrote to a priest about it. The utmost he could say was that after all the worm, like man, was a creature of God, that St. Peter had been warned definitely against calling any creature unclean and that theologians had since the foundation of the Church discussed without finally solving it the problem of evil, which he must therefore presume to be beyond the natural power of man's intelligence. My mother was the practical one. She said: *Now have you got worms, or haven't you?* I had to admit that, so far as I knew, I hadn't. Well, then, my mother said, would I be so good as to hold my tongue . . .'

And then the core of the matter:

'. . . But I suppose that people with the proper feeling for worms are the people I'm looking for, Leckie. And Joe Passiful's one of them. Joe Passiful is a saint . . .'

'Wait a minute,' I said. 'The people you're looking for . . .?'

'. . . Now don't start trying to make me commit myself, Leckie. Leave it at that. Do you talk about the poem you're writing, before you've completed the first stanza? No, of course not. Neither shall I. But I'll tell you what possible sainthood means. It means kissing the dust, not because you've been bidden to do so but kissing it with a loving, passionate kiss. Not for display and not out of panic anxiety, but with a quiet, passionate and compassionate love, with all due patience and humility. Listen. We've mentioned worms. It isn't necessary to go so far as worms. Consider merely that everyone stinks of excrement and putrefaction. That goes for you and me, for the Prime Minister and the Hangman, for the highest in the land and the girls at the Russian Ballet. Let them bathe and powder themselves all day long, and still if you stick your nose in the appropriate place you'll catch the familiar whiff of excrement and putrefaction . . .'

Flora Massingham blew her nose, and her face was so softened that I expected to see that her nose had been left in the handkerchief. The cat in her lap adjusted itself to the upheaval, purred half-heartedly for a second or two and then fell asleep again.

She continued:

'. . . The salt taste and the smells of lust and perspiration are as strong in Cleopatra's bed as the ghost of a rose is. And the little girl in Hounslow or Tooting Bec, who won't be kissed under the mistletoe, who is so pure that she falls ill with shame once a month, if you lick her sufficiently hard she rubs the skin off your tongue. With her, too, if you stick your nose in the appropriate place, you get a whiff of organic matter reverting to its mineral state. Now, St. Augustine and Dean Swift thought of all this and thought it a reason for hating and belittling mankind. I think it a reason for being in love with excrement and putrefaction. It is a reason for choosing out, among all mankind, those who stink unashamedly, for consorting with lepers, thieves and whores, for choosing to be accounted scum. Scum, the rest of the world would say. The cream, say I. The *élite*. For you will have noticed that scum and cream both rise to the surface, leaving the clear, unfortifying, too easily digested common fluid behind. And here in this world the scum or the cream of mankind are those who suffer and rejoice, the idle, fecund and gay, those who cause the well-washed and well-fed to turn away with a finger to their nose. A man is worthless until he has touched rock bottom. He is worth only a little if, having once touched it, he then recoils in anxious haste or struggles against adversity. A man should make rock bottom his abiding-place, his nest. He should live continually in a desert, with the taste of sand in his mouth. It will give him a thirst.'

I said:

'The other day, in Charing X Road, I saw a man being strangled publicly for a few pence.'

'A Scotsman?'

'Yes,' I said. 'His neck was as red and scaly as a turkey's with continual strangulation.'

'I know him,' said Flora Massingham. 'It's Johnny Watt, and he's an awful swine. All he wants to do is show off his muscles. His wife left him.'

'So he won't do,' I said.

'No, he won't do. Now Joe Passiful . . . You will see the difference . . . Joe feels that he has no right to existence. When I first knew him he was a policeman. He got sacked for giving money to people he was supposed to run in, and as soon as he got sacked he left me because he didn't want me to be at the expense of his keep. He left me, and Heaven knows what he did before he took to letting himself be twisted up in a boxing ring. My little Joey. The things he does, and all the time he's paralysed with fear. He smells of fear, as you or I might smell of drink. If he's out shopping he avoids the time of day when little boys are playing in the street, but all the dogs bark at him, because they smell the fear, and make him drop his parcels and come home with the wrong change.'

'And what about Clifford?'

Flora Massingham said:

'I don't know Clifford well enough yet. He's got a nice, pink aura, but I don't know where he's got to with it. And besides, you know, it's rather up to him. Your wife, now . . .'

'Ah, yes.'

'. . . I must meet her soon, Leckie. But ring Clifford up. I want to take him to Paradies's again.'

'Where you took us ten days ago, off the Bayswater Road?'

'Yes, there.'

'As a matter of fact,' I said, 'Clifford was rather bored.'

'I know. But Paradies will be on his own tonight.'

'Is he the conjurer?'

'No, he owns the house, and the little private theatre's just one of his amusements. Clifford'll adore him. He's just the thing for Clifford.'

Paradies himself let us in. He was a tall distinguished gentleman with a white moustache. His clothes were excellently cut to reveal a chest enormously out of proportion to the rest of him and a waist ridiculously fine. As he turned to lead the way upstairs I noticed something sticking out through his coat, which might have been a dagger in his back or merely a handle to wind him up with. He took us into a large room full of rare works of art, but untidy, dusty and musty beyond belief, and served us with sherry and seedcake.

After suitable introductions and a little polite conversation, Flora Massingham said, in a tiny coaxing voice that was not her voice at all:

'Would you like to show us your shoe shop?'

Paradies coughed modestly and said that if we really wanted to see it, he would be very pleased. We all made appropriate noises and were led down into the basement, where there were hundreds of pairs of high-heeled shoes, riding boots with spurs, silver and brass fitted straps of all kinds hanging on the walls and a collection of riding and other whips from every part of the world. Paradies suggested modestly that we might care to try some of the shoes on and encouraged us to walk about in them. Clifford was the only one who entered into the spirit of the thing. He pranced about, clicked his heels together and sprang in the air. Paradies watched him with approval, if not, indeed, with excitement, and would most certainly have joined in Clifford's antics had not his position as host constrained him to preserve a mean between the various behavior of his guests. He did, however, put on a very fine pair of high-heeled riding boots of undressed yellow leather.

Flora Massingham, in the same little, coaxing voice, said to him:

'And now would you perhaps play the organ for us?'

Again we went upstairs. I insisted on taking off the shoes I had put on, but Clifford and Paradies only laced theirs the tighter and became more and more flushed and excited, and Flora Massingham kept on her pair of multi-coloured Russian boots out of pure amiability. The organ was a full-sized instrument built into the largest of the rooms, which I had seen before as the theatre. Paradies played it merrily, and Clifford danced. The tone of the organ was superb, and Clifford's impromptu choreography was fully worthy of it. In the end, Clifford began to pull down curtains and hangings from the wall, taking off his coat and trousers and draping himself in the curtains and hangings which looked as if they might be most expensive and rare. After a while, we all went back to the first room and had more sherry and seedcake.

Flora Massingham put on a wicked, secretive look and said:

'But would you like to show us the little animal now?' Paradies was confused. He blushed, coughed and giggled a little, but his eyes shone.

He said:

'Would you really like to see it?'

He seemed particularly shy of Clifford, now. But eventually he showed us the little animal. It was encircled, every half inch or so, with a fine, gold ring, and each ring was studded with every kind of precious stone and had an elaborate, pendent medallion.

In order to keep the conversation flowing, I told Paradies that among the Indians of Patagonia a ring of mule's hair is so bound upon the neck that the hairs project forward, while the Dyaks of Borneo, the *glans* having been flattened between two boards for several years, pierce it with a bamboo skewer and keep the passage thus bored open with a pigeon quill until the time comes to substitute the ampallang of copper, silver or gold with its pair of revolving balls. He was extremely interested and thanked me with genuine feeling for the information. We stayed thus in conversation for a few minutes longer, and then Flora Massingham went downstairs to put on her own shoes again, and she and I took our leave, leaving a happy, manifestly rejuvenated Clifford behind with Paradies. Flora told me that Paradies was really a most distinguished gentleman and a personal friend of several members of the Court circle if not, indeed, of the Family itself. I asked her about the instrument projecting from Paradies's back, and she said that she had forgotten to make him show me this, but it was the handle of a powerful steel corselet which Paradies tightened up a little each day. His waist was reputed to be already the smallest in the world.

We spent the rest of the night wandering. At a little nightclub we saw three very beautiful girls dancing with three young men in plus fours, with three little, damp moustaches. On the Victoria Embankment we heard a lovers' quarrel that was like a Cockney scene in a B.B.C. vaudeville programme and as moving as if it had taken place in real life. In Hyde Park and in the Bloomsbury squares, trenches dug hastily during the crisis of the previous year reflected the fitful light of the moon.

I said:

'Can bitterness be obstructed?'

I said:

'Is there no excusable wrath?'

I said:

'I committed three months ago an act of violence.'

And then I told Flora Massingham about Richard St. Hilda. I said:

'It was not my act. The world and a great many stars conspired to rob me of the power of free movement at a time when my forehead was creased with resentment and humiliation.'

I said:

'I hit this man because there was nothing else that I was able to do. Everything dropped out of my hands. I could not hold a loaf of bread, and so I threw it at this man and knocked his spectacles off. That immediately seemed to me to be such a stupid thing to do that I was forced to hit him. I hit him very hard. I hit him disgustingly hard. But all the time I was wanting somebody or something to stop me. If my wife had not presently come and tugged at my arm, I should have turned and implored her to do so. And when it was all over, I wept as I have never wept in my life.'

There was a pause.

'Why have you told me this, Leckie?'

I said:

'Perhaps I am afraid of the consequences.'

'The . . .?'

'Oh, not the immediate consequences,' I said. 'Richard St. Hilda has a scar over his eye. I "marked him for life." But we are still friends. He passes it off as a joke and did so from the beginning, as soon as the doctor had stitched him and the concussion had worn off. As a matter of fact,' I said, 'I think he rather enjoyed it. Enjoyed the exciting scene. Enjoyed behaving well. Enjoyed having his forehead bathed by Effie. Enjoyed the fuss made by neighbours. Enjoyed putting about an alibi to the effect that he had been kicked by a horse. And I still live in his flat, and when I have no cigarettes he gives me a little money to buy some. It isn't that,' I said. 'It's the process started or prematurely concluded in my own life. In what way shall I have to answer for the act? What are the obscure depths that it should have revealed and failed to?'

Flora Massingham said:

'This man has forgiven you. Have you forgiven him?'

I said:

'I don't know.'

I said:

'No, I don't think I have. I don't think he wants me to forgive him. I think he plays on my feeling of remorse. I was angry with him at first because he broke promises to me, and he has broken other promises since then, as if he were tempting me to hit him again. At this very moment, he is in the South of France with a young boy for whom he cares very little. When he gives me money, he gives me as little as possible so that it won't be long before I want more, and when I am without a cigarette he pretends not to notice the fact, perhaps for a whole day . . .'

I told Flora all this. I tried to tell her about 'Thea', but I did not get a chance, because she was more interested in the fact that I had a wife. I think she must have known that what I meant to say about 'Thea' was worthless. I was going to parade myself as a person uncommonly sensitive to his fate.

After returning from Kent and again taking up my abode at Richard St. Hilda's flat, I had in fact twice thought that I should see 'Thea'. There had been a further social evening at the Institute of Mystical Science, and there had been a demonstration of dancing by Fraülein von Stubenau's pupils at a hall in North London. I had intended to go to both these functions, and I had felt with certainty that 'Thea' would be there. In both cases, just as I was about to set off, friends had called and I had found myself inescapably involved in an evening's hard drinking. I knew that 'Thea' had been at the social evening. Edgar Voysey and Clifford Fantl had been there, and they had seen her.

'I didn't like the people she was with, you know. A typically disreputable refugee group,' Fantl had said, and he had held back from speaking to 'Thea', as he had promised he would if ever he saw her again.

I was going to recount this incident as a further example of fate's finger meddling with me, but I was not given a hearing.

As to my horoscope and its indications of danger from falling masonry, I did not try to mention it. At this time, that fear had receded into the back of my mind, and when I observed it I was a little ashamed, as one is of the fear of pain or of animals or of any irrational fear.

A little before dawn, we turned into the Lyons' Corner House in Piccadily. It was full of middle-aged men who looked as washed out as the fading moon outside. Some were taking breakfast with the young or less young women in whose beds they had but recently disported themselves. Others were simply taking breakfast. None of them spoke.

Dawn over London on a Sunday morning. The streets were bare, the pavements as comfortless as dirty ice. A wan light shone out of the sky, only half removing the shadows of a dusty Saturday. A priest hurried in at the door of St. Mary's Church in Soho Square. Flora Massingham was performing all next week, twice nightly, in Rotherham and the following week in Sheffield. I felt something not unlike desperation at parting from her again. Her great mouth plastered encouraging, moist kisses upon my face. I watched her turn and go towards her bus stop in Charing X Road. She had no corset, and the stuff of her light summer coat clung electrically to the massive, adorable geography of her bottom. I turned and walked off towards Holborn.

Five

I must now make a third statement liable to provoke disbelief. Having married Richard St. Hilda's mother early the previous year, Clifford was Richard's stepfather. The arrangement no longer had much reality and at the time had given rise to little but a momentary panic.

Upon his retirement, Richard St. Hilda's father, a diplomat, had fulfilled a lifelong ambition and married a chorus girl or, rather, a chorus singer in musical comedies. Upon the demise of Richard St. Hilda's father, his mother had taken to drink. Richard's adolescence and the childhood of his sister, Isobel, had been much disturbed by their mother's alcoholic crises. Isobel (the result, Richard insisted, of a pill) had sometimes had to be locked away in her nurse's room for protection. Once at least Richard had been impelled to strike his mother. Luckily, old St. Hilda (perhaps having seen all this coming) had left his money in trust to the children. On Richard's coming of age, they had been able to install their mother, with a monthly allowance, in a small house at Torquay and to pay as they arose such debts as she managed to incur.

I do not know whether there is (or was in those days) a theatre at Torquay. Clifford had perhaps taken a summer engagement with some pierrot troupe. At any rate, he and Mrs. St. Hilda had somehow become acquainted. It may be that a member of the same troupe had known Mrs. St. Hilda during her own brief theatrical career. If so, no doubt he told Clifford that she had married a rich man, for Clifford had most certainly assumed that she was a rich widow. Richard had learnt of the affair during the first months of our acquaintance. He had been too late to prevent the marriage taking place, but had managed to see that no serious harm was done. He had rather taken to Clifford, and Clifford, for his part, had shown no rancour at the disappointment of his expectations.

Clifford was now out of the picture. I later heard of him entertaining the troops. Mrs. St. Hilda took up with a priest and continued to drink. Every once in a while, Richard paid one of her enormous drink bills.

I never met Mrs. St. Hilda. Frequently, however, I talked to her over the telephone. It was usually evening when she rang, but sometimes it was afternoon. As the day's first alcoholic exhilaration gave way to loneliness and anguish, she would put through a long-distance call. Even when Richard was there, he would not himself answer the telephone. At first either Derek Sutler or I and then either Alison or I would calm Mrs. St. Hilda and get her off the line.

It must have been during that last fortnight before the outbreak of war that, exasperated by my noncommittal, yes-and-no voice, constantly interposed between her and the voice she wished to hear, Mrs. St. Hilda broke off our pointless conversation and positively screamed at me:

'Get out of my son's flat!'

Alison had gone to see her mother in the Isle of Wight. She was due to return on a Saturday which proved to be the day before our declaration of war. Richard St. Hilda was in the French Pyrenees, on the point of turning east towards the Cote d'Azur. I was alone in his flat, except for the woman who came in each day to cook my breakfast and clean up. And except for the two Siamese. As I had explained to Richard when he was driving off to Dover, at other times I would not for the world have cooked Tit and Nit their food, but when I was in charge it was different. I also mowed the grass. At moments I experienced resentment, because I felt that I should have been in the Pyrenees, too, and not cooped up in London through the dusty months.

I remember writing to someone at this time, to refuse an invitation, and saying:

> I am inclined to welcome the prospect of war, and this sets
> me apart from my friends, who dread it. Destitution is worse
> than war, and, for some, war is a remedy against destitution.

And at one moment I rang up a recruiting office and demanded to know the age limit for marines. They were still taking nobody over twenty-three, and so I was preserved from that folly.

On Friday, September 1st, I got up so pleased with life that I at once set off for Hyde Park. It was a hot day with an immaculately blue sky. I took a boat out on the Serpentine and fell into an ecstasy of contentment. The birds sang. The trees whispered together. The girls loitered in their coloured dresses. I returned home before lunch and sat in Richard St. Hilda's drawing room, with the balcony windows blissfully open. My attention was attracted by the cry of a child, a rare sound in that neighbourhood. I turned to the french windows, and it was a Chinese baby in the next garden, with black eyes and blue hair. A Chinese woman in black satin trousers and white tunic came out to comfort the child. I was ready to weep with pleasure.

In point of fact, our neighbours were the Chinese naval attaché and his family. I do not know whether China had a navy at this time, but certainly she had a naval attaché, and he lived next door.

At his front gate, there always stood a large black Ford bearing its C.D. disc and containing a pale-faced English chauffeur who read penny dreadfuls all day long. Earlier in the summer, I had been disturbed one afternoon by the sounds of a fowl in distress. I went to the window, and there in the neighbouring garden, tethered by one leg to the balcony post, was a Rhode Island Red hen. Tit and Nit were stalking her. Subsequently, I had several times seen poultrymen delivering a live hen at the front door, sometimes a Rhode Island Red and sometimes a Light Sussex or a White Wyandotte. I have no explanation to offer, unless it be that Chinese who wish to eat poultry are commanded either to kill it themselves with appropriate ritual or to eat it alive. It may have been that the attaché's family wished to adopt the English custom of keeping pets, but I have heard that the Chinese eat newborn mice alive, picking them up by the tail, diping them in a pot of honey and swallowing them whole.

I was deeply moved by the sight of the Chinese baby. For one thing, before she went off to Southampton, Alison had wondered if she were not in the family way herself. I had dismissed this as a rather painful joke, but now it came back to me as reality, and I even wished for a moment that it might be true. Babies were becoming dramatic. Not only did one cast horoscopes for the moment of their first cry, but that very morning the Germans had invaded Poland, and when I went out for a drink before lunch there were headings in the newspapers to the effect that Hitler was bombing every baby he could find.

The following day, Alison returned to London, looking very pretty. I met her at Baker Street.

She said:

'Darling, there *is* going to be a war, isn't there?'

I told her there was. All the astrologers had failed to notice it, but that was because they were looking at their charts instead of at the sky. The charts do not bother their heads about closeness to the earth. Mars stood in the evening sky like a young sun, closer to the earth than it had been for Heaven knows how many years.

Alison said:

'In that case, darling, hadn't I better come and live at Richard's? I know he'll let me, if you will.'

And then she told me:

'Darling, I *am* in the family way . . .'

Richard St. Hilda had reached Vence when the war broke out. Also living in Vence now was Edgar Voysey, who had deserted the astral plane in order to paint, and the two young men who had lived opposite Alison and myself in Marginal Road and one of whom had lent me an overcoat and made oracular utterances to me at Richard's party in the spring, not to mention a woman famous for her motion pictures in silhouette and an elderly pioneer in the photography of pure light. Richard took his friend to the pornographic cinemas in Cannes and Nice, drank apéritifs, sunbathed and flirted with sailors. The end of August arrived, and the natives of Vence began to look suspiciously upon their harmless English and American visitors. Poland was invaded. That same day, gentlemen from the *deuxiéme bureau* called and took them all off to prison. A few questions would have been all, but the elderly photographer had started to learn French, and in his possession was a notebook containing phrases in French and English. The local schoolmaster was called in to give expert evidence. Richard St. Hilda and the rest were released, but advised to return home at once.

Edgar Voysey decided to stay behind and attach himself to the American Red Cross. The others drove across France for three days, saw nothing but horses, thousands upon thousands of them, and reached London on Wednesday morning, September 6th.

I was lying on the divan in his drawing room when Richard came in. There had been an air raid warning during the night, and I was sleepy. Alison was out at work. She had a temporary job with some medical organisation.

Richard had not changed, except that he was very sunburnt. He had brought me several interesting works of philosophy to read. He seemed in perfect health, and I found myself very pleased to see him again, contrary to my expectations.

Some days passed. The weather continued good. It began to seem evident that the Germans had no intention of inaugurating the end of the world by bombing London to a powder. The cinemas and theatres reopened. Illustrated war papers began to appear. The evening sky was full of silvery balloons, looking at times like a still from some film of a Martian invasion and at other times, when they were going up on a windy day, like a stampede of enormous, plunging cows. The absence of electric lighting revealed new beauties in London at night, and in a night breeze the balloon cables sang distantly and sounded, until you had traced the sound to its source, like a music of the spheres. The world was changing slowly but demonstrably and, so far as the natural senses were able to tell, changing not for the worse.

Here I must turn back. My personal life appeared to have become reasonable, but the appearance was illusory. Three circumstances still disturbed me. I have mentioned one of them, the fact that on two occasions I had thought to see 'Thea' and had been unaccountably prevented.

Possibly more disturbing was the fact that during four whole months, from April to August, I had done nothing. I am by nature a lazy but I am not an inactive man, and even now, when I look back upon those four months, my scalp tingles. I must have spent the bulk of those months rotting in an armchair, while madness rooted busily in the motionless soul. When I think of this inaction, it is as if one had turned to his mirror and found that he no longer cast any reflection in it.

A third circumstance takes me back to the period immediately after I had struck Richard St. Hilda. I must recount it in detail.

As I have said, Richard bore the situation well.

He stood up, a great column of a man, topping six feet, with the blood arching out over his brows like a waterfall, and said, with a dignity and calm that were almost excessive:

'Alison, look after Caroline, please.'

He then walked steadily to the house, holding a table napkin to his face.

I sat down on a white-painted bench, trembling furiously and, I am sure, white to the lips. At the end of perhaps two minutes, I also was sufficiently recovered to go indoors. I remember that, as I passed where he had been sitting, I picked up Richard's spectacles, which had been knocked off by the loaf of bread before I hit him.

I went to the drawing room and sat huddled and immobile in my usual chair. Overhead, a tap was running in the bathroom. Presently, I heard Richard come downstairs and take up the telephone in the hall. He telephoned to three doctors, but could get none of them. He went round to Effie's cottage.

Alison came in. She stood for a moment, as if to give me the opportunity of speaking to her if I wished to. I said nothing, and she went out.

As soon as she had gone, the very substance of my lungs began to tremble, and before I knew it I was sobbing with a vehemence of which I should not have believed myself capable. Had anyone been within hearing, he must have supposed it a wounded lion roaring.

When this fit was over, I heard a car arrive and saw Effie's doctor pass the window.

Some time later, Effie appeared outside the window, in a large, haymaker's hat. She gave Alison a note from Richard and waited for a reply. The note said:

> DEAR LECKIE,
>
> I would like to hear from you before I venture to return to the other cottage. I am frankly afraid lest this lunchtime's incident should be repeated. If you feel so inclined, please go away. If you don't, please let Effie bring me some form of reply. I am lying down for a while and shall probably stay where I am until after supper, when I expect to be recovered.
>
> Ever,
>
> RICHARD.

Effie also told Alison, and Alison told me, that Richard had had two or three stitches put in and was suffering from concussion. I went round to where Richard languidly reclined on Effie's lace-covered divan and dumbly pleaded disorder of the psyche, holding Richard's wrist instead of his hand as if the wrist were less compromising.

The next thing was that Frances and Herbert Abell, who had been up to London for the day, came to the door, on what pretext I forgot. At any rate, they were on the scent. They pretended not to have seen Caroline since their return.

During the week or so which elapsed between this occasion and our return to London, the Abells never in fact rested for a moment. Richard, as I have said, invented for the benefit of the village an alibi to the effect that a horse had kicked him, and he and I presented an aspect of unbroken friendship to the world, but the Abells tried desperately to keep as it were the bad blood on the boil. They succeeded to the extent of keeping Effie in a great state of nerves and of inducing her to invite a psychoanalyst of her acquaintance down from London, but he only stayed for tea and told us stories of Alpine holidays. At moments, I very nearly ran amok again and hit everybody.

Our neighbours speculated. Richard himself brought me reports of their speculation.

Frances Abell said:

'It was jealousy, of course. You'll notice he went for the eyes, and you'll remember that the evening before we'd been admiring Richard's eyes.'

Herbert Abell thought it must have to do with Caroline. Effie said:

'Poor Leckie. He's so full of blind hatred.'

Then, on the morning of our departure, Richard did not take the trouble to go round to Cherry Orchard to say goodbye to the Abells. Frances and Harbutt came round as Alison, Richard, Tit, Nit and I were packing ourselves and our luggage into Richard's car. Frances Abell's morning face was heavily made up, and the rodent's eyes behind her glasses were full of loneliness. Harbutt was hearty as ever, but with a failing conviction. Eric was playing his flute in the house. Caroline, with her wonderful, peach-bloom legs, was not to be seen.

Something in my face told Richard that the presence of the Abell's worried me and that I was still hating them.

Frances Abell said to me:

'Are you feeling better now, Leckie dear?'

No doubt I flushed.

Richard said, quite openly:

'Don't mind them, Leckie. You're alive, and they're dead.'

Frances Abell's face seemed to consist of nothing but the rice-powder on it. Herbert Abell's distinguished heartiness froze. As Richard drove away, I looked back, and the Abells were two pillars of salt that would have crumbled beneath a light blow with the palms of the hands. Unseen by Richard and Alison, I crossed myself.

Isobel St. Hilda appeared, newly married to a man called Nigel Tillyard of whom Richard did not approve. Indeed, when the marriage first became imminent Richard had tried to persuade me to flirt with his sister and if possible to start an affair with her, in order, if it could still be done, to separate the two. That I did not respond to the invitation is no criticism of Isobel St. Hilda's physical charms.

I had met her once without Nigel Tillyard and twice with him. She somewhat resembled her brother in appearance, though she was small and brown-eyed. She had been head girl or games captain or something of the kind at Roedean when Nigel, out bird-watching on the Downs, first caught her in his binoculars. Any other former head girls at Roedean I have met went in for verse-speaking more or less professionally. Perhaps it is for this accomplishment that head girls of Roedean are appointed. In that case, Isobel St. Hilda must have been games captain or something else, for I am pleased to say that I have never known her show the least tendency to speak verse.

What she in fact took up under Nigel Tillyard's influence was the study of art, though Nigel himself had not until then taken up this pursuit. They also became members of the Hammersmith branch of the Left Book Club. This led to old raincoats, low-heeled shoes, ribbed, woollen stockings gartered below the knee, a hairband. In these garments, Isobel nevertheless contrived to look very well.

She and Nigel had just taken a house at Tottenham Rivers, beyond Hungerford, in Wiltshire. Richard was solicitous for his friends. His first act, on returning from France, had been to send Tit and Nit to a farm in Dorsetshire. I did not see them again, though I heard in due course from Derek Sutler that Tit, as often happens with emasculated tomcats, became dropsical. Richard himself proposed to go down presently to Bristol, where Derek had installed himself with his wife's parents.

Alison and I had no intention of leaving London for the present. Richard, however, was anxious that, if bombing started, we should have a country refuge prepared, especially in view of Alison's pregnancy. Isobel, despite her opposition to his wishes respecting her marriage, was still much under her brother's influence. She and Alison seemed to hit it off. And so it was arranged that at need we were to go down to Tottenham Rivers. We were simply to let Isobel know when we felt like coming.

Bristol pended. Richard, in the meantime, exerted his conscience with regard to the war. It had come as a surprise to him, and he felt that he ought to do something about it if only to prevent it doing something about him. He ran about to the Red Cross and St. John, to recruiting offices of the various services, to A.R.P. and A.F.S. centres and to the headquarters of the Peace Pledge Union, to investigate possibilities. One thing, he said, he would not do. He would not take anybody's life. I suggested that he should go easy for a week or two and let the war seep as it were into his consciousness and then see how he felt about it, but at the end of four days Richard had come to the end of his enthusiasm for immediate action and would spend most of the day lying on the divan, ruffling his hair and expressing the many degrees of perplexity upon his plump, gentle face.

At eleven o'clock on a fine morning towards the end of September, he was lying thus. I am unable to give the exact date. What follows so confused me that I forgot to note it down at the time.

In his disputation over the many issues involved in war, Richard tended to branch off into metaphysics and by way of metaphysics would arrive at personalities. He had always been deeply interested in the motives for human behaviour, and now that the occasion was safely past he frequently referred to my hitting him in Kent, in the hope of seeing to the bottom of the whole situation.

On this particular morning, I was inclined to be jocular. There were in Richard St. Hilda's drawing room four large pictures by the painter to whom Richard gave thirty shillings a week. One of these was a portrait of Richard. It depicted him leaning very grandly against an ornate mantelpiece, looking every inch a patron of the arts. At one point, I had suggested that we ought to put a piece of sticking plaster over the right eye of this portrait. Now I thought that perhaps, since the permanent extent of the scar was known, we might paint in a little scar.

It was all very jolly.

Again Richard indicated his interest in the motives for my act of violence.

'Perhaps,' he said, 'it would help me to understand this war . . .'

I said:

'It might help me, if I knew. But I'll tell you what I was thinking before I got up this morning. I was thinking what an anticlimax it was when I did hit you, and then I went on to wonder if perhaps there were such things as climaxes at all . . .'

'I've always rather wondered,' said Richard.

I said:

'. . . To hear people talk, you would think that climaxes were very common, that in fact everything had a climax. It is wishful thinking. People would like something to come to a resounding conclusion and remove them henceforward from the awful continuity of time. It is part of the death wish. The Victorian novel reader believed marriage a climax to love. We know better. How banal is the last half-movement of any symphony, compared with what preceded. Before the end, one has passed on to something else. Even in the embraces of the bed, I personally find that at the very peak of the act I am thinking that, when this is over, it will be some little while before I am able to start again . . .'

Alas, even for Richard, this was not the ultimate, binding truth. The war and his place in it were real perplexities to him, and he was not quite happy. He grinned and lay on the divan with ruffled hair, gazing through his spectacles at a ceiling in which there was no crack.

I thought coffee might be nice. I went downstairs to the kitchen, to ask for some to be made. The daily help had already left. I made the coffee myself.

Here I must ask the reader to consider a phenomenon connected with sight. So far as I know, everybody finds that an object will at one time appear larger or smaller than it does at another. This variation in one's estimate of size increases when the object is a human person, who can affect one by his own mood too. In health and manifesting vitality, his stature appears heightened. When he is tired or depressed, he shrinks visibly.

I offer this reflection in order that the reader may better appreciate my first reactions to the episode which I am now about to relate.

When I came upstairs again with the coffee, Richard St. Hilda was or appeared to be asleep. Moreover, he was or appeared to be smaller in size than he had been ten minutes ago.

My first thought invoked the phenomenon upon which I have commented above. In the case of Richard St. Hilda, this phenomenon was at all times particularly striking. A large man with an impressive presence and with the blooming, skin-bursting vitality of a milkmaid and perhaps the signs of a blood pressure to come in later life, he was optical illusion incarnate. When tiredness or depression withdrew him as it were within the limits of his skin, the diminution was considerable.

I stood there with a tray of coffee in my hands and considered Richard's apparent decrease in stature. I smiled. I put the tray down and poured out the coffee. I took one cup to Richard and touched his shoulder.

'Wake up,' I said. 'Here's coffee.'

Richard did not awake.

I put his coffee back on the tray and shook him.

Still he showed no sign of life.

'Playful, aren't you?' I said.

Eventually, I yielded to the incipient panic. I went round the corner to the house of the doctor who had attended my pains in the back. He was out. I returned to the flat.

This time there was no mistake. Richard had diminished to a size for which no degree of optical illusion could account. He had not wrinkled. He was still ruddy and smooth. He lay as he was before, his hair ruffled. Most extraordinary fact of all, his clothes still fitted him. But in stature he was a dwarf, a manikin.

I thought:

'Whatever happens next, I shall be held responsible.'

I thought:

'He is not shrinking visibly before my eyes. It is only when I am out of the room that he shrinks. I must not leave him again. I must find a priest or a doctor, but when I go out now I must take Richard with me.'

The thought that a priest would do as well as a doctor prompted me to wonder if perhaps some form of sacramental treatment by myself might not prevent the state of things from deteriorating still further before I had secured outside help.

I thought:

'How lucky it is that I have always kept a missal to hand.' I turned to the shelf on which I knew the missal was. What might have happened had it not been in the same room, I do not know. My eyes were turned away from Richard for no longer than a few seconds, and yet, when I turned to him again, he was fully three inches smaller. I found the text for ministry to the dying.

'Extreme unction,' I thought, 'may fix him at his present size.'

There was no oil in the room. I tried to remember the exact spot in the dining room where the salad oil stood. I flew out of the room, plunged down the steps three at a time, seized the bottle and flung myself upstairs again. Richard had lost perhaps an inch.

I loosened his clothes, uncorked the bottle of oil, dipped in my finger and anointed Richard's eyes.

I read out:

'Through this holy unction and through His most loving mercy, may the Lord pardon thee whatever wrong thou hast done by seeing. Amen.'

I tipped the bottle up on the first two fingertips of my right hand and dabbed behind Richard's ears.

I read out:

'Through this holy unction and through His most loving mercy, may the Lord pardon thee whatever wrong thou hast done by hearing. Amen.'

This was all wrong. According to the stage directions at the top, I ought to have a table covered with a white cloth and a dish on it containing cotton wool divided into seven distinct pellets, in order to wipe the anointed places. I ought to have some bread to purify my fingers.

There ought to be a lighted candle, holy water and a crucifix. I ought to be wearing a surplice and a violet stole.

I dabbed Richard's nostrils with my fingertips.

This time I remembered to do it in the form of a cross. I read out:

'Through this holy unction and through His most loving mercy, may the Lord pardon thee whatever wrong thou hast done by smelling. Amen.'

Also, I ought to have begun with certain prayers, a confession, penitential psalms and a litany. But I felt that if I did everything properly I might be too late. There was no time to waste. I must get Richard as it were sealed up.

I took my fingers from the mouth of the bottle and touched his closed lips.

'. . . The Lord pardon thee whatever wrong thou hast done by taste and speech. Amen.'

A cross on the back of each of Richard's hands.

'. . . Whatever wrong thou hast done by touch . . .'

His feet. But I dared not delay to take his shoes off.

'. . . Whatever wrong thou hast done by walking . . .'

The last thing I had better do properly. I unfastened Richard's fly buttons and touched him warily about the loins.

I read out:

'Through this holy unction and through His most loving mercy, may the Lord pardon thee whatever wrong thou hast done by the irregular motions of the flesh. Amen.'

There was a good deal more. I could not omit all of it. I picked out the last prayer but one.

I read:

'Look down, we beseech Thee, O Lord, on Thy servant Richard St. Hilda, bowed down by the weakness of his body, and revive the soul which Thou hast created, so that being amended by chastisement he may feel that he is made whole by Thy remedy. Through Christ our Lord. Amen.' I closed the missal.

I thought:

'I will now turn my head away and count ten.'

I did so. The sacrament was effective. When I turned back to Richard, he had not shrunk any further.

'Now,' I thought, 'I must wrap him up in the divan spread and take him to a doctor.'

I put my hands under Richard St. Hilda's shoulders and knees and lifted him up. Immediately, he dropped away to a powder so fine that my gasp of astonishment scattered him widely over the room, and he was no longer distinguishable from the motes of dust which all this while had been dancing in the sunlight from the window.

A sweat broke out upon my face and hands. I wrung my hands together in anguish.

I said:

'Oh, dear. Oh, dear.'

I hugged my shoulders and rocked from side to side. I chewed my top lip and then my bottom lip. I felt that I was bleeding between the toes. I shook myself and lit a cigarette. I tiptoed to the outer door and opened it. I paused and looked out. I walked into the street and then along the street, quickening my pace.

Six

To walk by night. I cannot know what reminiscence is provoked in other people by this phrase. To some, I fancy, who have little experience of solitude, it conjures up nothing unless it be that banality the moonlight excursion of lovers. To me and surely to a great many, it implies whatever lies deepest and most jealously guarded in their lives. It means hunger, homelessness and total frustration of the will. It means the piteous trade of a whore. It means restlessness at the full moon, when dogs bay and the lunatic cries aloud from the window of his room.

Above all, it means proximity to the divine.

But I need not go on. In those who understand, I have already touched the hidden spring. In those who do not, there is no apparatus for words to call into operation. I need only say that on the day of which I am writing I walked I know not where until the night fell, that all night I was lost to myself and that the morning, when it came, was like no other morning.

On the previous day, although it had been in my mind to look for a doctor or a priest, I had in fact made no search. Now, in the chill of the morning, I found myself by a church.

I went in.

Before a gilded ark, a tiny ball of light hovered. There were cage gates of heavy brass and of chromium-plated steel. A doll in purple sat askew upon a cupboard top, her black hair surmounted by an enormous crown set with pieces of coloured glass. It was ten years since I had been in such a place.

I walked up the near aisle and looked at the cards hung upon the confessional boxes. None of them bore the name of any priest I knew or had heard of. I thought that somebody was there, behind each heavy, green curtain, but I knew that all these were discreet men who would not disturb me. I walked in front of the altar, genuflected and walked down the farther aisle. Here, too, the names on the confessional boxes were strange to me. I wondered what church this was and in what city.

In the shadows, a young and an old woman were praying near one of the boxes. A priest in his cassock strode across the church, a surplice over his arm, and went in. I turned away.

I went towards the vestry. Two young priests were just inside the door, the one robing the other, tying a great cord round and round him.

I said:

'Excuse me. Is Father Berthold here now?'

The priest half-robed turned his shoulders, heavily muffled with the pale gaberdine.

'Berthold?'

The other said:

'A Franciscan, I suppose.'

'Yes,' I said. 'He was at Ambleside.' The priest stopping to knot a cord said:

'He never was at this church, except for the Easter sermon.'

'I'm sorry,' I said.

I turned to go away.

'If you can wait,' said the priest, 'Father Aspic will be here. He's a Franciscan.'

I did not wish to wait, but I thought it would be impolite not to. Indeed, I became very nervous at the thought of meeting a strange friar. I could not think what I should say to him. As a matter of fact, I had no particular wish to see Fr. Berthold or any reason to suppose he was still alive. I had asked for him because his was the first priest's name that came into my head, and I had known perfectly well that he would not be there.

I stood uncomfortably by the vestry door and waited. Father Aspic came. I was glad that I had waited. Father Aspic was evidently a saint, and I knew at once that I could tell my story to him. He was very old and small. The brown hood fell about his sunken temples. His eyes were blue and short-sighted, and a lorgnette hung beside the rosary upon his friar's robe. His nose was thick and fastidious, and there was very little blood in his face.

Of the two young priests, one, now fully vested, had gone away to celebrate mass in a caged chapel. The other retired into the vestry and closed the door. Father Aspic put his hand upon my shoulder and walked down the aisle with me.

I told him nothing He led me to the door and pointed out the direction in which, he said, lay the chief house of the Franciscan province.

I asked him:

'Am I in London?'

Father Aspic showed no sign of surprise.

He said:

'Yes, my son.'

He did not even ask me:

'Have you come far?'

He said:

'Are you a Catholic?'

'Well, I was sort of brought up one,' I said.

I turned my red, guilty face to the morning sunlight falling upon London.

Father Aspic lifted up the crucifix on his rosary and kissed it. 'The world is very beautiful,' he said.

I told him nothing, but meeting him had comforted me. I stood upon the steps of the church and looked out upon London, with the sun rising. I turned to Father Aspic, to thank him for his kindness. He was not there. Perhaps he never had been there. Certainly, had I invented him, Father Aspic is a name that I might have given him.

In the afternoon, I walked on Hampstead Heath. The grass was damp. I think it was the same afternoon, but I am not certain. I walked to the top of Parliament Hill and looked across to Highgate and out towards London. St. Paul's was clearly visible, and so I thought was the Tower of London. I talked with a man flying kites. He had four large, variously coloured kites with him and flew them expertly. An assistant, a hungry-looking man no doubt hired in the street for this purpose, kept one kite flying, while the expert brought in or sent up another. He tended the kites very carefully. Each, when it was done with, he rolled up in yellow oilskin.

I walked through Ken Wood. Eventually, I reached the Vale of Health.

After that, I was at a tea party. I think it was in the Vale of Health. It was a rather genteel tea party, and I do not know whether I had called on some old acquaintance or whether I had been invited home by some stranger with whom I had entered into conversation, for instance the kite-flier.

By now, I had begun to enjoy my wanderings for their own sake. I was no longer searching. Or perhaps I was searching, but did not know for what. All I knew was that I must not go back to the flat in the Bloomsbury square. Every now and then, I had a moment of panic, as if I had forgotten something of importance.

I walked into town and found myself in Oxford Street, just round the corner from Phelps Place, where the Institute of Mystical Science stood.

At the outbreak of war, a circular had been sent round to the effect that lectures at the Institute would be discontinued, though informal discussion groups would be formed at the private addresses of the various lecturers. (Now that I think of it, perhaps the tea party that afternoon had been at one of these addresses. Mrs. Verity lived in Hampstead.) Also, I had rather tended to hold aloof from these people, because of 'Thea'. Now I thought that I would look into the building. Mrs. Verity or Dr. Gloss might still have a room there. The main door was open. I went up to the top floor in the lift. I went into the lecture hall. The chairs, the piano and the permanganate-of-potash paintings were still there, but there was no sign of human life. I took the lift down again and walked away.

For some reason, my attention was attracted by a shop window. Perhaps it was the Burmese Gem shop, attracting me by its name and by the varied brilliance of its wares. Certainly it contained a mirror.

I stared into this shop window and felt extraordinarily happy. And then I turned suddenly. I had felt behind me the presence of somebody in great anguish of spirit. I turned and saw a man with his jacket collar up and drying mud on his shoes. Our eyes met for a second, then the man turned on his heel and walked away, his hands in his trousers pockets. I felt impelled to follow him.

It was already fairly dark, and at one point I thought I had lost him. I caught up with him in a side street unfamiliar to me.

There was an archway leading to some yard or mews that lay completely in darkness. The other side of the arch was a closed shop and, above it, offices or a warehouse. On this side, light and a murmur of voices came out to us through a pseudo-antique oak door, a leaded window with a galleon inset in coloured glass and leaded lights over the door. In the archway itself was another door, and just outside it, in the shadow, were two men with musical instruments, a mandolin and a guitar. The door opened, and a group of young men and a girl came out, the girl laughing loudly, her head thrown back, a bag of peanuts and a handkerchief in her hand, the young men joking as it appeared savagely under their breath, their hands thrust deep in their trousers pockets, their heads forward. As the door swung to behind them, one of the musicians pushed his foot in to keep it from shutting completely. Both the musicians were sallow and had dark, greasy hair.

As the man I was following stepped forward, one of the musicians stopped playing, held out a cap and said:

'Thank you, sir.'

The man I was following looked at the musicians, peering into their cynically cheerful, vaguely dirty faces. The one who had stopped playing, the one with the mandolin, coughed and then ignored him, pushed his cap on his head and started strumming again. My man stood close to the two of them for a moment longer, opened his mouth to ask them a question, was about to turn and go away and then at last moved up to the door in the archway, pushed it open and went in. I followed.

People turned to look at him, people standing in groups, talking and drinking. He held back, but in a moment everybody had looked away again. He went up to the counter and pulled himself on to an empty stool. There were rows of brightly labelled bottles, some of them inverted, with little taps on the nozzle and little tin cups hanging down from the taps. Above the picture rail were squares of tartan cloth framed in varnished wood beading. Below these and filling in the wall space behind the rows of bottles was a single great mirror, and in the mirror, now, the face of the man I was following, a face intelligent and mobile but here and there setting in excessively definite lines, the pale, submarine eyes tremulous, hurt and withdrawn, the fair, partly bleaching hair untidy, the outline of cheek and jaw a little rough shaved, perhaps yesterday.

A handsome girl with unusually high colouring stood opposite him, on the other side of the counter, her hands on the counter, her head tipped over to one side.

She said:

'Good evening, sir.'

'Good evening. . .'

He looked between the bottles and into the mirror. He noticed evidently that his jacket collar was turned up and set it right. He looked across the heads of the people near him and into the brightly lit corners of the room.

The girl was still there.

She said:

'Can I get you anything, sir?'

He looked at her, wrinkled his nose and half smiled. There was a glass on the counter beside him. He put his fingers to it and lifted it up. A face turned and stared up at him, a plump, pink little face with a small moustache and thin hair brushed straight back. My man put the glass down and pointed to it with one finger.

'What's this?'

'Scotch ale, sir.'

'Is it good?'

'It's the best, sir.'

'Give me some of that.'

The girl took a glass from under the counter and drew up his ale, tugging at one of four black, silver-bound handles that stood between her and him. He spread his fingers out on the wood of the counter, pressing down on them until they must have hurt, then sighed and looked about him with a great deal less restraint.

But even now it was as if he did not quite understand. The girl put his glass of ale in front of him. He took a sip of it, held it up above the level of his eyes and looked through it at the fine, sparkling texture of the under surface.

The girl said:

'Four and a half, dear.'

The little, pink face was looking up at him with interest again, a hand pointing to his side pocket, all the fingers of another hand held up and then the first hand knocking its thumb down, the face exchanging a look with the girl behind the counter and its mouth saying very carefully and distortedly, with a gesture of both hands:

'Money. Baksheesh. Ar-jong. The glass of beer costs fourpence-halfpenny. Four and a half pence.'

The man I was following felt in his pocket and pulled out first a penny and then a florin. He put them both on the counter, took a single gulp of his ale, swung himself off the stool and pushed his way to the door.

The hectically coloured girl was calling out:

'Your change, dearie . . .'

But he stepped out into the archway and let the door swing to behind him. I followed. The two musicians, the guitarist and the mandolin player, had gone. My man stood a moment in the shadow of the arch, staring into the deeper obscurity of the mews or yard to his right, chewing his top lip. He shrugged his shoulders, put up his jacket collar again, thrust his hands into his pockets and turned out into the street.

He looked worried. Rather hungry, too. In the street was a costermonger's barrow. He seemed to think he would buy some fruit to eat out here and began to feel for a coin in his pocket, but some vague anxiety stopped him. He looked down at his feet, saw that his shoes were caked with pale, dry mud, frowned, his lips parting, sighed, shook his head and tried to smile but failed. Turning a corner, he had the lights and the traffic of a main road about two hundred yards away in front of him. He took another turning. To his left were two restaurants side by side and then a further block of warehouses, offices or whatever they were. There was some traffic even in this side street, a taxi, a private car, two girls in shorts racing each other on bicycles. He passed a German-Swiss delicatessen shop, the unlighted window full of varied sausages and dusty bottles of wine, then a smaller café. Through the window, half-curtained with lace, I saw men with their hats pushed back on their heads, playing a game with wooden discs and a dice-box. I thought it was called either backgammon or *tric-trac,* possibly both.

It was a warm, dry evening. I could not think why the man's jacket collar was turned up, but he kept it up all the same.

At the next corner was a newsagent's shop. It was closed. Turning the corner, we had the distant blaze of a main road in front of us once again. The man I was following stopped and looked about him. Outside the newsagent's shop were torn placards, each pinned to a separate board and propped against the grimy stonework. They were pre-war posters which had never been taken down. KING AND QUEEN IN ATLANTIC DRAMA. ROYAL TOUR TO CANADA DAILY REPORT. ALLIANCE WELL RECEIVED IN TURKEY. AXIS TURNED DOWN BY JAPAN AND FRANCO. They were meaningless and distant enough to be reassuring. BLACKOUT FOR ALL LONDON. My man again managed the half of a smile. Another placard apparently startled him for a moment. SOHO MURDER CASE DISCLOSURES. He looked away and looked at it again. It can have told him nothing, but a sweat broke out on his top lip. SOHO KILLING. MAN QUESTIONED. He breathed in quickly and stared across the street, squinting as it were into the huddled shadows of his own mind. But he knew already that this was only a pretence. There was no clue for him in this.

Coming towards him now was a tall, thin negro, flatfooted, with hands swinging loose, a big curly-brimmed hat on the side of his head. The negro, too, was reassuring, being totally alien and remote. My man smiled at the negro and spoke.

He said:

'Is this Soho?'

'Yeah, sure.'

The negro said it like any English boy who has been to American films. The voice was not like any of the voices that negroes are supposed to have. That made the man I was following smile all the more.

'Thanks,' he said.

'That's O.K.'

The negro walked on, the large, flat feet turned in.

Then something was happening, and the man with mud-caked shoes and his jacket collar turned up was afraid. Two cars were hesitating round the corner, one grey and one blue. I heard the occupants of the two cars consulting with each other, shouting through the noise of clutches holding their engines hard.

A woman's voice was calling out to somebody by name:

'Leckie. Leckie . . .'

The man's first impulse was to run up and see what it was, see if he could help. A lovers' quarrel, a drunken lark involving a girl, possibly a genuine crime. He might be useful. Then fear warned him again to turn away. He turned at once and marched off towards the distant main road, his heart beginning to pump hard.

The thought pulsed in his head:

'I don't want to get mixed up in anything. I must go away. I've got to keep clear of things.'

He strode out as fast as he could. There was no thought in his head, except that he must get away.

But the two cars were following him, were alongside, were pulling up two or three yards in front of him. People were getting out of them and banging the doors, from the grey car a woman and a large young man with a scar over one eye, from the other a police inspector and a constable. The man I was following strode on. He meant to ignore them. They stood in his path.

The woman kept saying: 'Leckie, darling. Leckie . . .'

It was to him that she was saying it. He must have seen that she was handsome, rather tall, and that she had tears in her eyes, but he strode on.

He said, with his eyes now looking straight in front of him: 'I'm sorry. There must be some confusion.'

He tried to get past, but the two policemen barred his way. The inspector said:

'Now be reasonable, sir. You're only . . .'

He did not hear any more. His head went round faster and faster, until his body could do nothing but follow it. His shoulders swung round, and one foot crossed over the other. He toppled heavily in the gutter, knocking off the police constable's helmet as he went down.

Seven

On November 9th, 1939, I had a letter from Tom Johnson. Recently come to hand were certain assets of Thorpe and Leckie, Ltd., which had not been in a position to be declared at the time of Sam Thorpe's demise and my bankruptcy. After deducting a suitable charge, Messrs. Johnson, Snooper and Co. proposed to hand these assets over to me. They would be pleased if I would accept payment in a series of instalments, as they were themselves temporarily embarrassed by war conditions. In short, I possessed several hundred pounds, of which I was able to touch fifty at once, with further cheques for twenty pounds reaching me on the first of each month for at least two years to come. I did not enquire into the source of this income nor question in detail its extent.

The effect on my state of mind was powerful and instantaneous. I recaptured my belief in the existence of free will. Indeed, I began to practice the exercise of free will. I took a taxi where formerly I would have taken a bus. I shaved every day and enjoyed frequent baths. I ordered myself a suit of clothes from a range of tweeds which I had always admired at a distance. I became voluble in society. I made new friends and visited or entertained friends whom I had for some time past neglected. I rose earlier in the morning. I went to theatres, parties and dances.

Looking further for a new way of occupying my time, the first expensive object I observed lying about in Richard St. Hilda's flat was a

Leica camera. It had accompanied Richard on expeditions to Switzerland and more recently to the Pyrenees and the Cote d'Azur. With it Richard had photographed cherry trees blossoming in Kent. It had been used by young actor friends to photograph their colleagues and by the subsidised painter to record his frequently rather large paintings in more portable form. To me it was an expensive object, and not until now had I felt that I had the right to make use of it.

The art of photography is very simple. It consists in exposing a piece of chemically sensitised machinery in the neighbourhood of almost anything, though by preference certain portions of the selected area should be darker and others lighter than the rest, a condition far from difficult to fulfil. The image thus produced is then enlarged, and the photographer will select a portion of the enlarged image for further reproduction. This he will do with the intention of securing a printed area over which dark and light patches are evenly and pleasantly distributed or, in the more ambitious language of a school of modern painters, an area in which is apparent the play of spatial relationships and the harmony of masses of tone. The photographer is further able to interfere with the printed image by scratching or making black marks on the film, by striking a match while the film is being developed, by under-printing and overdeveloping images in which small patches of perfect black appear or by superimposing a negative and a positive film to make his print. Suppose, for example, that he has originally exposed his machine in the neighbourhood of a human face. By scratching and making black marks, he may remove pimples, warts, moles and superfluous hair. By striking a match, he may outline the image with a thick black line, an effect known as solarisation and considered by many to be highly artistic, and indeed, if he does not presently blow the match out, the whole printed area will turn out uniformly grey or reveal a chin, a nose and possibly a bumpy forehead disembodied and afloat upon a sea of oil. The under-printing   and   overdeveloping   produce   high-key   prints, etherealising the face thus treated, while superimposition of a negative and a positive film results in the illusion of a bas-relief. I learned these tricks of the art from Aloysius Smith. As a matter of fact, I never employed any of them myself. I contented myself with exposing film in suitable neighbourhoods.

I thought that female nudes were perhaps suitable for a beginner. The war rendered liable to suspicion anyone observed taking photographs in the open air, and the neighbourhood of female nudes would, I thought, remain agreeable to the photographer even when, as might happen, his interest in the art itself flagged.

At this juncture, the young man whom Richard St. Hilda had taken with him into the Pyrenees and along the Cote d'Azur and who, perhaps as a result of this experience, was turning over a new leaf, asked Richard if he might bring with him to dinner a young woman called Pat Mallard. Richard, at this time, was seldom in town, but when he was I found him in a rare good humour. I several times caught him looking at me intently, but when I met his eye he merely ruffled his back hair and grinned at me his slow, rosy grin of incomprehension. He must have decided each time he looked at me that, even if something needed to be done, he was not the man to do it, for he presently took himself off again, staying first with Effie in Kent and moving on from there to the farm Tit and Nit were on in Dorset, leaving behind him messages to the effect that he still had a little money if any were really needed. On this particular evening, although we had neither of us seen Pat Mallard or formed any clear impression of her from the young man's account, Richard decided to express his good humour by conspiring with me that he and I should impersonate each other. That is to say, he would address me as Richard, and I would address him as Leckie. I would do the honours as host. We hoped that the young man would quickly see and fall in with our little game, and we trusted to be amused by the reactions of the young woman, who had presumably heard a good deal and formed a definite impression of Richard St. Hilda, if not indeed of me too.

I mention this fact not because our little game had any amusing consequences of its own but because it reveals the attitude of mind which we cultivated towards Pat Mallard even before we had met her and which therefore must have influenced my later relations with her.

Pat Mallard was a big girl with spectacles and a clipped, schoolmistress manner of speaking. She lived in the Hampstead Garden Suburb alone with her father, a retired military man, and studied dancing of a daisy-picking variety at one of the numerous schools founded under the influence of Isadora Duncan. Richard's young man had made her acquaintance at the headquarters of a pacifist group in the West End, and we did not presume from her appearance that his interest in her could be other than that of intellectual comradeship. Richard and I abandoned our little game very quickly and without apologies, as though, with a young woman like this, it were hardly worth playing.

This was no more than a day or two before Richard's eventual departure for Bristol. The morning before, he left the flat soon after breakfast. He told me that he was meeting his solicitor in order to make a new will. He said this with a direct, lingering and rather bashful smile. I was told nothing more, but I interpreted the smile as an intimation that the matter could be regarded as one in which I had some interest. Richard went. Two or three days afterwards, I met his recent young man in the street. I wanted a model. It occurred to me to ask about Pat Mallard. She was strongly built, and her dancing, though it served no other purpose, would have developed just the degree of muscularity which looks well under strong lighting.

I said:

'Do you think Pat might come and pose for me? Do you mind?'

I felt certain she would come if the young man agreed and asked her, for the combination of ripe virginity and an interest in the arts is commonly pleased by a request to denude itself of workaday raiment. The young man agreed.

I said:

'I should think her figure is rather good, isn't it?'

The young man said:

'I should think so.'

Pat Mallard came to the flat in Bloomsbury on Saturday afternoon. I concentrated what lighting I had in the dining room downstairs, and Pat undressed in Alison's room which was also downstairs.

She said to Alison:

'Does your husband want me to take everything off?'

Alison lent her a dressing gown, and Pat Mallard came into the dining-room, where I had a gas fire going and, drawn across the windows, a print curtain of Vanessa Bell design.

I was deeply moved, when Pat removed the dressing gown and placed herself against this curtain, to find that her body was beyond criticism and that she posed with a rare sensitiveness. I must attempt to do my feelings justice. Here was a young woman whom almost anybody would have written off as one of the eternally unloved. Her clothes, her spectacles, her way of doing her hair (although it was nice hair), her interests, her manner of speech, all proclaimed the type of young woman of the English middle classes whom parental inhibition, influences at school and afterwards, attitudes of the people she met, had robbed of the capacity to go out of herself into a vivid, painful world. Yet here was this same young woman with her clothes off and her spectacles off, doing something which her training allowed her to think worth the trouble. Her body was lovable, and her movements were not only sensitive but free, free and lucid beyond the capacity of many a harlot. She lifted her arms above her head and, poising herself upon the toe of one foot and the ball of the other in a position which her school of dancing had taught her, parted them fastidiously from each other and extended her body in superb profile. Her head lifted and then bowed gracefully upon its column of neck, and even her face had proved itself to be charming. I could have cried.

I remember that I said to Alison afterwards:

'If somebody not a fool would only make love to her, what a change there would be.'

Alison said:

'Well, darling, there's always you.'

I said:

'No. I'm afraid it would be hard work. I should have liked to try, but I really don't feel that it's up to me. I haven't enough energy as it is.'

It was November. Alison by now was over three months gone and believed that she felt the child stir. She was working for three doctors in Wimpole Street. Every fortnight or so, she went to the Middlesex Hospital for examination and prenatal care.

That weekend, she went off again to the Isle of Wight, from which she was to return on Monday morning. The horror of the grave yawns conspicuously after tea on Sundays. That Sunday, I found Richard St. Hilda's Bloomsbury flat exceptionally desolate. Nobody had come in that morning to make the beds and wash up.

I had at one time hung around the ballet. I had been for almost a year consumed with hopeless passion for an Australian girl called Maimie Joyce, who was the star dancer in a small company called the Ballet Unit. The Unit Theatre was in Canonbury. I was no longer very interested in ballet or, at all acutely, in Maimie Joyce. I thought I would go to the Unit, all the same.

The first person I encountered as I entered the dingy little foyer was a girl called Midge Pettit. During the period of my hopeless passion for Maimie Joyce, Midge had been my confidante. One or two of the young men having volunteered for the R.A.F., she was now the Ballet Unit's business manager.

I said:

'Hello.'

I said:

'How's Maimie?'

I said:

'What am I going to see?'

Midge said:

'You haven't seen Tristram's new ballet, have you? It's rather lovely.'

Anything that Midge Pettit liked was 'rather lovely'. Her vocabulary of disapproval was less exclusive.

I found my seat.

The music was played on two pianos occupied by a plump young man and a lean young woman. They played a little suite by Erik Satie, after which the curtain went up for a ballet by one of Stefi Yefimovitch's lesser talents, a frisky, nostalgic thing in a taste which the advent of war had made seem curiously out of date and insipid. Maimie Joyce was not dancing in this, but Tessa Duveen was. I thought Tessa had quarrelled with the Ballet Unit long ago, but here she was, improved in style and feeling if not in technique. I must remember to find Tessa and be nice to her when I went behind after the show.

The second ballet was one of Tristram Panting's older pieces, done at a time when he was experimenting with the idiom of Javanese dance movements. I still thought it pretty good. Then the interval. Then the new ballet, *Le Retour d'Orfée*.

It was danced to music by Scriabine. Obviously, Panting had been reading Rilke. He presented Eurydice not merely as the female principle of teeming life and spiritual inertia but as a shadow of Orpheus's mind lost to him by self-love, turned now to reality by his acceptance of personal death.

I thought how perfectly managed it all was, how totally exteriorised upon the little stage. It was a ballet without a single cliché or a single end-stopped movement. When a dancer left the stage it was because the interplay of forms, as it were, relinquished him. When a dancer made his entry, it was as though the flow of movement passing from one to another compelled him to come.

I sat entranced. Maimie Joyce's long arms created a perfect harmony and froze it upon the air.

During the applause that followed, I heard a young man behind me observe to his neighbour:

'I must say, I do think Colin's costume was rather fetching.' I went through the foyer and the print room to the iron steps which led up to the dressing rooms.

Tristram Panting was having a row with the fair-haired young man who had just danced his Orpheus to perfection and who now, off the stage, looked undersized and ridiculous.

He was saying:

'Colin, how can you be so horrid?'

Colin tossed back his hair and said:

'I don't care. I don't. It brings out the beast in me, Tristram.'

I wanted to explain to Panting what I felt about his work. He was too engrossed in the quarrel. He was friendly for a moment and introduced me to Colin, who touched my hand with his long fingers and nearly broke me off at the elbow, but a moment later the quarrel had been resumed. I gave it up. This world was too full of contrasts for me. I looked for Maimie Joyce's dressing room.

Maimie's husband was already there. Dear Michael, who was as kind and sensible as Maimie herself and as free of passion. He loved her with an old man's detachment and a boy's attentiveness to detail. It was perfect. The lovely iceberg had found in marriage with this young man a climate totally suited to her. I had tried to blister the lucid slopes.

Maimie said:

'How did you like *Orfée?*'

'I liked it,' said I. 'I tried to tell Tristram, but he's too busy having a temperament with Colin out in the passage. I can tell you, though.'

I said:

'How's neuralgia this winter?'

Maimie's husband said:

'She doesn't have neuralgia since she got married. She nearly had appendicitis, though.'

I said that I myself had not been terribly well lately, but luckily I was not made to go into detail.

The little dressing room was all mirror, bright light, paper wrappings and cleansing tissues, floating powder, flimsy dresses, wigs, flowers and pinned-up greetings telegrams. Maimie had already got the powder and the grease off her face. She sent us out while she changed her clothes. The passage was narrow and crowded. In another dressing room, some of the boys were playing a gramophone. They were playing hot music to shock each other. A number of admirers and mothers had arrived. Girls were pushing past from one room to another. Everybody was in everybody else's way. Maimie's husband and I went and stood at the top of the iron steps. Tessa Duveen came out of the nearest dressing room. I had forgotten my intention of seeking her out and making a fuss of her.

'Meanie,' she was saying. 'You wouldn't have let a girl know you were here if I hadn't found out.'

I tried to look hurt and at the same time rather absentminded.

Tessa smiled. She said:

'It's awful nice to see you. My, aren't you smart? How ever did you manage to buy a suit like that? Are you going to speak to a girl, now she's here?'

I'm afraid Tessa Duveen takes rather a lot of explaining. Her act in public, indeed in private, too, was that of the bad little girl whom nobody understands. Nor was it altogether an act, for she *was* a bad little girl, and probably nobody in her world understood her except Maimie Joyce and myself. She contended that everybody else hated her.

She had other grievances. That she was not beautiful, for instance. That she was too fat. That she would never be a great dancer. These grievances were all to some extent true, though not sufficiently true to prevent her from being a little person very pleasant to look at and a character dancer whom any producer would have been glad to have to hand.

But one could describe Tessa Duveen's surface characteristics at great length, and the total impression would be more and more that she was a spiteful, affected and spoilt child. She was not. Or rather she was, but she was also a brave, spontaneous, vivid and hard-living girl.

She was short, plump, sensuous and highly coloured, with a variety of styles of coiffure which ended up in a fringe of rusty curls on the forehead, so that she reminded one of a Renoir girl or a Manet cocotte. When I first knew her, she was sixteen. She fell in love with me (I think, but it is always a little difficult to be sure) when I was hopelessly attached to Maimie Joyce. I kissed her a little, but for the most part I played big brother.

At seventeen, Tessa got herself into a scrape and married a young man as crazy as herself, a wild, hurt boy with very straight flaxen hair which drooped in an enthusiast's side-lock over his right ear, who poured jugs of beer over her and was conscientiously and tormentedly unfaithful from the beginning. The baby was born months late and showed a perverse desire to be born the wrong way round, but by this time the father had gone off to China to fly an aeroplane against the Japanese. Having lost the use of one hand, he returned and tried to set up house again with Tessa, but never succeeded for more than a month at a time. He hated me and in some of his jealous fits would accuse Tessa of having married him on the strength of a child that was mine.

Tessa Duveen was now twenty-one.

I suddenly felt homesick for her violent youth.

I said to Maimie's husband:

'Look, I'm going. Don't let Maimie think I'm rude. I'm coming again next week to take photographs from the wings. In any case, I'm going to ring you up and bring Alison to supper with you one night.'

I took Tessa's arm, and we went down the iron steps and out into the dark street. Tessa had changed her clothes, but she had not taken her make-up off. She had lost her tissues, and nobody would lend her any. We went into a little delicatessen and had coffee and a sandwich. The shop was full of every kind of sausage and every kind of bread hanging in rows. Tessa's made-up face, orange and red, with blue and silver eyelids and long, thick lashes, had a stimulating unreality beneath this ordinary light. We sat on high stools at the counter, our cramped knees touching. For the first time, I really felt desire for Tessa Duveen. I treasured it. I had often wanted to want her. At times she moved me, but I had never really desired her.

I said:

'Are you coming home with me, Tessa? Nobody's there tonight.'

Tessa made a wry face. Then she sat worrying.

After a while, she said:

'I don't like this place.'

We went out and stumbled through the blackout along a side-street that led into Charing X Road. Tessa held herself close against me. Neither of us spoke. Then Tessa stopped and faced me.

'Leckie,' she said. 'No.'

She said:

'You can't take things up where you left them years ago. It would have been nice then. It won't be the same now.' She pressed herself up to me.

'Oh, Christ,' she said. 'You never did before, and now you want to. It isn't fair. I'm not the same now, and I do want to so much.'

I said nothing. We kissed. We walked on to the bus stop. Tessa still said she would not come. We argued. We talked until the last bus had gone. Tessa said she would come, but I hadn't to blame her if it was a flop. I knew it would be a flop now, but I was obstinate. The real desire had been talked out of me, but I was trying to make myself believe that it would come back.

I remember Tessa lying with her arms crossed over her breasts. When I smiled and tried to pull her arms away, she would not let me.

She said:

'No, you mustn't look. They're not pretty now. You mustn't look at me at all.'

At the bus stop, she had said:

'I daren't go with you. I should be frightened. You see everything. You'd be making love with your mind. You'd be thinking all the time and seeing me.'

Eight

Derek Sutler, about to be called up into the R.A.F., came to sort out belongings of his in the flat. He discovered a copy of Richard St. Hilda's most recent will. At midday we went round to the Flying Dutchman for a drink. Derek told me what was in the will. Apart from Mrs. St. Hilda's annuity, he and I were to inherit the rest in the form of a life-interest to ourselves and our children.

It was embarrassing, but we speculated on what the size of Richard's total fortune must be, to judge by his normal expenditure. We concluded that his demise while this will remained in force could not mean less than a capital sum of thirty thousand pounds each for Derek Sutler and myself.

A figure who now appeared, prominently if not importantly, on my horizon was Aloysius Smith, whom in my earliest pages I described as 'a professional photographer who made his living by photographing mortuaries for a refrigeration company.' Aloysius Smith was at once the happiest and unhappiest of men.

He was unhappy in the sense in which animals are unhappy. This was a doctrine taught at the Institute of Mystical Science, that the animals are unhappy and that they are unhappy because this is a world created not for them but for man. I believe that it is a true doctrine. I believe that, as Mrs. Verity and Fraülein von Stubenau used to say, one can read the unhappiness of animals in their faces and in their limited movements and their cries. But now I must describe Aloysius Smith superficially and recall the general circumstances of his terrestrial existence.

I first met him in the company of the elder of the two young men who lived opposite Alison and myself at the house with the detachable ceiling in Marginal Road. I was standing outside the Dominion Theatre in Tottenham Court Road. I had arranged to meet someone there, turned up late and found him gone. A number of excitable young men passed, evidently in the course of a peripatetic party of some kind, and in the dazzle of a pre-war London evening I recognised my little friend from over the road. I was drawn into the group. I no longer care what impression I create in public, but in those days I was rather sensitive, and to be seen in this group caused me no little discomfort, for as the drink went down in one public house after another their excitable voices became more and more shrill, their movements and gestures more like those of mannequins or non-stop lovelies. I was aware of other drinkers tipping their hats back and regarding us with profound hostility. However, the evening passed without incident, and I reached home safely.

Aloysius Smith was one of this group. I was astonished to discover later that he was married to a wife and enjoyed the use of notable talents.

Aloysius was rather tall and big-boned, dark, with straight black hair combed untidily back, and steel-rimmed, very thick glasses behind which swam two eyes of indeterminate colour and startling concentration. He looked foreign and perhaps a little sinister and in wartime was often thought to be a spy, particularly as he always appeared to be going about some business of a private and incomprehensible nature. He lived in a top-storey flat in the Vale of Health with his wife and a cat. He made a fair income not only out of photography but, as his luck took him, out of book-illustration, architectural and fashion design, handicrafts, interior decoration, caricature and the erection of air-raid shelters. He painted, carved, collected *objets d'art* and played the violin. The most astonishing creations blossomed beneath his careless, rather large hands.

That was his happiness, effortless creativity and a fascination with inanimate things. But he was not fully human. He frequented the company of cats because he was more than half a cat himself. He collected musical boxes, Victorian glass, matchbox covers, strange headgear, weapons and lengths of Oriental stuff partly as a barrier between himself and the world and partly because it was only through the medium of inanimate things that he could make contact with other people. In conversation with him, I always had the uncomfortable feeling that he was paying no attention to what I said. His extraordinarily polite, attentive and indeed mellifluous way of saying, 'Yes, Leckie,' 'No, of course not, Leckie,' gave colour to this feeling. Yet, if one suddenly put a question to him to find out whether he had been listening, the answer was there, and it was obvious that his memory had retained every word.

His wife's name was Muriel Agnes. She was small and shy. It was easy to win her confidence. I do not think Aloysius made her at all happy, although she loved him. Indeed, Aloysius Smith's relationship with Muriel Agnes was perhaps the one thing about him truly rather than apparently sinister. He dominated her, and it is of the very essence of the sinister that other creatures should dominate mankind.

I have occasionally thought that Muriel Agnes was herself not entirely human and that she and Aloysius made an exemplary pair of babes in the wood, little lost animals in a baleful human world, two changelings holding hands in fear of their sad incomprehensible destiny. But then I have reflected that, as St. Paul and the Christian fathers held, women are of their nature without souls, that they commonly receive a soul from some man and that Muriel Agnes had been shut off more than is common from male, humanising influences.

Interested people tried to put a narrow interpretation on Aloysius Smith's relationship with his wife. Aloysius had once joined in a lively pub crawl by taxi with Richard St. Hilda, Alison and myself, the two young men from Marginal Road and a number of other male and female characters. Under the liberating influence of drink he had gone round kissing all the males in his vicinity. After the party, the two young men from Marginal Road told stories of Aloysius' agony when confronted with the sexual problem before he married Muriel Agnes, their contention being that he should not have married or indeed had relations with the opposite sex at all. I did not accept this view. As for that particular alcoholic incident, it was the case that, apart from Muriel Agnes, all the occupants of the taxi in which Aloysius was riding had been males. If repressed desire was displayed in Aloysius' going round kissing everybody, it was desire of the changeling to enter fully into the human world into which it had been transported. It is true that Muriel Agnes had been observed to be agitated by the incident, but it is surely wrong to assume that her agitation was due to a feeling that her husband was betraying the failure of their relationship in public and not to natural compassion with him in a despair which she herself shared. It is true also that a certain nymphomaniac in the party was disgusted by Aloysius' behavior and declared her intention of never speaking to him again, but then females who have been sexually overstimulated become very single-minded and as it were puritanical in reverse.

Let me complete this survey by once again stressing the diversity of Aloysius Smith's talents and the rather quaint pixellated charm of his top flat in the Vale of Health and by adding that he possessed, in addition to musical boxes, cat and violin, a large number of books, not all of which had been selected for their attractive bindings. I doubt whether Aloysius ever read them, and if he did I am sure that what the words conveyed to him was different from what they would have conveyed to you or me. But there it was. Aloysius Smith possessed a library, and a library is said to be of all things the most representative of the human spirit.

I should also add that Muriel Agnes had long wanted to move from the Vale of Health for a human reason. On several occasions, drawing the curtains apart as she turned out the light to go to bed, she had observed in the street below a policeman carrying a large white bundle. Eventually, her curiosity had caused her to put on a dressing gown and run downstairs to find out the meaning of this occurrence. The white bundles were sheets enveloping corpses retrieved from the Vale of Health pond. This had upset Muriel Agnes in precisely the same way as it would have upset any young married woman. Also, Muriel Agnes had several times confessed to Alison in the kitchen that she would like to have a child. Whichever way you looked at it, the problem was a difficult one to solve.

In December and January I spent a lot of time in Aloysius Smith's company. I watched him developing film and printing from it. I studied some hundreds of his photographs and lost myself in the little world of his creation. I took him to the Unit Theatre, where he made pictures of Maimie Joyce that will immortalise (for a while) those long, expressive limbs, and where he met and amused and was amused by Tessa Duveen and protected me from further intimacy with her. More pertinently, I invited him to share my sessions with Pat Mallard, for models, other than stereotyped professional ones, are not so easily come by and the nude was a territory which until then had largely escaped Aloysius' attention.

He came to Richard St. Hilda's flat on a Sunday afternoon in December. Alison had invited him and Muriel Agnes to tea and supper. Photography was to occupy the interval between the two, and the rest of the evening was to be social. Richard St. Hilda was in Bristol.

Aloysius bought his own lighting apparatus. Hitherto I had worked with lighting of moderate power and had therefore had to confine myself to a limited range of tones, in which the black was to be found only in deep hollows and the white only upon salient features. Aloysius brought bulbs of such brilliance that he could flood every surface with utter, transparent whiteness and yet leave a jet-black line wavering along the ridge of the bone. These bulbs gave off not only light but heat of such intensity that one actually felt (or received the impression that one felt) the waves of both heat and light progressing at their own tempo through the finer meshes of the air and the contained ether. These waves appeared furthermore to produce a musical tone.

It was December and therefore dark very early. How that heavily curtained room appeared from the outside I cannot say, but I imagined that an emanation of some sort must surely catch the attention of an alert air raid warden. Perhaps he would have put it down to the singing of the balloon cables which in those early days gave rise to legends of a metropolitan circle of buzzing, invisible rays.

To add to this hypnagogic, hyperaesthetic atmosphere, three finely blown glasses and two bottles of air-conditioned sherry were introduced into the room for the delectation of the two photographers and their model. Sherry was a drink which Colonel Mallard evidently permitted his daughter, for she showed no signs of nervousness in its presence. I had formerly sat for my portrait to one of Aloysius' cameras. His method was to bewilder his models and make them laugh while he dodged around them talking quietly and persuasively, deliberately wasting film until the last fixity of expression, the last uneasy tension of a muscle should have disappeared. In combination with the light and heat and the sherry, this method operated with full effect on Pat Mallard.

The most interesting passages in my own photographs are probably those in which a small Aloysius, peering through his Kontax's viewfinder, intruded for a moment upon the field of vision of the lens of my Leica. His own pictures are quite extraordinary. At first he let me choose every alternate pose, but I told him to ignore me entirely, to do what he liked with the model and the light, and if any desirable effect happened to present itself to my eye I would attempt to record it. I used perhaps a quarter of the film Aloysius used. Part of the time I spent in plying Pat Mallard with sherry. Aloysius photographed her raising the glass to her lips. He lay on his back and photographed half vertically up mighty columns of leg.

He leaped on top of the desk and photographed an upward-looking face with a perspective of body receding down to absurdly diminished feet. He was in every corner of the room at once, so that if he demanded Pat Mallard's face she did not know in which direction to look. He tossed her bits of drapery and photographed her as she caught them. He handed her a guitar or a Japanese sword or such other properties as I had been able to find, or snatched them away and recorded the turn of a bewildered arm and shoulder. Even visually, woman is inexhaustible in her variety, but that evening every detail of a superb body was, if not made captive, yet momentarily, lyrically acknowledged. The discordant personality of this inhibited girl was caught up and resolved. I believe that Pat Mallard was, between tea and supper on that Sunday evening in December, for the first time in her life, perfectly happy.

Then the lights fused. Aloysius' high-powered filaments had overstrained the circuit. Aloysius went downstairs, where Alison and Muriel Agnes were now conspiring by candlelight to produce the supper of the century, to fix the fuse. By the light which flickered behind the mica panels of a slow-burning stove, Pat Mallard put Alison's dressing gown over her shoulders and sat on the arm of a low, comfortable chair. I sat on the other arm.

I do not remember whether it was out of pure friendliness or from a mild, alcoholic lechery liberated by the sudden darkness, that I put my arm in the first place around Pat Mallard's waist, or was it her shoulders? In any case, Pat responded, and the large, warm, breathless, vital, sweet-smelling body, barely concealed by Alison's dressing gown even from the sense of touch, was pushing against my thin shirt the tips of two most pleasantly curvetted and resilient breasts, and two heavy, sensitive arms were meeting upon the nape of my neck to fold their hands behind my head.

Pat sighed, and as my tongue went in search of the sherried softness of her mouth, I remember wondering what I had done and what in Heaven's name I might be letting myself in for.

Aloysius put in a new fuse, and the lights came on. He returned. Pat's manner was not at all confused, but on the contrary, as a first reaction, rather triumphant. She remembered to ask Aloysius to do a simple portrait of her before he packed up, to use as a Christmas card. Her normal, timid self reasserted itself to insist that this portrait should not let it appear that even her shoulders had been uncovered when it was taken and to remind us both that she must see all our finished prints, to be assured that in none of them was she recognisable to her relatives and friends, before she passed any of them for publication. Then she returned downstairs to dress in Alison's room, saying that she really ought to go and see if she could help with the supper.

When I next saw her, she was once more wearing a plain jumper and skirt, and glasses covered her blue, naturally glassy eyes. She was being fussy and helpful with the other two girls, talking liberally in that hard, clipped voice. I believe she laid the table. At the same time, I seem to remember that there was a little more rouge than before upon her lips and that her hair was looking a little nicer.

Later in the evening, when all these visitors had gone, I confessed to Alison that shortly before supper I had kissed Pat Mallard.

Alison said:

'I'm afraid I knew that. It was rather obvious from her behaviour when she came down to help us with the supper. I don't mind, darling.'

Pat Mallard came again either on the Sunday before or on the Sunday after Christmas, 1939. I cannot remember which of the two Sundays it was, but only that it occurred during that bleak period at the end of December when one's friends are unavailable because they have gone away to be present at family reunions. Gabriel Fantl, who had no place in English family life, turned up to supper the same evening. His visit made photography impossible, for Fantl is not the kind of person to behave well at a respectable exhibition of the nude. He, Pat and myself went round to the Flying Dutchman. Alison, five months gone with child, would not come. Pat Mallard protested vigorously about the necessity of staying behind and helping Alison with supper, but Alison made her go with us.

The Flying Dutchman was my local. It stood in a little terrace off the square, and it had been very pleasant in the first days of the war to sit outside it in the evening sun and watch the barrage balloons slowly ascending. In winter it was a rather noisy pub, but not at Christmas, for the only people there at that time were those without families to visit. The landlord was a well-dressed person whom Richard St. Hilda had christened 'the Warthog,' though to my mind his facial resemblance was rather to the animal called a tapir.

We spoke French. Pat Mallard had spent two years at a convent in Switzerland, and her French was good. Indeed, it was pleasanter to hear her speak French than English, for in French she did not clip her vowels or over-insist on her consonants. Fantl was in high fettle. The ritual of English beer-drinking pleased him at all times, and tonight he was able to drink his beer in French. He related a new and more diverting account of the series of disreputable accidents which had first brought him to England. The black hair on either side of his otherwise bald head stuck up like horns, and his soft brown eyes gleamed with the purest, most tender malice.

Returning to the flat, Pat and I walked with our arms about each other's waists, and in the middle of the street we stopped and nuzzled like horses or pecked each other like amorous birds. Perhaps it was the recalling of her schooldays in Switzerland which introduced this new element of freedom into Pat Mallard's behaviour. Perhaps in Lausanne she had walked similarly entwined with a schoolfriend of her own age and the two had so pecked and nuzzled at each other.

This behaviour upset Fantl, whether because he himself had been running short of women lately or because we made him feel that he was no longer the centre of the picture.

Whatever it was, at the first opportunity he took me on one side and said:

'You want to leave her alone, Leckie. She's a halfwit.'

Fantl was rude and sulky at supper and left early.

Pat wanted to call on friends of hers who lived nearby. I walked round with her. We stood facing each other outside their gate. I do not know what goes on in the minds of girls like Pat Mallard, whether they have long brooded on imaginary scenes of love or whether everything comes to them in a flash when they are first stimulated. Tonight, Pat behaved like a girl who is used to admiration. When I kissed her, she went limp in my arms as though she had been exacting a similar tribute for years, and this despite her stature, which rendered kissing from an erect position a performance that required dexterity. Our conversation presently took the turn of discussing future relations in a matter-of-fact way.

I said, very tactfully: 'Pat, are you a virgin?'

Pat said:

'Yes, that's just it . . .'

Inwardly, I agreed. The whole business was beginning to look like the prelude to a surgical operation.

Pat said:

'There's Alison, too. I like Alison, awfully . . .'

When I left her, it was arranged that Pat Mallard should come to see me at noon on Tuesday.

Promptly at noon on Tuesday the bell rang, and there was Pat Mallard at the door. She evidently meant business, for she had left her spectacles off. I remember, too, that she was wearing Wellington boots, so there must have been snow. She took her Wellingtons off boldly without being invited and moved about the house in the little felt shoes that she wore underneath. I began to feel anxious. I stalled. I talked about the weather. I brought out the last batch of Aloysius' prints and discussed them. I suggested lunch. For the moment, Pat relaxed her grim purpose. She went downstairs to make coffee and a sandwich or two. We lunched. Pat took the plates away and washed them. I played the gramophone. We sat in facing chairs and avoided each other's eyes. At the end of half an hour or so, Pat came and sat at my feet. Her mood was easier now. As she was at this moment, I liked her very much.

I said:

'You'd better go and take your clothes off, anyway.'

I took off my coat, put a spool of film in the camera and fitted up some lighting. Pat returned in Alison's dressing gown. I went back to my chair. Pat came and sat once more at my feet. I kissed her. I bent down and untied the cord of Alison's dressing gown and exposed the full length of Pat Mallard's body. I pulled the dressing gown together. Pat turned her head and smiled up at me. We kissed again to hide each other's faces.

That I desired this body is hardly open to question. When I recall now those perfectly formed breasts, that smooth, youthful throat, firm belly and hips and the full splendour of those limbs stretched out before me upon the hearthrug, I am sorry that I did so little about them. I am sorry, and I do not understand it. I caressed those breasts with my hands. My lips pressed upon that throat and upon the open, sighing lips. My hands moved down the eloquent sides and rested upon those thighs which turned uneasily and barely restrained themselves from quivering. Pat

Mallard clung to me with a passion verging on folly. Her sighs were like the breathing of one in terror. Her fingers clutched, fell away and clutched at me again. I made no attempt to fulfil her desire or my own.

It may be that my true feelings did me credit, though I hesitate to think that anything did me credit at this period. My deepest thought may have been that, once I had given this girl the taste for amorous pleasures, it would be my duty to remain at her disposal until for the time being she wearied, satisfied and at peace with herself, and that this I was in no position to do. It may be so. I should like to think that it was.

I have not calculated the position and aspects of the planet Saturn for that day and hour.

Excited as she was, I made Pat Mallard go into the corner of the room that was lighted and pose for me. I did not keep her there for long, but it was enough to break the violent spell. Pat dressed and went away before Alison came home from work. Pat Mallard did not feel able to meet Alison that day. She said that she would ring me up on Friday at lunchtime.

When the telephone bell rang on Friday, I was finishing a plate of soft herring roes which I had fried in butter and served up to myself on toast with plenty of lemon and a sprinkling of cayenne pepper.

I went into the kitchen, put my plate in a large enamel bowl and ran cold water over it. I filled the whistling kettle, put the whistle over the spout and lit the gas with a small contraption which connected with the gas supply and emitted a small tongue of flame when I pressed a button in its flank. I then shook about two ounces of coffee into a cream jug and selected from the plate rack a saucer and my favourite cup, a deep blue one with white rings. The telephone bell stopped ringing as I ignited the second gas ring and put a saucepan of milk over it.

It started again less than two minutes later and was joined by the whistling kettle. This time it did not go on for long. And I was able to make my coffee, take it upstairs, drink the first cup and light a cigarette before it started for the third time. This time also, it did not go on for long.

I read. I think it was a book by C. F. Ramuz, *Si le Soleil ne revenait pas*, which Richard St. Hilda had brought me when he came back in a hurry from the Côte d'Azur. If it was not that, it was Jean Giono's *Colline*. I then dozed. The telephone bell woke me at twenty minutes to three. This time it rang for at least ten minutes as if the person at the other end had dismissed her (or his) first flurry of disappointment and had determined now to ring confidently, with a long full-throated ring. I let it go on. It being presumed that it was she, Pat Mallard, at the far end of several miles of telephone wire was not a formidable proposition. Fully clothed, wearing her glasses no doubt, her normal daytime self, inept, puzzled, hot and anxious, she had no power to coerce me from a distance. I let the bell ring.

After that steady, ten-minute peal, its morale collapsed. It rang in more and more agitated tones, at ever more erratic intervals. I lay on the divan with my hands clasped behind my head and listened to it, estimating how long it would go on, and in the intervals calculated, with an eye on the clock, how long it would be before it started again.

At four o'clock I made myself tea. At six I went round to the Flying Dutchman. As I closed the door behind me the telephone bell had started ringing again for the fourteenth time in five and a half hours. It rang with the voice of humanity's endless craving. *Brrr-brrr, brrr-brrr. Brrr-brrr, brrr-brrr.* I heard it from the street outside. It rang through the empty flat with the voice of humanity's everlasting frustration. *Ping-ping, ping-ping. Ping-ping, ping-ping.* Albert William Christ went round to the Flying Dutchman and buried his smiles in a pint of Charrington's bitter.

Nine

A great deal of snow fell, and the weather was extremely cold. I stood at the big french windows and watched the garden below me changing. Snow climbed up the boles of the trees and pulled their branches down. It obliterated the division between flower-border, path and lawn. It banked itself up against the walls, first one wall and then, as the wind changed, the other. It turned the small shrubbery at the end of the garden into a dense, septentrional forest, the haunt of red-jawed wolves and sleeping bears.

I became aware of the garden for the first time. Aware of it, that is to say, as a closed space and a separate entity. During the summer I had sat in it in a deckchair. I had taken tea and occasionally lunch in it. I had been occasionally enchanted by bursts of blossom and, especially in the autumn twilight, by songs of birds. But these things had taken place, for me, in a generalised foliate region made up of many contingent gardens, in fact of all the gardens lying between the side of the square I lived in and the adjacent terrace in which stood the Flying Dutchman. Now I became aware of the one garden's separateness. I do not know why. It may be that my thought had lost its power of diffusion and was narrowing down to a purposive narrowness. It may be that Richard St. Hilda's continued absence allowed me as it were to take possession of what he had left with me.

When there was no more snow to fall, I photographed the garden. I photographed it from the balcony. I went down into it and photographed the detail of bared and now heavily freighted trees. I scattered crumbs outside the window of the dining room in the basement and lay in wait with my camera on the floor behind the foot of the curtains to photograph birds that came to pick up the crumbs. I thought that when the spring came I would do something with the garden (study in detail the requirements of these four pear trees, this single walnut, perhaps dig the borders into a different shape and grow something). For the moment I could do nothing but acknowledge its separate existence and photograph it in winter dress.

At the Flying Dutchman I heard many lamenting frozen pipes and many asking the Warthog where on earth they were to find a plumber. Our pipes did not freeze. I ran hot water through them at intervals, and I saw that every room was heated at some time or other whether I needed to use it or not.

I was less successful with myself. I had only one attack of lumbago. I did not really notice it until Alison had gone to work. Then I found that I could only lie on one side and that when I tried to get up I worked my legs as if on a bicycle without producing any effect from the hips upward. I had to wait until the woman came in to make breakfast and call out to her and get her to come and pull me out of bed. This very soon passed, but I had an ugly chill from top to toe which lasted until the thaw. It may have been this which by association first caused 'Thea' to recur to my mind and to linger there.

This was January, 1940. The war appeared to be stabilised, if indeed it had not already ended. The only fighting was in Finland, and that little war pleased everybody. It appeared to be what people thought a war should be, the gallant few resisting an overwhelmingly large enemy who were overpoweringly in the wrong. It pleased us ethically, like the story of David and Goliath. It fitted our schoolbook view of history, like Salamis and Thermopylae and the Spanish Armada. It was a war in the British tradition with the further advantage that the British did not have to fight it. The newspapers showed groups of sad-looking Russian prisoners and explained that they were illiterate men who did not know what they were fighting for (which is likely enough, for Comrade Stalin could hardly tell them without upsetting the Germans). The newsreels showed us blazing farmhouses, Finns on skis in white cloaks (they did not show us Russians in white cloaks, for it would not do to have both sides looking equally romantic) or Finns taking Turkish baths and then rushing outside and rolling in the snow (the Finns were obviously a clean people like the English and hardy like the Scots). Nothing had happened for years of which we so wholeheartedly approved. The Labour Party, who had for some time hated Communists more than they had ever hated Tories, were loudest of all in their denunciations of Comrade Stalin. Athletes and younger sons clamoured to be allowed to go and join in blood-brotherhood with these sport-loving heroes. I heard a smart woman at a sophisticated party declare that she would give herself to any Finnish soldier at any time. But this was January, 1940.

I received from the Institute of Mystical Science a printed card, not black-edged but decorated with oak leaves, announcing that Dr. Leopold Gloss had been translated to another plane and that his physical body would be cremated at Golder's Green at 11.30 a.m. on January 24th, on the evening of which day there would be a meeting at the Caxton Hall, Vauxhall Bridge Road, Victoria, to which all members and friends of the Institute were cordially invited and at which Professor Dr. Unradt would speak of death, reincarnation and the future of Europe over the urn containing his dead friend's ashes. The ashes themselves would thenceforward be kept at Mrs. Verity's flat in Hampstead where they could be visited if due notice were given, until such time as continental traffic was fully restored, when they would be taken first to Vienna and then to Dornach in Switzerland, where they would be scattered to the four winds before the portals of the Goetheanum at the first international post-war congress of Rudolf Steiner's surviving pupils and disciples.

This mighty vision pleased me, but I did not attend either the ceremony of cremation or the subsequent thanksgiving. Fantl went, with Irene. He came round afterwards and reported that 'Thea' had not been there. He described the ceremony at Golder's Green, the bearing of branches of oak and mistletoe by Mrs. Verity, Fraülein von Stubenau, Siegmund Laufer and Professor Dr. Unradt, the little prayers and a benediction concerning the threefold nature of man and the columns of fire, water and air. Leopold Gloss's eyelids had fluttered once too often. He had gone too long without that effort to give utterance to his message which had from moment to moment brought him so vividly to life. I mourned him, but I did not go to the crematorium.

Fantl was looking very smart. A closely waisted overcoat of fine serge embraced his fragile body. A brown, porkpie hat with a hackle tucked into the band cast a sophisticated shadow over his soft, clownish brown eyes. He did not tell me how he came to be so rich, and I did not ask.

I did not know that 'Thea' would not be at the crematorium. Indeed, I thought she might be. I do not think that I should have gone had I been certain that she would. Perhaps it was the same feeling which had withheld me from seeing her on a previous occasion, a feeling that when I again saw 'Thea' it must be under marvellous circumstances, that I must not cheaply pursue her as if I were a person with a proposition to make.

The thaw came. The snow tumbled from the rooftops. It slid down from the branches of four pear trees, a walnut and the others whose names I did not know and eased them and allowed them to return to their former stance. Ice dripped from under the eaves and out of the mortar between the bricks. Over a window in the flat above, a crack opened.

I did not see it for a day or two. While the streets were full of melted snow I did not go out except by taxi. When the last of the slush had run along the gutters into the nearest drain or soaked down into the earth, I went out through the dining room window and examined the garden. A watering can and the garden roller had been left out in the snow. They were rusty beyond further usefulness. I looked up at the house. I saw the crack in the stone ten yards above the balcony windows. The lintel was split diagonally along most of its length.

The people who lived in the flat above were away. Richard St. Hilda had never told me the address of his landlady or who was her agent. I did not know Richard's own address at the moment but simply that he was in

Bristol. I thought of telephoning all the local agents until I found the right one. I thought of telephoning the district surveyor. I did neither.

I had a dream. In the morning I awoke feeling particularly wretched, but I did not remember a single image from the dream.

I remember only that I was crying out:

'It isn't time yet. I'm not ready to die. I'm not ready . . .'

After breakfast I found a brick and bits of crumbled mortar on the balcony. I went down into the garden and looked up. The crack in the lintel reached from corner to corner. A brick was missing from above the top half. The bottom half was cracking the wood of the windowframe. The people upstairs had still not returned. I called in a builder on my own authority, and he fitted some temporary props.

Francis Piazole of Padua was born on April 3, 1652, at 9.47 p.m., and baptized immediately as he was not expected to live. Nor did he live to be more than three years of age, for on the 7th of March 1655, at about the 20th hour he was drowned in a small quantity of water where chickens were used to drink. It was subsequently observed that at the moment of birth Luna in the radix had the declination of Saturn and the square of Mars, that the ascendant degree had exact parallel declination with Saturn and Luna and that the ascendant and the sign containing Saturn in the 8th house were both of the watery triplicity. When these facts were made known to the father of the child it is said that he shook his fist at the offending planets and with great vehemence invited them to pick on somebody their own size.

Richard St. Hilda joined the Navy. I found this very difficult to understand. It is true that sailors fascinated him, but usually those things which fascinate from a distance are the last things to which one commits oneself, and Richard St. Hilda had from the day of his birth developed the most elaborate defences against ever committing himself to anything. His own account of the affair was that he foresaw that he could not endure life in the Army, and therefore he joined the Navy before the Army could get hold of him, but Richard's logic had never been of that simple, energetic variety. However, there it was. Richard St. Hilda had recruited himself in Bristol and in a few days would report to the Depot at Chatham.

I met him at Paddington, had lunch with him in Charlotte St. and helped him across London with his luggage. Conversation was difficult. Really it was very brave of Richard. I felt sure that if I said much he would burst into tears, and so should I.

Presently I had a letter from him.

H.M.S. Royal Flush.

DEAR LECKIE,

The above, which sounds like one of Nelson's frigates or possibly Blake's flagship, is really a requisitioned holiday camp at Noggin-on-Sea. I share a little chalet on the beach with a young man who spends his evenings writing letters to his wife by the light of a penny rush. Everything is rather pink.

People really do say, 'Ay, ay, sir,' and at an improbable hour of the morning somebody bangs on the door and calls out, 'Show a leg,' or 'Wakey, wakey, rise and shine.'

Haven't heard yet when or by what means I'm going to be made an admiral. I think I've just contracted the disease and that it will take its normal course. I stand easy with the officers. The class-light gleams in our eyes.

How do I come to be here? Well, the idea of going into the Navy was suggested to me when I was about thirteen, my father's contention being that I should choose an outdoor life. The present circumstances found me, so to speak, with the germs of the idea still alive. After some weeks of trying to puzzle it out for myself, I was brought to a state of mind in which what I look upon as decision was no longer necessary.

Feeling awfully well. Bless you.

R.

Alison came home from her doctors one teatime and announced that she had just fallen off a bus at the stop in Baker Street. This was the second time she had fallen in the street and collected a crowd. She was now more than six months gone.

My attitude to the imminent baby was mixed. There were times when I thought that Alison with a baby might be amusing. There were times when I felt sorry for Alison because she was going to have a baby and because she was swollen and out of shape and because she looked sometimes so happy and at other times so sad and was obviously thinking about things that only pregnant women think about and because she grew tired easily and suffered continually from heartburn and fell off buses. There were times when I hated Alison for the same reasons, and there were many, many times when I hated the baby. Mostly, I did not think about it at all.

February brought black weather. On Monday, Feb. 18th, I went in the morning to book seats for a concert at the Wigmore Hall. On my way back, up the lower part of Barker Street, I called at my photographic dealer's. It was a misty, fretful day, and the fret was of that curious, shining quality in which, despite the gloom, natural colours stand out with more than common intensity. Paintwork gleamed. Evergreen foliage was of an angry viridian. Upon the pavement, the expectorations of catarrhal tradesmen suggested the presence of turquoise, amber and pea-green opals.

As I came out of my dealer's and crossed the road, my attention was drawn to a couple arm in arm looking into the window of a cake shop.

As I passed close to them, the woman, aged about thirty-five, was saying to the man, aged about forty-five:

'Darling, don't turn your nose up like that.'

I looked at the man's nose as I passed and barely restrained myself from open laughter, for if there was a nose in Christendom that could never, under any circumstances whatever, be turned up, that nose was it. It was not one of those arrogant, arched noses with rocking-horse nostrils. Those one could imagine being turned up in a crisis. But this nose resembled the nose of a sheep in profile, descending in a curve like that of one side of a pear, with no angular salience at either bridge or tip.

In this context, the woman's remark amused me so much that, after walking for twenty yards or so with a broad smile on my face, I had to turn and pretend interest in the contents of another shop window (a hat shop) to conceal a fit of giggles and if possible get it under control.

I have always found that the best way to subdue fits of giggles is to concentrate on something very solemn, such as Jesus Christ. The most solemn thing in my life at that moment was 'Thea'. I concentrated on 'Thea'. And I succeeded in conjuring up her features with a clarity that I had not before been able to achieve. 'Thea' was before my eyes, and my hilarity collapsed.

'Thea' was before my eyes. Or, rather, her reflection was. Here, before my eyes, was that heavenly pallor, that soft, pale hair parted so quietly upon the forehead, those quiet, infinitely sad features. I have no words left to describe 'Thea' or to describe her effect upon me. I can only call 'Thea' by her name and hope to be understood. 'Thea' was the naked impact of my own life upon me. She was truly to me 'the beauty of the world.' The reflection vanished, and I was left with no more than the picture in my mind's eye. I realised what had happened. 'Thea' had in actuality stood near me, looking into the same shop window.

I turned. Walking up Baker Street towards the Marylebone Road was that figure of miraculous precision. Stepping forward, one after the other, were those legs in which, above an ankle fine as the fetlock of a deer, the dancer's divided calf-muscle swelled and subsided a little with every step.

Then I clenched my fingers and toes, froze and sweated. I did not look up. With that prevision of fate which afflicts everybody at certain moments, I knew that the instrument of my death was within a second of striking. I knew furthermore from which direction it came, from directly overhead.

Sparrows had loosened a tile from the roof of this building against which I stood. At 10.30 a.m. this tile balanced dangerously upon the gutter's edge. At 10.34 it overbalanced and, corner foremost, descended in a vertical line which terminated above my right eye at a point corresponding exactly with Richard St. Hilda's recently incurred scar. This line was as clear in my mind's eye as the red lines connecting Christ's wounds to stars and other objects in certain early Italian paintings.

I died instantly and without pain.

Ten

Imagine a world in which every object is of animal nature. There are rivers, lakes and seas, but these are not the chemical fusion of hydrogen and oxygen in which float particles of every mineral. The land is clothed with trees, flowers and herbs, but these are improperly called 'vegetation'. These rivers, lakes and seas are as fully animal as the fishes and amphibious beasts which live in them. Imagine a diffuse, impalpable and lucid frogspawn. These trees, flowers and herbs are no more truly vegetable than are birds, insects and arboreal apes and reptiles. The land itself is animal. No veins of coal or mineral ore run through it. It is like yeast. Endless proliferation takes place among the roots of its animal turf, a proliferation not of plant cells but of ovum and spermatozoon, the budding and extension of a culture of bacilli. Imagine, moreover, that all this is real and yet is not physically discernible to a physical eye.

The effect of a typical landscape in this world is not unlike the effect of certain paintings by the surrealists. That bush will suddenly disclose a staring eye. A cactus growth, which attracts attention by the livid hues in which it is represented, reveals on closer examination features appropriate only to the human form. The vines and liana creepers betray a muscular contraction like that of the painter's intestines.

I stood upon an eminence in the middle of such a landscape. From what I had heard at the Institute of Mystical Science and from my reading of Rudolf Steiner, I recognised it as the spiritual realm of Luna, in which man had lived before he attained his present degree of physical incarnation and inhabited the earth. I leaned against a spur of rock which was truly not rock but the excrescence of a substance resembling horn.

To the ordinary human imagination, it must appear that such a landscape was horrible, eerie. I did not find it so, presumably because I was there by right, by necessity and in a state consonant with its nature. In point of fact, I felt extraordinarily happy.

I stooped to trail my fingers in a lucid, animal pool. I was content as I had not been since as a boy I first sought companionship with woods, grassy banks and streams.

But this spiritual realm of Luna is not the abiding-place of the recently dead. I must presently go away. The restless will awakened within me, and as it did so I became aware of the pain in my head. It grew worse.

I leaned my head against the rock of horn. I stood erect and looked about me. I reeled. The landscape faded slowly from my vision.

A period supervened in which I was almost bereft of consciousness, but not totally. It was as if, translated down from plane to plane of existence, I became momentarily alive to each and was able to form rudimentary, nascent impressions. I was chiefly aware of the sensation of movement, a peculiar form of movement. The brief, rushing wind which follows in the wake of a heavy vehicle or drags at the periphery of a circle of bomb blast seemed to travel towards a diminishing centre, and I was drawn with it, not impetuously but with a trance-like slowness in which I was nevertheless aware of jolts, shudders and cross currents perceptible to the ear-drums and the heart and the root of the stomach. Before me rose the portals of a large building of brick and white Portland stone. It was the Middlesex Hospital.

I thought:

'This is evidently my spiritual home. I visited this building as a pauper one year ago. My wife will presently take up her residence here in order to be delivered of our offspring. Already she comes to the building each month for prenatal care (perhaps she is here at this very moment). And now it is the first place which I posthumously revisit.' A brief panic shook me.

I thought:

'Hell is repetition, and I am drawn again into the orbit of my private history. I am in Hell . . .'

In the hall, I accosted a young woman in a white overall, possibly one of the almoner's staff.

I said:

'Excuse me. I am looking for my wife. I fancy she's in the pre-natal department. Could you find out for me? Leckie's the name. Mrs. A. W. Leckie . . .'

The young woman hurried past. Either she did not see me, or she found my appearance distasteful.

I accosted another young woman, a nurse.

I said:

'Excuse me. I believe they're operating on me somewhere in the building, but I'm afraid I don't know where the operating theatre is . . .'

The nurse also hurried past.

I walked upstairs past seven or eight landings. At the very top of the building I saw a door open and a nurse walk out, go into another room and return with a tray of surgical instruments. I followed her into the operating theatre and stood for a moment leaning against the door. I was breathing heavily after my long climb.

It was a most impressive picture. In the middle lay my chloroformed body upon a table. It was shut off from my physical vision by a group of doctors in white, with masks over their noses and mouths and semi-transparent gloves of red rubber. On the far side of me stood a row of students similarly attired, and behind the doctors, also wearing masks and gloves and with their backs towards me, were the sterile nurses. Nearest to me were the dirty nurses. I recognised the second dirty. She was the nurse who had been so charming to me during my treatment for a non-existent renal stone. I tried to speak to her, but she turned and put a finger to her lips. I ignored her injunction and addressed the group.

I said:

'Look here, all of you. I don't like to interfere in matters relating to the medical profession for which I entertain the highest regard, but you're wasting your time. Can't you see that the patient is dead? After all, I am in a position to know . . .'

Nobody paid the slightest attention to what I said. I pushed past the first and second dirties and the sterile nurses and watched one of the doctors extract a long sliver of slate from my forehead, while another swabbed the wound, took the foreign body from his colleague and passed it, together with the swab, to a sterile nurse who in turn passed them on to my little friend, the second dirty. My detachment was extraordinary. For the first time, I observed the expulsion of blood without feeling in the least nauseated or faint. As the group of doctors broke up and the senior sterile nurse took a length of gut to stitch my forehead, I walked out on to the landing and set my foot upon the top stairs.

Now I stood in a shadowy realm, in the remoter distances of which I was aware of figures both stationary and in movement, though even the stationary figures presented an appearance of movement, for about them drifted a swirl of mist which at times hid them completely from my view and at other times disclosed a part of them, greatly magnified or diminished according to the play of light. I saw a white horseman and other personalities from the Apocalypse. I saw lovers coldly and unhappily entwined. I saw huge, solitary figures sitting with their shoulders hunched and their knees hunched up before them and the image of cold horror upon their faces. As I looked upon them, each in turn receded to an infinite distance, as figures sometimes do in a dream or a half-dream and left me at the centre of a loneliness so intense that I turned both sick and dizzy with it and could have cried aloud.

I was alone. And then I was not alone. I was in the presence of a tall, impressive figure whom I recognised. There was no door or gate to be seen, for there was no wall into which a gate or a door might have been let. At most there might have been an illusion of shadowy curtains, a little like some stage setting by Gordon Craig. Yet one knew immediately that this lofty, spectral figure guarded as it were a door. It was not merely that his presence, like a commissionaire's, was full of majesty, nor was it that he bore any facial resemblance to St. Peter in a painting. Rather was it that one received the direct spiritual apprehension of his function. He was beyond a shadow of doubt that personage whom Mrs. Verity had described as the Guardian of the Threshold.

His function was to prevent the spirit from passing prematurely from one plane or spiritual realm to another. I could not remember which particular realms or planes they were. I rather fancied that at the moment I was in my etheric body, in which case the Guardian of the Threshold would be there to prevent me from passing from the etheric to the astral plane, but I could not be sure.

I was a little worried about this. In a short while I should obviously have to enter into conversation with the Guardian of the Threshold, and I had always found on earth that, however kindly their disposition may be, august personages do not care to have the young address them in a vague state of mind, especially if their guidance is being sought.

Luckily I did not have to open conversation at once. The Guardian of the Threshold was at the moment listening to a thin, ill-looking man with a red beard, dressed in the fashion of the late twenties. I walked away to a distance, sat down and tried to collect my thoughts about death and in particular about my own death.

I thought:

'My God, what a predicament death is! This is really final. This is the one scrape out of which nobody can talk his way. No amount of bluff will help a man now. It is too late to clutch at straws or to hope for the last-minute happy inspiration, the timely assistance of an old friend.'

The mood changed. I was overcome by a blissful sensation not unlike that which on earth accompanies a deep feeling of gratitude.

I thought:

'Here is peace. Here is an end to all strife, division and anxiety. No longer have I anything to fear. The worst that can befall me has already befallen, and I am still happy. Responsibility and care . . .'

I checked myself. This was not true. I still nourished the seeds of anxiety in my heart. Already I had begun to worry again.

I thought:

'Oh, the unreality of death! I am unchanged!'

But I must concentrate. After death, one lingered for a certain period of time in the vicinity of the physical body. In the next phase, one relived one's earthly life in reverse order. I wondered if I were going to be one of those awful, earthbound spirits. At the Institute of Mystical Science in Phelps Place, they used to tell hair-raising stories of what happened to people whose attachment to material things had affected even their etheric nature, so that they continued to haunt (according to the nature of their attachment) homes, brothels, hoarded possessions or public houses. I hoped that none of my vices had eaten so far into me as all that and that there was going to be no initial difficulty about disengaging my etheric body.

I turned my head and perceived that the Guardian of the Threshold was gazing in my direction with a stern benignity in which there was nothing forbidding. He had finished with the red-bearded, thin man, who appeared to be stamping away in a fury.

This individual came up to me. His eyes burned with martyrdom, and it seemed to me that he was eaten away inside by some painful malady which interfered with his breathing. Two spots of crimson had appeared upon the cheekbones of his white face like rouge clumsily applied.

As he spoke, he pressed both hands into his stomach.

He said:

'This splendiferous imagery is distasteful to me.'

He said:

'Serve the poor. Well and good. But whom are the poor going to serve? John of Patmos answered it. The poor are going to serve themselves and attend to their own self-glorification.'

He spat, and there was a thread of blood in the spittle. He strode off. I went up to the Threshold and cleared my throat. The Guardian of the Threshold gazed compassionately after the man's retreating figure.

'An interesting case,' he said. 'He has been here for ten years, and nothing that I can say humbles him. A generous, sensitive spirit, but on earth he was one of those who hate falsehood more than they love truth, and his pride is illimitable.

Then he turned to me and smiled.

'I am not sure that you ought to be here,' he said. 'But I think the general feeling was that you stood in danger of paralysing your will by too much concern with the past.'

'I did try to lose my memory,' said I.

'That will not do, either,' said the Guardian of the Threshold. 'Had you succeeded in losing your memory, you would have spent the rest of your life attempting to recapture it. To lose the memory is merely to lose a certain form of connection with the past. It does not destroy the past. A man suffering from amnesia is not a man without a past. You tried, in this as in all else, to destroy not the past but the future. Once you were a man without a past. It was lifetimes ago. You were a child in the dawn of the world. In striving to recapture the dewy wildness of that time you were striving to destroy all that you have since become. No, your task is to face the future as you are. Your knowledge of the past is precious. You must accept it with gratitude and turn elsewhere. You must neither use the past as a means to shield you from the future, with all its uncertainty, nor must you strive to destroy the past in order that you may face the future without a burden, formless and impressionable as a column of water.'

'Yes, I think I see that. I have been allowing the death wish to predominate.'

'The death wish? That is a phrase just now current on earth, I believe. It is a misleading phrase. It implies that death is peace, freedom from responsibility.'

'Is there no peace, anywhere?'

'There is peace to be found in death, and there is freedom from responsibility. But death alone does not provide them.'

'There is peace also on earth,' I said.

'Yes, sometimes in the midst of battle. Sometimes, too, upon the bed of sickness. Your lack of boldness in life was complicated by an abnormal apprehension of physical pain. You had suffered very little, I understand.'

'Very little,' I said. 'I had a virgin's apprehension of physical pain. I had kissed him. I knew his form and intention, but I had never lain with him. I frequently prayed to be relieved of this virginity.'

'There is no release from the fear of pain,' said the Guardian of the Threshold. 'Be glad of it. Rejoice that in your lethargy there is one thing that will never fail to bring you to your feet, stinging you to life with terror. Physical pain is very kind to the spirit of man.'

I was about to speak of 'Thea'. The Guardian of the Threshold forestalled me.

He said:

'You received on earth a glimpse into the life before you last died. A secret of the periodicity of the soul was revealed to you. It is a privilege granted to few men. Accept it, and be grateful. "Thea" belongs to the past.'

'But she is alive today,' I cried. 'Was it not reasonable to wish to approach more closely to her? Surely, the past and the future are not separate. In knowing her, perhaps in loving her, could I not have worked out more carefully my future destiny, and she too?'

The Guardian of the Threshold was silent. An enigmatical smile played upon his lips. The omniscient lustre of those eyes did not appal me. In the presence of this being, I was fortified. Even in my perplexity, I felt happy.

I began to wish that I had not died. I wondered. I did not know how long I had been away, but perhaps on earth they had not yet buried my physical body. I remembered that dreams of apparently interminable length take place within a few seconds of earth-time. Perhaps on earth my body still lay anaesthetised upon the operating table, and not even the doctors knew that I was dead. Perhaps it was not yet too late. I wondered how best to put this matter to the Guardian of the Threshold. Indeed, I wondered whether to raise it at all. It would be a terrible thing if I were sent back to earth to find a body already in the throes of putrefaction.

I said:

'I have a wife who very soon will bear a child.'

The Guardian of the Threshold raised his celestial eyebrows.

'So,' he said, 'you are not long in regretting the earth.'

'Supposing,' I began, 'that I . . .'

Again the Guardian of the Threshold forestalled me.

He said:

'That does not rest with me.'

I left him discouraged. I attempted once more to concentrate upon immediate necessities. As I did so, I became once more aware of the pain in my head.

A doctrine taught at the Institute of Mystical Science was that after death the soul sought out and attempted to communicate with that person who had been its friend on earth. I did not know whom I could regard as my friend. It might be Richard St. Hilda, but I did not feel that I wanted to see Richard just at the moment. It might be Flora Massingham, but she was too full of riotous life to suit my present mood. One person who occurred to my mind was a man I had not seen or even thought of for a year and a half. It was an old bricklayer called Ezra. He was responsible for the one truly happy image that I retained from my period of actual work with Sam Thorpe.

At a site on which we were building a small factory in North London, a swarm of bees had settled on a lamppost. Neither the foreman nor I had the least idea what to do with them. Eventually, a labourer remembered that Old Ezra was a countryman. Ezra was fetched. He picked up an empty cement bag and with a whitewash brush brushed the bees into it. The others supposed that the swarm would fetch a tidy price, but Ezra said that, no, you couldn't sell bees for money. He would take them to his pub in the evening and find out who wanted a swarm. He would let the man have them for nothing, but he would of course expect to be treated to a certain number of drinks.

That was the only time I had been in close contact with Old Ezra, but I remembered him with a quite disproportionate warmth. I had made enquiries about him from the foreman and learned that he was a widower living with a widowed daughter and a roomful of canaries and budgerigars. That was all. Why he now recurred to my mind as my possible life's friend, I do not know, unless it was that I had a great need of simplicity.

Thinking thus of the doctrine of the friend, I became aware of the earth and could see it as it were from a great height (I associate my sensation with that of the Blessed Damozel looking out from the gold bar of Heaven). I saw its green fields and the red smudges of its towns, and it was spinning. Its pathos overwhelmed me, and at once the swirling mists closed over the view and I was back in a shadowy realm.

The Accusers awaited me. I was aware of them gathering behind my back. I did not turn for a while. I was afraid. Beads of sweat gathered upon my top lip, and my scalp tingled. I turned, expecting to see a hostile, gesticulating crowd with stones or weapons in their hands. Instead, I saw a few quiet figures, perfectly still or moving very slightly. They were not very close to me, and they were very humble. I knew that I could expect no action from them. They waited with infinite patience for me to accuse myself.

I will not specify here who these Accusers were, nor what passed between us. But it was immediately after I had faced them that it dawned on my slow mind what the Guardian of the Threshold's last words had meant.

'That does not rest with me . . .'

I had fancied that he meant that whether I was allowed to return to life or not depended upon a higher authority still. Now I understood. He meant that it depended upon myself. With a cry like that of one emerging from an anaesthetic, I lost consciousness and sped towards my body.

I lay in bed. My wife was standing beside me. It was damp downstairs. I slept on the divan in the drawing room. Alison slept in one of Richard St. Hilda's twin beds in the next room, at the front of the house. She had come into the drawing room to ask me if I was all right.

She stooped to smooth my hair and then stood up, leaning her thighs against the side of the divan, her belly resting on the deep red counterpane like a huge, sacred egg on a cushion of quilted satin.

Over this belly, and indeed elsewhere too, clung a thin, rather worn nightdress of a pale green silk. It was an object very familiar to me and one of which I was rather fond. How often I had seen it swish and crackle with the electricity from her warm, vital body as Alison pulled it up over her head in the morning. It was a very old nightdress. Alison had worn it when we were very poor, and she had had it first when we were very rich. Now it cave to her belly as though it were drawn inward by the life of the child insolently sitting there or perhaps already standing on its head. This belly fascinated me. I was especially taken with the tiny navel two-thirds of the way up, stretched until it was as small as the navel of a brazilian orange.

I asked Alison if she would pull the nightdress up about her waist, so that I could press my cheek against the smooth, tepid flesh of the great belly. There was palpable life within. My wife shivered and placed both her hands upon my head. A little later, she bent down as well as she could to kiss me. Her mouth was dry and hot, breathing a breath which came from deeper sources than I was accustomed to.

I was at Polperro in Cornwall. I stayed at a low-beamed guesthouse with a stream rushing outside my window and plunging into a tunnel beneath the house's foundations. The big room was full of copper jugs, Flemish brass dishes and harness ornaments, coiled rope, witch-balls of crude, stringed glass, ships in bottles and galleons with leathery parchment sails. In the dim lamplight, one or two quiet people crossed this room. They were people who had left their homes in London because these were now haunted for them by the fear of what might one day fall from the sky.

Outside, there was still the long twilight of late February. I walked towards the harbour bearing, left.

Never had I seen a place so female, so closely shut in as this inhabited cleft between two plump hills, opening out at the front into a harbour over which one felt that hands were crossed in modesty. As a place to inhabit in the ordinary way, it was horrible.

I bore left along the crease between the right buttock and thigh, a little above the level at which this mighty, inverted limb plunges into the water.

There were two cottages standing one above the other on the steep hillside. I climbed up the narrow stone steps past one of them and to the base of the second. A man of perhaps fifty was stooping over a yellow hyacinth close by the fence. I saw by his cap that he was not English. His cap was panelled and bore a large cloth-covered button at the point upon which all the panels converged.

I said:

'Are you Kamtschatka?'

The man had already got up from his contemplation and smiled at me.

'Yes ...'

I said:

'I have a letter to you from Flora Massingham.'

'From whom?'

I repeated the name. Kamtschatka took my letter and opened it.

'Ah,' he said. 'From Florizel.'

And a little later:

'Ah, you are the man whose little poem we read. Come in, please. How is Florizel? She was down here with us.' Kamtschatka went in first.

He called out:

'Mom, here is a friend of Florizel. Come, please.'

To me, he said:

'I am sorry, but I did not remember Florizel's patronym.'

Mom was a tall, powerful girl with a fine, brutal face, black hair, heavy black eyebrows and a dark, rather coarse skin. Her voice was deep but not very assured. It came from the back of her throat, generous but a little unsteady. Her English was better than Kamtschatka's.

During the conversation, my eyes strayed continually to an easel set up by the window. I had seen none of Kamtschatka's paintings. I had seen only a set of Goyesque drawings, in which the terrors of the refugee soul were personified. My eyes were now painfully drawn to the picture half-finished upon the easel, for it was the only picture in sight, but for a number of watercolours laid carelessly upon the mantelpiece and almost completely hidden by a cigarette box. In the picture upon the easel, my eyes met for the first time that strange palette from which no colour is excluded, but out of which the liverish dazzle of pink and turquoise attack first and turn the soul dizzy, faint with disequilibrium.

As a young man before the first world war, Kamtschatka lived in Vienna and devoted most of his time and energy to the theatre. He worked in close collaboration with another young Czech whose name I cannot remember but whom I will call Palanek. Palanek had a great deal of red hair and was a small man, very nervous and unstable.

One night, he and Kamtschatka were drinking together on the terrace of a small café. When they had paid their bill and were in the street, Kamtschatka suddenly fell to the ground. He tried to rise to his feet, but he could not. Each time, some inexplicable force dragged him to one side and tumbled him over upon the moonlit cobbles. Neither of them had drunk very much.

Palanek thought that his friend was pretending to be drunk and became annoyed at what appeared to him to be a childish display and refused to help the two passersby who in the end carried Kamtschatka to a chair in front of another café. When Kamtschatka presently recovered and did his utmost to explain the incident, Palanek would not listen but quarrelled with him and went off in a rage. That was the end of their collaboration.

To Kamtschatka, the incident was inexplicable. Without apparent reason, his sense of balance had suddenly been disturbed and the force of gravity had acted upon him in a manner without precedent. The incident and the sensations accompanying it were not repeated, but Kamtschatka the artist made use of them. At the time, he was engaged upon a picture of a girl looking out from a balcony over a wide valley. This picture had offered problems in perspective which after many trials had begun to seem insoluble. Now they were solved. That inexplicable tumble in the street, that moment at which natural laws had appeared to be miraculously suspended, had solved them. Out of his memory of the incident, Kamtschatka evolved, for this and for succeeding pictures, a new form of perspective.

During the First World War, Kamtschatka served with the Austrian cavalry. In a retreat, his detachment had to swim their horses across a river under heavy shell-fire. There were few survivors. Kamtschatka himself received a piece of shrapnel in his skull. One eardrum was destroyed. It is well-known that the eardrums control balance, and when Kamtschatka was allowed out of bed he at once tumbled to the hospital floor under influences identical with those which before he had experienced as it were hysterically.

When a man's eardrum is destroyed, it normally takes some months to re-educate him in walking straight and with confidence. Due to his aforementioned studies in perspective, Kamtschatka's sense of balance was restored perfectly within a fortnight.

Kamtschatka told me this and other stories at Polperro in Cornwall on the occasion of our first meeting, and I remember how quickly the thought came to my mind, with mingled panic and delight:

'Here then is my life's friend.'

'. . . She was fair, pale and of moderate height,' I said. 'I do not know whether to call her beautiful or pretty. Her face was not haughty as some think a woman's face must be to be called beautiful. On the other hand, neither did it display the piquant irregularities, the hint of improvisation characteristic of the pretty woman. It was a gentle face, perfectly composed and a little sad. In the same way her figure and carriage were perfect. Their perfection would unhesitatingly engage the eye. Yet they had nothing about them of that animal pride by which desirable women are commonly recognised. I have said that she was of moderate height. There are legends in Ireland and elsewhere that Christ, alone among mankind, was exactly six feet tall, neither a hair's breadth more nor less. If there is a height which correspondingly represents perfection in womankind, she was of that height, neither a hair's breadth more nor less. She left Vienna in June, 1938, after the German occupation. She was a dancer but had not danced lately. She had stayed in England previously, to study dancing under Legat. Her English was very good.'

Kamtschatka meditated.

'She was a little of the sixteenth century, perhaps? A little the Lady of Pollaiuolo?'

'Yes, I suppose so.'

'A little too sweet, perhaps?'

'Ah, no'

'Moment,' said Kamtschatka.

He went to the kitchen door and called:

'Mom. Come please'

To me he said:

'Moment. You shall see.'

Mom entered, lofty, black and powerful. A woman with the strength of ten virgins, submitting her life to the whims of this man's genius.

'Mom,' said Kamtschatka, 'have we the picture I made of Jo and Robert, please?'

Mom demanded further details. These were provided in German. Mom went upstairs. Kamtschatka fussed about the room we were in, hands fluttering with excitement among his folios. Mom returned with a canvas of medium size. Kamtschatka took it from her and set it upon the easel, from which Mom removed the half-finished picture.

'There, you see,' said Kamtschatka. 'Their mother was a Dutch woman, but she married and bore these children in Vienna. You see that Robert is like yourself.'

In all Kamtschatka's portraits, the background contains figures, landscape and symbolical images. Kamtschatka will never do a portrait of anybody whom he dislikes or to whom he is indifferent. In the case of strangers to whom he may have taken a fancy, he will ask for photographs of their parents and of themselves and will not begin work until he feels that he understands their history. Childhood scenes and faces of parents are likely to appear in the finished portrait.

In the double portrait now confronting me, the arrangement of the two faces was conventional, the brother's head set a little higher upon the canvas and in greater depth, protective but leaving his sister the frontal light. Jo and Robert. They were undoubtedly 'Thea' and the young man with whom I had seen her leave the little hall at the top of a building in Phelps Place. As Kamtschatka said, Robert in the portrait bore a marked resemblance to myself, though he too was pale and very fair. The background contained the representation of a large house and bushes of lilac. At the top of broad steps stood a figure who may have been 'Thea's' mother or grandmother in her youth. I did not have time to observe any more, for at that moment Kamtschatka had to go and sit down in a fit of giddiness. Mom went to fetch him a glass of water. I stood anxiously by in case I were needed to chafe his hands or perform some other service.

A little later, I said:

'Then you know this girl.'

Mom said:

'Her parents were friends of Kamtschatka's.'

She said:

'Jo and Robert are very lucky. They got their visas and sailed a fortnight ago. They will go to Paraguay.' I sat in the dining car of the Cornish Riviera. The old head waiter in his brown uniform, gold-rimmed pince-nez, white hair and white, yellow-edged moustache, was engaged at the far end with a group of celebrities. I do not remember who they were. They may have been Jessie Matthews and Sonnie Hale. Or perhaps they were Lady Astor and her friends. In those days, there was always a group of celebrities on the Cornish Riviera, and if there was not the old head waiter would tell you stories of celebrities dating back to Lawrence of Arabia. Whoever these particular celebrities may have been they were at the moment the only occupants of the dining car beside the old head waiter and myself.

It was four o'clock. I had sat here since noon watching the pink fields of Devonshire, the creeks and estuaries, the woods, hills and streams of Somerset and Hampshire go by. Just now a narrow, disused and overgrown eighteenth-century canal ran alongside the permanent way, but failed to keep up with the train. Five minutes ago, among its reeds and between two hanging willows, I had seen a tall, grey heron standing upon one leg and apparently fast asleep in the failing light. I had treated myself to the only 1929 claret I could find on the diminishing wartime list. I had lingered over a series of coffee-cups and two little glasses of Cointreau tasting and smelling of fennel seeds steeped in weak hydrochloric acid. I had dozed and daydreamed until it was half-past three and the old waiter had asked me if I would care for tea. Now I had tea. I do not like the taste of tea, but am very fond of the sound of spoons rattling against china and the hour of the day at which tea is made and the lucid, fragrant steam rising in the first twilight.

The telephone bell woke me. Where the heavy dark-blue curtains were parted, I saw that a pale sun shone and that the sky was cloudless. I had not moved the telephone to my bedside last night, so to answer it I had to get up. It was Gabriel Fantl. He sounded very woeful and said that he could not speak about it over the telephone but would like to come and see me. I thought that perhaps he was cleaned out of money or that the police had been round again to threaten him with internment. I said he was to come immediately. Fantl told me over the telephone that Edgar Voysey, driving his ambulance in France and the Rhineland, had received both the Croix de Guerre and some British medal and that he was now on his way home to America. In the letterbox was a letter from Richard St. Hilda, now in Chatham, which suggested that I might care to sue the hat-shop in Baker Street for pain and anguish.

I had just finished breakfast and was sitting in sandals and dressing gown drinking a last cup of tepid coffee over a gas fire in the dining room downstairs when Fantl arrived. He was not in need of money, nor had the police been worrying him. Nor had he ferreted out for me any news about 'Thea'. His trouble was the Czech Legion. Fantl had never been in Czechoslovakia, and he could not speak a word of Czech. Moreover, he considered that the Czechs were a bunch of savages. But he carried a Czechoslovak passport, and the Czech Legion were after him. He had therefore reached the painful conclusion that the only way to avoid being conscripted among a bunch of savages and halfwits was to join the British Army, and the previous day he had visited a recruiting office and volunteered for the Auxiliary Military Pioneer Corps, into which he would presently be called up. I suggested that he could have returned to France and joined the French army, but he pointed out to me that French soldiers received only fifty centimes a day and that in any case he now regarded himself as an Englishman.

Poor Fantl. He was the last man on earth to be a soldier. His First World War service in the Austro-Hungarian Imperial Army had consisted chiefly in consolation of the wives of his superior officers and those more perilously engaged in Russia, Rumania or the Italian alps. Fantl was very small and frail. I could have lifted him under the arms and carried him about as easily as a doll and had indeed so carried him to the door on one occasion when he was troublesome at a party. I could not see him wielding pick and shovel side by side with tough but superannuated reservists and regulars with hammer toes, Bombay livers and huge, tattooed arms.

I dressed, and we walked out into the garden. This was manifestly the first day of spring. In the little shrubbery at the end of the garden a flowering almond whose existence I had not suspected was already in bloom. I cut out a single branch and set it in a large Nanking blue jar on the drawing room floor so that a pattern of thin black stems traced itself upon the wall, holding there a number of small, pink rosettes.

Eleven

At the Flying Dutchman, they wanted to know what I had done to my eye. I told them I had been kicked by a horse.

I said:

'Oh, I've been down to the country for a bit. Had a row with a horse, you know.'

I said:

'Been riding in Cornwall. Had a bit of trouble with the farmer's mare.'

I said:

'Oh that. Horse took a dislike to me, you know.'

This increased my credit at the Flying Dutchman. They had not regarded me as a man who knew about horses.

Not that the Flying Dutchman was a horsey pub. It was a mixed pub. Songwriters, film men, journalists, music hall comics and the proprietors of garages were equally welcome. But they did like a man to be active in some way. There was no prudery. Irregularities of every sort were permitted and indeed encouraged, but it was felt that even these could be pursued with a proper heartiness. Virility was encouraged but not *de rigueur*. Cleanliness, affluence and a good school met with general but not universal approval. Feelings of patriotism had no need to conceal themselves, but they were optional. All in all, the Flying Dutchman was the pleasantest pub in the neighbourhood, and the Warthog had a great many friends. He gave credit, made loans and cashed cheques liberally but judiciously, keeping his eye on the till. He was an extremely well-dressed man, and a ludicrous physique had by no means undermined his self-assurance. He strutted about on short legs, kept his chest jutting a hair's breadth in front of his stomach, and with that great, porcine nose discovered truffles rooting in the air. He wore a red carnation in his carefully pressed lapel. Many young women and others old enough to know better brought their troubles to him and were advised, sometimes generously.

The wound above my eye had now reached the stage at which it was protected by a mere piece of boracic lint and two parallel strips of sticking plaster. The stitches were out. I was allowed to change the dressing myself. As the last suppurations dried, I observed that the hardening scar ran slantwise, like a piece of white string just beneath the skin, in a line which slightly raised but otherwise simply extended that of the eyebrow itself. I was not at all displeased with the general effect. It had, however, one disconcerting feature. My facial expression was modified, and it was so modified as to bring out resemblances between myself and Richard St. Hilda which in his case the scar had merely accentuated but which in my case were wholly aborigine. I had developed, as it were, a glazed and supercilious eye.

As March developed, the occasional pains in my head vanished and I removed plaster and lint. The scar lost its remaining traces of inflammation. I was changed, but once more complete. Out of the damp, black soil of the garden thrust up the leaves and flowering stems of tulip and daffodil. The almond tree shed its petals and produced leaf.

A barrage balloon took its ease in the street outside. Eight or ten houses had been requisitioned and demolished at the corner of the street. We expected at least a battery of guns. Now the shadows of war had been reduced to the jovial, silver presence of a balloon and a group of aged men in Air Force uniform who marked out a court on the surface of the road and played badminton.

Alison and Richard had both kept in touch with Effie. Richard had several times driven down to the cottage in Kent and had stayed there for a while before going to Bristol. Alison had written once or twice and had visited Effie in a London nursing-home when she had come up for one of her periodical operations.

The news of Frances Abell was that she had gone to Bristol a little before Richard himself, the reason being that Eric wished to register as a conscientious objector and that the Bristol tribunals were said to be the most lenient. It was also rumoured that Harbutt Abell had taken up definitely with a student from his art school and that he and Frances were separated and contemplating divorce.

I was moderately interested in these reports. I had been fond of Effie in the days before Richard St. Hilda had stolen her from me and begun as it were to stage manage her, and at this distance it was possible to feel pity for Frances Abell. I wondered whether Caroline's frocks had been let down to cover a little more of those golden limbs. But I did not wish to see any of these people and when towards the end of March the bell rang and I answered the door to find Effie on my doorstep, I was unprepared. I warmed to her at once.

She floated in on a cloud of perfume, dressed in a lemon coat and wearing a hat of black, varnished straw not in the least reminiscent either of haymaking or of a garden with hollyhocks.

'Leckie dear,' she said, 'your eye!'

I stalled about that. I kissed Effie, took her coat and suggested tea.

Effie was not alone. Elizabeth and Tim were with her. Elizabeth was Effie's talented daughter. Tim had recently married Elizabeth. I discovered that I was glad to see them too.

Tim Jacobs was new to me. I had heard of him. When Alison went to see Effie in the nursing home, Effie had told Alison rather proudly that Elizabeth was living in sin with a young man called Tim, a plant biologist. Effie had encouraged the affair, but I do not think it can be inferred from this that she was a dirty old thing. On the contrary, she wished her daughter to behave properly within the framework of current tradition, and in the circles in which she moved Elizabeth's virginity really had become a problem, if it were not indeed a definite social liability. I took a fancy to Tim. Like other young scientists, he had developed that slightly pompous scepticism which is in reality the height of superstition, but he was diffident and receptive at heart, and his pale, serious lankiness was by no means devoid of charm. I imagine that he had made up his mind from the start to marry Elizabeth and that he endured the illicit preliminaries out of pure good humour.

Elizabeth herself had improved out of all recognition. When I first knew her, she had worn jade, puce or mustard-coloured stockings and at parties was liable to dance solo in the middle of the room. She had been easily prevailed upon to read poems by herself in which as a child she hid behind curtains in Edwardian drawing rooms, and at night she heard strange rappings and dreamed dreams of painfully obvious significance, which she would recount at the breakfast table. In fact, she had been a girl in whom virginity was a palpable mistake. The changing of her condition cannot have been easy, and it was very much to Tim's credit that he had seen how very much worth his pains the operation would be.

Tim and Elizabeth Jacobs had come to live with Tim's mother in my neighbourhood. This was at the moment necessary on financial grounds. The professor under whom Tim did his research had promised to put him very shortly on a national plant breeding station. Effie had put on her best town clothes and come to visit them.

Effie talked about these things and about the danger in which Elizabeth's equally talented brother stood of being called up into the Army, about her financial worries and her reluctant attempts to sell or let both cottages in Kent, about her garden (the frost this year had killed her mulberry tree), about local characters, favourite tramps and the behaviour of her ghosts. Then she reverted to my eye.

'Leckie dear,' she said once more, 'your eye!'

I thought Effie deserved a version all to herself. Besides, she had heard the horse one when it was first used as Richard's alibi, and knew in any case that I did not ride.

I said:

'It was Richard. The fact that I had marked him for life preyed on both of us. It was all right when we were sober, but after a drink or two I would begin to stare at Richard's scar, or he would begin to finger it, so that conversation became impossible. In the end, I came to the conclusion that Richard had to do the same to me as I had done to him.'

Effie said:

'Yes, I think I understand that, Leckie dear.'

Elizabeth said:

'Don't be such an awful liar, Leckie!'

Effie said:

'But this is so much Leckie, Elizabeth.'

Tim Jacobs smiled quietly to himself.

I said:

'It wasn't easy to make Richard hit me, as you can imagine. Whatever else you can say about him, he's terribly good-tempered. I had to get him really drunk one night and then taunt him. He . . .'

Elizabeth said:

'What did you taunt him with, Leckie?'

Effie said:

'No. This is serious, Elizabeth dear. I can imagine it all so well.'

Tim was on my side.

I said:

'Eventually . . .'

But at that moment Alison came in from her three doctors. Tim had to be introduced. Effie, Elizabeth and Alison had to do one of those long girlish reunions. I hurried downstairs to put the kettle on. I remember how Alison looked that afternoon, a high colour in her cheeks and carrying the child superbly, her eyes laughing.

Jill was an ordinary cat. She was a nice, friendly creature, but unremarkable. Friends who had given up their house asked us if we knew anyone who would take her, and the prolonged absence of Tit and Nit had permitted a colony of mice to establish itself in the basement. So Jill arrived by carrier's van one afternoon in a wicker cage. She was black and rather small. I lighted the gas fire in the dining room, put a saucer of milk beside it and locked Jill in. An hour later, I went down to see how things were going and found that Jill had drunk the milk and was washing herself, one paw behind her ear. Her initial tendency to pace restlessly to and fro had gone completely and when I fondled her she purred. I allowed her to come upstairs. She sat on the arm of my chair and presently fell asleep.

I mention Jill because she added to the prevailing atmosphere of fertility. She made friends with the black and white torn next door and before she had been with us a fortnight had swollen visibly. She became a baggy little cat and ran about the house with a bellyful of kittens swaying from side to side beneath her.

The daffodils bloomed. Alison filled the house with them. The pear-trees had borne leaf and threatened to do more. New shoots thrust out from the old rosewood, which I belatedly pruned. Another pink-flowering shrub was out, whose name I did not know.

On Tuesday, April 9th, the war ascended to new heights of unreality. German vessels were sighted in Oslo Fjord, but the shore batteries were ordered not to fire. A single battalion of German troops marched through the streets of Oslo and settled down in the bandstands, where they unpacked their instruments and played before a population which had been told nothing. On the same day, Denmark was occupied without fuss. A naval battle ensued in which British vessels inflicted great losses upon the German navy in Oslo Fjord. Parts of the Norwegian army retired to the hills, where they were presently joined by French, British and Poles. The British force had been assembled in the first place to assist the romantic Finns.

Alison was standing at the door with her hand on the light switch.

She said:

'Are you awake, darling?'

I turned over.

'Yes. At least, I think so.'

Alison said:

'Shall I put the light on, darling?'

'Yes, do.'

Alison was dressed.

She said:

'I've been having pains every three-quarters of an hour or so. Do you think I ought to go now?'

It was three o'clock in the morning. This was the first I had been told. It was now April 13th. Alison had as usual been to work in Wimpole Street all day yesterday. We had spent a quiet evening, reading, drinking coffee, playing the gramophone, listening to the news and sewing. I had been round to the Flying Dutchman.

I put on a dressing gown and went downstairs to fill the kettle. I made tea.

Alison said:

'They're supposed to get worse and closer together.'

'I don't know, I'm sure,' I said.

Alison said:
'It's not a good time of night for getting a taxi, is it?'
In the end, we both went back to bed. Alison woke me again at six.
She said:
'They're getting closer together now.'
I rang up two or three taxi ranks, but there was nobody there. Alison had her little attaché case packed. We drank some more tea.
I said:
'Can you walk a little way till we pick up a taxi?'
'Of course, darling. I'm perfectly all right.'
It was a fresh, clear morning. A taxi passed us in the main road. I stopped it. We had to go round by the outpatients'. I was kept waiting for about half an hour. I went upstairs. Alison was lying under a blanket in a tiny anteroom. She was a bit pale.
I said:
'How are you feeling?'
'Fine, darling.'
I said:
'Good luck, sweet.'
I felt a bit sheepish. I could not think what the correct behaviour or even the appropriate feelings were. I kissed Alison.
'I expect they'll start by shaving you,' I said.
'Darling,' said Alison, 'they've shaved me already. Kiss me again, darling.'
The nurse went out.
Alison said:
'Darling, do you love me?'
'Yes,' I said. 'At least, I think so.'
The nurse returned and sent me away.
I said:
'Shall I be able to see her?'
'Perhaps,' said the nurse. 'Ring up this afternoon at four o'clock.'
'Darling,' I said, 'try and get them to remember the exact time.'

I returned to the flat. It was only a little after seven. The woman would not be in to make my breakfast for another two hours. I rooted in a cupboard under the stairs and found the spade. I began to dig. The daffodils were still in bloom, but I dug round them. The Michaelmas daisies were putting out shoots below the top soil, but I chopped them ruthlessly back to keep room for my own sowing. The sun was hot by breakfast time. After breakfast, I went on digging. I turned over the borders along both sides of the garden and broadened them by two feet. I dug until half-past one. At half-past one I had lost so much by perspiration that a visit to the Flying Dutchman became imperative.

After two pints, my hands had almost ceased shaking, and my power of speech was restored. I informed the Warthog that my child was now on its way, and then I began to eat Scotch eggs and some of the Danish blue cheese which he had laid away before the invasion, and to sip the third pint not with violent physiological need but with enjoyment.

My attention was drawn to two people who were playing the pin-table. At this hour, they were the only people in the saloon bar. They were a girl well under twenty and a man of about forty. Their manner of playing attracted me. They played with reverence. A pin-table is not by nature a highly responsive instrument, especially if it be such a highly mechanised affair of ringing bells and flashing lights as the pin-table which stood in the saloon bar at the Flying Dutchman. But these two played it with sweetness. They were rapt. And indeed, now that I came to observe them, they were a remarkable pair. The man was a thick-set, blond fellow with a broken nose. The girl was, I felt certain, very young indeed. Her figure was fairly well developed, and there was considerable assurance in her manner, yet I felt that she was too young to be allowed by law in a public-house, that she was no more than fifteen. I tried to make out her relationship to the man. He might have been her father, but if he were then they had but newly discovered each other after a long separation. As they were rapt in playing the pin-table, they were also wrapt in each other. The two were in love, and their love was silent and fulfilled so that it was able to go out and be extended to inanimate things and to betray itself in their movements at a pin-table, playing it amorously. The girl was a mere child, and yet the man of forty treated her with deference. The man had lived hard and was brutalised and already in many ways old and weak and vulnerable, and yet the girl laughed with him as though he were the embodiment of ardent youth.

I thought:

'The man's face is familiar.'

But I dismissed the thought. People to whom one is strongly attracted appear in a few moments to have been long known. I listened to the names by which the two called each other.

'Joey...'

'Ginny...'

Joey. Joe Passiful. Ginny. Virginia. Flora Massingham's Ginny. The little daughter at school. Virginia Massingham. The man grotesquely battling in a cheap wrestling ring, battling against a stupid, hostile crowd. 'Elbow' Enrico. Flora Massingham's tale of barking dogs and a violent man sweating with fear.

'Excuse me,' I said. 'You don't happen to be Mr. Passiful, the wrestler...?'

I had broken the spell. The happy lover at the pin-table became a man deficient in cunning, a man lacking in self-confidence, a hurt man, caught frolicking in public houses with a little girl. He was confused. His face sweated. His manner was servile, defiant, cornered. I could have hated myself for blundering upon this idyll. I must restore it. I was not sure that I had enough tact or delicacy, that I had what Flora Massingham herself called 'the polite soul.'

I said:

'I'm terribly sorry for interrupting your game, but I thought I remembered seeing you with Flora Massingham.'

'Yes, that's right ...'

Joe Passiful's voice was ugly, rattling in his throat.

Ginny stood undecided, ready to hate me for Joe's sake and to fight me with more than Joe's cunning if need be.

I said:

'Flora Massingham's a great woman . . .'

It was not enough that I admired Flora Massingham. Many admired and hated her out of envy.

I tried another approach.

'Look,' I said. 'I've only known Flora Massingham for two or three years, but I owe her a lot. I spent a lot of time with her just before the war broke out . . .'

Ginny asked me:

'What's your name?'

'Leckie,' I said.

'I don't remember hearing Mummy speak of you.'

The more I tried to put it across that I was all right, the more I felt like a confidence man, a sponger in public houses, a man trying to sell something. I don't know what it was that finally broke the ice. I think Ginny had enough of her mother's instinct to see that it mattered to me to make myself known. She accepted me first, and Joey accepted me because she did. He was obviously used to taking his cues from Ginny as he would have taken them from her mother, trusting their woman's instinct, knowing that they were more reliable than himself in matters which required guile.

I bought drinks. We played the pin-table together. I took down Flora's present address. The acceptance, now that it had come, was full and complete. I joined in their rapture. I was not the third who make a crowd. There was no exclusion and no constraint. I told the two of them about the child that was coming, and at once it concerned them as deeply as it concerned me.

At closing time, they came round to the flat. We took some bottles in. I hunted round for food. There were pies and sweets that I had not expected.

'That's how it is,' said Joey.

'He means,' said Ginny, 'about your wife leaving pastries for you.'

'Yes, that's right,' said Joey. 'It was the last thing she thought of.'

His battered, stupid features were full of light. He rolled his head and sighed. His thick hands, wrapped like a lump of dough about the lager glass I had brought him for his beer, were inhabited by an angel.

Ginny touched my hands and said:

'Don't worry, Leckie. It's natural. It isn't like illness pain.' The wiser her mood, the more like a mere, dumpy schoolgirl she looked.

I thought:

'How marvellously she is her mother's child.'

We were all three drinking down lumps in our throats, but the beer we had brought in did not last very long. We began to sober up. Jill walked in. She trotted restlessly from corner to corner, the bag of kittens swaying beneath her. Her look was very purposeful.

'She's going to have them today or today,' said Ginny. 'Let's make a place for her.'

We tore up newspapers and put them on top of some old flannel in a box and put the box in the cupboard under the stairs, where it was dark. Ginny soothed Jill and took her to the box. Jill stayed in the box, purring continuously, perfectly still. Ginny put a saucer of milk beside the box. Jill did not touch it. We three-parts closed the cupboard door and left Jill inside, purring like a Rolls engine.

It was four o'clock. I rang up the hospital. Ginny and Joe Passiful sat holding their breath. I got through to a nurse in the maternity wards.

The nurse said:

'Your wife is in labour.'

Slowly, the hair rose up from my scalp.

'Yes,' I said. 'Yes. Thank you.'

The nurse said:

'Ring again at six.'

'Yes,' I said. 'Very well. Yes. Thank you. Thank you.'

I put the telephone down. My lips obeyed the injunction to stop quivering. Out of a dry mouth I told Virginia Massingham and the solemn Joey that there was still nothing.

The doorbell rang. It was Tim and Elizabeth. I told them Alison was in hospital. Ginny and Elizabeth made tea. I felt embarrassed by my company. Tim and Elizabeth were fine young people. They could have made friends with Ginny and Joe. But it would have needed an effort on my part. I should have needed to draw them together. I was not just now capable of making the effort. The company of four had to sit there in two camps, wondering about each other.

At six, nobody had gone. They were all four making difficult conversation. I could have made it easy for them, but I did not. They were trying to meet in a labyrinth. I did not help. I wanted to be left alone.

I went downstairs. The telephone had an extension downstairs. I closed the door of the little downstairs room and tried to empty my heart of confusion. I dialled the number of the hospital.

The nurse said:

'Is that Mr. Leckie?'

'Yes . . . ?'

'The child is a little girl.'

'Yes, yes. But my wife?'

'Your wife is quite well. She is tired.'

'When can I see her?'

'Any time between eight and nine.'

Then I sobbed audibly, and tears forced their way into the corners of my eyes. I walked in the garden. I could not think about it all yet. I must first get myself under control, and then I must send my guests away.

I went upstairs.

'Look,' I said, 'I was supposed to ring up the hospital again at six, and I'm feeling rather edgy . . .'

All four went, and there was no offence. I had Flora Massingham's address. I said I would make contact over the weekend. Elizabeth was the least intelligent.

She said:

'Leckie, will you ring us up as soon as you know?'

But Elizabeth felt herself more personally involved than the others. She had made sure during the week that she too was in the family way.

In the evening, I saw Fantl. He was in Bertorelli's with a girl who looked ill and had one eye larger than the other. He was reporting to a military depot tomorrow. Each of us was too full of himself to communicate much. Fantl wanted to know if he could come round to the hospital with me right away. I told him no. He said he would send in some flowers tomorrow morning, before he went to report. It was miserable, meeting like this and being able to say so little and that in the presence of the girl.

At the hospital, they had put the child in bed with Alison for me to see. The light was dim, but I could see that Alison had put some make-up on her face for me and that her weariness was a happy one.

It had not been an easy birth. Alison was torn a little and had to have stitches put in. They had given her a chloroform mask to hold to her face when the pain grew too bad, and she had gripped the plump, red arm of a nurse for a long while. Alison herself had kept her eyes on the clock, and when the child first cried it was ten minutes past five.

The child was sleeping. I had been led to suppose that newborn children had malformed heads and features for a day or two, especially after a rather difficult birth. This one had a shapely head, and its features were perfectly formed. The head was covered with fine, red-gold hair. The features already suggested a likeness to myself.

I looked at the child. I looked at Alison.

Alison said:

'Do you like it, darling? It's rather underweight.'

I looked at the child again. I looked at Alison. I kissed her. I fled.

When I returned to the flat, Jill was still purring in the cupboard under the stairs. Alison had beaten her by a quarter of a day. Jill bore her kittens during the night, three black and white ones of various marking and one that was all black.

Visiting time on Sunday was from three to four. I called at Flora Massingham's in the morning, stayed for lunch, went to the hospital and returned to Flora Massingham's. The new address was near Paddington. There was a bookshop under it, empty at present. Nothing was yet in place, but it did not matter. Flora Massingham did not need a home or even a background, though none was better able to create both. She was her own stability, her own roof, light and sanitation. If she did not choose to extend herself into a suitable environment, one did not feel the lack.

She said:

'I am fallow land.'

And it was enough. Flora Massingham was doing nothing, discovering nothing and drinking nothing. Her appearance proved it. She looked almost commonplace, waiting for the spirit to stir, waiting for the crop to be sown in her.

'But,' she said, 'Joey has come back to me.'

I told Flora that I had visited other worlds.

She said:

'I'm sorry.'

I was surprised to hear her say that.

I asked:

'Why do you say that?'

She looked surprised that I should ask.

'You don't want that sort of thing,' she said. 'You're not ready for it, Leckie. Are you?'

That was all that was said about other worlds or about any hidden thing. The day was spent in finding a name for my child. At the hospital in the afternoon, I showed Alison five postcards that we had covered on both sides with possible names. I wrote them out with my surname following, to see how they looked. After tea we filled three more postcards, and at eleven o'clock I had still not made up my mind. The calendar did not help. The day's saint was St. Hermenegild. As soon as I got back to the flat and was alone, I decided on 'Judith', which did not appear on any of the eight postcards. I sat up till dawn doing Judith Leckie's horoscope. One day I would take the chart to Flora Massingham for her reading. For the present, I made out what I could without help. The Sun stood in Aries, conjoined with Jupiter upon the cusp of the eighth house and in a fortunate sextile with the Moon. The child ought in physical appearance to favour both her parents, for like Alison, she had Virgo rising, but rising with it was Neptune, my planet. Danger came from Mercury in opposition with Neptune and with the ascendant degree and from the square of these to the Moon, hinting at nervous maladies or inflammatory weakness of the lungs. Mars also stood in Gemini at the zenith.

I took daffodils in to the hospital. I took daffodils to Flora Massingham (not to decorate her room, for it was a room that would have resisted decoration, but because I could think of no other thing to take). I took tulips to the hospital. I bought a dwarf broom in a pot and took that in, too.

The shoots of the roses increased and I trained them against walls. The pear trees would be in full blow when Alison came out of hospital. I bought seeds of hardy-annual flowers, candy-tuft and larkspur, sweet alyssum and mallow, love-in-a-mist, cornflower and night-scented stock, mignonette and Collins's toadflax, scarlet flax, Shirley poppy, Californian poppy and gypsophila. I showed the packets to Alison in hospital and then went back to Richard St. Hilda's flat to rake the soil and sow them.

Jill and her kittens were installed in the dining room. Three that were marked like three different maps in black and white fed lustily. The kitten that was entirely black like its mother was pushed to one side at feeding time and did not grow so fast as the others, but became the most venturesome of the four. I lived my life to the accompaniment of Jill's purring.

Against her doctor's advice but with encouragement from all the nurses, Alison fed Judith out of her breast. When I visited the hospital I did not again see the child and her mother together. To see the child, I was taken to the door of the common nursery from which the children were fetched to their mothers only at feeding time. On my fourth visit, I found Alison in tears. Judith had a cold, had been as it were born with a cold. I hurried home to examine the position of Saturn in my child's horoscope, but I found nothing to the point, and the cold presently dried up.

The crumbling lintel of the flat above met my eyes several times as I laboured in the garden, but I felt no fear of it even when the wood of the window frame itself split and one of the temporary props staggered out of the vertical.

Alison was in a ward containing four other recently delivered women. One of them was a Jewess, and one day a crowd of the faithful assembled by her bedside to see a robed and bearded Rabbi perform circumcision upon the fruit of her womb. This woman talked in her sleep about Germany and the need for keeping Germans away from the hospital until she and the little Jewish man-child were safely out of it.

Twelve

I took a taxi down and had it wait. A little nurse who had made friends and told Alison her secrets carried Judith in the lift and across the wide hall and put her into Alison's arms in the taxi.

This was my first sight of Judith at close quarters and in full light. Truly, she bore an astonishing likeness to myself.

I thought:

'Who is she? What is her history? The likeness to myself will pass. A likeness to Alison will develop and pass. For some time to come, this child will seem to belong to Alison, to be a part of her. But she is not. She is herself. A child's body may be the creation of her parents, but no child yet ever inherited a soul.'

I thought:

'I must bear it in mind if I am one day tempted to assume a right and to make demands upon this Judith Leckie. It may be that parents have a duty towards their child, but a child has none towards them. A child is born free, and this means free of parenthood.'

Alison was looking very beautiful. It was as if the delivery had consumed her with its intolerable pain and dissolved away whatever traces of strain or harshness the years of our life together had formed in her.

I did not at once dare to hold Judith in my arms. When I did my fear of dropping her was so great, my feelings of tenderness so grotesquely out of proportion, that anything else remained hidden. Later, I discovered that to hold my daughter in my arms excited me sexually. I do not know whether this is a common experience, for it is not the kind of fact which even today is openly discussed. I did compare notes with two recent fathers and elicited from them a similar confession.

Life was reshaped. Every three hours, Alison unfastened her bodice and drew the child's mouth to the neighbourhood of her breast. Anything else became subsidiary.

At first, Judith did not gain sufficient weight. At this period, the two spinsters who had long lived noiselessly above ventured into neighbourly prominence, their withered hearts blossoming helplessly at the sound of a child's cry. One of them had been a nurse. She said that Alison was not leaving her child long enough at the breast. One of Alison's doctors, who turned up one morning with a pair of scales, confirmed this. They had been wrong at the hospital. There a feed was measured by the clock, but it appeared that children have their own tempo.

A more disturbing feature was that the navel did not heal. Each morning, as Alison unstitched the web band about Judith's belly, the navel lay open and bled a little.

Alison's doctor, himself childless, was most helpful. He appointed himself family physician. I found one comment of his particularly to the point. He said one day that Judith was crying because she felt chaotic. This comment illuminated for me the nature of a child's misery (and I dare say of adult misery, too). I had myself not been capable of imagining causes other than hunger or wind. In consequence, when Judith cried, I felt now that I knew in what tone of voice I must speak to soothe her.

On May 10th, German troops invaded the low countries. German aeroplanes bombed Rotterdam and killed, it was said, a hundred thousand people. A quarter of the Dutch army was also said to have been killed. British and French troops invaded Belgium, but had to be evacuated by sea when the Belgian army cracked. I cannot now recall what impression these events made upon me. I think it must have been slight, though I remember very clearly many of the details that were reported.

My head was full of cotyledons. Wherever I had sown seed, pairs of what I took to be tiny leaves appeared, but Tim Jacobs said that they were cotyledons. In damp weather or after watering them, I pored over these tiny vegetable forms, thinning them out and sometimes transplanting trowelfuls of them, until my head contained nothing else. When I closed my eyes, I saw a banner of cotyledons pricked out against a background of black soil.

Animal, human and vegetable growth surrounded me. Even the mineral kingdom exposed itself to my gaze and came to life, for the two spinsters upstairs had the builder in at last and the stricken lintel was replaced behind a scaffolding. The very stone healed.

Aloysius Smith, who came to photograph Judith but was more interested in Jill's kittens, reported seeing Pat Mallard in a public house in Soho, with two young men in tow. According to Aloysius, Pat had completely changed. Her clothes, her hair, her lipstick, were fashionable. She gave off glamour and sophistication.

Judith became very beautiful. Pseudo-smiles, the effect of wind, gave place to smiles proper and then to laughter. Judith kicked her legs all day, chuckled and formed bubbles upon her lips. Yet the likeness to myself persisted. I would look at Judith Leckie, and it was as if I were looking at myself through the wrong end of a telescope. At times, this threw me into a panic so that I would rush out of the house and round the corner to the Flying Dutchman to pour mild liquor upon the flames.

On June 15th I registered for military service. Faced with the necessity of stating my profession, I hesitated. What was I? I thought to put 'gentleman', but decided that I did not look the part. 'Bankrupt'? Accurate, but liable to cause prejudice. By what had I kept myself alive for the greater part of my adult life? By faith. Faith and appeal to motherly instinct in the middle-aged. Should I not then write 'gigolo'? Evidently I had no profession. Something entirely outrageous would be best. I might try 'ponce's clerk'. In the end, I was guided by vanity. I put 'author'. I was classified by the cipher '2MM'. Two days after I had registered, Marshall retain assumed control of the French government and asked for an armistice. Mr. Churchill, our new Prime Minister, made the gesture of offering to the already defeated French a solemn bond of union with ourselves. For me the bottom had dropped out of the war. France was the only country of which I could ever at any time have conceived myself to be a citizen. When France collapsed, the world had ended. The outside world, that is to say. Throughout May, June and July, my inner world was firm and secure, and its people lived together in a state of natural bliss as though I had already fought and won and lost my war.

It was a village hall of wood and corrugated iron. Half a dozen young men —all twenty-eight or twenty-nine years old—were already there, sitting on wooden chairs in front of the porch.

One said:

'They're full up.'

But I went inside the porch and pushed open a wooden door painted plum colour. A clerk in his shirtsleeves looked up at me with anguish, half a dozen further young men (on a form in front of him) with dubious grins.

I said:

'I'm sorry, but I want to ask somebody about something.'

The clerk said:

'Listen, I want my lunch sometime today.'

I went out.

A clerk who was unoccupied had heard me from behind a screen. He came out.

He said:

'What is it?'

I said:

'I have glasses for reading, and I've forgotten them. Does it matter?'

The clerk said:

'I don't know.'

I said:

'Well, I thought if it did . . .'

The clerk said:

'It's too late to do anything about it now, isn't it? I should mention the matter to the eye doctor when you go in. He's the first you come to.'

I went outside and sat on a chair. The other young men were establishing fraternity. I couldn't be bothered. Others came. One was a good-looking Air Raid Precautions warden with a club foot. A doctor appeared in his car, from the interior of which he brought out a packet of sandwiches. He waved to us as he went in. My bladder was aching. I wondered how long I should have to wait and whether I ought to empty it and trust to it partly filling up again before I went in.

A clerk came out and said:

'Three married men, please.'

Three who were nearer to the door beat me to it.

Another clerk came out and said:

'All single men, please.'

Those who looked married all went in. I remarked on this to a man near me. He didn't see the joke.

Presently we all went in. The place was divided up by asbestos screens. The clerk in the first compartment gave us forms to fill up for our marriage and child allowances. A fat young man with wavy hair and a moustache, who looked like a butcher and had been the centre of fun and fraternity outside, couldn't understand the form. We all peered over each other's forms to some extent.

A second clerk checked up our particulars and sent us into little cubicles to undress to our coats and trousers. In the next cubicle to me was a Roumanian. He said he came from Cernauti in Bukovina, occupied a few days ago by Soviet troops. The A.R.P. warden was running about stubbing the foot of his short leg against screens and pieces of wood. The urine doctor fetched us to a room at the far end and gave us jam pots and lager glasses.

Halfway through, I said:

'I'm afraid this isn't going to hold it.'

The urine doctor handed me a pail that I could switch over to.

The young butcher was looking sheepish.

He said:

'I can't go yet, sir.'

The doctor said:

'Go outside and turn the tap on. That might help you.'

The eye doctor wasn't interested in my reading glasses. He only wanted to know how far I could see. I read three lines of letters, and that satisfied him.

He looked at my form and said:

'You're an author, eh?'

I said I was.

'You'll be able to write a book about this,' said the eye doctor. 'There's plenty of material.'

I was passed on to the weight, measurements and distinguishing marks doctor. It was the urine doctor, but now he had finished with urine. He discovered the scar over my right eye, and told a clerk to put down 'scar over right eye.' This I did resent. It was noted down in case I became a deserter. I felt a mild claustrophobia. But then it might also come in useful for identification purposes if I were blown unrecognisably to pieces.

The joints doctor, who was the chairman of the board, was the first to require total nudity. While I was lying down on a camp bed, the shameful parts doctor came up to him.

'You see, he's quite hairy,' said the joints doctor. 'He can't be a hermaphrodite.'

'He says it does come out occasionally,' said the shameful parts doctor. 'And his voice is normal.'

They giggled.

'Well,' said the shameful parts doctor, 'I've always noticed that the larger the man the smaller the penis.'

It was the Roumanian they were talking about. He was plump, bald-headed and gentle, and at a first glance he had no shameful parts at all. There was a normal mat of hair, but only a small valve nesting in it. The joints doctor probed my stomach and made me stand on one leg.

He also looked at my form and said:

'Author, yes? What sort of books do you write?'

I invented a number of books.

'You'll be able to write about this,' he said.

'It's been done,' said I.

'By whom?'

'Lawrence.'

'Whom?'

'D. H. Lawrence. A long chapter called "The Nightmare" in *Kangaroo*.'

'I don't read D. H. Lawrence, but my son does,' said the joints doctor. 'Is it good?'

'A bit overdone,' I said. 'He thought it the final insult to human dignity.'

'Yes,' said the joints doctor. 'He was always a bit—er . . .'

'Touchy?' I suggested.

'Yes,' said the joints doctor. 'Wasn't he?'

I said:

'He was, rather.'

I passed on to the shameful parts doctor. I had to turn my head to one side to cough. That made it seem curiously polite.

I touched my toes, and the shameful parts doctor coughed in his turn.

'All right,' he said.

The chairman gave each man a last general inspection and filled up his card. I sat in a little cubicle to wait my turn. I was able to inspect the Roumanian a little more closely and to watch other people going round. At any given moment there were only two or perhaps three men completely naked. This fact allowed them to retain a certain individuality. However cursorily studied, they were not just so much meat. It pleased me to see the toughest men unable to stand on one leg, much less to go up on their toes on one leg. Also, I seemed to be one of the only two men who didn't have ugly little paunches. One man's paunch stuck out like a small, bracketed ledge. He was a marsupial.

The chairman who had also been the joints doctor asked how much exercise I took and whether I felt well in myself.

He filled up my card and said:

'What did you say the title of your last book was? I must get it.'

He took down the title I invented for him and gave me my card. I was marked Grade One. This pleased me. I dressed and went round to the military officer, who was sitting in a little box quite apart from all the doctors and clerks. He was quite different in temperament, too. The doctors were tall, gentle creatures of a rather fluttering, ineffectual charm. The military officer was squat and bald, a horrid little man in a bow tie. He asked me whether I had ever belonged to the territorials, what languages I spoke besides French, and whether I had any hobbies —'apart from your writing, of course.'

I went off to the tube station and took a train back to Russell Square. I was very pleased indeed to be Grade One and made the same joke to everybody I met during the evening—namely, that I was a perfect specimen of British manhood and that they were sending me in for a beauty competition next week.

Round at the Flying Dutchman, the Warthog was limping round with a stick and groaning. This public house was the meeting-place of the Local Defence Volunteers, and the Warthog had been drilling last night at a barracks, under a sergeant of the Guards who made his men stamp hard. The Warthog had clicked his heels together so smartly that he burst a blood vessel in his ankle. He had been to hospital and was told that he would need a small operation in the groin. The sad thing was that nobody believed him. As soon as his back was turned, the young Irish barman said the Warthog was supposed to be on guard tonight and didn't like the thought.

Thirteen

At the beginning of August, Alison and I got up one morning with the idea separately fixed in our two heads that bombing was about to start. Alison took Judith to Tottenham Rivers the following day. I saw them off at Paddington. As they changed trains at Reading, the sirens were going. At about the same time, I distantly heard the first bombs fall on Croydon.

The date on which the old world came to an end was Saturday, September 7th, 1940. That afternoon, Richard St. Hilda and I took tea on the second floor of Lyons' Piccadilly corner house. This is pretty high up. We appeared to be on the same level as the balls of cotton wool in the air outside.

Nobody quite knew what to do about air raids in those days. They were a thing which took place in cities we had never visited. Richard and I went down to the cloakroom and stood for a while on the marble steps between the basement and the ground floor. This seemed rather silly. There was a crowd, and it was nearly opening time. We decided to walk through Leicester Square, turn back down Shaftesbury Avenue and stand outside the York Minster until it opened. Richard St. Hilda was dressed like a railway porter, with a red badge in his cap and a service respirator over his shoulder. The costume of a supply assistant in the Navy is quite becoming to small, dapper men, but it did not suit Richard.

When it grew dark, there was a red glow over London, as, of course, there had always been before the blackout. This was a sign which made it plain to everybody that the world had come to an end. At the Café Royal, people we knew were getting up parties to go and see the docks on fire.

Richard had to go back to Chatham. I returned to the flat. It is better (at any rate, it is pleasanter) to be with other people when death brawls inexplicably in the neighbourhood. That night, I was frightened in the empty flat. I lay in bed in a corner, out of reach of any possible flying glass, and felt the walls of my stomach secreting acid, so that I knew if I spat it would burn a hole in the carpet. Sunday morning, the eighth day of September and the first of the new dispensation, was a morning of sun and of silky, ecstatic air. One's pleasure at having survived into the new world outweighed for the moment other considerations. That evening, however, it started all over again.

I went round to see how Tim and Elizabeth Jacobs were getting along with the baby they now had. Tim Jacobs thought this second bombing a typical example of German thoroughness and lack of humour. They were trying, he said, to exterminate the dead. Elizabeth put her baby under the basement stairs, and we listened to the noise outside.

I went out into the loud, posthumous street. It was a long, straight avenue. Not a soul was abroad. Light flashed across the street intersections, and every fifty yards or so the pavement had begun to rock.

On Monday morning, the sun came up as fresh as ever, but when the daily help arrived at ten o'clock I found that I was still sleepy. I decided to join Alison and Judith at Tottenham Rivers.

I caught the afternoon train from Paddington, reached Tottenham Rivers shortly before six o'clock and walked the two miles to Isobel Tillyard's house. It was a large cottage in a narrow lane. An overgrown yew hedge darkened the kitchen windows.

The equinoctial gales blew, and it rained. Even indoors, one was buffeted. The birds in the forest were blown out of the trees. Isobel's first child was born. Nigel Tillyard, with a cadet's white band about his cap, was at first frequently and then more rarely home for the weekend. From time to time, senior Tillyards appeared, with hams, turkeys and cases of whisky. Then they bravely returned to the Savoy.

Judith's age increased to eight months. She crowed, foamed, gesticulated like Hitler and fell out of her pram. The night overhead was full of aeroplane engines with a double pulse, and next morning the centre of Coventry lay flat. Although I had duly notified the Ministry of Labour and National Service of my change of address, my call-up papers were delivered at Richard St. Hilda's empty flat. Unfortunately, they were discovered a fortnight later, when the once-daily help let herself in to find something Derek Sutler had written for. They were forwarded to me at Tottenham Rivers.

I wrote to the adjutant of the unit requiring my presence. It was a field artillery unit and had been stationed in Durham. My further joining instructions showed that it had moved in the meantime to Ulster. The earliest of the morning light appeared at eight o'clock, for this was December and far north. The train slipped between successive groves of laurel and came to a station with a single platform, where it stood for an hour and a half. Light increased and the colours of day assembled between the grimy boards of the station and the dripping glass of the train, between the train and the laurels. At ten o'clock, the light was still feeble, for a mist hindered its diffusion. From the train, I could not have told the time by a pallid clockface placed at a level above the eye, beneath a long penthouse. Because of the war, they had blocked out station names. I might, I fancy, just about have read this one if it had been there to read. I should have liked to know what it was. Not that it would have meant much to me unless I had long ago heard Aunt Sheena or my parents use it. To the best of my information, I had been born not a hundred miles from here, though, since I attained consciousness and memory, I had not visited any part of Scotland. My few very early, physiological memories lacked any local colour whatever.

A series of shudders passed through the train. Steam rose with evident difficulty from the wheels of the engine and tender and the first coach. The train entered further corridors of frozen laurel. Noon sounded from a distant church as the train eased its weight against the buffers of a railway quay which lay alongside the quays of this grey port.

I thought:

'It has taken me twenty-four hours to travel from a little way the other side of Cheltenham.'

And I found that I no longer believed in the real existence of Cheltenham or of any place further south than Carlisle.

I was tired. My hair was full of grit, and the stubble had grown about my mouth and inside my collar.

Formalities took place upon the boat itself. Cameras were brought to light and films extracted with a polite assurance of their eventual return. I was carrying only a rucksack of bare necessities, and a military warrant accelerated the passage through of my flagrantly civilian and faintly disreputable person. I climbed up to the steerage deck.

A perfect monochrome confronted me. On the quay, the faces and the clothes of men desultorily freighting the boat made patches of degraded colour, but towards the open sea there was no colour at all. Upon the water, a line of seaplanes diminished in size and visibility. It was impossible to say how many. At first I counted up to eight. Then I made it nine. The tenth, if it lay there, had become lightened in tone until it was assimilated to the mist itself, and any that lay beyond were irrecoverably lost.

I thought:

'Yesterday was Friday the thirteenth. I sat in the waiting room at Tottenham Rivers high-level halt with Alison. It was misty, and there was a frost. It was difficult to keep warm. The train was very late. A pilot officer wanted to talk to us. Did Alison bring Judith to the station? I can hardly remember. No, Judith would not be there. Alison would not have kept her there in the cold.'

As the train was leaving, Alison had said:

'I shan't smile again until I hear from you.'

I wanted now to arrive quickly at my destination. I could not write until then, and Alison must smile. I must let her know that I had stepped safely into this new dimension and that time was annihilated.

At Cheltenham, the line had been wrecked by a bomb. We had to get out of the train at the station before it and by-pass Cheltenham in motor-coaches.

While I stared into the mist, a congregation of figures had taken place behind and to either side of me, accusing figures perhaps, like those in the afterworld. At any rate, I was too conspicuous. With rime upon my hair, I stepped back into the partial shelter of the working deck, on which a gun had been mounted and was now manned.

I thought:

'The five men immediately to my left are political desperadoes. Shabbily dressed, they nevertheless betray a certain care for effect. Two of them are more in need of a shave than I am, but the features of all are fine. This is what makes me certain that they are political desperadoes. In England, the poor are not handsome, their looks are spoilt by sheepishness. Fine features, shabby clothes and an assured, self-respecting air betray the foreigner, and a foreigner is suspect, particularly at a port and particularly when the port is drenched with mist and it is wartime.'

To the right were soldiers. One had his wife and child with him. He was small and florid. His eyes were blue, his hair black, and he wore a red and blue artillery cap and no greatcoat. Other soldiers stood colourless and silent, their collars up and their hands deep in greatcoat pockets. The mist had tarnished their buttons, and their faces were grey with lack of sleep.

The best I could hope was that I should be like one of these, inconspicuous and wraithlike. Military service is a form of death. The greatcoat is a winding sheet, impenetrable and full of dignity, if the face is properly covered. I did not wish to behave unseemly, to exhibit gaudy colours or to be one of those who riot in death. I remembered a drunken Scotsman in the refreshment room at Crewe last night. I did not like these angry, jovial soldiers.

Engines throbbed. There was falling soot and a smell of blistering paint. Half an hour later, the screw turned. The boat did not yet assume horizontal motion, but kicked and plunged at the harbour water so that a faint swell was set up and the stomach responded with the first, propitiatory symptoms of what one knew would become seasickness if one were not a good sailor. The motion of departure was then a relief. Water rushed like a millstream from the labouring screw, and the quayside folded up its cranes and put away its long sheds in the mist. The first of the seaplanes raced across the water, mastered the low air and turned about to circle over us.

The boat swerved under green cliffs and attained the open sea. To the north, Ailsa Craig appeared like a ghostly sugar-loaf in the mist.

'Paddy's milestone,' the English and Scottish passengers informed each other.

They began to throw up. Some leaned over the rail and splashed the iron side. Some threw up where they stood, producing round pools of vomit like cow-claps. A hatch opened to serve beer and cigarettes.

We came again to green cliffs, and the heaving of water decreased. This was Ireland, and the cliffs were not so high. Houses of grey stone and red brick appeared, and the slender barrels of several pieces of ordnance were visible for a moment between stunted palm trees.

At the head of the gangway stood two red-capped military police, officious and red-faced. Two civil police stood silently at the foot of the gangway. The contrast implied disdain. The full-skirted, well-tailored black uniform, the holstered revolver and the harp on the black, peaked cap contained for the unaccustomed eye a suggestion of the Balkan picturesque and of real violence.

The train appeared to cross the lough at water level. It skirted ten miles of coast, rode into a second lough and turned inland between a jagged escarpment and a wilderness of tall cranes urgent with imploration in the failing light.

To reach Killing, one had to change stations. At the Great Northern station, there was an hour and a half to wait. In the grill room, the girl who brought me fried eggs and ham looked as I had always expected the Irish colleen in a big city to look. I became very drowsy and shook my head.

I was sitting in a signal box. There appeared to be neither material nor spiritual logic in this. A signal box had never been one of my dream-symbols. Indeed, I could not remember that I had ever dreamed I was in a signal box. The supposition that this might be an echo from a previous life was untenable. According to the best information, a man rarely becomes incarnate more than once in two thousand years. Two thousand years ago, there were no signal boxes, nor, so far as I knew, any structure resembling signal boxes. Indeed, I doubted whether glass had even been invented. The whole thing must have come about by empirically determinable means.

I remembered. This was the station at Killing in Co. Tyrone. I had arrived here an hour and a half ago. The stationmaster had telephoned to my regiment. They had explained that they would send a truck to fetch me, and the stationmaster had invited me to come up here and sit by the fire. On the verge of sleep, I had been sitting there for an hour and a half.

The signal box at Killing is a tall structure set high on piles as though to outride expected floods, though I cannot imagine what use a signal box would be if the railway lines were submerged. It is glazed on three sides, so that its occupants can see for miles in several directions.

It had been ten o'clock when I reached Killing. There was no mist now, and the sky was plastered with stars. This signal box must be the local clubroom. Seven or eight men sat around the stove, smoking their pipes. They had already discussed horses, cockfighting and the war. At first they had tried to draw me into the conversation, but I was too sleepy. Occasionally, one of the men got up and set his foot to its base and with both hands pulled out one of the tall, handsome levers or with the tilted weight of his shoulders hove it into its place. I had sat here among the levers and the stars for an hour and a half.

A vehicle kicked up pebbles in the station yard below. 'That'll be the truck now,' said one of the party in the signal box.

I picked up my rucksack and climbed down the steep flight of wooden stairs. Three figures were grouped beside the vehicle in the moonlight. They were the stationmaster, a soldier in a leather jerkin and an officer. The officer was plump, jolly and young. He danced from leg to leg and smiled continuously. The soldier felt in his pockets and produced a half-inch piece of cigarette, which he ignited from the stationmaster's pipe.

The officer danced furiously, chuckled and took three steps backward. He said:

'Can you prove that you are Gunner Leckie?'

I flushed (or so I suppose). Could I what? . . . I came awake. He wanted me to prove who I was. Didn't they want me? If I failed to offer proof, could I go back to Tottenham Rivers, to Alison and Judith? . . . I made an appreciable pause. The officer danced forward.

'I suppose it doesn't really matter,' he said.

I brought out my wallet and displayed in the moonlight my identity card, my ration book, a printed message from Mr. Anthony Eden and the adjutant's peremptory letter.

The officer and the soldier sat in front of the truck. I climbed into the back. We drove through a village. The officer asked me if I was hungry. If so, he would knock up one of the cooks. I was not hungry. I was sleepy. We drove out of this village and to the next village and turned into a stable-yard.

A number of doors in this yard bore incomprehensible legends. The officer knocked at one of these doors. It was painted green. It slid open and revealed a sergeant with ammunition pouches strapped about his middle.

'Are there any beds?' said the officer.

The sergeant withdrew behind the green sliding door. There was indistinct conversation punctuated by ejaculations which I imagined to be indecent.

A waif of a man with large, tender eyes appeared. Playing cards adhered to his fingers. From his turn of head, he seemed to have been impelled from behind.

The man said:

'Is he clean, sir?'

The officer looked at me begrimed and marked by stubble in the moonlight.

'I should think so,' he said, and skipped and laughed.

'He can have my bed, sir,' said the large-eyed, fragile man. 'It's the fourth from the end upstairs, left side. Top bed, sir.'

I walked along a dim corridor between double-tiered bunks. Every twenty yards, a lighted hurricane lamp stood on the floor. Men were groaning, blowing and turning in their sleep. At the far end was a large stove red hot at the top and for several feet up the pipe.

THE CONNECTING DOOR

I

AT WHATEVER TIME I AWAKE, BELLS ARE RINGING. THE DEEPest-toned is that of the Minster. It is some distance away, and how clearly I hear it depends on the wind. It is as massive as the *gros bourdon* of Notre Dame in Paris or that of Sacré Coeur, which, if you are sitting at a café table in the Place du Tertre, distinctly raises your iron chair at each stroke.

Much closer is a bell of medium weight. It comes from Old St. Peter's, a hundred yards away. Mass is said there at six o'clock, seven and half past eight.

The first trams clang round the corner from the station square at half past five. I have not personally confirmed this. It is what Joseph told me on arrival, when I enquired if one heard station noises from the hotel.

I suppose that it is the bells themselves which awake me. Last night or, rather, in the small hours of today, I was even awakened by a telephone bell in the next room, at a quarter to three. These telephones have strangled, uncouth voices. I lifted my own telephone and began speaking into its mouthpiece. The walls are thin. The tone of the man's voice next door was distinctly evident to me. If the dialect had been one I understood, I should, I suppose, have made out half his words. I imagine the call to have been simply one from the night porter, rousing my temporary neighbour for an early departure. The man's head and mine were, I suppose, a foot or two apart, separated by two half-inch thicknesses of plaster, a space crossed by a few thin laths and two sheets of wallpaper identical in design, small roses over a lattice. Had I conscientiously stayed awake, I might, half an hour later, have heard from the station the sound of departure of the train in which my sleepy neighbour sat.

When I finally awake, I try to discover the hour from the coalition of sounds at that moment. At first, failing, I got out of bed and looked at my watch. It had stopped. Wound to a customary tightness, it stops no doubt at the sharp change of temperature as it is transferred from my hot wrist to the square of cold marble.

At first, the children at the school across the road merely confused me. My experiences at the École Alsacienne in the Rue Notre-Dame-des-Champs in Paris have cured me of any simple British assumption that, if there are schoolchildren in a playground, it must be getting on for nine o'clock, but, still, the sound was the same, whether it was eight o'clock or nine. From the point of view of guessing the time, it is clearly better to wake between the hours. Then, if I hear the children singing, I shall know that it is after eight.

They sing French folk-songs. Because their nursery background has not been French, they are learning the familiar ones. They sing 'Alouette', for instance, and even '*Au Clair de la Lune*' and '*Sur le Pont d' Avignon*'. I have not yet heard that delightful gavotte tune, with the absurd and quite non-youthful words, '*j'ai du bon tabac dans ma tabatière . . .*'

The light through the shutters is no help. It is, after all, daylight by shortly after four o'clock. This I established on the journey here. If, however, I already know the time, the light through the shutters gives me some indication of the weather. Real sunlight, for instance, is slotted through like parallel sheets of white metal.

Eventually, I patter barefoot across the brown oilcloth, kneel on the shabby, blue-green *chaise longue* with its bursting backrest (Jeanne places the cushions so as to hide it) and pull at a piece of white braid which raises the shutters. The tall windows are covered with cheap net. There is nothing to hold the windows open, so that, with the wind in certain directions, they close themselves firmly or intermittently bang.

The church across the road is St. John's, a building in Dominican style. Only the far wall remains, with a cupola at the end to my right. This is at eye-level (I am on the fourth floor). In the bombed space stands a new church, as austere as a Welsh chapel and smaller. The classrooms of the *école maternelle* to the left are prefabrications of wood and plasterboard.

Old St. Peter's stands, undamaged, sixty or seventy yards beyond St. John's. It is built in red stone. It has a hexagonal short spire on top of a square tower. The oblong belfry is separate. Hitherwards of Old St. Peter's runs the canal, St. John's Quay on this side, the Quai Desaix on that. If I crane forward and look to the right, I see the top of a green bank which is in fact the earthwork lying across the main sluice gates, the *grande écluse*. Nineteenth-century barracks lie adjacent to former prison-towers remaining of the old ramparts. Immediately beyond these is Little France, the extreme southerly point of the old town.

In Little France, the overhanging houses crowd together about three parallel locks. Their balconies are crowded with flowers, and in the water are municipal bathing establishments and moored washhouses. This is where the olive-green, still water is clearest.

My room has double doors, between which it is possible to become awkwardly wedged. In addition to the *chaise longue* and the brass double bedstead, it contains a large, built-in cupboard, a washbasin and a *bidet* fixture with hot and cold running water before which a screen has been placed, the cane-bottomed chair and this minute and infirm table, over it a slippery white cloth. On it stand yesterday's *Dernières Nouvelles*, a guidebook, a bottle of ink, an ashtray, eight packets of neatly stacked yellow *gauloises*, a novel called *La Peste* by Albert Camus and an open exercisebook, its stiff covers blue-mottled, three and a half pages of which have been filled with small handwriting.

THE MAN IN THE TOP BUNK WAS ALREADY ASLEEP. THAT WAS THREE and a half days ago, eleven o'clock in the evening at the Gare de l'Est.

The window was open and the blind drawn. It was too cold under the one red blanket. I slept badly. By five o'clock, light showed round the edges of the blind.

Then it vanished. We were under the Vosges. Over our heads rose contorted masses of clay and pink stone, clothed with shaggy fir-trees. Then light again. I dressed and went out into the corridor.

The Pullman attendant still lay on his let-down bunk, but I was not the first up. A narrow road ran parallel with the railway. Along it moved an oxcart. No doubt it creaked or rumbled, but, to me, shut in with the train noises, it was silent. The bullocks were long-horned, cream or pale buff, silky.

Under their brown tiles and their washes of pink or pale-blue, lemon or orange, the square, timbered houses had a prosperous air. The fields were laid out in narrow strips at right angles to the road. There were hops, potatoes, maize, tobacco, asparagus, pale-mauve opium poppies. The Erckmann-Chatrian country, Phalsbourg and Saverne, was already behind us. Villages slid past. They had German-looking names, Hochfelden, Schwindratzheim, Mommenheim, Brumath, Stefansfeld, Niederhausbergen, Schiltigheim.

Suddenly, to the left, the improbably tall spire of the Minster reared up out of the plain and rushed towards us. The sun stood behind it, the glare breaking its fine, fretted silhouette, black but with a red glint, whether from the stone itself or from hot light widening through fissures of stone. Then came the chimneys of breweries and tanneries, here and there square outlines broken into heaps of bomb débris, perhaps as much as eight years old. The train slowed down and steamed to a halt.

The man from my top bunk, a business man of some kind, found a porter at once and was gone, raising his hat. I looked about for someone with the name of this hotel on his cap. I had asked to be met. In the station, the light was grey and cold. The two of them found me, young Harold in his silver-grey flannel plus fours, not-quite-so-young Atha in a sports coat of pale Donegal tweed with too many buttons.

An elderly porter took my enormous, wood-banded, pale-green-canvas-covered trunk on his shoulder. We followed. At the station entrance stood a young man who looked a bit like the Austrian film actor, Anton Walbrook. This was Joseph from the hotel. He wore no cap.

The enormous square was empty but for kiosks in the middle and a few stationary trams, the small, leisurely, cream-coloured trams which tug each other about the city in twos, threes and fours. On the far side, one of a row of hotels was a partly cleared square of builder's rubble. Young Harold stared across at it thoughtfully. Then the two of them left me to Joseph, promising to see me again after breakfast.

Joseph spoke English. He had been, how you say, *incorporé de force* in the *Wehrmacht*. He did not look strong. He wore an ordinary blue suit, rather shabby, a black tie and not-very-clean white shirt. At the hotel, he spent some time running up and down stairs to get the lift to descend.

On the fourth floor, Jeanne ran me a bath. Jeanne's features are coarse, but not irregular. Her friendly smile displays gold fillings. A black jumper contains her big, round breasts. A black skirt encloses her round buttocks. Her complexion is pale. Her strong, shapely legs are pale, with fine, white hairs catching the sunlight. She is, I suppose, a country girl, sophisticated in one or two obvious ways by hotel life. The dark hair is piled carefully on her head.

At first sight, she aroused coarse thoughts. She came on duty early in the morning. If there were few visitors, she had at first little to do. The commercial traveller, on an early call but with some minutes to spare, must often have thought of pulling her into bed. One did not feel that she would mind. To feel the temperature of the water, she leaned over the bath. The so vulnerable grooves in which the hamstrings lay at the backs of her round, white, rough knees added a stab of tenderness to the coarse thoughts.

These, however, I can see, will continue to recur. They recurred this morning, when I awoke early and heard her already in the carpeted corridor outside my room. Jeanne is not, I am sure, an intelligent girl, but neither is she mentally defective. Yesterday she helped me to make out my laundry list. I gave her some sweets, boiled sweets shaped like raspberries and with something like raspberry jam inside.

I went downstairs (this is again my first morning, Tuesday morning). Without a special key, you cannot, from an upper floor, call the lift up.

Unless somebody has left it with the open gates on your floor, you walk down. The stair carpet is red.

The young woman at the reception desk is capable and intelligent, helpful and, in essence, friendly. The complexity of her duties has stiffened her manner. The severity of her expression is due, one feels, to the fear that, if she too far relaxed, she might forget some of the many things she must bear in mind. This makes her seem plain, though, clearly, there is somewhere a man for whom she would make a wonderful wife. From her I buy my *Dernières Nouvelles*. Sometimes I also buy a picture postcard off a revolving stand, a photograph of a stork's nest or of the Minster. I have now bought from this young woman four copies of the *Dernières Nouvelles*. That makes twenty francs. I must note even that, though whether I should charge up my morning newspaper to Mathew Latimer's or *The Examiner* is not yet clear to me.

A door to the left of the reception desk takes me into the dining room. It is quite strictly a dining room, in use only for dinner. At breakfast time and even for lunch, I pass through it to the restaurant beyond.

I like the restaurant. I now like the dining room, too, but the restaurant was my first love. The morning of my arrival later turned cloudy, and by midday there was rain. At breakfast time, sunlight still winked enticingly through the revolving doors. The room is square and ample. The plump-armed women behind the counter, among the urns, the dishes and the cash register, wore friendly smiles and joked energetically in the dialect with each other and with familiar breakfasters.

The landlord strode among us, smiling and waving his plump, white hands. Joseph (a person, I quickly found, very little regarded at the hotel) had looked like Anton Walbrook. The landlord was a prosperous, well-dressed, smiling version of Erich von Stroheim, a Stroheim perhaps at last happy in love.

One eats, of course, national bread (three slices). This year, it is like coarse English brown bread. Last year, at Puits de la Lisière, it was bright yellow and indigestible. The coffee is not quite *du vrai*, but it is at least *du bon*. There is a tiny, plated jug of hot milk, a flat oblong of sugar, a metal dish in the shape of a scallop shell on which lies butter the size of Mrs Beeton's walnut, a glass dish of thin, brown jam, probably rhubarb. It is a better breakfast than can be normally had in Paris this year. It costs ninety-nine francs, *service compris*. The table-covers are paper, but crisp and fresh.

I am bound to say that, even on the morning of my arrival, I did not rejoice in this waiter's company. Abnormally flat-footed even for a waiter, with a face like a monkey and dark, wavy hair, not old but not very young, he struck me as unintelligently rapacious, as one who had heard pre-war tales of gullible Englishmen. He is a sad soul. I do not wish him any harm. He works only in the restaurant and, at the end of the week, will be replaced even on breakfast duty by the youthfully charming Pierre or the long-faced, happy Italian, Serge.

The *Dernières Nouvelles* carries three or four pages of local advertisements, in addition to birth, death and marriage announcements and a marriage mart. It contains some national and even international news. It appears that we have lent the French ten million pounds. This can only stand me personally in good stead. M. Schumann has received a vote of confidence in the Chamber of Deputies. Count Bernadotte hopes for a truce in Palestine. The Russians are being troublesome to the British and the Americans both in Berlin and in Vienna. In London, the future of the Rhine is under discussion. But the regional news is clearly more important.

A woman in Metz has been done to death with an axe. There is a wine-fair at Colmar, and on Sunday there will be a rose-feast at Saverne. A milk van crashed into a tree at Wissembourg, and on the Rehtal road two lorries met head-on and fell down the mountain side. At Sarrebourg (where Annelies lived), a landlord who wanted to get rid of a tenant has taken the roof off a house. There was a slight earthquake yesterday, with its epicentre at Baden-Baden (I did not notice). Two peasants have had fatal accidents in the fields. One fell off his manure-cart, and the wheels went over his head. In the other case, a haycart overturned, and its driver was smothered under the hay.

*

THE DATE OF MY ARRIVAL WAS JUNE 1ST. YOUNG HAROLD (HE IS NINEteen, rising twenty) arrived on the 1st of April, All Fools' Day, a Thursday, at four o'clock in the afternoon. He felt a bit of a fool, but did not mind.

He came via Tilbury-Dunkirk. On the boat, he took up with a girl who was going to Switzerland as a children's nurse. It was a night crossing. In adjacent deckchairs, the two snuggled together under one hired rug, their foreheads and noses tormented by the same smuts. On the Bale express, they had breakfast and luncheon together. At lunch, they shared a bottle of sweet Muscat. Afterwards, they went on embracing in the compartment. Harold attempted to persuade the girl not to go straight on to Bâle but to alight here and first spend a day or two (and, what was more to the point, a night or two) at a hotel with himself. These overtures it seems that the girl resisted, though not without some regret.

When the train jolted to a halt at the station here, young Harold was taken by surprise. He assembled his belongings in a hurry and climbed down from the train. He then stood on the platform, one hand stretched up to the window, held, as he thought, in affectionate reluctance by the girl. When the train began to move, however, he found that it was simply the sleeve of his overcoat caught on the doorhandle.

He disengaged it in time, but at that moment two policemen approached him. They took him to a cell on the station premises, where they searched him comprehensively. (The following day, as in due course he read in the *Dernières Nouvelles*, two German spies were picked up as they alighted from that afternoon train.) The first three nights Harold spent at the Hôtel des Vosges, across the station square.

It was on the Sunday afternoon when he installed himself with the Willms in the Place de Bordeaux. At nine hundred francs a month with full board, this was an expensive lodging, but it was very much pleasanter than the others to which advertisements in the *Dernières Nouvelles* had led him.

On Monday morning, Harold crossed the Contades, a small park of no great amenity but containing a restaurant and a bandstand, and, by way of the Quai Koch, reached this wide square before the university, that solid building in grey stone, with Zwingli's name oddly prominent among those gilt-lettered over the architrave. He enrolled himself with Mlle Kuntz, in charge of foreign students. As he walked out of the building, he met Umpleby.

This was a surprise. It was not altogether a welcome surprise. After three days adrift in a strange city, it is always quite nice to see a familiar face, and Umpleby's was a very pleasant face, though a bit comic (wide-mouthed, the small nose a bit pink and shiny, the fair hair stiff and calf-licked). But Harold had not expected to meet anybody he knew. That had been one of his reasons for coming here, instead of going to Clermont-Ferrand, say, or Besancon or, for that matter, to the Sorbonne. Umpleby had the best possible reasons for coming here, since he also did German. Although Harold had taken to writing verse, the greatest figures in his pantheon were the German symphonists, but he knew no German, apart from those lyrics of Heine and others which had been set to music by Schubert, Schumann, Brahms and Hugo Wolf. A fair number of these he knew by heart, though only with the melodic line attached.

It rained the day after Harold's arrival (it rained the day of mine). A week earlier, there had been snow. A week later, it was already hot. In the Place de la République, magnolia blossoms cupped the moonlight. The scent of lime-trees in flower was, he states firmly, thick in the air in the Place Broglie ('the Breuil'). On the cafe terrace in the Orangerie, bumble-bees drunk on lime-nectar would (he says) plop into your beer from the foliage overhead, then, picked out, stretch one quivering leg after another and walk across the blue-and-white-checked tablecloth, buzzing with indignation. It was Fritz Willm with whom, during those early weeks, Harold walked in the Orangerie of an evening. Among the foreign students, he and Umpleby first made friends with a Polish-Jewish girl called Cesia, her friend Mieczyslas, a dark and luscious Russian girl called Sonia Sobouttian Soboutnikoff, Marie (a Lithuanian), a pair of Austrian-

Jewish twins (female) and a Turk called Attila. Between lectures, they would gather in this square about the Pasteur memorial fountain. Harold fancied Sonia (still does). He sat next her in lectures, and on at least one occasion, to the astonishment of a professor with beard and *pince-nez*, she put her apricot-coloured arms about him, her black hair covering his face. Presently, however, this Sonia began to display an unfortunate preference for a tall Czech, who wore one of those attractive shirts with an embroidered neckband. In 1918, the Soboutnikoffs had got out of Russia by the Tiflis route and been naturalised Persian.

After Sonia's defection, Harold went out several times with Maria. Maria, it seems, is less exuberant than Sonia. Indeed, the reason why her family sent her to study here was an entanglement with a married man, which has left Maria with a broken heart. She is, moreover, fair, and young Harold is attracted by dark colouring, not so much in itself as because he feels it to be more exotic and thus more poetic. Maria is, however, finely made and delicate-featured. She also has a rather pretty voice, and in this she once sang heartbroken little Lithuanian songs in a grotto in the Orangerie, much to Harold's delight, so that he wrote a poem about the occasion.

It is not a very good poem, I'm afraid, though I remember, as sufficiently vivid, drops of water from a fountain being rendered as 'cold pearls upon the night's face softly blown'. There occur the lines:

All pain is silent, listening for the birth
of a more perfect song within the air.

Also characteristic is the couplet:

And as the baffled heart in silence lies,
Moss-covered phoenixes stare with sightless eyes.

From an acquaintance with the conventional architecture of grottoes, I was inclined, before this afternoon, to suspect that the phoenixes would in fact turn out to be sphinxes, but certainly they are moss-covered in part.

You take a No. 3 tram along the Allée de la Robertsau. It is a long, broad avenue running north-east, and the trams move along it faster than when they are describing their unbelievably intricate manoeuvres about the town. You alight, and your feet crunch softly on gravel. From Harold I understood that, here at the entrance, always sat a beggar-woman, her leg and her crutch stretched forward, emerging from the folds of a black or navy-blue shawl, but this afternoon she was not there.

The Orangerie is a fair-sized park, and it contains a pavilion intended for residence by the Empress Josephine. There is a real orangery, with the trees in tubs. Birds sang. There was a breeze. I walked through green aisles of lime trees, plane trees, horse chestnut, acacia, and came to formal French flowerbeds, with begonias and the sharply patterned leaves of koleus. The gardeners were potting out geraniums. There were palm-trees in tubs, and there were fountains.

To one end of the Empress's pavilion, the English taste in gardening is observed. There are delphiniums, Canterbury bells, dwarf Michaelmas daisies. One group of statuary displays a chimpanzee sitting on a dolphin's back and forcing the water out of its mouth. Another shows a goose-girl in clogs. As I turned away from it, a jolly father and his two small children came towards me, playing marbles along the path. Click, click. The daughter accused her father of cheating. He laughed. They were gaily enchanted with each other's company. The marbles clicked sharply along the path.

The pavilion has a little clock tower. The clock struck three, with a hard, metallic ring. My heart was suddenly wrung for the Empress Josephine. She was missing all this, by which I suppose I mean just being alive now (and here, for, truly, this place and these people do cause the heart to expand). Besides, Napoleon must have been an awful fidget. And she was barren.

I turned into the main walk, by one end of the boating lake. Over there was a little zoo, to this side of it an open-air restaurant, at which I am told that the food is very good, despite the fact that the waitresses (none of them at the moment visible) serve you in regional costume. Across the lake is Harold's big café terrace, with trees. Below this, he was sitting on a park bench.

He seemed, I thought, just a trifle discontented, though, on the other hand, extremely fit, more sunburnt than on Tuesday, his hair yet more sun-bleached, a kind of sun-dazzle (though this afternoon the sky was a little overcast) in the pale-blue eyes. Perhaps it was simply fatigue, which, it appeared, he had every reason for feeling today. He still wore the same silver-grey flannel plus fours, his jacket loosely over his shoulders in what appears to be the local undergraduates' fashion.

Before I turned about to sit beside him, I looked at the trees on the cafe terrace behind. They were horse chestnuts, not limes, rather closely planted and much-trimmed. Still, at the right time of year, bees, I suppose, could get drunk just as easily on chestnut blossom. I had similarly noticed that there were only plane trees in the Breuil.

There seemed no point in mentioning either discovery. The lime tree is important in the Goethe-Schubert, Heine-Schumann world.

Am Brunnen vor dem Tore,
Da steht ein Lindenbaum. . . .

Though, now that I come to think of it, that may be Schubert, but it is not Goethe. For the moment, that was young Harold's world.

He had stayed only four weeks with the Willms, though he continued to frequent Fritz Willm in the evening. It was purely a matter of expense. Full *pension* at the Willms was rather more than Harold's father had counted on, and he, by no means a rich man, had refused to augment the monthly amount first agreed on. Harold, too, had lost money on two occasions, once during an evening of riotous drunkenness in the German student tradition and once, presumably by pickpocket, while he stood in a crowd watching the Joan of Arc Day procession. So he had moved in with Umpleby. They had taken a room together over the École Pigier in the

Avenue des Vosges. They took their meals, including breakfast, at the Gallia, the students' restaurant, where they paid by student's voucher. It was cheap and convenient, and the food was good, though not quite on the Willm scale, the standard there being set by the Swiss consul and people from the British and German consulates-general, who came in daily for luncheon.

Fritz Willm would be at his office in the railway administration. Umpleby had gone to a lecture. Recently, both he and young Harold had been cutting their lectures. After some weeks of hiking and climbing small mountains in the nearer parts of the Black Forest, Umpleby's conscience had smitten him.

'Mine hasn't smitten me yet,' said Harold.

Although he sometimes used learned circumlocutions with ease and had clearly read a great deal, young Harold's accent was decidedly, though not distressingly, from beyond the Trent. His speech was unemphatic. There was a hint of singer's resonance in his voice, which normally sounded between the eleventh and thirteenth below middle C. The sun had bleached a reddish tinge out of his hair. He did not possess much in the way of a profile, but the face was mobile and not altogether displeasing, the head rather markedly brainy.

I asked if there were any more poems.

'One,' said Harold.

Out of the left-hand pocket of his jacket he fished a small notebook, with stiff, marbled covers. In it, written out in violet ink, were already some twelve or fifteen short poems. The most recent was called *Waldesrauschen*. While I read it, young Harold brought out of his right-hand jacket pocket a folder of ungummed cigarette papers and a packet of German tobacco. He rolled a cigarette.

'Umpleby and I,' he said, 'both prefer German tobacco. We go over to Kehl and smuggle it back in our plus fours. Umpleby smokes a pipe. Fritz's brother, Jean, taught me to roll cigarettes. The trouble is, without gum, they sometimes fall apart.'

From the café behind us and at a level well above our heads, a loudspeaker had begun to play a song from *The White Horse Inn*. A girl passed, stepping rather prettily, perhaps even mincingly, her colouring very fair, the lips bright without make-up, the forehead a bit German and bulging, young, very young really, but full-busted in the cheap, often-washed, pale-blue jumper, nice legs without stockings, small, flat-heeled shoes, toes carefully placed as she walked, books under one arm. I give all this detail, but in fact only glanced at her briefly as she passed. I was reading the poem. In essence it was a first-cuckoo poem, though combined with sunbathing in the woods, so that, although it was newly done, its reference must have been a month old.

I read it twice and then turned to Harold to say that I liked this poem better than the last one, though . . . But he was not there beside me. He had been sitting on my right. I looked along the path in that direction. The girl had almost rounded the boating lake. Young Harold was not quite a hundred yards away, in what was not quite hot pursuit.

He turned and waved, then with his finger attempted to describe his intended movements to me. Clearly, he should not long remain so if any shadow of encouragement were offered. I waved back, rather hoping to indicate that I hoped to see him again presently.

I read the poem once more. The idea was that a state of delightful near-insensibility, induced by forest-sounds and the sun overhead, was shattered by the first note of the cuckoo's call and that sudden sharp consciousness was lulled again as it completed the descending third. I looked up again. The young woman was sitting on a bench directly opposite, across the lake. Harold was, as one might say, bearing down upon her, though still some twenty or thirty yards away.

It would not have been friendly to watch the next minute or so. I looked down again at the violet ink, the immature but mannered handwriting (its Greek ϵ's, for instance). Overhead, the loudspeaker sang in a vigorous tenor:

Adieu, mein kleiner Garde Offizier,
Adieu, adieu,

Und vergiss mich nicht, and vergiss mich
  nicht. . . .

It would sound louder across the boating lake. I looked up again. Harold and the girl were sitting side by side in easy discussion. At one moment, I thought he was looking my way, I showed the mottled notebook, pointed at it, slipped it into my pocket. Then I got up and walked on. I passed through the grotto, with its moss-covered sphinxes and bubbling spring.

By way of a rather dull tract, though with well-grown trees, you come to gates and a road on which stand new suburban houses. These are the fringes of the elegant Quartier des Quinze, where stands, for instance, our consulate-general.

As my friend the Hon. Bert has already twice reminded me, it must not be long before I call and pay my respects to the consul (strange, how respectable I have become). He thinks it will do, though, if I turn up without fail to the *cocktail* for the King's birthday next Thursday. The Hon. Bert's own office is in town. From there, he runs a kind of one-man British Council, though in fact he belongs to the consulate-general.

You turn left. The suburban houses give out. There is a wooden bridge over the Rhine-Marne canal. By it stands an inn called '*Le Joyeux Marinier*'. Rue des Bosquets. Rue . . . The guidebook doesn't go beyond the bridge. The Rhine still lies north-east, so if you take what I suppose is (in essence) the towpath . . . That would be where Harold and Annelies and Annelies's plain friend and Attila will turn off. No, not Attila, that Sunday afternoon.

There are distant harbour noises, hammering, faint hooters. It is a long, desolate road, but planted with chestnut and plane trees. The port could be reached by any of those three water-lanes to the right.

To the left, it might already be open country. There is a cottage. There is a white goat tethered in its front garden. Beyond, a field, then trees, the Robertsau woods.

On the right, three barges, tied up. Seven white ducks play follow-my-leader on the poplar-shaded water. At the water's edge grow familiar English weeds, knapweed and bindweed, thistles, willow herb (great hairy, not rosebay). There are reeds, rushes.

The hammering is closer. In the distance, a dog barks (sounds carry over the still water). You pass a wooden café. A rusty railway line comes to the water's edge, not in use now.

Where this canal and the last water-lane meet, there is a sort of coastguard station in new brick, pink geraniums all round its verandah. Ahead lie tin shacks, coal dumps, petrol in what look like small gasometers.

A petrol engine starts up. In the boat are two customs officers and a policeman. You come to a congestion of barges and paddle steamers. At the road's edge, the dull-white, narrow-petalled stars of traveller's joy, old man's beard, on ragged bushes. A heavy barge is going out, two dinghies rearing at the swirl of the screw behind it. The boats are called by the names of writers, Flaubert, Anatole France (unimaginable in England). The port flag is like a Union Jack without the cross of St. George.

The road lies uphill. From the crest, you can see what may be the water of the Rhine and what are certainly cranes and gutted warehouses on the German side. A breeze springs up. You cross an iron bridge and bear left. Turning, you can see the distant spire of the Minster, and, yes, the breeze, coming up behind you from the heart of the Old Town, bears the sound of the great bell to your ears.

To the left are the Robertsau woods. No cuckoos there today, or, if so, they are silent, but from that direction comes the heavenly scent of what, this time, must truly be limes. As it does when you approach the sea, the air has suddenly brightened.

On the far bank, that must be the spire of Kehl church, standing among the ruins. French families are living there now. But, indeed, Kehl was founded by the French. There Beaumarchais printed the dangerous thoughts of Rousseau and Voltaire. At this point, the only trees are on the right of the road. They are sycamores, perhaps maples. On the grass bank, there are poppies, yarrow, St. John's wort, sage, meadowsweet, brambles, other plants I don't know, perhaps not in the English flora.

Now the canal lies behind you, and this, this is the open Rhine. This really is the Rhine, churning impatiently towards the sea, though with a détour of three hundred miles yet to go.

At the bend, to the left, a rock stands out into the water. A kind of Lorelei rock. You might think she sat there, combing her golden hair, luring those who sail the Rhine to destruction. A rock? No, shattered concrete. A French gun, or machine gun, emplacement, built nine years ago, if not seventeen or eighteen, more recently blown up by one side or the other. The twisted, rusty iron is like hair, and the concrete clings to it like scurf.

Further along, somebody at the water's edge is fishing. You cannot see him, but you can see his rod waving slowly up and down.

I LOVE THE RECEPTIONIST DEARLY, BUT I SHALL NEVER KNOW HER name. It is an advantage of the French mode of address that one might easily for years maintain polite and even friendly relations with a person without ever learning, or feeling that there was any need to learn, his or her name. The receptionist will remain 'Mademoiselle'. It may not even be accurate. It seems quite possible that she is the adored, intelligent wife of a working-class husband and that, on her way to the hotel, she takes their two quiet, spotless children to the *école maternelle* across the road.

Her desk is at two steps above street level. In the dining room, I sit at that level and with my back almost exactly to hers through a wall more substantial than that between the bedrooms, at any rate on the fourth floor. The greater part of the dining room is at street level.

The thinness of the bedroom walls could become a bit of a trial. There are more people in the hotel. They are, I suppose, assembling for the Festival. Three nights ago, it would be a commercial traveller's early call which made me, almost in my sleep, begin speaking into the mouthpiece of my own telephone. Last night, the bed in the next room creaked rhythmically for an impressive period of time. Before and after the rythmical creaking, there was the sound of dance music on a gramophone. Before, yes. That I can understand. Afterwards, no, since, when it stopped, there was no subsequent rhythmical creaking.

In the early morning, Jeanne is busy. Just pulling her into bed is no longer a practical proposition. The lavatories, too, are clogged with newspaper, so that to flush them may produce unspeakable results.

The flat-footedness of waiters is one of the saddest things. Even my nice Pierre (I would guess, recently married, but have not yet discussed this subject with him) is a bit flat-footed at, say, twenty-five. Usually, in the dining room, I am served by him. On his day off, I am served by Serge. Pierre is handsome and, in essence, a dashing, independent fellow. Serge has great charm, but was, I fancy, brought up more resigned. Essentially, he likes being a waiter. This does not make him a better waiter than Pierre, who is admirable.

I have had no direct dealings with the head waiter, called, I believe, Jean. He never ventures off the street-level part of the dining room. He pulls, and smells at, a great many corks, but does not therefore necessarily serve the bottles out of which they came. He is middle-aged, with spectacles and a moustache. Pierre and Serge wear their white jackets even for dinner. Jean wears a tailed coat.

He is, at present, being rather beastly, in a negative sort of way, to a young woman who just wants an omelette. She wears a brown jumper and is probably English. I, therefore, ought perhaps to go to her rescue. On the other hand, she may not be English. I am afraid that Serge and even Pierre are, in a negative kind of way, participating in this beastliness. They are leaning against doorposts, napkins over their folded arms, pretending that they have never heard of such a thing as an omelette, though, conceivably, they may consider mentioning such objects when they next have to go through the restaurant on a more respectable errand.

I really don't quite know what to do. If, somehow, I could be appealed to *as an Englishman* (and, given the right circumstances, Pierre would, as our relations stand at present, put this thing to me squarely), I could act. Or, at least, I could speak. I could say that the very nicest young Englishwomen did sometimes go into restaurants unaccompanied and order a simple omelette, which might well be all that, with the present currency restrictions, they could afford. I might have added, critically, that, after all, if they wanted that table for somebody else, the quickest way to get rid of the young woman would be to serve her at once with her omelette. I could have begun such a conversation if Pierre had come to my table for any reason whatever. I could have called him if there had been the shadow of an excuse. But it is understood that my *truite pochée au bleu aux amandes* will take twenty minutes. The right trout will first have to be located in one of those mountain streams in the Vosges. Then it will have to be caught. I have clearly indicated that the huge soup tureen could be taken away. I have my white wine in the little blue and grey jug of local stoneware, gothically lettered, *Trinkt wie Eure Väter aus Stein den Wein.* I have an ashtray. I have the menu. I have a basket of bread. I have butter.

And the girl may not be English. I think she is. I think she is a schoolteacher, abroad on her personal allowance of twenty-five pounds. But she speaks adequate French and is yet unperceptive of all that she has come up against. I can only renounce my position as an ambassador of my country, to say nothing of my position as a knight errant.

The walls of my part of the dining room are largely occupied by colour prints depicting peasants in the various regional costumes, for the black head-knot is strictly local to the immediate neighbourhood, where, indeed, like the surname-allocation of Scotch tartans, it developed only last century. In Geispolsheim, the head-knot is red. In Wissembourg, it is replaced by a small, cylindrical lace coif. At Hanau, the Protestant skirt is green, the Catholic red. The shawl, the corsage and the apron also vary, and so do the hats and waistcoats of the men. Against corner posts and in alcoves, there are wood carvings, fishes and mermaids such as are traditionally placed like figureheads on the ornate wine barrels.

The food here is excellent. There are several four-star restaurants in town, with trout pools and whatnot, but I can see that I shall normally dine here. For one thing, I am usually pretty tired by the evening, and it is convenient to clean up in my room, flop on the *chaise longue*, dally briefly with Jeanne as she comes in to take the bedcover off and turn the sheets down, then unhurriedly descend the four flights of red-carpeted stairs, exchange a few words with the receptionist, sit here undisturbed at what is now regarded as my usual table and discuss the menu and the day's news with Pierre or Serge or, once in a while, the immaculate, beaming Erich von Stroheim.

I suspect that young Harold does not dine regularly at all. Brought up to a north-country high-tea and late supper routine, he still thinks of the midday meal as his dinner. One bad habit he has formed is that of drinking beer with his breakfast or, rather, before he calls for his *complet*. Except when they are out hiking in the Black Forest or the Vosges, he and Umpleby then also lunch at the Gallia, normally at the same small table served by a young, fair, wispy-moustached waiter called Paul, recently married.

As he darts, sweating, around his tables, Paul regularly avers:

'*La vie est dure, et les femmes sont chères!*'

Umpleby and Harold are fond of Paul, who in turn seems devoted to his only two English. The food at the Gallia seems respectable, though young Harold finds it sometimes too redolent of garlic and is contemptuous of the *poudings*. The two boys never drink wine at the Gallia, but the beer is first-rate. They drink Schutzenberger in preference to Tigre Bock. On their hiking days, they dine at the Gallia. I am not sure what they eat for the rest of the day when they have lunched there. Perhaps, when out with Fritz Willm, young Harold simply crunches an occasional *pretzel* or calls for a sizeable hunk of *kugelhopf*.

They are aware of other students, but do not mix with any of those who eat at the Gallia. There are two main large groups, one of Roumanian and one of Bulgarian students. The Roumanians strike the two boys as the more civilised-looking, the Bulgarians being apparently swarthy and tending to long side-whiskers. Attila is never at the Gallia, but there are other Turks in evidence, one of them fabulously handsome, so that all the girls are lined up to be seduced in turn by him. To be found not infrequently with the Bulgarians is a young woman Harold finds intolerably attractive. Her black hair, parted in the middle, is drawn back to a heavy coil in the nape. She commonly wears a two-piece tailor-made costume in navy blue, over a bright red jumper. Sometimes she leaves the jacket off, and then the forward thrust of her violent breasts makes the boy feel quite ill with a desire he regards as hopeless, since he recognises in her a woman of such high sexual voltage he cannot imagine himself approaching her. He is astonished by the easy familiarity with which the raffish young Bulgarians treat her. At times, she even seems to bore them and has been known to step quivering off as though insulted.

These groups of students do not take any of the same classes as Harold and Umpleby. They are established at the university for more than the semester which is all that the two English youths, along with Cesia, Mieczyslas, Attila, Maria, the Austrian-Jewish twins and Sonia Soboutnikoff, are up for. None of these eats at the Gallia.

Jean has vanished. Serge has brought the schoolteacher in the brown jumper her omelette and is being charming to her. This is a great relief. At least that young woman has not gone abroad in order to eat, and, more specifically, to eat steaks, which is what a great many Englishmen are still doing. It is vulgar, though understandable. I have eaten steaks enough and am now in a veal phase, though a *carré de porc* would also go down very nicely. But here comes Pierre with my *truite aux amandes.*

THE RHINE AGAIN, A MILE OR SO TO THE SOUTH (AND UPSTREAM), THE port area lying between the two points. This is the highway into Germany, and today the sun blazes.

The string of little yellow trams wanders southward through industrial suburbs and rides up a slope between great spaces of cleared debris. There was once a pinnacled bridge, with the French and German custom houses on it. It may still be seen on picture postcards. The present footbridge is a sappers' construction of wood, with pointed breakwaters upstream. The French customs are on the far side, in Kehl.

You walk along the path upstream to the right, and the first thing you see is a rough-hewn slab of pink stone, polished on one side and bearing the names of nine men, aged between twenty-four and forty-one, who were murdered at this point and their bodies thrown into the Rhine by the Gestapo in flight, in November 1944, three and a half years ago. Before the unimpressive monument, people have placed poppies and white campion in food tins.

Further on, a larger white stone proclaims that here General de Lattre de Tassigny, bringing the French First Army back from Germany five months later, crossed the Rhine to confirm the liberation of Alsace. Further again, another wrecked concrete emplacement.

And now the open river. All that sliding surface of water, dimpled here and there by what are probably very awkward currents, death to swimmers. A powerful barge curves downstream at a remarkable speed and sends long waves pulling at the reeds and grasses.

I turn back. Between the end of the tramlines and the footbridge, the last house on the French side is a block of workers' flats. The concrete surface is badly pitted with bullets. At an open window on the third floor, a young workman in a blue and white striped jersey plays the accordion.

Too hot to eat a big lunch. In the cool interior of any of these large inns, I could get a plate of small fry, Rhine whitebait, a small jug of white wine, cherries. It might turn out to be the inn I hear of from not-quite-so-young Atha.

Young Harold and Fritz Willm sometimes come out this way on a Sunday morning. Not today.

The fair girl in the Orangerie turns out to be called Annelies. She is only fifteen. This seems a bit young even to Harold, though, as he says in somewhat less elegant terms, her person is mature. *Il y a du monde au balcon.*

Annelies lives in Sarrebourg with a widowed mother, but during the week is a boarder at a commercial school, sometimes going home on Saturday evening. The girl and her mother are of German origin, but naturalised French. A further meeting has been arranged.

THE ILL, FLOWING MORE OR LESS PARALLEL WITH THE RHINE, BRANCHES to form an island, and on that the Old Town was built. Inside the city boundaries, old or new, there is nothing which resembles a river. There is, instead, a complex system of canals. The Ill, however, enters at the south-west as a river and leaves as a river in the north-east, towards Robertsau. Also, I suppose, towards Fuchs-am-Buckel, where the Hon. Bert and I had lunch on a terrace beside the river.

This guidebook cost sixty-five francs at the bookshop on the *far* side of the university square. It is evident for how long young Harold has been cutting lectures. He still insists that it is on *this* side, next door to the Gallia.

Harold a bit cross. The girl did not turn up. He thinks she must have gone home for the weekend. Hung round the school at midday today without success. He and I are, of all things, to visit Ste-Odile by charabanc on Wednesday. This must be kept from the Hon. Bert.

He lives and functions in Titmouse Street. My hotel is just off the island. I am on it, here, in the Street of the Old Winemarket. There one turns right towards the Place Kleber or carries on to where, from a first-floor window, projects the pole from which a large Union Jack droops. Hon. Bert takes it in at sundown.

Hon. Bert is plump, dark, jolly, quick in his movements, not really at all shrill. Far nicer than anyone in either London or Paris said. A friendly soul. He clearly feels that my social deportment is his concern and was at first greatly afraid that I should disgrace him. This did not stop him at once beginning to lay himself open. Now I believe he feels that, however doubtful my accent and however horrible some of the shirts I wear, I shall not seriously compromise his position here. With the Phinelius *château* today, he has, I feel, already produced his prize exhibit or, rather, exposed me to his most exacting judges, his acid test. The occasion went off quite nicely.

Of course, my forthcoming luncheon at the Prefecture *en toute intimité* did not fail to impress him. I did not expect it to.

In addition to his own flat, what Hon. Bert has at the Rue de la Mésange is a twofold office, with a French (or, more exactly, an Alsatian) and an English (or, rather, an Irish) secretary, and a reading room in which are displayed all the main British periodicals, including *The Daily Worker*. His charwoman cooks admirably, with a little help from himself. I buy duty free English cigarettes from him.

He gets some return. I paid today at Fuchs-am-Buckel. He also got out of announcing the Berlioz *Requiem*. True, this was to my advantage, since I get paid in francs. Perhaps it was also a demonstration of faith in me.

It was at Holzheim that I saw my first stork's nest, a ragged heap of twigs on the chimney stack of the presbytery. The parent storks stood erect in the nest, seem never to leave it. No doubt they catch frogs in the early morning and again at sunset, and that is their day. They return year after year, wintering in North Africa.

The village nearest to the Phinelius *château* is said to have been very collaborationist in the war. In one respect, it shows an admirable spirit. Its church is used by both denominations. The Catholics hold their services in the choir, the Protestants in the nave. Try to imagine that in Ireland.

The *châtelaine* is religious and literary, her husband a landscape gardener. A long south wall has Stations of the Cross, commissioned from a young sculptor. A bit like Eric Gill, who, I suppose, never carved in this pink stone. About the plain below, yews have been disposed to look like cypresses. As the Hon. Bert says, you would think you were in Italy.

Here and there, a narrow pyramid, the top of a church tower, rose above a dark ring of trees and roofs, and that was a village, yawning the afternoon away. Very hot. One saw where the Bruche valley opened into the Vosges. Up there lies the site of the Struthof concentration camp (we read of it as Natzweiler) and the new French army's battle school.

Mme Phinelius served us with afternoon tea very much in the English manner, except that the pastries were better. They had seats for the Berlioz *Requiem*, and the two of them drove into town with us for dinner.

Just after eight o'clock, we came out of a deeply shaded side street into the Minster square. The sun blazed full on its west front, whose particles of quartz gave back the light. The stone is not uniform in colour. It varies from a delicate shell pink to brown in which there is only a dull red glare, but, in the direct evening sun, virgins, apostles, pinnacles and glass were all one iridescent salmon, a vast dazzle of pink and gold.

By half past eight, the light was gone. The vast nave of the Minster was illuminated only by huge candles in iron brackets. The archbishop had yielded, and the Catholic choirs of the Minster itself and Young St. Peter's had been joined by Protestant choirs from St. Thomas's and the Temple.

The RDF engineers had their apparatus in a small vestry. The microphone for the announcers was outside in a buttress corner, with a lamp about as strong as a night-light to read by. I expected to find some official with the announcements translated, typed and distributed in multiplicate. Miss Lenepveu would bring them, I was told. Miss Lenepveu was the French announcer.

At twenty-eight minutes past eight, no Miss Lenepvue. The orchestra had tuned. Charles Munch stood alert on the temporary rostrum. The engineers exchanged their final signals with London. The susurrus in the packed Minster was like a fever. At twenty-nine minutes past, a tall, handsome blonde in slacks appeared. The chief engineer showed her where the microphone had been placed. Miss Lenepveu asked after *le speaker anglais*. I was pointed out to her.

'I go first', she said, 'and then I give you.'

She held up a piece of paper. A light flashed. The chief engineer snapped his fingers and pointed to the microphone by the night-light. Miss Lenepveu bounced at it and began to read. I stood behind her.

When she had finished, she turned quickly and gave me her piece of paper, on which her own announcement was written in French only and in highly characteristic French handwriting. The difficulty was knowing whether to speak of the orchestra as the Orchestre National de la Radiodiffusion Française or as the symphony orchestra of the French national broadcasting organisation or as the French national radio orchestra and whether M. Jouatte should be described as 'of the Opéra' and what pronunciation of the name of Charles Münch would be most acceptable in London.

I must have managed, because in no time Münch was giving with the brass. When I looked inside the nave of the Minster, all the candle flames lay flat, pointing towards the great doors.

It seems that I worried unnecessarily. France heard my opening announcement, but, when I presently wandered into the vestry, Miss Lenepveu slapped her thigh, shook her fair curls and delightedly told me that London had been incorrectly plugged in and had missed the first two or three minutes of the music. The chief engineer was on the telephone, trying to make head or tail of some B.B.C. official's French and at the same time to establish his view that the fault lay with London.

He asked me if I would speak to London. I told the voice in London that I was a mere bystander who knew English and that I could not even undertake to interpret in a matter involving technical terms. It was an educated voice.

It said:

'Oh, well, never mind. I suppose our Paris office will find out. All we heard was a conversation between, I suppose, two engineers. They sounded very bored. I only hope it wasn't too obscene. Lovely performance going on now. . .'

And indeed there was.

TONIGHT WAS CANDLES, TOO, BUT THEY WERE SMALL ONES. EACH MUsic desk had two in a crystal globe. The idea would be to recreate eighteenth-century musical conditions out of doors. The occasion was described in the programme as a *soirée-sérénade*. Linguistically, this seems a bit redundant.

It was in the courtyard of a palace built in the eighteenth century by the archbishop uncle of that cardinal prince de Rohan-Guéménée who was implicated in the Queen's Necklace affair. This palace stands opposite the south porch of the Minster. It was damaged in the war and has not yet been fully restored, so that you cannot go through the palace on to the great terrace which lies, to the other side, along the M. There is, however, access, by way of a tapestried staircase, to a walk on the walls surrounding the courtyard and over the main gates.

We began with Couperin's *Concert dans le Goût Théâtral.* The music and the setting were of a period. Couperin was sixty years old when the architect began work in 1728, and he died while those red and beige stones were being laid patiently one upon another for thirteen years. There was some Lully, some Rameau, and then René le Roy played a flute concerto by Leclair.

All round the courtyard are sculptured heads on stone brackets. In the flickering light from so many candles, these periwigged heads seemed to nod sagely in time with the music. (Not too wild a fancy. What with expulsion of breath and movement of bows, the candles themselves must to some extent have flickered in time with the music.) Beyond that intense fairyland of candles, on top of the walls, life-sized ladies in classical garments sat on stone lions. Beyond, I could dimly make out the shape of the Minster and the south tower, if not the spire, lost in the darkness.

Periwig, ivory fan, turbaned black boys bearing cushions. The careful paces of minuet and gavotte, the formal bow which is a dance in itself. The ages circled warily about each other, for it was in Rameau's and Lully's time that Gibbon described in formal periods the German hordes lunging towards Rome, with their long moustaches and cross-gartered legs, in the fourth century. It was Julian the Apostate who drove them back across the Rhine and saved Belgian Gaul for another fifty years.

Here, too, a new language, French, was first recorded in the Merovingian oaths. That Minster, which took so long to build, was finished the year before John Gutenberg invented printing here. Half a millenium later, an English writer, D. H. Lawrence, saw the Minster as I saw it two hours ago, 'a darkness within darkness'. Two days before, I had seen it as a brightness within the light.

The interval. I stood up. Those wooden garden seats were very hard. I turned round. There was the palace itself. A pity one could not walk through to the riverside terrace beyond. I walked there this morning. In the still river, brown children bathed. On the terrace, art students sketched. There, the cardinals used to organise water sports for their royal guests, with fireworks.

People were crowding towards me. I turned again, up the tapestried staircase. White, dimly lighted walls, exquisite ironwork. Most of the figures in the tapestries are dressed like ancient Romans, with greaved, hugely muscular legs, but among them are cardinals with red hats and bishops with croziers.

You come to the walk along the walls and over the gates. I looked down upon that forest of candles. Their heat, as they burned down in the crystal globes, rose up to my face. I keep reminding myself that I am here as a journalist. I count the garden seats. Fifty to each row and forty rows. An audience of two thousand. I count the classical ladies on lions as I pass.

The Minster towered above me, very near, a comforting, giant shadow. A darkness within darkness is sometimes a good thing, but Lawrence added that here were 'long, long prisons of stone'. He thought it a disease of the spirit that men should wish to build so high and so permanently. He was, he says, himself always glad as a boy when his card-castles fell. Well, he has had a part of his wish. The Americans made a nice hole in the north aisle.

Lawrence came here in the depth of winter, a sick and dying man with only two years to go. The city, to him, was itself dead. It was still winter when not-quite-so-young Atha arrived, though, in point of date, it cannot have been more than a month before young Harold's arrival, and, when *he* came, it was spring.

Though neither dying nor sick in any demonstrable sense, moderately-young Atha clearly had something of Lawrence's feeling about the place. In his circumstances, of course, he ought not to be here at all. I ought, I suppose, to note down that the age of fairly-young Atha (the *pseudo*-Atha, as I begin to think of him to myself) is in fact twenty-four. He is thus five years older than Harold and twelve years younger than me. Fritz Willm I think of as still in his early thirties.

II

B Y AND LARGE, YOUNG HAROLD IS A CHEERY SOUL. AT THE ÉCOLE PIgier, the headmaster's wife, herself full of those French brave smiles, would, if the language in which she expressed herself were English, call him 'Smiler' (without any of that British anti-phrase which makes soldiers call short men 'Lofty'). *'Il sourit tout le temps.'* He does, indeed, whenever she is there. As soon as she has closed the door, his face becomes pretty expressionless.

Nothing of the sort could be said about after-all-quite-young Atha. In consequence, though no great smiler myself, I do not like him as well as I like young Harold, though Harold is a bit sorrowful at the moment. This is because of Annelies, the girl in the Orangerie.

Atha's bad circumstances were financial, amatory and religious. His London address is a rather old-fashioned Bohemian one. When I get back, I ought to inspect it.

He is supposed to be in love with a dancer, a *ballerina*. His handwriting is pretty but illegible. One at first thought that he was in love 'with a *ballista*'. This seemed odd. One hoped that it was not *a tergo*. It is not. On the other hand, its normality is in doubt. This love grew more acute as it appeared that the young woman in question did not mean to expose herself to frontal attack.

The religious question had presented itself as follows. Brought up as some kind of nonconformist, Atha had wished to find himself a Catholic, having flirted meanwhile with various high-minded notions. He had got himself involved with English Catholicism both at its smartest and at its most liberal-minded. To his religious instructor, he presented this travelling abroad as a pilgrimage. There had been some talk of him spending a while in retreat at a French monastery. The sum with which he travelled abroad was less than twenty pounds, for some piece of writing.

I have mentioned his jacket of pale-grey Donegal tweed, bought, out of the original twenty pounds, from a shop in Charing Cross Road whose clientele, to judge by the signed photographs in the window and inside the shop, consisted otherwise wholly of boxers and music hall comedians. His trousers are ordinary, unpressed grey flannel bags, belted and trailing. Apparently, he possesses no overcoat. I should have thought this a serious deprivation in winter (it does not matter in June), but pale and emaciated Atha is clearly a good deal more hardy than he looks. He wears his fine, fair-to-sandy hair too long, but his fingernails are clean.

Like me, he came via Paris, but the crossing had been Newhaven-Dieppe steerage, not in my subsidised 'Golden Arrow' style. He had not expected company, but in fact got that of a young Catholic married woman to whom, in a quite special way, he was devoted. She was off to join her husband in Paris.

I know both the husband and Benedicta, and I do not in the least marvel at frightful Atha's devotion. My connection with the Kings is somewhat involved, but, certainly, I am aware of them in at least one of the capacities in which they exist for him. It was in connection with Fr. Arbuthnot that religious Atha was introduced to Michael and Benedicta King. Even so, this was in part because of Michael's position as the young editor of *The Cross and the Sword*, which also concerns me, even professionally. Poet-and-intellectual Atha might, conceivably, have something to offer them. They, certainly, had space he might contrive to fill.

It must, in fact, be eight months since I saw either Michael or Benedicta. It is nice to hear of movements I heard first projected. For, of course, the Kings have always been, not precisely globetrotters, but heart-of-Europe frequenters.

At any rate, pilgrim Atha, as he walked along the platform at Victoria, without overcoat and carrying only a rucksack, saw Benedicta's head projecting from a carriage window and talking animatedly to a man younger than himself, whom he had met and who was not merely devoted to Benedicta in his own way but positively her slave and also, to some extent, Michael's errand-boy, in connection with *The Cross and the Sword.*

This young man has, it appears, declared his intention, once he has reached latchkey age, of entering a Trappist monastery. In the meantime, he goes in for action with the Kings, who themselves, however, are sometimes attracted by contemplation. The young man is rather talkative, and censorious Atha does not quite see him keeping vows of silence. He likes, nevertheless, the heroic ambience in which such possibilities are seriously debated by young men.

It was a grey day, and, out of Newhaven, the spray-laden wind was icy on the boat deck. It was five years since Atha had last crossed the Channel. Until last year, I myself had not set foot on the European mainland for eleven years.

'*Le voyageur solitaire est un diable,*' says Henry de Montherland, who ought to know.

It is true that the shedding all at once of our ties both to person and to place leaves us open to unholy possibilities. We are suddenly irresponsible, or responsible only to ourselves. But it is not only devils who are irresponsible. Angels are irresponsible, or responsible only to God, which is much the same thing. A year ago, I was the type of angelic traveller. As we measured the hem of the white cliffs of Dover, I sat in my second-class carriage, a dedicated spirit, dedicated, I suppose, to the new.

Of course, I had read Horace, and I knew, in theory, that to travel changes nothing, that nobody can leave himself behind, that, as soon as we step beyond the Gare du Nord, our daily habits and preoccupations will take us by the elbow. This year already, I clung to my Pullman accommodation. I stayed below, sipping brandy with a girl from the British Council, no amateur of winds like whetted knives, no connoisseur of spray. I coldly noted the town hall clock tower rising above young Harold's shattered Calais. When, from the heights of Montmartre, the domes and minarets of Sacré Coeur gathered speed and raced to meet the train, I did not suppose that, before the last franc was spent, my secret self would have translated itself into action on the boulevards.

On my first post-war trip abroad last year, however, I stood all the way from Folkestone as near the prow as I could, although such a wind blew up-Channel that the boat never rose upright until she was inside the breakwater off Boulogne. I thrilled to the cries of the French porters running aboard like a pack of untrained beagles. I thrilled to the different smell on shore, a difference, I suppose, which is chiefly one of tobacco.

Still, that was in June. I don't suppose I should have stood on the boat deck in February, with or without Benedicta King, let alone without an overcoat and far less from Newhaven to Dieppe.

If it has been correctly reported to me, I might, I think, even have found the conversation boring. For it appears that Benedicta and ridiculous Atha together recited Keats into the wind and that they talked about saints in what I can only regard as a childish manner.

Atha, moreover, states unashamedly that at one point he said:

'Perhaps it's a mistake to cross the Channel except with a person you're in love with.'

Benedicta thought there was something in this.

'It's a pity,' said Atha, 'we're neither of us in love, at any rate not with each other.'

'Yes,' sighed Benedicta.

Then, apparently, solemn Atha said:

'Benedicta, what *colour* is contemplation?'

And, straight off the cuff, Benedicta replied:

'Oh, blue! Blue as the note of a flute!'

This was also thoughtful Atha's opinion. It is, I may say, not mine. At any rate, I am more conscious of a quite different type of mystical thought, the result, no doubt, of reading Kierkegaard. I am not much disposed to mysticism in summer. From March onward, a healthy paganism prevails. Categories remote from common experience belong to the winter months. I feel that 'the light of truth' is a thing one seeks for in the long, dark nights. It is artificial light, if not, indeed, more specifically, electric light. The very sound of Kierkegaard's name makes my eyeballs ache. He lived in the crackling, hyperborean light of the Baltic. His winters were very long, and his relaxations were to sit in brightly lighted theatres and cafés. Then he went home and 'burned the midnight oil'. No wonder he went unread until the age of electricity, for which clearly he yearned through northern winters a hundred years ago. No wonder that it was only during the war he came into his own. At first, the blackout had seemed more artificial than the preceding blaze of light. I first really took to Kierkegaard only after we'd laboured and stumbled through it for over five years.

Still, it may be that, essentially, contemplation with Roman Catholics is blue. This would have something to do with the Mediterranean, no doubt. I put the above conversation on record because it does seem to account for certain lines in a curious poem written shortly thereafter.

MY HAND STILL SMARTS FROM THE IMPACT, THROUGH ITS BLACK, threadbare skirt, of Jeanne's salient and attractive bottom. While her gold fillings yet flash in the doorway and before the *rictus* has faded from my own face, I think of Arlette, and the muscles contract about my navel. Except through man's incessant lechery, there is no connection between the two. It is not the same kind of lechery, moreover. Moreover, but for Blod, I should never have seen Puits.

In her time, the house was a-building. The de Moors then lived in Paris, near the Parc Monceau, into which Blod took the children each morning. Puits-de-la-Lisière was simply a fact on Blod's horizon.

When, last year, I proposed to go and look at France again, Blod wrote to Mme de Moor, who promptly invited me, of whom she had never previously heard, to stay for three weeks. Three years previously, part of the house at Puits had reacted unfavourably to the fall of an American bomb on the next estate. This sinistration had left Mme de Moor a widow, M. de Moor having died shortly afterwards, '*sans doute*,' as Mme de Moor wrote with admirable laconicism, '*d'émotion*' .

At the Gare du Nord, Noémie and Yves stood by the engine. Noémie was to be wearing '*un tailleur aux petits carrés dans les beiges*', and I wore the green hat which met with such disapproving glances from young Harold and not-quite-so-young Atha on my arrival here the week before last. It is shaped into a flat porkpie, and it looks as though it were made of dehydrated turf, so that, when I bought it in 1945, I half expected that at the first downpour it would melt and run down my face. For purposes of recognition, it could hardly be bettered. The young de Moors and I recognised each other without difficulty, and they took turns to drive me out to Puits-de-la-Lisière, which lies about twelve miles to the west of Paris, on the fourth or fifth bend of the Seine. To reach it, we passed through less elegant suburbs.

Their name suggests that the de Moors were by origin Dutch. If so, the strain has been corrected by marriage. The conversation at table was of the most lively Gallic, and the eyes of all but the mother were dark, brilliant and restless. In the course of those three weeks last year, I became most intimate with the eldest son, Michel, who still lives at home. The recently married second son, Roger, then lived in the lodge, but has since moved into Paris. Yves is about to be married, and there is some hope for Noémie.

Michel de Moor, though younger than myself, is already a figure in the French banking world. He is strongly Anglophile. He reads *Time, The Continental Daily Mail* and the memoirs of Mr Churchill. He drinks whisky (at a thousand francs a glass), extends himself frequently in a long bath, eats fried eggs for breakfast on Sunday morning and practises his silences as well as his English on me.

The area is dotted with tapestried *châteaux*, chromium-plated *bars américains* and racing stables. Across the Fora St. Germain stretch sandy gallops for the horses which nowadays habitually win our English classic events. Last year, for instance, in a Boussac stableyard, I patted a Derby winner on the nose at two o'clock in the morning.

That is as intimate as I have ever been with a horse. It is true that I seem to have a very early memory of actually sitting on a horse. This would be outside the Co-op stables behind Waterside Lane in Hinderholme. It would be an enormous, dappled-grey carthorse, and my paternal grandfather held its head. I cannot have been more than three years old, perhaps four. I suppose that my father held me. I have other memories, but I do not think that, since my legs were more than two feet long, they have straddled a horse. I have sometimes regretted this fact, though I cannot say that I have ever felt much drawn to people who rode, and especially to women who rode, in England.

That first Sunday morning in Puits-de-la-Lisière, Noémie de Moor told me about her equitation and asked me the (really, when you come to think of it, very curious) question:

'*Savez-vous monter?*'

And, clearly, the short answer was:

'*Non.*'

I did not know how to mount. I made no equitation. I had never made serious equitation.

Noémie no longer wore her two-piece, tailor-made costume in pale check. She was dressed in white sweater and chocolate-coloured jodhpurs. That was also the costume in which I first saw Arlette the following week, except that her jodhpurs were in narrow-grained, creamy silver corduroy, which went better with her fine, very fair hair.

I had gone to mass with the de Moors. This was not altogether a popular move. As there was an English Protestant church in the neighbourhood, Mme de Moor clearly felt that I ought to have gone to that. I had tried to explain that not all English Protestants were of the same denomination and that in fact I felt closer to Catholicism than to the C. of E., but to Mme de Moor this was idle sophistry. However, she had permitted the intrusion. It was a big, new church, quite full. Mme de Moor and Noémie wore black lace mantillas. A number of faldstools in the second row bore their name engraved on silver plates.

Outside church, there was much social behaviour. Mme de Moor and Noémie went home with friends. Michel and I, with others, drove to some place at a crossroads in the Forest, where we sat outside drinking a mixture of vermouth and blackcurrant liqueur, with ice and soda. Even Michel drank this. Perhaps, after Catholic righteousness, he felt it wrong to thirst for a Protestant thing like whisky.

A bit shaky about the colours of horses. Most white horses, I know, are greys. I'm told that a pure Arab can be called white, but, although I can tell a beautiful horse from a utilitarian one, I'm not sure when the beautiful horse is all Arab. At any rate, it was on a sort of cream, whitish horse that a girl with fair hair streaming came gloriously to the end of the *piste* and then, reigning and turning, saw us and guided the beast delicately across. She walked him round while she shook hands from the saddle, took a sip of *vermouth-cassis* not from Michel de Moor's glass but from mine, then was across the road again and into a gallop along the far *piste* in no time, hair streaming.

That same afternoon, I saw Arlette in a frock (a white frock, with some kind of iris or lilac pattern). She was of a nice height, small-footed, slim-legged, the head perhaps a bit large (but that, after all, is womanly), the shoulders not narrow, but the hands slim, well-cared-for and soft, the elegantly trimmed mane of fair hair soft. I recalled the few young English horsewomen I had met, big-jawed, square-fingered, slangy, not unpleasant girls by any means but horribly confused about this and that. I am no judge of the matter, but I should think Arlette rides superlatively well. Heraldic on horseback, on her feet she is quite in her right mind. At this particular moment, I refuse to speculate upon her in other positions.

Here I am, on my fourth floor. It is a fortnight since I saw Arlette. The bedcovers are neatly turned down. After dinner, I shall go the the Aubette to hear the Calvet quartet with Gérard Souzay. My palm is pink with Jeanne's rump, but my fingers hold a pen. I am concerned with travelling Atha. In effect, it is the end of February.

Though he knew other parts of France, Atha had never before been in Paris. So far as I can calculate from his accounts of the matter, he quitted the place within thirty-six hours, yet not because of any previous arrangement. To anyone who loves Paris, this must seem incomprehensible. The reasons he proffers seem to me quite unsound.

It is, of course, true that the end of February (or the beginning of March) is not a well-chosen time for a first glimpse of Paris, though it seems that the weather, if cold, was clear and exhilarating. The Dieppe trains come into St. Lazare. Benedicta King parked Atha at a hotel near the station. St. Lazare is also the station for Puits-de-la-Lisière, and to me it is rather an elegant station, though I do see that to one side there is a row of somewhat inelegant hotels, and I do see that, even at the age of twenty-four and however hard-up I might be, I should not much have cared to stay at any of them. Still, that is a trifling matter.

There were, in the rucksack, a number of letters of introduction. That same evening, after an excellent dinner at the price of seven francs including wine, reasonably well-connected Atha boldly introduced himself to all the complications of the *Métro* and attempted to deliver one of these letters, addressed to a wild and powerful American expatriate writer. He failed, because this writer had just gone to London.

Next day, he met Benedicta in the afternoon. He recalls standing with her at the back of a bus which passed Notre Dame, afforded him a glimpse of the booksellers' boxes on the quays and presumably went up the Boul' Mich'. At about six o'clock they joined Michael King at the Café de la Paix, but that did not last long. When Benedicta called for him at his hotel the following morning, she was told that impulsive Atha had packed up, paid and gone the previous evening.

HE SAT ALL NIGHT SLEEPLESS IN THE CORNER OF AN OTHERWISE EMPTY second-class compartment. In the false dawn, he saw white mists swirl curiously away from the train as it battered its way across the plain.

This was the hour at which spies might have been expected to be abroad, but none of the *gendarmerie* approached him. It was dark in the enormous station square, but on the island in the middle there were lights in some kind of all-night refreshment room. Frozen Atha had coffee and a roll.

It was still dark outside. He bore left past the Hotel des Vosges and turned up the Rue Kuhn. Had I been here at the time and already awake, I might well have heard his steps in the street, for there were no trams yet running, and the first bell did not sound until he had crossed the Ill and, by way of the Old Winemarket and the Place Kléber and the Arcades, was very near the Minster.

It reached up into the darkness above him, 'a darkness within darkness, . . . long, long prisons of stone'. Not-yet-unconverted Atha had none of D. H. Lawrence's thoughts on that early Sunday morning in a cold February. As a boy, he says, he trembled with rage and frustration when his card-castles fell.

He passed beneath the shadowy arch of the wise and foolish virgins. Their smirking or downcast lineaments were invisible to him. At a small altar in the south aisle, mass was already being said. The altar was backed by a lifesize painting of Christ as the Good Shepherd, a pastoral crook in his right hand, a lamb under his left arm, others about his sandalled feet. The outlines of the whole were picked out with fairy-lamps. Atha shuddered, though he remembered Fr. Arbuthnot saying that the horrors of repository art were not legitimate obstacles to faith. He had conceded the point.

Further east, beyond the boot-soles, the purple-vested priest, his sleepy choirboy and the religious art, the astronomical clock whirred faintly in the shadows. Atha left the group of faithful before the altar and walked out into the paling darkness.

In the Breuil, the lime trees were not yet budded. Before the mayor's house, shadowy on the left, stood the figure of Rouget de Lisle, who there composed and first sang the *Marseillaise*, a spine-chilling song for the Army of the Rhine, who, being Alsatians, marched into Germany singing it in German.

He now had the municipal theatre on his right hand. This is closed at present. From playbills still adhering to one of those cylindrical structures (at the other end of the Place Broglie) to which we seem to have no equivalent and for which therefore we probably have no name, the season finished with a Jouvet company in Molière. Earlier, young Harold saw a *Tales of Hoffmann*, a Parisian farce gabbled so fast he recalls catching only such aphorisms as that every husband in Paris has a mistress and some rather dubious jokes about the Polish corridor (the husband in question had a Polish mistress) and a performance in German of Strindberg's *The Father*, with Paul Wegener. Harold is not yet well-acquainted with feminine geography. The young ladies of the ballet in *The Tales of Hoffmann* wore, it seems, grey tights without any form of tutu or apron, and Harold was at once appalled and enchanted by the spectacle of so many plump, cloven bottoms running about the stage. Lugubrious Atha did not so much as look at the playbills.

I had always supposed there were nine Muses. Only six stand, each topping an Ionian column in red stone, before the municipal theatre, a German building, the original theatre having suffered from the bombardment of 1870 (this from the guidebook). Atha would no doubt glance up at the Muses. He then crossed a canal, walked purposefully, though without haste, along the Avenue de la Marseillaise and, by way of the Pont Royal, left the medieval, islanded, predominantly French or autonomously Rhenish old town and came to wide avenues, open squares and all the ponderous monuments of the first period of German rule, none more ponderous than the pale-grey university.

The statue of Goethe is grey. Across the red-stone base of the Pasteur memorial fountain, somebody had painted in huge, ragged, red letters:

VIVE REX!

Atha wondered about this. It did not seem to him to be quite the kind of political slogan one would have expected to find so prominently exposed here. The square had been deserted. From the far side, a military command was shouted in French, and, as he watched, a detachment of tall Negroes in khaki uniforms and red fezzes emerged from mist under the pollarded trees and shuffled across the square, doubtless toward the barracks at the Porte de Schiltigheim.

It was almost light. The doors of the Gallia (formerly the Germania) were open. Atha pushed his way through the glass swing doors. There were no other customers yet, and many of the chairs were still upside down on the tables. He sat at the small table normally used by Umpleby and young Harold. He looked around him and saw the Schutzenberger and Tigre Bock posters, long unchanged. A raw-boned, unsmiling, lantern-jawed, clean-shaven waiter appeared. Atha ordered a *complet*.

'Where is Paul?' he asked.

'Paul, *monsieur*?'

'There was aforetime a boy who called himself Paul ...'

'There are no longer boys who call themselves Paul, *monsieur*. There are those who call themselves Maurice, Carlo and Robert, and there is one, a French of the interior, who calls himself Yves. As for me, monsieur, I call myself Albert.'

'You do not recall to yourself any Paul?'

'But no, *monsieur*.'

'It was a small boy, mince and frail,' said Atha. 'He carried a species of moustache, in colour yellow or sooner orange. He was at the time gay and melancholic. He spoke frequently of his family and repeated constantly, "*La vie est dure, et les femmes sont chères.*" '

'No, *monsieur*, we are not phenomena like that, we others. Paul is without doubt dead. As you describe him, he has the air a little phthisic, if not even degenerate. He coughed perhaps in speaking of his family?'

The little dialogue achieved itself. Atha broke his roll and plastered butter on one bit, pushing it into his mouth. Albert left him.

Atha, bemused, sat facing the inner room, reserved for residents. He looked to his right, at the window seat where a honeymoon couple, students married to each other, had once sat embracing over breakfast. He turned to his left and again contemplated the Tigre Bock and Schutzenberger advertisements. He half-turned his chair and looked over his shoulder at the Bulgarians' table, towards the door. He shivered. He poured out coffee.

He walked across to the picture-postcard stand, selected two cards, showed them to Albert, who, at the sound of footsteps, had showed his nose again, and returned to his table. One card showed the Minster spire, the other a stork's nest. Atha addressed this one to Benedicta King, explaining his sudden departure from Paris.

It was almost nine o'clock. Mme Willm should be up by now. A strap of the rucksack over one shoulder, Atha walked along the Quai Koch and through the Contades, by the bare trees, the bandstand, the long glass front of the restaurant. The street door in the Place de Bordeaux was shut. He rang the first-floor bell.

Fritz Willm appeared in a dressing gown, a man in his thirties, sharp-faced, wearing spectacles, but broad-shouldered, deep-chested, short-necked, so that his strength might have been taken for a deformity. They went upstairs. Mme Willm was away, staying with relatives at Mulhouse. In what had been young Harold's room, Jean was sleeping off the *bombe* or *noce* he had made the night before, Saturday. Fritz made coffee. He and Atha sat drinking it before the brown, porcelain stove.

No, there had been no letters. Yes, the *estomac* and the *névrose* were unimproved. Things went badly. The Willms could no longer afford a *bonne*. There were no lodgers or midday eaters. The Swiss vice-consul had gone, and the German consulate-general had adopted a new policy. As Fritz Willm said this, his eyelids drooped, and he raised a hawk nose. He looked Jewish. Atha supposed he was Jewish, despite fair, straight hair. That would account for the withdrawal of German consular staff.

Until Mme Willm came back from Mulhouse, Fritz said Atha could stay. In due course, Jean rose and washed away his hangover, a big, puffy youth with horn-rimmed spectacles atilt upon his nose and the wet butt of a hand-rolled cigarette stuck to the lower of his two fat lips.

Fritz was out to lunch, his afternoon occupied with some erotic duty, the prospect of which appeared to give him no pleasure. His Sunday afternoons were spent with some widow or with a nursemaid picked up in the Orangerie. Atha went out with Jean, who had friends to meet. They drank and finally ate. Atha went to the station and caught a slow train to Sarrebourg.

The February sun came out and burned through the windows. Peasants in wide-brimmed black hats or huge knots of black ribbon shuffled in discomfort upon the ribbed, buff-painted seats.

The Rue des Remparts rose steeply out of the town. The house stood at a corner. A lane descended even more steeply, no doubt to some river. Annelies was out with her *fiancé*, the owner of a hotel in which she now worked as receptionist. She would not be back until after the last train had gone. Atha had seen photographs of Annelies's widowed mother, but had not met her before. She was not very old, darker-haired than her daughter. She seemed well-disposed. No doubt Annelies would write.

IN THE MORNING, UNCERTAIN ATHA WALKED IN THE LEAFLESS, COLD Orangerie. The pollarded limes on the deserted café terrace seemed unbudded. They were black, barbaric candelabra. No boats plied on the lake. In the grotto, the pale-grey stone of the sphinxes, faintly mottled with dry lichen, stood in the bald light without shadow or mystery. The few drops of water were melting ice. In the afternoon, he took a slow, empty tram out through Neudorf and up the long ramp to a point just short of the pinnacled Kehl Bridge.

The German customs house and passport office stood on the bridge. A brisk officer took every penny and franc of Atha's money from him and gave him a receipt. The Rhine was in spate. It raced along, whole trees and great swathes of grass on its tossing, icy surface, chequered olive and jade.

In Kehl, the main street had been renamed the Adolf-Hitlerstrasse. In the shop-windows, swastika-stamped notices assured indifferent Atha that business there was conducted wholly by and with Aryans.

It was already dusk. As the lights came on, Atha saw one sad little storm-trooper, a family man or an elderly bachelor wearing *pince-nez*, glad perhaps of an excuse to get out in the evening. He stood at a street corner like a stray dog and sniffed the evening.

Back at the Willms', no letter stood on the ledge over the brown porcelain stove. Atha went out to dine at the glass-fronted restaurant on the Contades.

Then he walked to the Place Brant and took a tram out to the Rhine again. He turned left and came to the port where black water slapped against the sides of barges.

It appears that he stared for a while at this black water. The next thing he distinctly remembers is sitting in a café, where also a number of workmen were drinking. It may have been the same café-restaurant at which, on a Sunday morning, I recently ate Rhine sprats. On this occasion, it was cool shade away from the blistering sun. To February Atha, it had been brightness and warmth out of the cold, agitated dark.

His mind had undergone a partial blackout, though he seems to recall leaving the black, comparatively still barge water for the near bank of the open Rhine, icier and less easy simply to drop into but irrevocable and slower to yield up its corpses. For, at dinner on the Contades, it had emerged clearly into Atha's mind that his purpose in coming here was suicide. He had thought of this as the happy place, but he had also thought of it as a place in which he could disappear, whether by way of the great, unswimmable river or from high up the tallest of all Gothic spires known to him.

For the moment, a protective amnesia had intervened. A letter from Sarrebourg might yet come in the morning, the renewal-of-happiness dream be revived, the other postponed. No letter stood on the Willms' mantelpiece in the morning. After crossing the Contades and turning along the Quai Koch, white-faced Atha crossed a bridge to the central island by St. Stephen's and the statue of a boy luring titmice and, through narrow streets, came out by the north porch of the Minster, where St. Lawrence toasted on his gridiron, and continued to the open square, turned left past the west front with all its portals and statues, turned left again and yet again through a small, rounded arch and up five or six steps to a *guichet* at which he bought the kind of ticket which now costs twenty francs.

To the main platform, there are three hundred and twenty-eight echoing, corkscrew steps, rather worn, spinning (rather slowly) anti-clockwise. At a slit in the red stone, one is already above the roof of the nave, which there lies before one in all the turquoise tenderness of weathered copper, protected at every corner and pinnacle by a jungle of gargoyles dripping from nose and mouth.

That morning's Atha did not count the steps. He made angry fun of me for counting them this morning. It was, he gave me to understand, the kind of thing that only a journalist would do. As a matter of fact, he is right. I do not quite like the way he spits out the word 'journalist', for I doubt whether I should be here at all were it not for *The Examiner*. However, I am here in part as a journalist. If I were not, I should not have counted the steps.

As I did this morning, he passed through a wooden shed containing lavatories, little storerooms for brushes, pails and mops, a souvenir counter and a post office (though perhaps, at that time of year, these last two were closed). It is the south tower one has climbed. The spire rises from the north tower.

From the platform, the view to the ground is already vertiginous. The tiny people walk there like seraphim without bodies, their legs waving feebly to and fro beneath them. I am not much prone to giddiness, even now. The Hon. Bert, happening to glance down, clutched my arm and closed his eyes. He must, he said, go, but I must not think of coming down with him. I could see how lines which to my eyes were merely vertical or horizontal tilted drunkenly across his mind.

Everywhere, there are names scratched and chipped in the stone. It is a hard stone, little defaced by weathering centuries. The pinkness, on which, I fancy, I have already sufficiently insisted, is by no means uniform. In later buildings, and conspicuously in the eighteenth-century Prefecture, the builder has sought homogeneous stone, often the lightest and so the most radiant pink, but, among the vast quantities of stone in the Minster, itself a whole mountain of stone, so that building it must have emptied quarries and laid hills low, there is everything from chocolate to dove-grey, various tones of red or pink merely predominating in the mass. The base of the spire, a vaulted chamber invisible from the ground, shows almost no colour. The names there are deeply chiselled. Now you must hurriedly do what you can while the attendant's back is turned, but in earlier days it is clear that the name-chipping on fashionable Gothic was never improvised.

'You left servants behind,' says the Hon. Bert, 'or perhaps a resident stonemason plied for hire.'

The name of Voltaire is half-defaced. 'Mme la Dauphine' was Marie Antoinette, who stayed here on her way to the French marriage and was entertained with a picnic on the Minster platform. Goethe was here at the time. His name occurs twice, once externally and once under the vaulting, in both cases with a list of his boarding house companions, including Herder. Both entries are dated 1776, five years after the close of the Sessenheim idyll and Goethe's first departure, six years after the visit of Mme la Dauphine, on her way to play at shepherdesses.

It is a pity Hon. Bert could not look steadily down upon the rooftops. They are not pink, but brown and cream. A shower in the night had washed them clean, and the overcast sky made near things luridly clear. They are very steep roofs. If a monk's fine, praying hands suggested the Gothic arch, these are the domestic but urgent prayers of broad, peasant hands. They were drawn and engraved by Gustave Doré, and much else in his drawing seems to conceal the image of their crowded, imbricated forms. In each roof, there are three, four, even five storeys, each with its row of attic windows projecting not horizontally but at a downward slope, so that snow would scarcely hold even there, or hold long. The chimney stacks are topped with flat platforms on which, no doubt, it was hoped that storks would build. This year, there seem to be no storks in the town. Looked up to from the street, these roofs are lovely. Looking down upon them from a fair height, even the hardened Asmodeus may yet pause to dash a tear from his demon eye.

But now you climb higher. Two hundred and seventy-two more steps, five hundred in all. This morning, there was quite a strong wind. At each long slit, the wind pulls at you. You pass the great bell. You hope it will not ring just now (you remember how the great bell of Sacre Coeur lifts you out of your seat at a café table in the Place du Tertre). You are above all bells.

You come out into the open, on top of one of the four delicate external ('free-standing' is, I believe, the architect's term) *tourelles* (but, of course, they cannot stand quite so free as pillars). This, I suppose, is the upward limit of 'the lantern'. By a walk which is a kind of gutter with parapet (you edge sideways along it), the rounded bays of the *tourelle* tops connect with each other. Above your head now rises what Goethe's translator calls 'the neck' connecting you with 'the nob or crown' (which is what, I suppose, my guidebook calls 'the helmet'). I must look up that quotation* again and show it to the Hon. Bert or, if I can't find a *Dichtung* and *Wahrheit* here, send it to him later from England.

You can't now climb beyond this point. There is an iron grating, how recent I don't know. Neither young Harold nor cold-weather Atha remembers it, but perhaps that isn't strange. In my journalist's role, I

---

*This is how it in fact goes, in its Victorian translation: 'I had to fight, both inwardly and outwardly, with quite different circumstances and adversaries, being at strife with myself, with the objects around me, and even with the elements. I found myself in a state of health which furthered me sufficiently in all that I would and should undertake; only there was a certain irritability left, which did not always let me be in equilibrium. A loud sound was disagreeable to me, diseased objects awakened in me loathing and horror. But I was especially troubled by a giddiness which came over me every time that I looked down from a height. All these infirmities I tried to remedy, and, indeed, as I wished to lose no time, in a somewhat violent way. In the evening, when they beat the tattoo, I went near the multitude of drums, the powerful rolling and beating of which might have made one's heart burst in one's bosom. All alone I ascended the highest pinnacle of the minster spire, and sat in what is called the neck, under the nob or crown, for a quarter of an hour, before I would venture to step out again into the open air, where, standing upon a platform scarce an ell square, without any particular holding, one sees the boundless prospect before, while the nearest objects and ornaments conceal the church, and everything upon and above which one stands. It is exactly as if one saw oneself carried up into the air in a balloon. Such troublesome and painful sensations I repeated until the impression became quite indifferent to me, and I have since derived great advantage from this training, in mountain travels and geological studies, and on great buildings, where I have vied with the carpenters in running over the bare beams and the cornices of the edifice. . .'

---

have a note here which clearly indicates that it wasn't there a hundred and fourteen years ago.

JAMES AND ELIZABETH WATSON
PANTON, RICHARD AND EDWARD COBBETT
THOMAS COOK
1834

It still looks professionally chiselled. As you read through the grating, you feel you ought not to be looking upward, the space there being so largely occupied by the rustle of Mrs Watson's skirts. Intrepid young woman.

The map in the guidebook comes to life, though you must edge along from one *tourelle*-top bay to another to get it whole. From the south-east bay you look down upon the nave of the Minster. The dull shapes far out to the east are the Black Forest. The faint gleam in front of them is the Rhine. From the south-west bay you look down into the Minster square, before the west front. The tiny, walking seraphim are three hundred and fifty feet below. In the distance here, there is little to see but a prospect of industrial suburb, with brewery and tannery chimneys, but it is clear that you are upon an island. The avenues and squares surround it, to the north-east a park, the Orangerie. As you move round the bay to the right, you see the sharper, more dramatic line of the near Vosges.

The north-west bay has a clear drop on two sides, either into the Minster square or into a narrow street. A jump into the square would land you in front of the north door of the west front, somewhat to the left (looked at from outside). To either side of the door stand four stone ladies in long tunics and crowns, each in her separate niche, each resting the point of her spear on a squirming Vice. None of the eight Virtues (there is another round the corner) seems particularly interested in what she is doing, though one in the right-hand group who is very plain (some burgess's wife of the time?) looks as though her long indrawn chin might be sitting on a horrid chuckle. The two girls on the extreme left are the prettiest and most charmingly posed, their expressions of a perfect amiability. No doubt the sculptor carved these first and thereafter asked his older models for a little more expression.

All nine are 'living' enough (the one on her own *looks* a bit left out). It is not difficult to imagine their reactions to the sudden descent of a male human body. The two pretty young things on the left would be nearest. Both their spears would clatter to the ground (some ten feet below). The first would stand pop-eyed with hand to mouth, the second, after looking about her to see whether at this height it was safe to faint, would clutch nearby ribs of stone and stand shrieking, 'Daddy!' The lean, plain, humorous, warm-hearted third would use her spear to get down to the ground and calculate sharply what she could do to help. As nothing directly helpful would be possible, she might then be sick.

And so on. But idle fancies of this kind were not in the mind of Atha, aged twenty-four, in late February, while even his calculations as to height lacked the precision of mine. He did not fancy the side-street. The choice from the north-east bay was side-street and nave, from the south-east bay nave and platform, from the south-west bay platform and square. The best views (of Black Forest and Rhine) lay to the east. The drop to any part of the nave was greater than that to the platform, and the act itself would be more likely to escape observation. But that turquoise surface sloped. One could not hit it squarely at right angles and be sure. As a solid surface to be confidently met at right angles, the platform was ideal, and the drop looked adequate (it is just over a hundred and thirty feet). There were, moreover, no awkward projections on that side, the most awkward elsewhere being at platform level. To land on the platform seemed a bit squalid, however. The pails, brushes and mops were just too handy. A full drop to the ground would have more poetry about it. If brought off to perfection, it was also more certain. Atha had even read somewhere that, in falling from a great enough height, a man would be dead before he reached the ground.

Atha decided on the south-west bay and on that side of it which faced the Minster square. He looked over the parapet. The projections below were intricate and no doubt more considerable than from so far above they seemed. A great leap would be needed to clear them. It would not matter so much if one struck some projecting edge a glancing blow which then bounced one's body further out, but it would not at all do to be caught and to hang there, perhaps with a thigh-bone already driven through one's liver, but conscious. It would not be easy to make a great leap. One had to stand on the narrow parapet, whose upper surface was lightly curved, and there was no handhold against which to steady one's balance, nor any means of getting one foot placed well behind the other and thus first swinging shoulder weight back. It was not even very easy to get on to the parapet, which projected towards one from awkwardly shaped footholds among the carved lozenges of stone. One might trip and simply tumble over, quite helpless. Apart from the greater likelihood in that case of the most unattractive of imaginable physical consequences, that would be undignified. One's fate would have been taken out of one's hands. One would have been deprived of the last act of will.

With the side of his clenched fist, Atha beat upon the cold, rough, quartz-glittering pink stone. The heavy charge of adrenaline in his blood made his knees tremble. He looked at the distant Vosges, then addressed himself to what had to be done. With his left hand, he gripped the outer edge of the parapet, with his right hand the edge that lay towards him. His left heel found a hold among the carved shapes below. Necessarily leaning back a little, he took all his weight on braced left leg and flexed left arm and raised his right foot from the ground, to bring it up and place it on the parapet. No doubt his breathing was rapid.

From below came the sound of climbing steps. Then they were out in the open, and the intruder was edging his way from north-east to south-east bay and round towards an Atha who stood as though raptly contemplating the landscape, though his knees almost visibly shook.

A voice said:

'*Schön, nicht?*'

It was a young man, with open-necked white shirt and leather jerkin, fair hair loosely waving, in height an inch or two shorter than Atha, pale-complexioned but stocky. With all the dreadful, checked strength of his overcharged bloodstream, Atha was hard put to it not at once to lay hold of the intruder and bundle *him* over the parapet. Instead, he contrived by facial expression to intimate that he did not understand German.

The young man knew some French and a few words of English. It quickly transpired that Atha was neither French nor local Rhenish. The young man ventured to explain that all that lay about them was German land. Atha did not take him up on this. The young German came from Lübeck. He was on holiday. That summer, he was going to the Olympic Games in Berlin.

'We shall show them,' he said.

'You mean,' said Atha, 'that you will win all the events?'

The German had a sense of humour. He laughed.

'Perhaps not all,' he said, 'but many. We are a folk of great athletes. We are not any longer degenerate like the French . . .'

He looked sideways at Atha, as though he would have liked to add:

'. . . and the English.'

But, evidently, he thought better of it.

As Atha left him, the young German turned.

'Is beautiful,' he said, 'this German land.'

Back in the Place de Bordeaux, a letter for Atha stood propped on the Willms' mantelpiece, over the chocolate-coloured porcelain stove.

THIS MORNING, IT WAS I WHO TOOK MY DEPARTURE IN SOMETHING OF a hurry. On Atha's face, I felt sure there remained an expression indicative of his distaste for my journalistic preoccupations.

These notes on the astronomical clock are what I was on my way down to make. It goes through all its motions only once a day, at noon or, rather, at two minutes past noon. I had five hundred steps to go down. I had to leave the Minster by one door and go in at another, where I must again pay, the main part of the building being closed shortly before midday. Besides, I seemed to remember that the big bell did some tolling about that time, and I did not want to find myself passing it then.

Going down the *tourelles*, you hardly know where to let your eyes rest. At every long slit, if your gaze turns where it will, the streets reel below you. On the other hand, if you keep your eyes on your feet, the tower itself spins with you inside it.

You are safe. You have passed through the low, wooden shed again and are descending the south tower, three hundred and twenty-eight steps. The wind has dropped. Your steps echo. You pass other people mounting, girls with French or American soldiers. The great bell is tolling overhead. Somewhere inside the Minster, the organ is being played with evident virtuosity, perhaps the advertised organist Grunenwald practising for his recital.

As you emerge into the square opposite the Palais des Rohan, the street clocks are already chiming, but there is no cause for alarm, the astronomical clock is two minutes slow.

Its mechanism whirrs as you push your way in among the other gapers. An impressive, bearded guide, in a skull cap and long robes, bearing a staff, is already giving tongue.

The first chimes. The interval is a minor third, the upper note sounding close and the lower somewhere behind the great face of the machine, which rises almost to the roof. To the left, a brass dial behind glass shows you the moveable church feasts. To the right, a similar mechanism gives you the position of the planets. There are rails to prevent you touching anything, and indeed you stand as far back as you may, so as to see the figures passing overhead and, highest of all, the cock which will crow three times and beat its wings.

In a curious French which is either local or Swiss, the guide declaims:

'*La mort qui sonne!*'

It is the first stroke of twelve. A skeleton strikes the model of a bell, which makes a wooden, tapping sound at the same time as there sounds a clear ringing chime from elsewhere. A figure passes in front of the skeleton, and another appears, waiting for the next stroke. The best, however, is reserved until the hour has struck.

The guide intones:

'*Les apôtres passent devant le Christ!*'

He points with his staff, and, it is quite true, Christ standing in a niche above the skeleton makes signs of the cross and blesses twelve apostles who click shuddering before him.

And now :

'*Le coq chante!*'

Yes, the wings are raised and lowered three times.

They make the sound of a flapping handkerchief. The beak opens. The sound, in cock-a-doodle-doo rhythm, is like that produced by the 'musical submarine' you hummed through as a child (it was made of tin, and a little disc of parchment or tissue paper was held in place under the funnel). Air is no doubt mechanically blown over a vibrant membrane.

That's all. The guide switches off a light, and the crowd disperses.

Before you follow them, look at the beautiful *pilier des anges*. Above the four evangelists, four angels with trumpets are blowing up the Last Judgment. Above them are Christ and three more angels bearing the instruments of His crucifixion. The draperies are thin, the faces gravely quiet like those of rested children. The lines of the wings enclose all, like the petals of a water lily or magnolia. There is no weight, no urgency. The eye dwells upon these upward convolutions without fatigue.

AT OBERNAI AND OTROTT, THE CHARABANC DRIVER STOPPED HIS vehicle and pointed out storks' nests, the old gates of villages which had been fortified towns, renaissance wells in drowsy market-places. The monastery of St. Odile stands at three thousand feet. The hill is surrounded by a pagan wall, and the regional poet, who is a disciple of Rudolf Steiner, argues that the saint's miraculous recovery of sight means that she was an initiate recovered from the spiritual blindness of orthodox religion.

Other charabancs are lined up in the road outside the gates. The chapel is decorated in the same kind of modern, gilded *kitsch* as Sacré Coeur or Lyons' corner houses. In the precincts are blue letterboxes and men's lavatories. Since tourists come daily in hundreds, the life of the nuns can hardly be one of strict contemplation. They must have a duty roster at the souvenir and postcard counters, for instance.

From a raised garden, there are spectacular views. Variously placed are semi-circular maps of fixed orientation. By directing your line of vision from their centres, you may discover the identity of any object in sight. On a clear day, the Minster spire is clearly visible, thirty miles to the north-east. This afternoon, the heat-haze made it uncertain whether you saw a spire or not.

Somewhere beyond the nearer pines and firs, there was artillery practice. First, we heard the shell lamenting overhead, then distantly the sound of the gun being fired, a sound like that of a door being shut.

I asked young Harold about the Orangerie girl.

'I must be psychic,' he said. 'It rained, you'll remember, on Sunday afternoon. I didn't go out. Neither did Umpleby. We slept. Suddenly, I woke up. I knew if I went straightaway to the Orangerie, I should find her. I knew exactly where she'd be sitting, and she was. It had stopped raining. There was a friend with her, another girl from the commercial school. We left the Orangerie and walked along the canal by the *Joyeux Marinier.*'

'The friend, too?' I asked.

'Yes, she's a plain girl. We're all going boating at Robertsau tomorrow afternoon. I'm taking Attila for the friend. You know, the terrible Turk. He says he can row.'

Attila, the Turk, had just bought himself a powerful motorbike, which it appeared he drove without licence or much knowledge of the mechanisms involved. He and young Harold (on the pillion) were proposing to do some widespread mountain excursions the following week. Attila was very keen to go to Turkheim, a name, he insisted, commemorating the fact that his countrymen had overrun the whole of this area in the eighteenth century.

The road back lay through Hohwald and Barr. As we descended in low gear into the vineyards, combed over plain and foothills, I heard, against charabanc engine, scattering stones and the exclamations of our neighbours, young Harold several times catch his breath, presumably at the beauty of the scene, which, I am bound to say, made my own eyelids prickle, my lips stay foolishly parted. Roadside calvaries were juxtaposed with vines growing on crossed stakes, the crucified Dionysus. The pale soil of this plain is incredibly fruitful. They say, if you merely scratch it with a stick, crops shoot above your head.

Along the roadside, cherry trees are planted. They belong to the commune, and different families pick them each year.

THE KING'S BIRTHDAY PASSED OFF VERY WELL. THE CONSUL, THOUGH painfully English, is utterly charming, and the archbishop in puce gloves was beautiful. There were a number of handsome, friendly young women in hats, among whom I talked longest with a blandly intelligent French girl from Nancy, where she works for the British Council.

The port authority with whom I talked had a tiny flag in his buttonhole. It looked like a Union Jack, a touching expression, I thought, of his Anglophily. It was the port flag. The port authorities are, it seems, dissatisfied with British policy on the Rhine. I am held personally responsible, since, unlike Hon. Bert and other members of the resident colony, I was in England when the London talks began. I shall put all this to rights towards the end of next week. I am to take a train to Bale and sail back here on a barge. I don't know how long this will take. On re-arrival, I am to be met by a motor-launch, which will conduct me around the port. For, in a manner which I do not understand, this inland place, more than two hundred miles from the nearest sea, constitutes nevertheless the fourth port of France. As a result of my excursion, I shall be in a position to tell England the truth about the Rhine. The motor-launch bit sounds tedious, but all the rest sounds wonderful. I shall take bathing trunks and sun glasses. Sharing the simple food of the bargees, I shall lie daylong deck-top as the green banks go by, with their intermittent castles. I must get a few Swiss francs from Erich von Stroheim.

This morning, I visited a brewery. Tomorrow, I am to study *pâté de foie gras* with the regional poet. In the morning, we are to call on a dealer at his warehouse in the town. Then, with the regional poet's wife, we are to be driven by a friend of theirs to Wantzenau, where the geese are reared. We are to lunch there. The friend is a widow. Her name is Mme Zix.

Young Harold has kissed the Orangerie girl, whose name is Annelies. It came on to rain while the two couples were boating at Robertsau. They tied up and landed in the woods. Harold kissed Annelies under a dripping willow. The 'sweet, hot lips you offered without shame' are to be celebrated in a poem. It does not appear that the plain friend was similarly kissed by the Turk, Attila, who rowed without skill and took a long time to make land.

THE ENVELOPE WAS OF A FAIRLY EXPENSIVE TYPE, OF AN OPAQUE, INwardly marbled, blue-grey paper, with grey, transparent lining. Over the point of the deep flap had been stuck a small gilt lozenge bearing, embossed, the letters A and L interlaced as a monogram. The notepaper was like that of the outer envelope, folded, with ripple edges. The handwriting, bigger on the envelope than within, was generically Continental rather than specifically either German or French in style (but rather French than German) and handsome enough without either great distinction or perfectly easy legibility. The letter read:

Cher Othon,

J'ai été tres surprise hier soir en rentrant d'apprendre votre visite—et je regrette de tout mon coeur de ne pas avoir été là—j' etais pour [sic] affairs à Haguenau.

Si je savais Othon que c'est uniquement pour moi que vous avez fait ce voyage de Paris, je me ferai des reproches cruels de ne pas vous avoir répondu à la lettre, mais vous savez Othon, je ne suis plus libre je suis fiancée depuis deux mois et je compte me marier bientôt ne me reprochez rien, car c'est vous le coupable de n' avoir plus écrit—mais tout de même Othon j'aurai été très contente de vous revoir car vous êtes si gentil—et si fin—seulement je n'ai pas une minute à moi je travaille toute la journée mais vous saver Othon—si après ce que vous venez d'apprendre cela *vous plairait encore de me revoir—envoyez-moi un mot et je viendrai le soir après fermeture du magasin.*

Je vous prierai de ne point venir à Sarrebourg car cela ferait des racontars—et mon fiancé est très jaloux.

Alors j' attends un mot de vous—oui ou non si je dois venir et je serai là.

ANNELIES

And there it is, on the rickety basketwork table in my hotel room, with the stacked *gauloises jaunes* and matchboxes, *La Peste* and the guidebook, the ashtray, three letters from Blod, picture postcards and stamps.

Richly aware as I am of the absurdities of Atha, I cannot honestly claim that I think he was wrong to base some expectations on the letter from Sarrebourg. The girl was to marry an older man. She was marrying for position, her own and also that of her widowed mother. Once married, she would be faithful. Even now she was discreet. Her mother must be covering the proffered visit, had clearly taken to Atha, whose return journey was romantic, whose departure almost at once ensured discretion. Let them spend one night together and go their separate ways in the morning, each with a memorable, a charming burden of renunciation.

A note was despatched to Sarrebourg, and Atha devoted himself to the task of passing twenty-four aimless hours. He recalls very little of what he did during the earlier part of Tuesday. He apparently went to the bookshop next door to the Gallia, enquired what they had by Léon Bloy and bought a book called *Le Sang du Pauvre*, which is a high-flown diatribe against the rich.

In the afternoon, Mme Willm returned from Mulhouse, a small, dark woman, bespectacled like her two sons, her speech rapid, her eyes

---

* It would be possible, perhaps even, from certain points of view, desirable, to put in a [sic] at several points in this letter, but it must be remembered that the girl was not French. The name 'Othon' apparently came into use as follows. Pedantically, Atha had once said that, although it was found as a surname in the north of England today, his name was really an Anglo-Saxon prenom, presumably the same as the German 'Otto'. So to this girl he became 'Otto' or its equivalent in French.

darting. Her manner struck Atha as totally unwelcoming. This surprised him. He could well understand that she might be momentarily annoyed at finding an unexpected visitor in the house, but, once she had expressed her annoyance to Fritz, it seemed to Atha that she might well have relaxed and viewed himself with a degree of friendliness. Certainly, whatever happened with Annelies, he would not stay tonight with the Willms.

'You permit,' he said, 'madame, that I pay you something?'

'Yes, *monsieur*,' she said, with glinting sarcasm, 'I permit it.'

Atha was uncertain what time Annelies would arrive. He fancied there was time for him to walk across the Contades and to the public baths and back. In case Annelies came early and he was out, he trusted that Mme Willm might be kind enough to let the girl come in and sit down for a while. Mme Willm assured him that she did not propose to ask strange young women into the house, under any circumstances whatever. Atha concluded he must wait about. Mme Willm must be in a state of considerable fury, he could not guess why.

From this point, Atha's account of his doings no longer strikes me as perfectly reasonable. The young woman had to leave her place of work and travel a distance of forty miles by train, probably by a slow train. At the earliest, therefore, she could hardly be expected in the city before six or in the Place de Bordeaux before a quarter past, and, indeed, seven o'clock would be more likely. Even with Continental time in force, it can hardly, in late February or at the beginning of March, have remained light until seven o'clock so far to the east. It must have taken a good forty minutes to cross the Contades, walk along the quays, cross the Ill and reach the *bains munieipaux*, buy a ticket, run and use a hot bath, dry and dress, return to the Place de Bordeaux.

Atha must therefore have decided, not much later than a quarter past six, that Annelies was not coming, after all. There are in fact other considerations which suggest that his desire to see Annelies was less urgent than much of his behaviour might seem to pretend. No doubt Mme Willm's presence irked him. No doubt he was conscious that his presence irked Mine Willm. No doubt the appeal of a deep bath of very hot water was strong. At any rate, when clean Atha returned to the Place de Bordeaux, he was informed that a young woman had called at the house and asked for him, that his probable movements had been indicated to her and that she had then gone away. Atha took his bundle of dirty clothes upstairs and stuffed them into his rucksack. He then left the house again.

On the cindery, trampled earth of the Contades, between the bare trees, he met Annelies returning. It was still light enough for the two to recognise each other. It was, apparently, too light for the young woman to feel that they could, with any propriety, at once kiss.

They walked by way of the Place Brant and the Arcades to the Place Kléber, the west side of which is almost wholly occupied by the enormous Café de l'Aubette. It was in the concert and banqueting hall of the Aubette that, on Tuesday evening, I heard Janine Micheau and Gérard Souzay, with a string quartet giving the first performance of a new work by Florent Schmitt, whose big-grey-bearded, cravated, black-sombreroed, brown-corduroyed figure is still to be seen about the streets, as though it were still the nineties and this Montmartre.

One afternoon last week, sitting outside on the terrace of the Aubette drinking tea in the nevertheless hot shade, I caught a sudden whiff of Virginia tobacco, like new-mown hay, and heard a very English female voice say:

'Darling!'

As its owner settled beside a man, four tables away, who was reading what might have been the *Continental Daily Mail* or *Times*, the voice of the woman, swooping with parcels, continued:

'Darling, I've spent *all* our money! we shall have to *walk* back to Calais!'

The answer was, all ungraciously, a grunt, at which the wife softened her tone.

'Darling,' she said, 'I haven't *really*!'

In February, however, the awning was up, the pavement free of basketwork tables and chairs. Atha and Annelies went through the revolving glass doors and sat at a table of brass-rimmed marble. I cannot gather with certitude what 'Othon' ordered. I suspect it was simply white wine. At any rate, there the two sat, pale-faced, intense Atha, a man then temperamentally ill-equipped for seduction wearing a pale-grey jacket of Donegal tweed with a dark-blue shirt, and the girl of twenty, with soft, very fair hair over a somewhat bulging forehead, her rosebud mouth prominent, her opulent (and, I gather from snapshots, somewhat flaccid) bosom in a white jumper caught up with a belt.

Two bits of dialogue strike Atha as salient. Indeed, they are the only points he recalls distinctly.

There was some talk of international affairs, of Hitler and the Nazis, on 'Othon's' part. Annelies's comment surprised him.

'Even so,' she said, 'we are all German. . . . *Quand même, nous sommes tous allemands.*'

It may have been:

'After all . . . *Après tout . . .*'

The collocation of '*tout*' and '*tous*', of 'all' with 'all', is stylistically unattractive, and Atha's reflecting mind may have substituted a '*quand même*' for that reason. He does not, he confesses, know what the '*tous*' was meant to include, whether simply Germans in the Homeland together with such denaturalised expatriates as Annelies and her mother, or the people of this area as a whole, ethnologically conceived as Rhinelanders estranged from their birthright by the temporary accident of French rule, or, indeed, whether he himself might not also be included as an Englishman and therefore *nordique*. At any rate, he did not pursue the matter, though his thoughts were dark.

In due course, he raised the more important question, how the two were to spend their evening and, not to put too fine a point upon it, their night. The response to this was even more disappointing.

It was:

'If I'd known you were just after a bit of lovemaking, I shouldn't have come.'

That is to say, as quoted in French:

'*Si j' avais su que vous vouliez faire des amours, je ne serais pas venue.*'

From evidence contained in the young woman's letter, it seems possible that, here too, reflection has supplied a minor stylistic improvement and that what Annelies really said had been:

'*Si je savais . . .* If I *knew* that all you were after . . .'

However, the sense is the same. Inwardly, Atha's reaction was rather of anger than disappointment. As far as his 'chances' were concerned, a keen disappointment, eloquently urged to the point of tearfulness, would, beyond a doubt, have served his turn better. As he confesses he was a little inclined to do (to himself) some three hundred and fifty feet above the ground, thirty-six hours before, he might have quoted wildly:

> *Qu'as-tu fait, infidèle,*
> *Qu'as-tu fait du passé?*

There were, indeed, other passages from Musset, Lamartine and Victor Hugo, all known to and frequently meditated by Atha, which might have served equally well. The result might have been quite gratifying.

He behaved, he assures me, with formal politeness, though he does not seem to have carried it very far. The small bill paid, Annelies gracefully helped on with her coat, the two went out through the swing doors into the cold and turned left along the frontage of the Aubette. There was some poignancy and regret now. Annelies was quite pretty. Fully conscious of her body's worth, she carried herself well, head and body erect, toes carefully pointed, perhaps turned in a little, her gait perhaps a bit mincing. But the main thought in miserably raging Atha's head was that he must get away from this horrible city at once.

The two turned left again and, by way of the Arcades, came to the Rue de la Haute Montée, where frequent trams pass on their way to the railway station square. Here, indifferent Atha ('Othon' no more) left his *inamorata* and turned right. By way of Titmouse Street, the Breuil, the bridge behind the municipal theatre, the Place de la République, the quays and the Contades, he reached the Place de Bordeaux. This was the route he had followed, very much more slowly and with different thoughts, on Sunday morning, eighty-four hours ago.

As though to make amends for his mother's poor welcome, Fritz Willm insisted on accompanying Atha to the station. They studied fares and train times. Atha discovered that, after he had paid Mme Willm, he possessed too few francs to take him as far as London. Fritz offered to lend him money which he could return through the post. Atha refused, at which Fritz, though conscience-stricken, seemed relieved. Atha booked a second-class ticket as far as Brussels. He would, he said, like to see Brussels. From there, he could write to various people in England for a loan or a gift of the necessary money. Fritz Willm said that he had never been in Brussels, but that he understood it was a beautiful and interesting city. Atha states that his principal reason for not accepting Fritz Willm's offer of a loan was that he did not wish to retain any link whatever with the city in which he stood at that moment. He was not, in any case, sure of ever getting beyond Brussels.

III

THIS TIME, I STAYED ONLY ONE SATURDAY NIGHT WITH THE DE Moors. The greater part of last month, I was put up by Alain Thomas, who is one of our authors at Matthew Latimer's. One of my authors, really. Not Matthew's cup of tea at all. His wife cooks incredibly badly. This, I fancy, is to punish Alain for not making more money and to show that it is not what she was brought up to. He does not mind. I should not have minded the constant plates of spaghetti without sauce or the occasional poached fish (also without sauce) if they had ever been served hot. But, in fact, I did not mind so very much even so. I ate out frequently elsewhere. The Thomas's flat, though untidy, is large and not inelegantly furnished. They live up the interminably winding Rue Notre Dame des Champs, about a hundred yards below the Closerie des Lilas.

Alain rather goes in for being the absent-minded man of letters. He wears *pince-nez* and a small beard which make him look more French than Frenchmen under sixty ever look now (Alain is forty-two). His father was a great man in the time of Alfred Vallette and the *Mercure*. Old poets like Paul Fort and Fernand Gregh, men like Paul Leautaud, remember him as a boy (he took me to see Gregh in that seemingly remote village inside Paris, the Hameau de Boulainvillers). At the same time, he is *persona grata* at the NRF. No sign of this starting up again yet, though Paulhan talks of it. Alain took me to the first Gallimard *cocktail* of the season. That would be the last or last-but-one Friday in May. They were all there, '*toutes ces têtes d'écrivains*' , as he said. I talked to Schlumberger and Supervielle. I only saw the glaring dwarf Sartre, the tall, amiable-looking Camus, like a less embittered Humphrey Bogart, Jouhandeau, still *mal vu* and publishing only in Switzerland, Gide, looking *parcheminé* but well. I was rather congratulating myself on being the only Englishman present at this prestigious assembly when in walked two young persons from *The White Review.*

I told Deirdre that I should be coming along here for several weeks.

'Oh,' she said, rather nastily I thought. 'Is that a good idea?'

I explained that for me it was.

The first Sunday afternoon, I saw the Dunoyer de Segonzac exhibition at the most upholstered of all art galleries, Charpentier's. The following morning, Alain got me up early to show me the flowers in Bagatelle. It was a beautiful morning, and there was still dew on both flowers and grass. Parties of schoolgirls, under the protection of nuns, sketched the roses and the irises.

A film unit was at work by the lake. It was a costume piece, late seventeenth century. A nobleman and a priest, both wearing bright orange make-up, the cleric in broad-brimmed black hat and black cloak lined with scarlet, stepped down the rocks in earnest but inaudible conversation, preceded by a young man in a yellow jumper, stepping backward, who dangled before them a microphone like a carrot to entice donkeys. A long cable lay behind him, connecting the microphone to the interior of a black van. The cameraman sat in a tall chair to one side.

The shot had to be repeated several times, and it was some time before the park-keeper and a policeman would let us step over the trailing wires and skirt the black van stationed in the lane. Marvellous rhododendrons bloomed along the forest path leading uphill towards the great promenade of the Bois de Boulogne.

I saw the new Sartre play, *Les Mains Sâles*, twice. The second time, I took Alain and Marguerite Thomas. No London theatre creaks like the Antoine, which is evidently constructed wholly of basketwork. We had three seats in a box containing six. Arriving in good time, we considerately grouped ourselves so as to leave one front seat vacant. Two quiet, unprotesting young people arrived with a formidable old lady, who raised a lorgnette to the felt brim of her black hat and who bore proudly before her a Queen Mary bosom strapped up in black taffeta, to a cameo brooch upon which the lorgnette was attached by a gold chain. She insisted to the *ouvreuse* that she had been assured of three front seats. Having failed by these means to disturb our tightly wedged composure (I can't think what you do if you get pins and needles in one of those *loges* when it is full and contains even the best-disposed strangers), she proceeded to comment incisively upon our generation and its *moeurs périmées*.

It would be Thursday when I established contact with Michel de Moor at the huge bank of which he is assistant manager. We lunched together that day, and I was duly invited to Puits de la Lisière for the weekend, i.e. for Saturday night. I took a crowded suburban train from St. Lazare and reached Puits in time for lunch on Saturday.

Noémie, Yves and Michel still lived at home. The married Roger had vacated the lodge, and this was now occupied by two American ex-Army students and their young wives, whom the de Moors had not yet come to know by sight. The servants were new. Last year, we had been waited on at table by a slow-witted, scrawny, ageless Breton called Jean, who, on occasion, would appear without collar and be (by Michel) smartly sent back to the kitchen to put it on before he served us. He had never been viewed with much favour, but was dismissed in the end for homosexual activities blatantly conducted with the gardener. A grandniece of Mme de Moor's had observed the two men behaving curiously at dusk upon the disused tennis court.

We drank our brandy and *nescafé* on the terrace, beneath a fine red maple which repeatedly ruffled its green skirts to display purple undergarments. Michel wondered how I wished to spend the afternoon. The day was hot, and *canotage* meant first carrying a heavy wooden canoe some fifty yards from beside the tennis court to where a small branch of the Seine lapped against a kind of allotment extension to the vegetable garden. I could think of nothing pleasanter than to sit on the vast terrace of the restaurant at St. Germain en Laye, with its breathtaking view over a bend in the Seine.

Michel got the car out, and we called round to ask the Guilloux next door if they cared to join us. Mme Guilloux, small, slight, of perfect figure and with reddened hair which exactly matched both her eyes and the jumper through which her tit-mammaries poked like venereal headlights, is a mannequin at one of the great Parisian fashion houses. The car broke down in the middle of the Forest, and Guilloux, a big, very handsome fellow in a green corduroy jacket, took charge. Though not so wholly devoid of mechanical knowledge as myself, Michel is rather helpless in such emergencies. His impulse would have been to abandon the car, walk to the nearest telephone and get another car driven out to us. Very properly, he is impatient of machines which go wrong, the sole purpose of machines being to serve human convenience.

Guilloux opened the bonnet. The carburettor was full of what seemed to be a mixture of rust and sand, deposited by an assortment of black-market petrols. The cup itself was chipped and leaked heavily, so that it was at the risk of a fire that Guilloux eventually restarted the car and drove it slowly out of the Forest and to a garage at the far end of Puits.

We stood in the garage yard. Along the road, three or four carts driven by gypsies trundled towards Paris. Perhaps ten horses and ponies of various sizes were harnessed to the shafts. Perhaps ten others, skewbald or pinto, followed or walked ahead, intermittently nibbling at the grass banks on either side. The scene was a peaceful one.

To console the Guilloux for their ruined outing Michel proposed dinner out at a hotel restaurant in the park. It was frequented by small, plump and noisy people with expensive clothes, Alsatian dogs and markedly underbred faces. Guilloux said they were all B.O.F.'s, i.e. black marketeers, the initials standing for *beurre, oeufs* and *fromage*, all forms of dairy produce being commodities still in short supply.

Fur-coated women sat alone, smoking thin cigarettes through holders. Perhaps it was to these women that the Alsatian dogs belonged. There were also a dozen or so young men in white plimsolls and track suits of black denim caught up at the ankle. They sat on the lawn in deck chairs and then, as the dusk deepened, were shepherded into the lounge by anxious-looking men who wore shoes and ordinary trousers. Like pugilists shadow-boxing, the young men, as they moved aimlessly among the other guests and customers, now and then rose up on their toes and sketched a movement of dribbling or evasion. They were the French football team, trained to a hair (next day, they beat Scotland). These tame and harmless animals, under the perfect control of their manager and trainer, clearly aroused lustful thoughts in the fur-coated women, who, however, were also counter-attracted by the vulgar little men with too much money and a knowing look.

From the tall windows of my room, I saw lights twinkling across the Seine. That was a more densely populated proletarian suburb towards Paris.

I awoke late. Michel was cutting Mass. The bathroom was full of steam. Downstairs, Michel, in a very English dressing gown, brown, with twisted cord, was frying an egg in a two-handled vessel made to fry one egg at a time. The napkins of the others lay beside places empty but for breadcrumbs. From a wireless set in the kitchen, there was the sound of dance music with vocal refrains in English, the Light Programme or Radio Luxembourg.

Arlette and her younger sister appeared before Mme de Moor came back from church. It was Arlette who drove me back to Paris in the afternoon. I dislike motorcars, on the whole, but there is something quite specially moving about the fingers and wrists of a finely bred girl (who clearly drives 'well') on the steering wheel of so dangerous a mass of hurtling, well-polished metal. Arlette has taken a job with a travel agency and has a flat half way up the hill towards Montmartre. I shall see her again in three weeks.

On Monday, I bought presents for the Thomases. At some time after ten, I went to the Gare de l'Est and found my place. The man in the top bunk was already asleep, snoring gently. I think he'd pinched one of my blankets. I had only one, a bright red, and I was cold during the night, so that I did not sleep much.

There were the pale-cream, silky oxen along the road, the houses, the crops and the Minster spire, the grey station, the two of them there to meet me, young Harold and not-so-young Atha, then Anton Walbrook, my room, Jeanne, breakfast, the parallel sheets of light through the white iron blinds, the sounds from the next room, the telephones in the small hours. At whatever time I awake, bells are ringing.

NO AUTHORS FOR MATTHEW LATIMER, ONLY POETS. *THE EXAMINER* seems satisfied with my first piece and looks forward to reading me on the military celebrations. In the meantime, they'd take paragraphs on the local industries or the state of political feeling. I looked round the brewery which supports a literary *salon* in the Rue Goethe (i.e. the husband owns the brewery, and the wife runs a literary *salon*). Vats, malting floors and so on. I gather too much maize has to be used, as in the bread. No paragraph in that.

Because of the heat, too many children swimming in the Ill just in front of the Palais des Rohan terrace. Three drowned yesterday. I might try the hunting-horn society or the beekeepers' syndicate. I had great hopes of the *pâté de foie gras* industry, but nothing much doing at this time of year.

The regional poet read his verses at the *salon*. So did a chubby little Franciscan, in brown robe, *béret*, heavy horn-rimmed spectacles and sandals. As he read, standing up, I watched his white toes wriggling under the table. Franciscans are fairly numerous in the city. The Hon. Bert tells me one of them is a good poet. That means he is published in Paris.

Not but that the *pâté de foie gras* expedition was a great success in its way. In the morning, the regional poet and I went round warehouses in the town. Stocks low. The stuff soon goes off in this heat. Then he, his wife and I were driven out to Wantzenau for lurch. The driver was a friend of theirs, a neatly made, red-haired widow, Mme Zix. Mme Zix is descended from a notable line of regional painters and men of letters. Oddly, she reminded me a little of young Harold's Orangerie girl, Annelies, of whom, of course, I had only the briefest glimpse.

This *café national* is not too bad. The rhubarb jam runs down my fingers. One thing the English do know is that rhubarb, which has no pectin, needs binding together with apple, which has a lot. Apart from breakfast time, the whole of this area is a gastronomical paradise, but the luncheon at Wantzenau stands out. The people in that one village have long specialised in ill-treating birds with delectable results. There must be some historical reason for this, but neither Mme Zix nor the regional poet knew what it was. Apart from stuffing geese in such a way as to give them swollen livers, they dwarf chickens. The Wantzenau chicken (which may in fact be a hen several years old) is a delicacy for one person. But also I do not remember having those thin chips called *pommes alumettes* cooked to such dry, brittle perfection. The wine was a *Gewürztraminer* of delicate fruitfulness, heavily iced.

The restaurant was cool and shady, the country roads outside shuddering with heat. It had been arranged that we should call after lunch at a certain farm, there to be shown the apparatus with which the geese are stuffed. You hold the bird between your knees, fit its beak over a steel tube, then pedal as if at a sewing machine. You thus force ground maize into the bird's drop. But this is not the season for stuffing.

Lunch today, *en toute intimité*, at the Prefecture, in its way, I suppose, the most admirable large building in the place. Mme P. an old friend of Marguerite Thomas's I thought Hon. Bert seemed a bit huffy when I told him, but admits both P. and Mme P. very nice, with attractive children.

FASHION NOTE, SATURDAY JUNE 12. THE POLICE ON TRAFFIC DUTY HAVE suddenly appeared in solar topees. They have also shed their tunics and stand displayed in navy blue shirt, white truncheon, white gauntlets the revolver holster and *casque coloniale* blancoed a dazzling white. A highly successful feature of the heatwave. Everybody likes it, not least the policemen.

I suppose General de Lattre de Tassigny duly held his military review and afterwards proceeded to the university, where the original documents of the Treaty of Westphalia, brought from Paris, were read aloud and expounded by learned gentlemen from the École des Chartres. I slept after lunch and missed all this. In the late afternoon, I passed in front of the university and observed the red carpet still lying on the pink steps, a curious colour clash and oddly forlorn. No doubt I shall pick up enough from some newspaper in the morning, and by Monday I shall be able to see the documents themselves on exhibition in one of the city's numerous museums, between the rows upon rows of French uniforms, a feast for moth and rust since Napoleon's time.

It really is terribly hot. In the hotel lift this evening, a perspiring fat man mopped his brow and told me that it was hotter here than in the Midi, as he ought to know, since he was from the Midi himself. It is a dreadful, steamy heat, though less so with nightfall.

Returning to the hotel about three hours ago, I was, however, before I reached my room, engulfed in horrible noise. There was choral singing, speechmaking, dance music. Sometimes it grew worse. It was drowned in a howling, a blasting. Then it broke off, and again you heard it distantly and undistorted. The Tannoy system wasn't working properly. This din has only just stopped. It is after midnight.

Across the road I could see rows of blue, white and red fairy-lamps, now extinguished. That is the bombed space beside St. John's, of which remains only a bare wall, with a small belfry against the sky. I had noticed advertisements for a Foire-Kermesse, to pay for the new building. I seem to remember church bazaars as being rather quiet affairs in England.

THIS MORNING, I WENT TO THE RHINE AGAIN AND BATHED AND LAY ON the spit of gravel where the Rhine proper and the Petit Rhin divide. I had a meal of Rhine sprats in the same cool restaurant, which I imagine to have been not-so-young Atha's February salvation. This afternoon, I slept again, with the iron shutters down.

Yesterday's parade (or, rather, Saturday's parade, and by the calendar I ought already to speak of yesterday morning on the Rhine and yesterday afternoon with the shutters down) has left a certain glamour in the streets. Zouaves, Spahis, Goumiers, stroll about in full regimentals. As I dined by an open window in the hotel, two strode past, 'dusk faces with white, silken turbans framed' (if I have got it right, Milton, though I dare say the turbans weren't silk), in long white, blue-lined, hooded cloaks, sandals on their brown feet, happily arrogant, much admired (by Serge and Pierre among others).

In the overheated concert hall, Fritz Munch (brother of Charles and principal of the Conservatoire, as their father was before them) conducted the massive Honnegger-Claudel *Jeanne d'Arc au Bûcher*, with Ida Rubinstein as Joan. One sweated in sympathy with the musicians, rather than listened.

Back here, I heard much the same din from St. John's across the road. The best way of not minding seemed to be to participate, if one could. I went over.

Young people were dancing on a tiny platform, to a band consisting of drums and accordion. The only stall left sold kitchenware, the rest of the open space being occupied by trestle tables at which older people, the very young with them, sat to drink beer and the regional champagne, which is called Dopff. There were brownies, wolf-cubs and young priests. Aged, toothless grandmothers sat and smiled happily at the generations around them. I felt very close to the heart of the people, yet spoke to nobody (except in getting myself a glass of Dopff). In French and in pre-war German films, one has seen shots of the faces of old peasantwomen smiling, faces so 'photogenic' that one wondered why the cameraman bothered taking shots of anything else. Under the massed, blue-white-and-red fairy-lamps and in the flicker of kerosene flares, there were all the faces of that kind.

A small tear did in fact form in the corner of one of my two eyes, the left one, I think. I suppose that, in essence, it was a tear of loneliness, for the aesthetic tear often turns that way. However, that corporate din is now all silent, and I am back in my room.

Tomorrow, lunch at the Prefecture again, with the flautist Rene le Roy. Hon. Bert distinctly green-eyed. Now too much persuaded I won't let the side down.

It is almost two o'clock. People are still walking about in the street. What they are seeking is the desire to sleep. I wish I could feel it myself. Turn in, anyway.

THE WEATHER BROKE WITH A CRASH. NOT SURE WHOSE IDEA THIS TRIP to Upper Alsace was, Hon. Bert's or the broadcasting director's. Possibly the two conspiring to meet some half-expressed wish of mine. Certainly, luncheon at Ammerschwihr had been laid on beforehand, so that the staff were on tiptoe when we arrived a good hour late. The *châtelaine* at Osthouse must also have been warned that we should call upon her in the morning. It was a first-rate idea, despite the storm.

The director of broadcasting is a Gascon. He was posted here at the Liberation to clean up broadcasting in the neighbourhood. His family are still at Tarbes. The lady to whom he refers as his 'necessity' here is, the Hon. Bert thinks, Mlle Lenepveu. His complexion is ruddy, his eyes brown, melting and salient. He speaks French with the stutter of a machine gun. My local affections are so far chiefly shared by him and by Mme P., a woman of great intelligence and perfect simplicity.

Like Mme Phinelius, the *châtelaine* at Osthouse speaks perfect English. The *château* dates back to the last crusade. The Germans The Germans did the most extraordinarily stupid things during the Occupation. They banned the wearing of *bérets*. In the city, they destroyed the statues of Joan of Arc, Rouget de Lisle and others and would have destroyed the portly figure of Kléber if the people hadn't themselves taken it down and hidden it before it was discovered that he was one of Napoleon's generals. They rased the Pasteur memorial in the university square. They altered the names on tombstones. At Osthouse, whose library contained irreplaceable treasures, they burned one volume out of each complete set of first editions.

Thunder, lightning and monstrous rain hit us as we came into Upper Alsace. I should have thought rain as bullet-like as that would be fatal to the infant grapes, like hail, but the director of broadcasting assured us that, on the contrary, it was raining wine ('us' included Hon. Bert's Irish secretary). We passed through Bennwihr and Mittelwihr, villages of which not one stone is left standing upon another as a result of American shelling. This is the area of which one used to hear on the wireless as 'the Colmar pocket'. The Gascon broadcasting director called it 'the graveyard of Alsace'. He said that, when the Americans approached Mittelwihr, a little walled paradise bequeathed us intact by the Middle Ages, it was defended by twenty-five German soldiers in all and that a whole division's artillery shelled the place flat before the American infantry would go in after those twenty-five. I do not know how true this is, though certainly it is better to be British than American in these parts.

The people cannot leave their ruins. Vineyards are not portable. After last year's record grape harvest, the people are prosperous again, for a lot of old wine too was saved. But they have nowhere to live except their precious cellars and prefabricated hutments. In the rain, gangs of German prisoners and Arabs were at last clearing the débris.

It was just beyond Mittelwihr that we ran through a lake in the road. The Hon. Bert could hardly be blamed for not seeing it. Too much rain was running down his windscreen for the wiper to deal with. Pale yellow mud washed over the car, and the engine stopped dead, drowned. Hon. Bert said there was nothing to do but sit there until it dried. Director of broadcasting insisted on us getting out and drying it. We got to Ammerschwihr, not quite so badly hit as Bennwihr and Mittelwihr, but pretty bad, and ate marvellously in a temporary restaurant built of planks.

The proprietor said the director of broadcasting was wrong about the effects of the storm. It wasn't a question of immediate damage to the infant grapes, but of soil being washed away from the roots of the vines. In several places, the roads were blocked with soil washed down from vineyard terraces which had collapsed. A cellar had been struck in Ammerschwihr. A man on a bicycle had been struck and killed.

Riquewihr is intact. The rain had cleared. As we alighted from the car to look at the buildings, we were accosted by an old man who spoke copious English with a Lancashire accent. He had been interned in Manchester at the outbreak of the Kaiser's war, the Alsatians at that time being German citizens. He invited us down to his cellar.

The trouble with drinking in cellars, if there are four of you, is that only one glass is used, so that you have to drain it each time before passing it to your neighbour. In this way, you drink an unusual amount of wine in a very short time and emerge blinking and fuddled into the sunlight.

On Friday, travel in the same direction again, but by train. It is the anniversary of General de Gaulle's first speech from London. The Hon. Bert is to address a Gaullist reunion of old comrades, arranged by a lawyer, Maitre Kalb, who during the war broadcast from London as 'Jacques d'Alsace'. There is even to be a small wreath-laying ceremony before dinner. All this strikes me as politically compromising, especially for an official representative of his country like the Hon. Bert. He doesn't agree.

'Isn't,' I said, 'de Gaulle now a politician and rather Fascist in tendency?'

'If you *will* read *The New Statesman*,' was Hon. Bert's slightly huffy rejoinder.

Hon. Bert is Conservative, royalist, Anglo-Catholic (and, for all I know, classicist). On the other hand, in his reading room off Titmouse Street, he fairly displays *all* the main English periodicals, including *The Daily Worker*. He assures me that all respectable people in the Colmar area are Gaullists and with reason. To be Gaullist there is non-political.

As Saturday is my day for joining a barge in Bâle and sailing back down the Rhine, the Colmar trip fits in quite well. The Hon. Bert further proposes to join me on this Rhine trip. We shall both take bathing costumes, dark glasses and Swiss francs. Erich von Stroheim will let me have ten Swiss francs.

THIS MORNING, I WALKED ROUND TO THE PLACE DE BORDEAUX. NOT much point in it, I thought. Three years ago, as soon as there were normal posts, I wrote to Fritz Willm. The letter was, as I'd rather expected it to be, returned, marked '*parti sans adresse*'. Still, I thought I'd see if any of the tenants knew anything. None did.

After lunch, I met the Jewish doctor who knows Marguerite Thomas. He'd left a note at the hotel. He took me round the marvellous hospital. Marvellous in several ways. A lot of the new, glass-walled structures I can only assume to be admirable, but the old buildings follow the line of a part of the city walls and contain some very beautiful staircases.

My guide himself had survived Auschwitz. During the war, the German medical faculty installed at the university here was heavily involved with the Struthof concentration camp. It was, as the doctor several times repeated, a small, experimental camp. Before his elevation to a larger sphere, the infamous Josef Kramer was its commandant. There he organised the first gas chambers and prepared cadavers for the medical faculty, whose head was one Josef Hirth, who is still at liberty.

A colleague of the Jewish doctor brought out and showed me the big albums of evidence prepared against Hirth's eventual trial. There were Kramer's accounts of the first gassings of women, which he observed through a specially constructed peephole. The women, for the most part Jewish, were thrust into the gas chamber naked. Kramer (or a stenographer sitting with him) noted down, second by second, their symptoms, from mere screams to the defecation which invariably took place towards the end of the proceedings, normally brief but sometimes experimentally prolonged. There were also numerous photographs of dissected cadavers. The identity of some had since been established by the branded numbers still visible upon attached or severed arms.

My reaction to all this was, of course, coloured by a good deal of organic nausea and horror. No doubt I should have felt this equally if confronted with some cadaver innocently pickled and dissected. The doctors, to whom sights of that kind were customary, were alone capable of viewing the matter with a balanced moral displeasure. Yet we appoint juries of medically untrained minds to appraise cases in which are involved things likely to provoke organic disturbance, to which even his many years of legal training can hardly render even the judge immune.

*

COLMAR IS A JEWEL OF A TOWN, AND STORKS HAVE NESTED ON TOP OF the Burgundian-tiled pro-cathedral itself. Its Unterlinden museum houses the famous Issenheim retable by Matthias Grünewald, always wrongly described as a 'German' painter, as well as a great many paintings by Martin Schongauer. The suffragan bishop and the commander of the garrison were present at the Hon. Bert's lecture, which he delivered very well. The colonel stayed with us, and we went to the house of another lawyer, General Leclerc's *aide* during the war, where we drank and talked until after midnight.

Hon. Bert and I thus occupied our hotel rooms for somewhat less than two and a half hours. By three o'clock, we were up again and waiting for the train to Bâle.

At Bâle, we battled through the crowded customs. At a spotless hotel, in the morning sunshine, we ate a wonderful breakfast of snow-white *croissants* with mountains of butter and lakes of fresh milk. Then we set out to find St. John's Bridge, where our instructions were to embark.

By nine o'clock, we found our vessel. It was not a barge. It was a paddle steamer. Under awnings were already sitting dozens of barge owners and their wives and daughters, navigators of the Seine, the Rhône, the Saône, the Scheldt. At the head of the gangway, girls in Swiss national costume gave us chocolate, literature and cigars. Swiss guns fired a salute as the steamer turned about in the river and departed from the land of hard currency and perpetual peace. I put it on record that I have now spent some two hours of my life in Switzerland.

That was ten hours ago. Clearly, the Hon. Bert and I would not have needed our bathing costumes and dark glasses, even if it had not come on to rain. It has just stopped raining.

At eleven o'clock, the steamer halted in the lock at Kembs. We disembarked and were shown over the vast electricity generator, a sort of Dnieprpetrovsk of the Rhine. It was grandiose, but wet. The dynamoes hummed. We steamed.

Once more on board, we sat down under the awnings to a luncheon of trout, chicken, rum omelettes, Riesling and Mirabelle and listened to speeches on the future of river navigation. The two banks of the Rhine are identical. There are poplar trees. Every few hundred yards, there is a smashed concrete gun-emplacement. It rained. It was very cold. The awnings dripped.

We came in sight of the spire of Kehl church two hours ago. Hon. Bert and I agreed. Even if this were now the fourth port of France, he and I did not propose at the moment to float round and round it in a motor-launch and be shouted at by a man with a megaphone. We had done our bit. We deserted, at whatever peril to international relations.

Let the harbour area be 551 *hectares*, with a water surface of 133 *hectares*, 18 grain warehouses and a coal-storing capacity of 600,000 tons. Let it. Let the Rhine question remain forever unanswered. Once our feet were on dry land, Hon. Bert and I ran for the first tram. Back at the hotel, I got Jeanne to run me a hot bath and now write extended on the *chaise longue*, the pamphlets they gave me on the marble-topped table at my side.

It is dinnertime. I shall walk slowly down four flights of red-carpeted stairs. In the dining room, I shall flirt with the two serious American girls at the next table, beneath the delighted, conspiratorial and benevolent gaze of Serge, Pierre and the old head waiter whose name is Jean.

A COCKTAIL PARTY AT THE REGIONAL POET'S. HON. BERT ASKED, TOO. Also Gascon head of broadcasting. Also Festival organiser, a doctor. Jolly, short, sensual, with a moustache. Was in England before the war, likes us, was particularly impressed by Oxford, but wonders how all those young men, obviously compelled by college regulations to do without women, manage, when they eat so much roast beef. Head of broadcasting very appreciative of this point.

Also Mme Zix. After a drink or two, very attractive. Short, broad, dyed-hair, but firm, neat figure and white skin. Again struck by her resemblance to the Orangerie girl. Forehead, I suppose, and mouth. Older, I suppose, yet perhaps not. Less than forty, I'd think, perhaps a lot less. I don't think I'd respond if she was near forty. Mme Zix is the *femme de trente ans* with complications.

This not the point, however. Not yet desperate for women. Point is Fritz Willm.

I told Mme Zix about my visit to the hospital. By what to me was a natural association of ideas, I then told her about the Willms. Jews, I said. I wondered what. I suppose I was then a bit pompous with drink.

Mme Zix laughed. She knew the Willms.

Not Jews in the least, she said. A very good Protestant family. The Willms had spent the war at Limoges. Mme Willm was dead. Both Fritz and Jean were married. Fritz could be easily found at the railway administration.

THE HON. BERT HAS GONE AWAY FOR A HOLIDAY IN BRITTANY, LEAVING me his office to write in, a great blessing, as the weather is again poor, after a hot weekend. He is also spared rage and envy at my third invitation to the Prefecture, this time for dinner and to see the leopard cub Cornut-Gentil has sent his successor's children from Africa.

On Saturday, I went to tea at the Willms' in the new residential area behind the Orangerie. Tea consisted of ham, pineapples with kirsch and two bottles of good wine, apparently produced by relations of the Willms at Barr. We are to visit the vineyards.

The diminutive 'Fritz' was always understood to be short not for 'Friedrich' but for 'Frédéric'. The young Mrs Willm calls her husband 'Fred'. Her features are quite pretty, but pinched. She wears spectacles. Her fair complexion is admirable. Not quite sure whether she may be described without qualification as a hunchback. Fritz himself gives an impression of hunchedness. His chest is very broad, his shoulders powerful, his neck short and his head set a bit forward. This overdevelopment may, I suppose, have taken place in the attempt to remedy an initial weakness. For all I know, Mrs Willm may also be a strong tennis player, but there is definitely a hump. In the matter of clear eyes, good skin, vivacity, there is no indication of her being anything but physically healthy at the moment, but she strikes one as what is known as 'delicate'. One fancies she must have been very ill at one time over a long period.

I could not imagine myself being physically attracted by her. Fritz's sexual experience was always wide. He never had to make do with plain girls. There is something odd about the marriage. This is the kind of thing I don't like saying. To speculate on other people's relations with each other is vulgar at the best of times, especially if one is looking for oddities. I have no reason to suppose that the two are not happy with each other, given that Fritz is not of a happy temperament.

Mrs Fritz also works in the railway administration. She is terribly proud of her husband. Much of her conversation is an appeal to the listener to keep him safe. I tried to draw Fritz about young Harold and not-so-young Atha. All I got were references to a young woman called '*la Lithuanienne*', presumably Harold's Maria, the broken-hearted singer. Fritz did not seem to have heard of the girl at Sarrebourg. I could not pursue the subject. Mrs Fritz did not like it. She was unable to tolerate the thought of her husband knowing other women in the past, although it was not a question of his women.

I felt:

'Her jealousy is a poniard from whose hilt she never takes her fingers.'

I also felt that, much as one respected her pathos, one might never experience real compassion towards her. In some way, she invited the blow to fall. By anticipating it, she hoped that, when the time came, she would know how to laugh it off. One knew that she would not. She knew that she would not.

Another thing I felt was:

'He has married a deformed girl so that his mother in Heaven will not visit him with jealousy and punishment.'

Of course, it is equally possible that Fritz feels himself to be deformed and that he has married a girl with the same but worse, deformity in order that they may play hunchbacked babes in the wood together. But Fritz was mother-dominated. Mme Willm was a vampire mother. In England, vampire mothers tend to produce homosexual sons. Not so abroad, where the duty to the mother is anal, economic. Still, oddities must ensue. It seems possible that Fritz Willm, able to seek handsome girls when his mother was alive (though either socially inferior or widowed), felt that only a cripple was possible after her death.

But, really, all happiness is precarious. Unless they are people of quite exceptional real strength or mere complacency, the recently married could be expected to feel and show anxiety in proportion to the happiness they have discovered. Because she is not attractive to me, that does not make Mrs Willm's anxiety less simply charming, less touching, less delightful. So far as their temperaments allow, I am sure Fred and she are happy, and I hope they remain so.

Economically, Fritz too is worried. He talks about the cost of living, and I suppose that the office worker feels it worst here just as he does in England. The notion is that Fritz is to hire a car to take us to Barr, but of course that I pay for it. He seemed to want to avoid finally committing himself to the excursion until he had talked to the garage proprietor. He felt, it was clear, that the price demanded might be too high and that, when it came to the point of paying, I might abscond.

He kept saying that it might cost so-and-so or even so-and-so and watching me closely to see how I reacted. Somebody must have stung him very badly at one time, for I am certain that he himself is agonisingly honest.

The weather is settling down to intermittently showery gloom. I hope it is brighter for the Hon. Bert in Brittany and for Blod and the children on Cardigan Bay. I am possessed by the quaintest thought about Blod. I want to drink sherry out of her navel. For more than ten years now, in all my happiest moments, there she has lain, old Flowerface, belly upward, that tiny cup quite unused, except once, before our marriage, when, doubtless under the influence of *Lady Chatterley's Lover*, I tried to arrange violets in it, there being in the garden outside a cold frame in which these sweetest, most unobtrusive flowers bloomed in December. It would be silly with most girls. They would giggle, and the sherry would run out over the sheets. With, possibly, one quiver because the liquid is so much below blood heat, Blod's belly will be still, and I can lower my face to drink up the sherry, and she will be looking at me with those friendly eyes.

Cook's in the Place Kléber can't get me a sleeper to Paris till Friday or a place on the Golden Arrow till next week. I shall see Arlette in Paris. This evening, I am taking Jeanne to the big fair, where no doubt we shall ride on erotically stimulating roundabouts, switchbacks and cakewalks and where I shall display male prowess by knocking coconuts out of deep cups. I was never a tremendous cricketer, though not bad at football of any kind.

On a pole fixed through this window hangs, over Titmouse Street, a Union Jack, which Hon. Bert always pulled in at sundown. I suppose the secretaries do this in his absence. They type and talk and make coffee beyond that door. Beyond them is the reading room. There are exposed all the periodicals and pamphlets and books illustrating the British way of life. Two north-country voices audible a few minutes ago at first from there and then nearer in consultation with the Irish secretary might have been those of young Harold and Umpleby but are in fact the voices of Smith and Taylor from Manchester.

FROM ARLETTE'S FOURTH-FLOOR BALCONY, HALFWAY UP THE HILL TOwards Montmartre, I look down into a sunny side-street. From a house on the other side, an old lady on a stretcher has just been carried out to a waiting ambulance. A group of children are playing some game with a ball. There have been first communions. Their brassards do not impede two boys, but a girl immobilised by her ankle-length muslin dress looks wistfully on. Arlette is engaged in cooking a *carré de porc* as it should be done.

The afternoon yawns emptily before us. An art gallery threatens. It is Sunday.

I was in Paris for breakfast yesterday. I recall the low-grade bread and coffee at the Gare de l'Est and the unshaven young soldier already drinking *marc* at the same table.

The fairground lay in a part of the city I had not visited before. I suppose that markets are held there, or perhaps that vast concrete space is normally used as a military parade ground. Stalls, booths, roundabouts, swings and the rest were distributed in orderly formation, their lights on. It was already near dark, and a fine drizzle fell.

There is something quite particularly eerie about a deserted fairground or, rather, about a fairground fully manned but with no other customers than oneself and a companion. The attendants stood at their lighted stalls, holding out to us rifles or handfuls of wooden balls. The mechanics were to hand by the buttons and levers of motionless dodgems, cakewalks, chairoplanes, dippers, walls of death. A steam organ blared, stopped, blared, faltered and stopped. I accepted a rifle butt and fired at a celluloid ball kept up by a jet of water. Jeanne aimed darts at large numbers and hit small ones. It was hard to decide whether we ought to ride on anything. We felt we ought to encourage these men faced by imminent ruin, but on the other hand it could hardly be worth their while to start up those mighty wheels and pistons for twenty francs. We twice climbed the steps of, and on mats slid down, a helter-skelter, which required no mechanical aid. In the end, we got some chairoplanes started up and whirled centrifugally round, but without a surrounding hubbub of other voices Jeanne couldn't even squeal properly. The man seemed quite pleased to have two customers.

I was reminded of the Sartre film, *Les Jeux sont faits*, which I had seen in London earlier in the year. The lovers danced on an empty café terrace to the faint sound of an invisible orchestra. They were dead, but did not quite know it, as they whirled in slow motion round and round. Jeanne is not an imaginative girl, but I felt that it all seemed posthumous even to her. It was a bit cold in the drizzle, but that hardly accounted for her suddenly shivering as we left the big fair and made our way to a stationary tram.

Jeanne, it turns out, has a baby which she leaves with her aunt at Schwindratzheim. The father was a German sergeant. In those parts, that kind of thing met with more tolerance than it seems to have done elsewhere in France, at any rate among the working class. There was not much immediately post-war hair-clipping of young women by the neighbours. There may have been some unpleasantness with rich employers belatedly much concerned to be French. Jeanne's working at a hotel in the city has something to do with circumstances of that kind.

If I had known so much about Jeanne a month ago, I wonder if I should have got on to the same terms of teasing friendliness with her, to say nothing of the subsequent horseplay. I might not. I couldn't regret it now, of course. I am no great admirer of my own character, but I couldn't, I hope, ever be left without some tenderness for a woman I'd been at all intimate with. Still, to collaborate with the Germans was not a good thing, even in those parts, even among feather-brained young women, even with comparatively inoffensive and good-looking young Germans, even although the collaboration itself was of a wholly non-political nature and, indeed, not even commercial except in so far as it might result in an extra bottle of milk or half-pound of meat. As to any possible harm to one's neighbours, it might even have resulted in somebody not being arrested.

But I suppose that was not collaboration, merely fraternisation. I fancied that Annelies might have collaborated in another sense. That is why, three years ago, when I wrote to Fritz Willm and got the letter back marked '*parti sans adresse*', I did not also write to Sarrebourg and why, during the past month, I took no train there.

Perhaps I was coldly censorious on inadequate grounds. Perhaps I have been a bit bloody-minded (or lazy). Young Harold seemed to think so, when it had all been explained to him.

It was on Monday evening that I took Jeanne to the fair. On Tuesday morning, I called at the *syndicat d'initiative* kiosk in the station square, to pick up fact-containing leaflets which might help with any further pieces *The Examiner* wanted. As I left, young Harold was emerging from the station entrance, he too being somewhat half-heartedly concerned with his departure.

The scene of my arrival was, so to speak, re-enacted in reverse, except that our middle term was omitted. Although it was almost two and a half hours later in the day, the effect was helped by an alternation of cloud and sunshine. Uncertain of his next movement, Harold stood in shadow before the station entrance. I joined him. He was staring across the vast expanse of the square.

'Oh, hello,' he said.

Across the square, one of a row of hotels lay in ruins. 'You've noticed?' I said.

'Yes. That's where I spent the first two nights, before I went to the Willms.'

'There was a war,' I said.

'Yes, there was going to be a war.'

'You knew that?'

'He knew. Our middle term.'

'The pseudo-Atha?'

'*He* doesn't like being called the pseudo-Atha. He says, if anybody's the pseudo-Atha, it's you.'

'He didn't seem very friendly,' I said.

'He felt that about you.'

'Well,' I said, 'I'm sorry about that. It was only because I felt his disapproval.'

'I think he was afraid of you condescending.'

'He disapproved of what I was up to. He didn't like my clothes. He resented the fact that I was staying comfortably in a hotel and eating at good restaurants and meeting all the local celebrities. He didn't understand. I was paid for. I couldn't have got here at all, otherwise. I had to take a job because I have four mouths to feed. As to the natty gents' pin-striped suiting, it's my demob suit, a present from the Army. It's the only suit I've got, apart from a dinner jacket. I don't much like it myself. For one thing, of course, clothes are rationed. Even hats. I don't like that turf hat myself. You can't nowadays "starve" in that picturesque manner. As to my hair being short, when you've got as little hair as I have . . .'

'Yes,' said young Harold, 'that was a bit of a shock.' There he stood, in his silver-grey plus fours, the slight reddish tinge sun-bleached out of his hair, the pale-blue eyes in the brick-burnt face looking at me with gentle, earnest puzzlement. The northern accent was strong.

'That war . . . ?' he said.

He looked across the square again at the rubble-strewn gap in the row of hotels.

'I suppose it would be an American bomb,' I told him. 'At least, it was an American bomb which made that hole in the nave of the Minster.'

'You mean that the Americans and the French . . .?'

'No,' I said. 'No, wars are different now. You drop bombs on your allies for strategical reasons.'

I was made to explain, of course. That took some time.

'I remember,' said Harold, 'something about a war. I remember seeing the Place Broglie. There was a tram overturned. I looked up, The Minster was still standing. Then I . . .'

'*You* remember?' I said.

'You're not the only one who remembers!'

'All right,' I said. 'Tell me, then. What were you doing . . . yesterday, for instance?'

'Yesterday? Why, I—I . . .'

'You were doing nothing,' I said, 'because I didn't think about you. In the past seventeen years, you've lived in occasional flickers, when I had you in mind. You forget, or, rather, you haven't quite realised, that without me you don't exist.'

'And yet I do remember! I remember the tram and the spire of the Minster, and then I remember the Rue des Remparts in Sarrebourg, where . . .'

I cut in.

'Yes,' I said, '*I* was at the pictures. In Rome.'

He looked at me sharply.

'And there on the screen, in a newsreel, were the two scenes you describe. There, when the camera moved to Sarrebourg, was a French 75 in action. You could see across the valley to where the Germans were firing, and there behind the gun was that house in the Rue des Remparts where Annelies's mother . . . I gulped aloud in the cinema. But wait a minute,' I said. 'You never saw that house. You were never in Sarrebourg. *He* was.'

Young Harold's pale-blue eyes registered trouble. Then he shrugged.

'Yes, that's true,' he said.

He looked at me critically.

'I wouldn't have thought you were the sentimental type,' he said.

I modestly pretended that I wasn't. Then, of course, he began to pin me down about what I'd done. I told him about the Fritz Willm letter returned marked '*parti sans adresse*' and had to admit that there had been no '*partie sans adresse*' letter back from Sarrebourg in respect of Annelies, that in fact I had done nothing about her. I told young Harold about the headcroppings of young women who'd collaborated and my feeling of certainty that collaboration would have been Annelies's line. I had to face the question whether *he*, our middle term, not-so-young Atha, would have been equally unforgiving or lazy or whatever it was, since it was only he and not I who might reasonably have felt some annoyance with Annelies and, indeed, only on *his* account that I claimed to feel anything at all, *he* being, we both agreed, in a singularly unreliable frame of mind at the time.

'At any rate,' I said, 'it's too late now.'

And I told Harold about my visit to Fritz Willm's and our evening trip by car to his cousin's vineyard and the rather delightful drinking that went on there. By this time, we had crossed the station square, turned up the Rue Kuhn and were passing the hotel, behind whose restaurant windows late breakfasters and mid-morning coffee-drinkers sat. Young Harold was displeased with me, and no more was said until we came into Titmouse Street. There I pointed out to him the Hon. Bert's Union Jack drooping from its second-floor balcony. This failed to arouse Harold's interest.

In the Place Broglie, he distended his nostrils and sniffed the air.

'Too late in the summer for lime-blossom,' I said. 'Besides, I'm afraid they weren't limes.'

I got a look which began with quick fury and ended with helplessness.

'Those on that side,' I said, 'are pollarded horse-chestnuts. Those both at this end and by the theatre are plane trees. On the terrace at the Orangerie, the trees over the tables are pollarded horse chestnuts.'

In front of the mayor's house, I reminded young Harold, there had once stood a bronze Joan of Arc. The Germans had melted it down. In the Place de la Republique, there was talk of magnolias.

'Yes,' I admitted, 'those were magnolias all right.'

'They cupped the moonlight,' said Harold.

'Yes,' I said, 'I'm sure.'

In the great space in front of the university, the first thing that struck him was that the bookshop had moved to the opposite side of the square. The Gallia was intact and still, or again, the Gallia. Then he saw that, in the middle of the square, the most important landmark of all had gone. There was no Pasteur memorial fountain, with its gilded obelisk. Where it should have stood, red and gilt, against the red steps before the pale-grey university, there was only a great circle of uneven concrete, like a fairies' ring in asphalt. My regret about this was so obviously genuine that young

Harold's mood towards me softened. I could almost see in his mind the image of Sonya and Cesia and Maria and Mieczyslas and the Austrian Jewish twins and Umpleby and himself grouped about that fountain on a sunny morning in late April or early May. It had not been, in itself, an object of any great beauty.

'You'll see,' I said, 'that the French have not, in revenge, taken Goethe's statue away or changed the name of Goethe Street. The French are rather less awful than the Germans.'

This last was a bit of a dig, but my companion didn't rise. (Not satisfied with that sentence. Clearly, one doesn't 'rise' to a 'dig'. I suppose the sense also is clear, but perhaps this is my cue to look out over the street again. Nothing. No first-communion dresses or stretcher cases. And go kiss Arlette behind the ear, while discovering how far the *carré de porc* is from being *au point*. That took longer than expected, because, despite the cooking instrument in her hand, she turned to me. I love her, I think. In fact I'm sure I love her, if that kind of intelligent, resigned thing is love. I can't believe my luck. Ten minutes. With the asparagus and the baby marrows, perhaps twenty.) Young Harold. Yes. We got on a tram to the Rhine.

'Have you got your passport?' he said.

'Passport?'

'Don't say the world has got rid of passports at last.'

'Oh, no, more than ever. But the other side is French territory now. I dare say you have to show some kind of permit to get beyond Kehl.'

'The bridge isn't there.'

'Not that bridge.'

'No shabby French soldiers this side, smart German ones that, unconvincingly ignoring each other.'

We set foot on the wooden bridge. There were concrete pillars remaining of the old bridge. The wood was hot through my soles of post-war leather. The church seemed to be the only building left standing in Kehl. No trains crossing the High Street. The church. It struck eleven.

He wanted to cross. He liked Germany, he said. (That had been the point of the 'dig', if digs have points.) I let him go. On the near side, there was something odd floating towards me. It was a human head. There were two human heads. Very strong swimmers. They pushed themselves off from a spit of land and knew, I suppose, where they would land up. Then a Swiss barge, rounding the bend at no end of a speed. Its ripples pulled at the reeds.

That evening, I saw the panther cub. They had a Minister's wife staying at the Prefecture. I cannot remember a more strictly desirable woman, and that is odd. I can see that she might have been just a short, dark peasant woman, with good features but with a moustache and hairy legs. In fact she was a blissful creature, in, I suppose, a pale-green taffeta (not sure about taffeta and satin) evening frock, with either palegreen-and-silver or just silver evening sandals with moderately high heels and, unexpectedly, bare legs rather brown and without a trace of hair or even down, the feet very small and beautifully formed, the well-shaped, flat nails on the short toes varnished in some colour expertly chosen. There might well have been, with the supposed-underlying peasant woman, *du monde au balcon*, but one might then have guessed at a few long, dark hairs clustering about the *areolae* of the nipples. About those unexamined, presumably dark-coloured nipples, one felt sure there was no such thing. It was a queen of smooth, beige bosoms mildly concealed by pale green taffeta or heavy satin calculated by some *haut couturier* for no other purpose. And yet the eyebrows were thick and strong. There was no trace of a moustache.

The point is that the panther cub had claws. It scratched me, and then it scratched her. One understands pornographers. One only regrets that, including Pierre Louys, they are so crude. The delicate claws at those legs, those shoulders and that bosom, the curious *fearlessness* of legs, shoulders and bosom to the delicate, transparent claws, nearly drove me out of my mind.

The Minister's wife was staying. I could not stay. I think the Minister was of Education. The P.'s have adorably well-brought-up children. They are handsome, the daughter a younger Arlette, very fair, like Mme P., P. being dark and rather small. There is nothing I more admire than good upbringing. I must try to bring Blod's children up well.

The human animal responds. From the beauty and simplicity of their mother's nature and manners, the young P.'s become adorable. They won't know why people love them. Of course, they are handsome. They are more handsome than their mother.

The leopard cub will become unmanageable. It is to be given to the zoo at Mulhouse. The *carré de porc*, the asparagus and the *courgettes*. Blissful, intelligent Arlette brings them lovingly to the table. I make a last-minute attempt to help.

THEN, OF COURSE, I SAW HIM AGAIN ON MY LAST WALK ROUND THE ORrangerie. The clock over Josephine's pavilion struck four. Nearby stood the goose-girl statue. The gardeners were potting out geraniums.

I walked in the direction of the little zoo and the restaurant where the waitresses no longer wore Alsatian costume, then turned left along the main walk on the near side of the boating lake. Birds sang, but it was an illusion that from across the lake one heard Tauber singing:

Adieu, mein kleiner Garde Offizier . . .

The trees were very tall overhead.

There he sat on a park bench, dwarfed in the green aisle, notebook on knee, the black and white marbled notebook, the black pen loaded with violet ink, the knee covered with pale-grey flannel. He wrote an immature hand, affecting the Greek ε. The lines on the left-hand page went:

> In the water, a simple medallion
> Softer clinks, where line relaxed and substance
>> Fall thinly starred;
> Where the gaze cools and rests easily on
> The crumbly round and steaming split-glance
>> Of a bedded moon-shard.

> But onward, and between the drowse of trees
> Two final lamps in the palace windows twitch
>   And die.
> But upward, and a watcher starts and sees
> A tongue of cloud creeping over . . .

I prompted him:

> . . . that licks . . .

And he completed the stanza.

> . . . A tongue of cloud creeping over, that licks
>   The moon from the sky.

'The previous stanza's a bit clotted,' I said. 'You'll have to clean it up.'

'Yes,' said young Harold, 'or throw the poem away. Those last two lines aren't too bad. Of course, it wasn't a palace, just the lights turned off at the restaurant over there last night. And the moon in this water just in front of us.'

' "Steaming"?' I said.

'Hot day, yesterday,' he explained. 'At any rate, you can imagine a ripple splitting the reflection, then decomposing it.'

'Decomposing it first,' I said, 'then leaving it just split. This is goodbye, I'm afraid.'

'Where's . . .?'

'Our middle term? The authentic Atha?'

'Yes.'

'He couldn't bear it. He's gone.'

'Back home?'

'I think he meant to, but his money gave out. He's stranded . . . in Brussels.'

'That's not a bad idea.'

'At any rate,' I said, 'Brussels is full of churches. And Easter comes early this year.'

Young Harold grinned. He was clearly about to tell me that it was long past Easter and Whitsun, too.

'In his world,' I said, 'it's always Lent. The images are covered.'

'The what?'

'It's a thing they do in Catholic churches, towards the end of Lent. They drape pieces of violet and purple cloth over all the holy images.'

'Because there's a bad time coming for old Jesus?'

'That's not the way to put it,' I said. 'It's "in anticipation of the mysteries of Good Friday".'

'I like that,' said Harold.

'Of course, on another plane of time, he got back home months ago. Well, home. London. Since then, he's been staying very comfortably at two places in the country, and he's just off to a third. If he did but know just what was in store for him in the near future, he might feel a bit more cheerful. He'd certainly be surprised.'

'What's in store?'

'Oh, well,' I said, 'there's a sort of Welsh girl, with a romantic, unpronounceable name. She turns out all right. They get married within a year. Legally, I mean, within a year.'

Young Harold didn't know what to make of that. There'd been an Eirwen at Rhyl and a Gwyneth in Hinderholme just before he left. He was prepared to have views on Welsh girls, but not on marriage.

He wanted to know what was in store for him. I couldn't tell him much. I told him he'd win the composition prize. I told him he ought to work harder at the university, but he paid no attention to that. I sketched out the next few days for him.

Apart from the discomfort of nearly ten hours on an unpadded pillion, he'd have two narrow escapes on the projected excursion with the terrible Turk. In fact, if Attila didn't accidentally turn the gas off when hitting a pile of gravel by the side of a winding, ascending mountain road, young Harold's leg would be torn off. Still, it would turn out all right. Then Attila would start expatiating on Turkheim and the Turks overrunning Europe and the last war and begin casting aspersions on

French valour at an inn in French-speaking Lorraine, near the Petit Armand and its catacombal memories of Verdun, and young Harold would have to get him away fast if the two were to avoid being lynched. A thunderstorm would then begin travelling backwards and forwards between the Vosges and the Black Forest, and they would be drenched, and young Harold would puke his guts up all night. Still, the experience would have no lasting effects.

I showed young Harold the scar on my top lip.

'That's funny,' he said. 'My father has a scar there, just under his moustache. He got it before they moved into Hinderholme. They were playing at hide-and-seek around the farm, and another boy came looking for him with a hayfork.'

'Well,' I said, 'on the way home, you pick up with students from other universities who've been at Besancon, Bale, Lille and Nancy. The boat's gone, and you have to spend a night in Dunkirk. There are quite interesting brothels in Dunkirk. At one, when some unsuspecting sailor gets on to the job, they wind up a partition between the room he's in and the café next door. When you troop out, pretty well oiled, you find, in a pool of blood under a lamppost, a Lascar's top lip. I don't think it's your idea. I think it's the idea of a sophisticated youth from Birmingham. However, you've all read a good deal of Baudelaire and so on, and you decide that cannibalism might be a thing to boast about afterwards. At the hotel, you toast the top lip and then cut it into small pieces. You're lucky. You get a crisp bit without moustache. You're the only one who gets it down. At the end of it all, you're the only cannibal among them.'

'Well,' said young Harold, 'I don't see how that gives you a scar on your top lip.'

I will say this. The conversation didn't appeal to Harold. I nevertheless persisted. I asked him whether he'd noticed a scar on pseudo-Atha's top lip. He hadn't. Quite right. There wasn't a scar on pseudo-Atha's top lip. I'd got mine two years later. In a pub off Charlotte Street, I'd met the sophisticated youth from Birmingham, now a flourishing journalist, a crime reporter when he got the chance and in his own mind an authority on the underworld.

He told everybody about this episode of the Lascar's lip in Dunkirk, made a hero of me and threw his money around. He was very keen on his own virility, which wasn't conspicuous, and he'd nursed resentment against me for seven years. Because of his intimate knowledge of criminal ways, he carried a razor in his boot top. Resentment and razor came out in Rathbone Place after closing time. He was quite easy to knock down and disarm, but he'd got in one slash as I stepped back. I was with a girl called Felicity Deems.

I said:

'As you see, the scar isn't much. But it's astounding how much blood there is in a top lip and how the lip will swell, way out beyond your nose . . .'

Young Harold didn't like this talk. At any rate, he'd vanished.

IV

A THING WHICH THE NEAR FUTURE HELD IN STORE FOR ME WAS that my father died. This left me, technically, head of the Atha family, although my mother is still alive and although I shall never quite feel head even of my own brood while my father-in-law, Idwal John, J.P., lives.

Early this year, we moved our London accommodation from Pitt Rise to Lower Green Road. The neighbourhood is less elegant, our rooms more numerous. The year's chief incidents so far have been my jaundice, Blod's miscarriage and an amusing conference in Oxford. The effects of jaundice are said to be lingering, and it may be that I view life with a jaundiced eye at present. Certainly, at the moment, I seem a bit queasy-gutted, but perhaps this is due to the dust and the heavily chlorinated water, which in its turn is due to the continued presence of bodies under the ruins.

This is Frankfurt-am-Main. My room is on the second floor of the American Press Club, formerly the Carlton, grandest of the remaining hotels. Johann Wolfgang von Goethe was born in this city two hundred years ago. My presence here is due to that fact. *The Examiner* has also agreed that I am to cover the Sessenheim idyll, and so by Friday evening next week I shall be on the other side of the Rhine again.

It is quite a pleasant room. The ceiling is high. The wallpaper, though faded, is clean, the faint design a pleasant one of flags and reeds, of Japanese inspiration. Four doors along the corridor, Heinz Friedenthal is no doubt cleaning his teeth with the bottled spa water he brought up for that purpose.

Odd, to think I had almost reached the age of thirty-eight before I ever went up in a civilian aircraft or flew by day. I can't say I much enjoyed the accompanying sensations, though my ears seem unbunged now and I suppose my soul has at last caught up with my body. It was interesting to discover that there is an horizon in cloudland. A bit disconcerting to see no angels sitting on the clouds.

Friedenthal, who became a Catholic five years ago, furtively crossed himself at the takeoff and again at the landing. Last year, in Hamburg, he had one of those apparently providential escapes, missing a plane which crashed (so that his wife in London thought he'd been killed). In the air, he drank a fair amount of brandy, but appeared confident that the plane would stay up, even when it started bounding and ducking over mountains, a shining river, at one moment the Rhine, at another the Main, vanishing and unaccountably reappearing, and the small boy in front was sick. I wasn't so sure. However rough it may be, there is always visible water under a boat. An aeroplane is kept up by hypothesis, by scientific 'laws' which, for all one knows, may be disproved while one is in the air.

We bumped gently several times, and the aeroplane neither turned over nor burst into flames. We'd gone forward to land, at the steward's suggestion, and one's eyes were troubled by the dazzle of retarded propellers, which, before the takeoff, I'd thought was the quivering of the fabric and that it would go on. Except for one's eardrums, one felt suddenly comfortable and rather tired. We taxied for miles around the airport. As the engines finally stalled, we heard the tannoy system.

'. . . Calling Major *Raabinson*. Major *Raabinson* report to A Block immediately, please. Calling Major *Raabinson*. Will Major *Raabinson* report immediately to A Block. Calling Major *Raabinson* . . .'

The sun burned down. In the end, we had got everything stamped that needed stamping and been issued with everything that needed issuing for the moment. Woods had been cleared for the Rhine-Main airport, and the bus drove along a cobbled road through woods, then out on to the *Autobahn*, past allotments, factories, ruined houses, then wooden, makeshift shops, a gay wine tent, banners and flags in a main street, the new German flag (red, black and gold), the blue and white municipal banner. Over the station entrance, in massive green bronze, a figure of Atlas, with two helpers, bearing the weight of Frankfurt on his shoulders.

Before the dark, smooth but frightened civilian receptionist could give us our rooms, a stocky, blond, tough-looking American colonel angrily scrutinised our passports and threw us hostile glances. An American bar, American drinks kept in a big, dark-red refrigerator advertising coca-cola. American voices, American food with a German accent which improves it, good coffee.

The bridge near the Carlton used to be called the Iron Bridge. Now they're rebuilding it, the Americans call it the Golden Bridge. Iron means something quite special to the Germans. No other people would have an iron cross as its noblest military decoration. In American military notices, the Germans are called 'indigenous personnel' (what they may use and must not). The other bridge is called the Old Bridge, but even before the war it was the *new* Old Bridge. These topographical details from Friedenthal.

He knew this town before the war. He remembers it chiefly in 1932, just before Hitler's advent to power, still a 'sober' town (not sure what the German word would be). It was, he says, probably the only German city which had remained 'sober'. One 'escaped' to Frankfurt, he says. He remembers a group of intellectuals who centred about the *Frankfurter Zeitung*. They'd sit in a smoky little *Weinstube*, drinking Palatinate wine served in jugs, talking art and philosophy. There were Walter Benjamin, Ernst Bloch, Paquet, Martin Buber. Benjamin poisoned himself in Paris in 1940, when the Nazis occupied that city. Paquet was killed here in an air-raid in 1944. Buber's independent Jewish state now exists. Friedenthal says he last heard of Ernst Bloch, a philosopher, washing dishes in a San Francisco hotel.

There are still black-marketeers loafing around the station entrance and elsewhere in the streets. One sees American soldiers with girls, and the German youths jeer at the girls. I thought one lot were going to start a fight this evening. Friedenthal describes this American occupation as the meeting of two barbaric cultures.

Gaily decorated brewery horses. Quite nice by the river. The church with the cross was the *Paulskirche*. We opened the only serviceable door in the remaining fabric of the cathedral and were confronted by the boot soles of worshippers packed into a vestry for Benediction. We shall be able to look inside the nave and sanctuary tomorrow, when the workmen are there. At the other end of the town, a medieval tower intact, the *Eschenheimer Tor*, and a bit of the old city walls. The past is very obstinate.

A flat, extensive town, with its heart torn out. A muttering, hateful town. No, a silent town. In the other, my rose-red city, rather less than half as old as time, the bells ring so loud all day you seem to hear them at night, too. Not here. A city without a tongue in its head. Silent, formless.

A siren. A police car, I suppose. It approaches, recedes. Then silence again. The smell of that chlorinated water from the tap. I don't fancy even cleaning my teeth with it. I must get bottled water from the bar, like Friedenthal.

MOUNTAINS OF PINK DUST AND RUBBLE, WITH FRAGMENTS OF HISTORY sticking up out of them. Willowherb, yellow ragweed, just like the parts of London that haven't been cleared. Worse, though. Much worse. The streets are choked with that dust.

Still, plenty in the shops. More than at home. Apparently, this has to do with a recent revaluation of the mark. Last year, Friedenthal says, if you smoked a cigarette in the street, anywhere in Germany, people would follow you, hoping to pick up the dog-end. Not now. We, of course, use the PX and buy American cigarettes for almost nothing, but even the indigenous personnel smoke, and most of them look well-fed. Every now and then, you see an ill-fed man in an old military uniform, walking fast with a stick, looking neither to right nor to left, a prisoner, it may be, not long released, who's walked all the way from Russia and is going as far west as he can before he drops. It seems one in eight of the population is now a refugee from the eastern zone.

Young men in *Lederhosen*, very brief. Young women in what is still called 'the new look', rather long, so that the male leg is more in evidence. It is rather a plump and often a carefully bronzed leg. The absence of the male leg is also in evidence. There are too many young men on crutches, far too many. I suppose that a nonexistent War Department cannot supply them with artificial limbs.

The Römer. Behind us the cathedral. In front, it was just possible to make out the shell of the old council chamber so lovingly described by Goethe in *Dichtung und Wahrheit*. A few stalls laid out on the slope, for the centre of Old Frankfurt was built on what, in a flat land, passes for a hill. At the midpoint of all that desolation, a bronze figure of Justice, eyes bandaged, right hand holding a pair of scales, remained intact on her pedestal. Highly symbolic, though of what it is difficult to say.

Odd circumstances bring the past to life. Goethe, for instance. He says:

> We did not fail to repair to the cathedral, and there visit the grave of that brave Gunther, so much prized by friend and foe. The famous stone which formerly covered it is set up in the choir. The door close by, leading into the conclave, remained long shut against us, until we at last managed, through the higher authorities, to gain access to this celebrated place. Ah, we should have done better had we continued as before to picture it merely in imagination; for we found this room, which is so remarkable in German history, where the most powerful princes were accustomed to meet for an act so momentous, in no respect worthily adorned, and even disfigured with beams, poles, scaffolding and similar lumber, which people had wanted to put out of the way.

Friedenthal and I did not fail to repair to the cathedral, a lacey, late-Gothic pile of no very great beauty, the spire intact, the walls broached. Workmen were going away and closing a rough door of dusty planks. They opened it for us again. Entering a cathedral, one expects the muted ringing of feet on stone, the reverent murmur of other visitors, an organ softly rousing the echoes, the pedal notes throbbing. Instead, we trod on bare earth, picked our way over bricks and timber and were suddenly appalled by what might have been the shriek of a pig with the knife at its throat.

It was a circular saw, of course, shrieking as the wood met it. In the sanctuary, they were turning out new choir-stalls and other church furniture on the spot. The cathedral was a mere shell, full of dust and debris. I didn't see Gunther's grave, but then, as I don't know who Gunther was, it doesn't matter. This Victorian translation of *Dichtung und Wahrheit* is full of words I can't quite attach a meaning to. I wonder if 'conclave' means the chapterhouse. Herr Lissner, of the *Frankfurter Rundschau*, is a Catholic and a scholar and may know.

A charming man and a good man. He adopts children. His latest is a black child, son of an American negro father, a G.I., and some local woman, his charwoman perhaps. Friedenthal has the *entrée* everywhere. Recorded something or other for the local broadcasting station this morning. Two important figures there called 'Bopp' and 'Herr'. Their office doors on the same landing bear the legends 'Herr Bopp' and 'Herr Herr'. Perhaps this strikes nobody but me as amusing.

The Goethe house also being restored, in time, they hope, for the centenary date. This also, by coincidence, connects up with the first chapter of *Dichtung und Wahrheit* and shall, certainly, thus connect up in *The Examiner*, which eases my work.

> At this time, too, my father undertook the reconstruction of the house. In Frankfurt, as in many old towns, when anybody put up a wooden structure, he ventured, for the sake of space, to make not only the first, but each successive storey, project over the lower one, by which means narrow streets especially were rendered somewhat dark and confined. At last a law was passed, that everyone putting up a new house from the ground, should confine his projections to the first upper storey, and carry the

others up perpendicularly. My father, that he might not lose the projecting space in the second storey, caring little for outward architectural appearance and anxious only for the good and convenient arrangement of the interior, resorted to the expedient, which others had employed before him, of propping the upper part of the house until one part after another had been removed from the bottom upwards, and a new house, as it were, inserted in its place. Thus . . .

But that, too, will do for the readers of *The Examiner*.

From the Römer, Friedenthal and I made our way along a path cleared through the débris. In a square hole which must have been a cellar, an old man was trying to lay out an allotment. Odder still, at a dizzy height, where a piece of floor projected from the solitary wall of a tall house, three women sat in deckchairs enjoying the sun.

We climbed over one of the smaller mountains of dust and came into the *Grosse Hirschgraben*. The house is being rebuilt to its original specifications. At present, it is a mere skeleton of new beams and joists, with a few of the original stones carefully inserted into their places over the doorway. A museum to the right of the house is already open. At the back, part of the house stands intact over a courtyard.

THE FLEISCHERFACHAUSSTELLUNG. FRANKFURT IS THE TOWN NOT ONLY of Goethe, Hölderlin, Schopenhauer, but also of the sausage and other pig products, indeed of meat in general. To young Goethe, the meat stalls were disgusting, and he flew past them in horror, but Victor Hugo lovingly described the old butchers' quarter in 1838. His description is printed in a German translation in a pamphlet we picked up at the butchers' exhibition. Friedenthal and Herr Lissner translated it for me. It seems to go:

Nowhere else are there such black, such ancient houses, leaning over such luscious piles of raw meat. Their curiously carved and ornamented facades are suffused by I know not what gluttonous merriment; their basements open like a dark abyss to swallow up countless carcases of sheep and oxen. Bloodstained butchers and rosy butcheresses chat pleasantly, with the joints of mutton strung in festoons over their heads. A blood-red stream, its colour scarcely softened by the rush of two fountains, flows noisily down the middle of the street. Butchers' boys, with faces cruel as Herod's, were even then preparing a bloodbath among the piglets, and servant girls with baskets on their arms yelled with laughter at the shrill uproar.

A butcher's boy was carrying one little pig by its hind legs: it did not squeal, for it had no idea of what its fate was about to be. I confess I wanted to buy the creature to save its life—but what on earth should I have done with it? A small girl of about four, noticing my pitying glances, implored me with her eyes to save it—but I did not do what the child's eyes demanded; I disobeyed their sweet, beseeching gaze, and I reproach myself for it. . . . But odder people than either Victor Hugo or I have written about this city. De Quincey wrote about it for the seventh edition of the *Encyclopaedia Britannica*, of all things, in the year of Hugo's account.

The present *Fleischerfachausstellung* is laid out on a great cleared space beyond the shopping centre. There are various pavilions, and stalls set out in them sell liqueurs, *bouillon* cubes, gleaming chromium-plated machinery for the manufacture of sausages. The arms of the butchers' guild show a portrait of St. Luke, the patron saint of butchers.

And so, what with Goethe, there are exhibitions both of *Geist* and of *Fleisch*. As Friedenthal says, the latter is the better attended. A defective language, German. The ghost is willing, but the meat is weak.

Friedenthal, Lissner and I went into a pavilion where you get sausages and beer at a counter and sit down at little tables to eat and drink. Three vast glasses of iced lager and three plates, on each of which reposed a freshly cooked Frankfurter sausage and a large dab of mustard. The sausages really were first-rate, pink and succulent. The ladies behind the counter were the wives of the richest butchers, the most elegant of rosy butcheresses.

Herr Lissner once wrote a *Kulturgeschichte* of the sausage, with an appendix on the haggis. Haggis is apparently mentioned in Homer. The suitors gave Odysseus the stomach of a goat filled with meat. Homer also says that at night a sleepless Odysseus turned over and over like a sausage on a spit. Herr Lissner recited the passage to us in Greek, a language I understand even less well than German. His declamation was accompanied by the sound of a barrel-organ playing Viennese waltzes by the pavilion door.

THROUGH THE AMERICANS, WE HIRE A VOLKSWAGEN AND DRIVE OUT beyond Bad Homburg into the Taunus mountains, winding through and above pretty mountain villages, pine forest. The Feldberg. A mass of rusted iron and concrete, where the R.A.F. wrecked an observation post. Beyond this to jutting rocks, with an incredible view over the plain.

This is Brünnhilde's rock. Here, ringed with fire, the daughter of Wotan awaited the hero's awakening kiss. Heinz Friedenthal reflects on vanished glory.

We return via Wiesbaden and try the *Spielcasino*. Friedenthal plays and wins a little. It is a small room, decorated in a gilded *Kitsch* which reminds one of Lyons' corner houses or the chapel at Ste-Odile or the interior of Sacré Coeur. Not many people. One very beautiful, shockingly well-dressed girl and an immaculate old boy perhaps her father, more likely a rich old *roué* with the incredibly beautiful *fausse-ingénue.*

The liturgy of roulette sounds very odd in German. In a singsong voice, the croupier's dark, heavy-lidded face emits, languidly:

'*Ein neues Spiel, ein neues, bitte . . .*'

A click. The ping-pong ball rolling down a slope.

'*. . . Nichts geht mehr.*'

The ball bounces over the ridges of the purring wheel, finally settles. '*Rot*' . . . '*Schwarz*' . . . '*Zero*' . . . or a number. According to this morning's paper, the croupiers of Monte Carlo, the aristocrats of their profession, are in America learning to shoot craps. They are going to introduce crap-shooting into the casino at Monte Carlo.

'*Ein neues Spiel, ein neues, bitte. . . . Nichts geht mehr . . . Rot.*'

On Sunday evening, after the last film performance, there is women's all-in wrestling at a cinema in Wiesbaden. We shall need the *Volkswagen* again for that. Tomorrow, we escape by another route. From the Valkyrie to Rhine-maidens. After Brünnhilde's rock, the *Lorelei*'s, down the romantic Rhine and back, as it might be to Southend, six marks fifty. The steamer, what's more, is called the *Rheingold.*

MUSIC ALL THE WAY. THE MOST PROMINENT CITIZEN ON BOARD WAS the gentleman who played the accordion. He was the *Stimmungsmacher.* His job, that is to say, was to keep us all in a jolly mood. He called out the places of interest and played alternately fore and aft.

The remarkable thing is how he keeps his own *Stimmung* up. He is a freelance, lives on tips. He goes to bed at one o'clock in the morning and gets up at half past five.

We started at seven and breakfasted on board. As you approach the *Lorelei*'s rock, the gorge narrows. We took a pilot on board. Till now there had been a merry traffic of barges, from Switzerland, Belgium, the Netherlands. In keeping with the romantic scenery and the ruined castles, even the entrance to a railway tunnel was decorated with Gothic pinnacles. But now, as if entering into the spirit of the thing, the sky grew suddenly darker, and it was cold. The water swirled, and it was easy to believe that inattentive boatmen had rushed here to destruction.

As the air grew colder, the German heart warmed. The *Stimmungsmacher* struck up the tune on his accordion, and they sang :

> *Ich Weiss nicht, was soil es bedeuten,*
> *Dass ich so traurig bin . . .*

Even the Nazis hadn't been able to stop people singing that. As Heine was a Jew, they'd gone on printing it in songbooks with the words attributed to 'author unknown'. On the way back, we stopped at the village of Assmanshausen, whose hotels and restaurants are recommended in the best guidebooks. Some of the passengers took an overland route to the *Niederwald Denkmal* 'Germania' monument and rejoined the boat a mile or two upstream. A woman who'd gone off that way with her pretty niece from the country confessed to us that she'd been so overcome with emotion up there that she'd sung 'The Watch on the Rhine', which is forbidden, like walking on the grass.

THE GIRLS HAD GIVEN THEMSELVES APPALLING NAMES. ONE, FOR INstance, was 'the Bull of Westphalia'. The most amusing was Rosie, 'the Wild Cat of Berlin,' whom the referee (male) had to warn repeatedly for biting, gouging, hair-pulling and other foul play. A concert of female grunting, shuffling, snarling, panting, whinnying with fright and the occasional shriek. At one point, Rosie claimed that another girl had bit her, and, when the referee wouldn't allow this, she attacked him.

A young man in front said to his girl:

'*Ich glaube, wir machen's doch Lieber auf die alte Art.*'

'*Benimm dich, Egon!*' she said.

He laughed. She viciously clawed his hand. I asked Friedenthal what the young man had said.

'I think we do it the old way,' he translated.

It was all very much rehearsed. One or two of the tougher-looking girls made one think uncomfortably of what one had read about sadistic female gaolers in the concentration camps, but for the most part they were handsome, intelligent-looking young women. They avoided the dangerous holds, and they had a certain technique. It was not quite *Freistil.*

I seem to remember Sachsenhausen as the name of a concentration camp. Sachsenhausen lies across the river, a bit downstream. One goes there in the evening to drink cider at old inns with a wreath or bush over the door. One eats cheese and *pretzeln*, and a fiddler strolls playing between the crowded tables. Very *gemütlich.*

This morning, an orchestra played Mozart and Lehar in the open air at the *Palmengarten.* In the afternoon, we looked in at an alleged Latin American revue in the *Tiergarten.* Quite ludicrously bad. A keeper at the *Tiergarten* has been arrested on a charge of poisoning the animals. Today's paper also reports five suicides in Frankfurt during the past week.

The weather still hot and dry. Better if it rained, with all that dust. Still, no wind to blow it about. *Rosenkavalier* tomorrow, in a patched-up public hall. Both the playhouse and the opera were destroyed. Hope better than Latin American revue.

A FRIENDLY AMERICAN JOURNALIST HAS OFFERED TO DRIVE ME ALL THE way, on Friday. This is marvellous. As he is going to Stuttgart, he will have to drive pretty well a hundred miles out of his way. Tried, by murmuring about petrol, to suggest payment. He says I can buy him a dinner on arrival. Friedenthal off to Munich tomorrow.

Have written to the regional poet and the Gascon head of broadcasting. Hope to see him, and the regional poet should be helpful about Sessenheim and local apocrypha about the idyll.

Rosenkavalier excellent. Really very creditable to keep up municipal singers, full-time municipal orchestra, first-rate musical director to the municipality, under those conditions. What a good opera *Rosenkavalier* is, especially Act II. Still, that's about all I shall remember with any great pleasure. In 1765, when he set out for Leipzig, Goethe avows that he left Frankfurt with indifference. So do I.

AND NOW I AM BACK AT THE SAME HOTEL, BUT NOT IN MY OLD ROOM on the fourth floor. I preferred that room. I suppose that here I face in the same direction, but, from the second floor, I have no clear view over the shell of St. John's or, craning to the right, despite a rudimentary balcony, any glimpse of the *ponts couverts* and the *grande écluse*, let alone of gable-tops in Little France. Even the sounds of bells does not reach me with the same distinct clarity, but penetrates confusedly through the street murmur, in which I am more nearly immersed.

I have not yet seen Jeanne. A thin, older woman makes the beds on this landing and never, I am sure, lies vigorously in them. I have not seen Joseph, who looks like Anton Walbrook. I haven't yet even seen Mademoiselle. When I arrived, late yesterday afternoon, after those fast, smooth, sunny miles down the otherwise deserted *Autobahn* and the dusty half-hour in the customs shed at Kehl, Erich von Stroheim himself stood behind the reception desk, with beaming smile and plunging handshake.

Pierre and Serge are still here, still gay and charming. They recognised me at once and came across to thank me for the English cigarettes I left for them last year. There is no great festival this year, but the hotel trade is booming, because of a pan-European conference next month.

The Hon. Bert has gone. His successor no longer occupies the separate premises in Titmouse Street, but is installed at the smart new consulate-general. This morning, the only person on duty there was a young and very pretty secretary. Either Hon. Bert's successor looked in, or she telephoned him at home, for this evening there was a note in my pigeon-hole inviting me round to his house for afternoon tea or a glass of sherry tomorrow.

Also looked in, this morning, at the railway administration, just round the corner, in the station square. The man who shares an office with him told me that Fritz Willm is away on his holidays and will be away all next week, in the mountains.

No doubt the Gascon head of broadcasting will be off somewhere over the weekend, fishing perhaps. I shall look him up on Monday morning. Even if she is not away, Mme P. will have all her family at home, and there will be guests. I look forward to a somewhat desolate Sunday. My late afternoon is fixed, of course, though I can't expect the new press officer to be quite up to Hon. Bert's standard in the way of amusement, and there is all the rest of the day to consider.

In Kehl, the French customs were rather tough with us. Perhaps that is why I feel a strange disinclination to make that point on the Rhine the object of my Sunday morning excursion. Or perhaps, having circumvented them on arrival through the kind offices of my American friend, I don't want to see ghosts rising yet. For that reason, too, I don't fancy hanging around the Orangerie. The only ghost so far is that of myself last year.

FIRST MISCALCULATION. KNOWING THAT I WAS TO ARRIVE ON FRIDAY evening, the regional poet and the head of broadcasting got together and laid on a car for an expedition to Sessenheim on Saturday. While I considerately twirled my thumbs, reluctant to disturb the two men at the weekend, they waited impatiently for me, tapping their feet, looking at their watches.

Head of broadcasting not unfriendly, but clearly feels that no more can be expected of him. He misses Hon. Bert. The new man (he was playing tennis when I arrived on Sunday) is sufficiently amiable, but a little remote and quite without either Hon. Bert's vivacity or his social graces.

Of Hon. Bert, head of broadcasting said in his machine gun French:

'*Il a été fait sur mesure pour nous.*'

I rang up the regional poet. Forewarned, I was able to begin with profuse apologies, denunciations of my own stupidity and so on, thus disarming him. He is, in any case, not so busy a man as the rosy-hued, liquid-eyed, quick-moving, plethoric Gascon. So tomorrow the regional poet is laying on another car, to be driven by his son. I had rather hoped it might be Mme Zix, but could do no more than vaguely enquire after her health.

Respects duly paid to the consul. Invited to his house for dinner tomorrow, after the Sessenheim expedition with regional poet. Not sure if I met the consul's wife at the King's birthday *cocktail* last year. Head of broadcasting's family never installed here, still in Tarbes. Otherwise, no doubt he too would have invited me home to dine, despite the irritation I unwittingly caused him on Saturday.

WE DID NOT MAKE IT. THE REGIONAL POET LIVES IN A STATE OF CONstant irritation with his son, whom he blackguarded every time the boy was out of hearing and of whose driving he was critical at every turn. A battered little car started knocking already as we drove through Wantzenau and, after several times stopping and being restarted, finally settled down a mile or so short of what I suppose was Drusenheim.

It was very hot. After various attempts to start the car by pushing or by letting it run in reverse downhill, the regional poet and I sat in it baking (there was no hood, and there was no shade of trees we could get into), while the son, goaded by his father, performed various inexpert and hopeless tinkerings under the bonnet and under the car itself.

Eventually, I walked to the outskirts of the village at the top of the gentle slope in front. I found a grocer's shop which had a petrol pump beside it and which also served wine, nicely cooled. The proprietor was out at the moment, with his car. He might be expected back in half an hour or so, when he would no doubt drive us into town, taking charge of our abandoned car on the return. I returned to the regional poet and his exhausted, resentment-choked son. The poet viciously proposed that his son should stay with the car, but I persuaded him that we should all walk back to the grocery and drink a glass of wine. It was almost an hour before the proprietor appeared, but in due course he drove us into town.

Nice dinner with the consul, outside in a corner of his garden, where we stayed with the brandy after dark. Tomorrow, I shall be driven to Sessenheim by the consular chauffeur in the consular car. For this I shall pay, but the charge will be modest.

TUMMY UPSET, FEEL SORE INSIDE. ONLY THING IS NOT TO EAT. EMPTIness produces unpleasant sensations of its own.

Still, I have been to Sessenheim. That way Goethe galloped and, having wormed his way into the graces of Pastor Brion's family, seduced the younger daughter and left her with a baby, or so it is thought.

The nastiest of all the romantic sexual cads is Alfred de Musset, but the young Goethe runs him close. He did not also require the various girls and women to be his mother, nor did he afterwards write poems denouncing them and blaming them for his misfortunes, but he gave class reasons for leaving them flat. These, to us, are incomprehensible. It was not even a peer-and-shopgirl matter. To us, a clergyman's daughter of one's own religion is at least as respectable as the son of a provincial lawyer whose parents had been in trade.

The present-day incumbent (previously written to) was helpful, charming and intelligent, a young man. It is a fine tradition that Albert Schweitzer came out of. I saw the romantic furniture, more especially the boxed-in, lattice-fronted pew, painted green, in which Goethe and Friedrike held hands during the services, and the lightly wooded mound in the fields where they sat of an evening.

The old inn '*Zum Ochsen*' stands next door to the church with its shiny, black-tiled onion spire. The chauffeur and I drank beer at the inn, where I also bought postcards, some photographic, others reproducing engravings of scenes from the Sessenheim idyll, the two daughters spinning before the door, the family at table, Goethe and the girl sitting soulfully on a rustic seat on the mound, Goethe arriving on horseback. I am sick of this Goethe, though I dare say that is not the line my further piece for The Examiner should take.

Perhaps I ought not to have come here again this year. The currency restrictions being what they are, one is inclined to accept any job which involves foreign travel. All the same, I do not think I should have accepted the Frankfurt-am-Main assignment unless I had been able, cleverly as I thought, also to get *The Examiner* to let me cover the Sessenheim idyll and thus come here. Now I am here, and I wonder why.

Even the execrable Alfred de Musset discovered that to revisit the scenes of a former happiness is inadvisable. Not-quite-so-young Atha was doing it and was wretched in part for that reason. Now the pendulum has swung again, as I might have known it would.

IF I AM NOT GOING TO EAT, PERHAPS I OUGHT NOT TO EXERT MYSELF physically. However, here I am, three hundred and fifty feet in the air, having climbed five hundred steps. My stiff-covered exercise book lies open on a parapet of gritty pink stone. My knees tremble a little, but only with the exertion.

This second phase of hunger is faintly exhilarating. On awakening this morning with bells all about me, I felt dreadfully sore inside, could not think of breakfast, tried to cut down on cigarettes (which do seem to irritate even the stomach, though I can't think how, since that isn't where the smoke goes). I rang up Mme P., as I've been meaning to do all week. Inevitably, I was invited to lunch. I had to explain that I could not eat and suggest that I might perhaps look in briefly before lunch, which I did. No guests at the Prefecture. P. in Paris, both children away. The panther, no longer a cub, prowls behind bars in Mulhouse.

I went back to the hotel and lay on my bed until three o'clock. I had a sudden craving for tea. I could have got tea at the Aubette or at the *pâtisserie* in Titmouse Street, but the sight and the sickly-sweet smell of the pastries I should have had to order (even if I didn't eat them) would have turned me up. I described the situation to Erich von Stroheim, not very hopefully.

With a wave of his plump, white hands and a word or two of dialect in the direction of the plump, jolly women at the counter, he caused a chromium-plated teapot to appear before me, immersed in it a small bag of Lipton's tea attached by a silk cord to the handle. Bliss. After a few more pots of tea, without milk or sugar, I may be able to start eating again. Indeed, I have already managed two dry rusks, at E. von S.'s suggestion. This very evening, I might go so far as an omelette or a *soufflé* or a trout *pochée au bleu* or a bowl of clear soup.

Nothing to it really, apart from the emptiness and a gentle nausea. The whole thing may be nervous in origin, *anorexia nervosa*. A fast is symbolic, though I can't think what it symbolises in the present instance. A vigil, but I have no ordeal or initiation to face.

I am leaving this town, of course. And this time I do not think I shall want to come back. I do not feel anxious or even guilty, except perhaps very slightly about Annelies and, in a quite different way, about Jeanne, about, that is to say, the mere churlishness of not even going up to the fourth floor or enquiring. I feel that she's not there. I feel that she's either on holiday or that she's left the hotel. Mademoiselle is on holiday, resting before the conference rush next week.

In the spring, I gave Blod a pretty bad time, but a man with jaundice may be excused his evil temper. That's over. We shall meet happily again, old Flower-face and I. By now, she'll have taken the children down with her to Welshport. I shall join her there towards the end of next week. Then Oxford again, all of us this time. Arlette first, I suppose.

No trouble over the journey. This year, they have got first-class sleepers on the line between here and Paris, so no sharing, no blanket-snitching personage overhead. From Paris, a place safely reserved on the Golden Arrow, real comfort. No heavy chores on return, just see my Sessenheim piece through the press and collect a luxury fee and account for my expenses, which have not been heavy.

Finding Annelies would not have been easy, might well have been impossible. I feel certain I should have drawn a blank in Sarrebourg. If fate had decided . . . Not sure I believe in fate, but if fate had decided that we should meet, it would have been just as likely that we should meet on some unexpected pavement or at somebody's house or up here. Odd if that turned out to be why I had come up here this early evening. I hadn't really intended to do any such thing.

This is the bay at the top of the south-east *tourelle*. The round slopes of the Black Forest are largely in sunlight but with a dark quarter to the left. The Rhine is a bright ribbon. Suppose I heard steps from below, then out in the open, and Annelies stood beside me, like the young German beside after-all-quite-young Atha.

But he, wintry Atha, was so occupied with desperate calculations, it may be he needed some intervention by fate. I wonder what happened to the young German. Perhaps he was killed in Russia or still languishes in a Russian prison. Perhaps he made a fortune on the black market in (was it?) Lübeck. He served his turn. I ought to be grateful to him. It is summer now, outside and, by and large, in. I am not standing here nagged at by any dark thought.

At least, I suppose I am not. I am ghost-free. The sun is strong upon the back of my head. It brightens the Virtues and Vices, the wise and foolish virgins, the human seraphim walking past, insect legs waving feebly to and fro beneath them. It presses through the great rose window, filling the nave with contusions of red and purple light beneath the turquoise copper of that roof and the dry gargoyles.

The comfortable, brown-tile roofs and stepped gables are all about my feet. That green patch is the Orangerie. I could not, I think, jump clear.

There is no sound of ascending steps. A sound has in fact just started about fifty feet below me, but it is not the sound of steps. It is a dry, grating sound, with, somewhere beyond it, the hollow sound of irresistible traction, like the cough of hydraulic brakes. Metal surfaces yield and separate, first the dry, flaking surfaces, then the more cunningly jointed, closely married, oil-smooth. The great bell has tilted, and the clapper drops once. The bell swings. The clapper drops again with greater force, and the stone vibrates beneath my feet and my hands.

I could not walk down the steps now, past that bell, the ground tilting below me. I suppose it must be tolling for Benediction. It will go on for ten minutes or so. At two seconds between each peal, that makes three hundred. Either I must wait, or I must go down the other way. I could not jump clear, I am certain. I should catch one foot on an ornament of stone, then pitch forward, arms and legs flying, hit the green roof and roll over its ridges down to the gutter of lead behind its pinnacles, lying there until consciousness ended, while the bell shook and thundered overhead.

THE STEEL HANDBASIN PUSHES UP AGAIN INTO THE WALL AND CLICKS home, almost silently. The wall is a pale green-grey. I have folded the matching linen cover down, and the book lies open on two red blankets. I suppose that we must already be nearing Saverne and that shortly thereafter we shall go underground, appropriately near Sarrebourg.

I must either take this action or not take it. The action itself allows a variant. I could first knock, that is to say. In neither case do I need to do more than turn round before proceeding.

Neither of the two questions in my mind is susceptible of complete answer until the action is taken. If I have guessed the answer to one of them wrong, the other may never be answered. The possibility of it not being answered exists even if my guessed answer to the other question is right. There could be deliberate refusal of an answer. There could be hysteria, panic and denial of a right answer to the other question, viz that the catch was drawn back.

As to which of the two women it is beyond that door, I am half-committed to my answer, but part of my resistance to the alternative is simply due to the feeling that such a coincidence would be too remarkable, too marvellous, too poetically strange, too arranged (by fate, I suppose I mean). After all, the sum of my evidence was quickly gathered and is tenuous.

I had barely stepped out of the door of this compartment when the door to my right opened and a woman emerged, turned right and walked briskly along the corridor. I did not properly see her face, but merely felt that about the head there was something familiar. The woman wore a long, closely waisted dressing gown or house coat of lilac satin. The short hair was artificially red, the neck smooth and white, the hips certainly feminine but without slackness, the movement and the set of head and shoulders admirable.

Leaning against the window rail at a point midway between my door and that out of which the woman had come, stood a tall, angular young man with a small dark moustache and sharp, unattractive and unintelligent features. He seemed to me out of place. I suspected him of being a second-class passenger who had loitered this way out of curiosity, perhaps indeed with the distinct idea of striking up an acquaintance with some woman in a sleeper. It may in fact be that he has a sleeper further along the corridor, but in that case it was odd that he should choose to loiter in the corridor elsewhere than outside his own door. This stray young wolf is important only in so far as his presence may be thought to have affected the woman's behaviour when she returned to her compartment, inhibiting her in a minor degree.

The lilac *negligé*, the neat red hair, the neatly placed, rapidly moving feet in mauve slippers reappeared. From the front also, the immediate effect of her figure was that it was exemplary. No slackness *au balcon* either. And it was Mme Zix. That is to say, in the first instance, I did not in the least doubt that it was she.

She, of course, had not observed me at all when she came out of her compartment and turned right. At most, she might have noted that two men stood there. That stretch of corridor is not more than seven or eight yards long. She would cover it in less than twenty steps, and the time it took her, from her first reappearance, to take that number of steps and insert the key of her compartment into the door can hardly have been more than twelve seconds, was almost certainly less.

During that interval of time, she had to adjust her mind to the recognition of me, notice the wolf awkwardly placed between us, adopt a facial expression appropriate to her judgment of the circumstances and bow slightly to me as she turned left with the key in her hand. The face expressed pleased recognition. Of that, I think, there is no conceivable doubt. It was a split second between that and the inclination of the head, barely raised again when the key was in the lock.

My own behaviour was inhibited by the wolf. I should have begun to speak while returning the inclination of the head, but the first sound of a voice would have caused him to turn sharply. All propriety would have been gone. We could not talk across him, and he was not the kind of young man who would have collected himself and vanished with a brief apology. He would have stood foolishly there for at least as long as our momentary exchange of politenesses and the unspoken question and answer would have taken. I have some eye to propriety myself. Mme Zix is a well-bred, intelligent widow known to all the most respectable citizens of the town some twenty or thirty miles behind us and thus, conceivably, at least by sight, to half the people with sleepers on this train. As to the Annelies of thirteen years ago, we know that her sense of propriety was almost excessive.

For, as the woman entered her compartment, that was the alternative guess at her identity which presented itself to me. It might not be Mme Zix. It might be the girl from Sarrebourg, now older, certainly once married and possibly since widowed, with tinted hair. From my first meeting with Mme Zix, I had noted a resemblance between the two. I had not seen Mme Zix for a year.

I had not seen Annelies for thirteen years. Nor she me. It seems hardly possible that recognition, if it was she, should not have come with more of a shock to both of us. The expression on her face would have been worried, incredulous. Then either she would have dismissed the possibility of the man being me, or even the wolf would not have inhibited some overt reaction. It is not, that is to say, improper for people who have not seen each other for thirteen years to exclaim in the presence of any third party whatsoever. What there could never have been was the calm acceptance, the discreet intimation.

Moreover, Annelies was bigger-bosomed. Also, I should have thought her taller, though a different style of garment may oddly shorten a woman in appearance, as well, perhaps, as suppress the opulence of a figure.

So much I had reasoned possibly even before the door of the next compartment was shut. Within the next few seconds, I stared the wolf out of countenance, and he loped off. I, in my turn, then went along the corridor. I returned and came back in here.

It cannot have been, it cannot be, Annelies. And yet the impression persists.

That may have been as much as five minutes ago. I have since undressed, cleaned my teeth and so on. The tooth-cleaning I presume to have been audible next door. Not until it was completed did the catch either disengage or engage with a loud click.

I think it disengaged. These chromium-plated fittings are pretty new. Even a comparatively ill-fitting bolt may be pushed home almost silently. On the other hand, a smooth fitting may become so firmly lodged by slight warping or dropping that, on its eventual release, it will ring back with a sound like a pistol shot. I take that to be what happened under the small fingers of the woman next door. From the moment at which it happened, it would be reasonable to suppose that it had, moreover, been intended as a signal. If Annelies (or Mme Zix) had wished to be discreet about it, she would have disengaged (or, for that matter, engaged) the bolt while I was out along the corridor. Even supposing that she had not noticed that it was in what she regarded as the wrong position until I had come back in here, she could still have rectified it inaudibly while my tap ran and the tooth-cleaning routine proceeded. I see that the bolt on this side is drawn back.

Whatever happens, I must not be heard rattling the knob. I must put my hand to it and turn it silently. On meeting the slightest resistance from a catch on the other side of the door, I must knock, as though I had meant to do so in the first place. The knuckles of my right hand must be already raised before I put my left hand to the doorknob.

I am more than half-inclined to hope that the woman *is only* Mme Zix. If it is Annelies, there will be so extremely much *to be said*. A romantic tale, a human elaborateness completed, may afterwards be agreeable to tell, but may yet be distressing, at the time, to act out, as well as exhausting by the complications it leads to, as well, perhaps, as unexpected in its ending. I would rather, I think, that I were merely seeking pleasure, amusingly conspired at by circumstance, with an attractive and doubtless passionate widow.

That is what I expect. I count on no more than a firm-bottomed, small-breasted body, touchingly short in the bed, the flamy hair and the slightly worried eyes shining under a subdued light from the bed-head lamp. That is all. I shall be granted no revelation about the long significance of my own life. No imaginative creation will be finished.

Left hand to the doorknob, knuckles of the right hand raised. This is adult child's play. And yet, as I now move, I am aware of some thumping of the heart, a certain weakness at the knees and a kind of spreading lassitude in the shoulders.